PRAISE FOR SULARI GENTILL

The Woman in the Library

"Sulari Gentill's *The Woman in the Library* is a thrill. The library setting, the conceit of four strangers at a table, and the twisty story-within-a-story make Gentill's novel unputdownable. The book is a treat for readers who love books about books and who like their mysteries to keep them guessing until the very last page."

—Eva Jurczyk, author of
The Department of Rare Books and Special Collections

"*The Woman in the Library* is a delicious read—it's a book that makes you *feel*. Cunningly crafted, with layers that fold back and feed upon each other, charming characters, and revelations that will make you cringe and gasp. You will feel a rising sense of dread as you read it, but you won't want to stop."

—Daniel O'Malley, author of *The Rook*

"*The Woman in the Library* is a sophisticated mystery with more layers than an onion, created by a master hand. Clever plot twists in Gentill's signature refined style will make you feel smarter just by reading. Sulari Gentill has done it again"

—Ellie Marney, *New York Times* bestselling author

After She Wrote Him
(a standalone previously published as *Crossing the Lines*)

2018 Winner of the Ned Kelly Award, Best Crime Fiction

"A pure delight, a swift yet psychologically complex read, cleverly conceived and brilliantly executed."

—Dean Koontz, *New York Times* bestselling author

"A tour de force! A brilliant blend of mystery, gut-wrenching psychological suspense, and literary storytelling. The novel stands as a shining (and refreshing) example of metafiction at its best—witty and wry, stylish and a joy to read."

—Jeffery Deaver, *New York Times* bestselling author

"A delightful, cerebral novel featuring a crime writer who grows dangerously enamored with her main character. As the interplay between creator and created reaches Russian-nesting-doll complexity, it forces us to question the nature of fiction itself."

—Gregg Hurwitz, *New York Times* bestselling author

"This is an elegant exploration of the creative process, as well as a strong defense of the crime-fiction genre, as Gentill illustrates the crossing of lines between imagination and reality."

—*Booklist*

"In this intriguing and unusual tale, a stunning departure from Gentill's period mysteries, the question is not whodunit but who's real and who's a figment of someone's vivid imagination."

—*Kirkus Reviews*

"Fans of postmodern fiction will enjoy this departure from Gentill's 1930s series. It's an exploration, as one character puts it, of 'an author's relationship with her protagonist, an examination of the tenuous line between belief and reality, imagination and self, and what happens when that line is crossed.'"

—*Publishers Weekly*

"Literary or pop fiction lovers will enjoy."

—*Library Journal*

Shanghai Secrets
The Ninth Rowland Sinclair WWII Mystery

"Gentill exposes the thoughts of Chinese characters about their colonizers, highlighting the exoticization of Asians by their 'betters.' This alone makes the book stand out, but readers will also relish the murder mystery and the intermittent fictional news articles about the time, which bring to life an ebullient if naive era. For fans of the series and those who like stories that juxtapose the haves against the have-nots."

—*Booklist*

"Eccentric but authentic characters bolster a cracking good plot. Gentill captures in telling detail a political, moral, and cultural milieu."

—*Publishers Weekly*

A Dangerous Language
The Eighth Rowland Sinclair WWII Mystery

"A thrilling eighth mystery."

—*Publishers Weekly*

"Fans of historical fiction and murder mysteries will consider her treasure trove of novels to be a rich discovery."

—*Bookreporter*

Give the Devil His Due
The Seventh Rowland Sinclair WWII Mystery

"This is a great addition to a fun Australian mystery series… A fast-paced and captivating novel set during a turbulent period in Australia's history. Containing an intriguing mystery, a unique sense of humour, and a range of historical characters, this is a highly recommended read for lovers of Australian fiction."

—*Sydney Morning Herald*

"[D]evil of a good read."

—*Herald Sun*

"This 1930s Sydney is vibrant and authentic, and the inclusion of a relevant newspaper cutting at the beginning of each chapter is a neat touch... In order to get the best value out of this highly original series with its quirky characters...seek out the earlier titles and follow them in sequence."

—Historical Novel Society

A Murder Unmentioned
The Sixth Rowland Sinclair WWII Mystery

Shortlisted for the Davitt Award for Best Adult Novel for 2015
Shortlisted for the Ned Kelly Award for Best Crime Novel 2015

"Each chapter begins with a brief excerpt from an Australian publication, such as the *Camperdown Chronicle*, that offers insights into the popular culture of the times. Fans of historical mysteries will find a lot to savor."

—*Publishers Weekly*

"A charmingly complex hero whose adventures continue to highlight many worldly problems between the great wars."

—*Kirkus Reviews*

"This sixth entry in the Rowland Sinclair series, which blends historical figures seamlessly with fictional ones, clarifies and advances the family dynamics of its appealing protagonist, which should delight fans and win new readers."

—*Booklist*

"Sulari Gentill likes to tease, blithely slotting real people and events into a crime series set in the 1930s relating the fictional adventures of artist and gentleman of leisure, Rowland Sinclair...the sixth book in the series and by far the most interesting... As always, every chapter opens with a relevant snippet from a periodical of the time. Once again, telling the fictional from the real is part of the fun... Clever Gentill. Investigating the past has never been more fun."

—*Sydney Morning Herald*

Gentlemen Formerly Dressed
The Fifth Rowland Sinclair WWII Mystery

"This book has it all: intrigue among the British aristocracy, the Nazi threat, and a dashing Australian hero. I didn't want it to end!"
—Rhys Bowen, author of the *New York Times* bestselling Royal Spyness and Molly Murphy mysteries, and the #1 Kindle bestseller, *In Farleigh Field*

"Rowland's determined attempts to open British eyes to the gathering storm combine mystery, rousing adventure, and chance meetings with eminent figures from Churchill to Evelyn Waugh."
—*Kirkus Reviews*

"The pleasure of this novel lies…in observing Rowland at dinner with Evelyn Waugh, trading insights with H. G. Wells, and setting Winston Churchill straight on the evils of nationalism. Fans of upper-class sleuths will be in their element."
—*Publishers Weekly*

"With fast pacing, madcap characters, and intriguing historical personages like H. G. Wells, Evelyn Waugh, and Winston Churchill making appearances, *Gentlemen Formerly Dressed* is historical mystery at its most fun. Sulari Gentill has managed to capture the odd decadence of the British upper classes in stark contrast to the rising fascist factions in both Germany and England. Fascinating history, entertaining characters, and a hint of romance make *Gentlemen Formerly Dressed* irresistible."
—*Shelf Awareness*

Paving the New Road
The Fourth Rowland Sinclair WWII Mystery

Shortlisted for the Davitt Award for Best Adult Crime Fiction for 2013

"The combination of famous historical figures, detailed descriptions of a troubling time, and plenty of action makes for a tale as rousing as it is relevant."
—*Kirkus Reviews*

"This installment takes the aristocratic Sinclair into a much darker place than did the previous three entries in the series but does so without losing the stylish prose and the easy way with character that have given the novels their appeal."

—Booklist

"Stylish, well-paced murder mystery…cheeky plotline… This tale is told with such flair and feeling for those extraordinary times… Verdict: thrilling."

—Herald Sun

Miles Off Course
The Third Rowland Sinclair WWII Mystery

"Gentill's third reads like a superior Western, alternating high adventure with social and political observations about prewar Australia."

—Kirkus Reviews

"Set in Australia in 1933, Gentill's entertaining third mystery featuring portrait artist Rowland Sinclair will appeal to fans of Greenwood's Phryne Fisher… Gentill matches Greenwood's skill at blending suspense with a light touch."

—Publishers Weekly

"Rowland is an especially interesting character: at first he comes off as a bit of a layabout, a guy who feels he's entitled to a cushy life by virtue of his aristocratic roots, but, as the story moves along, we realize he has a strong moral center and a compulsion to finish a job once he's started it. A great addition to a strong series and a fine read-alike for fans of Kerry Greenwood's Phryne Fisher novels."

—Booklist

A Decline in Prophets
The Second Rowland Sinclair WWII Mystery

Winner of the Davitt Award for Best Adult Crime Fiction for 2012

"I thoroughly enjoyed the glamour of the ocean voyage, the warmth and wit among the friends, and yet all the time, simmering beneath the surface, was the real and savage violence, waiting to erupt. The 1930s are a marvelous period. We know what lies ahead! This is beautifully drawn, with all its fragile hope and looming tragedy. I am delighted this is a series. I want them all."

—Anne Perry, *New York Times* bestselling author

"Set in late 1932, Gentill's lively second mystery featuring dashing Australian millionaire Rowland 'Rowly' Sinclair takes place initially aboard the luxury cruise ship *Aquitania*, as it steams along toward Sydney... The witty and insightful glimpses of the Australian bourgeoisie of this period keep this mystery afloat."

—*Publishers Weekly*

"A delightful period piece."

—*Kirkus Reviews*

"Rowland Sinclair is a gentleman artist who comes from a privileged background but whose sympathies are with bohemians, lefties, and ratbags. It's a rich political and cultural era to explore, and Gentill has a lot of fun with a hero who is always getting paint on his immaculate tailoring."

—*Sydney Morning Herald*

A House Divided (formerly *A Few Right Thinking Men*)
The First Rowland Sinclair WWII Mystery

Shortlisted for Best First Book for the Commonwealth Writers' Prize for 2011

"As series-launching novels go, this one is especially successful: the plot effectively plays Sinclair's aristocratic bearing and involvement in the arts against the Depression setting, fraught with radical politics, both of which he becomes involves in as he turns sleuth. And Sinclair himself is a delight: winning us over completely and making us feel as though he's an old friend."
—*Booklist*, Starred Review

"While the vintage Down Under settings might make this debut…comparable to Kerry Fisher's Melbourne-based Phryne Fisher 1920s mysteries, Gentill works in historical events that add verisimilitude to her story. There are more political machinations going on here than Phryne could ever contemplate. VERDICT: Thanks to Poisoned Pen Press for bringing another award-winning Australian crime writer to U.S. shores. Her witty hero will delight traditional mystery buffs."
—*Library Journal*, Starred Review

"It takes a talented writer to imbue history with colour and vivacity… *A Few Right Thinking Men* more than matches its historical crime contemporaries… It is rare to find such an assured debut. The novel deserves to be both read and remembered as an insight into the Australia that was; its conflicting ideologies, aims, and desires; the hallmarks of a country still maturing."
—*Australian Book Review*

"Fans of Kerry Greenwood's Phryne Fisher series, rejoice: here comes another Depression-era Australian sleuth! Along the way there is plenty of solid discussion of politics and social status, with enough context to both draw in those new to the era and keep those more well-versed in their history interested."
—Historical Novel Society

Also by Sulari Gentill

The Rowland Sinclair WWII Mysteries
A House Divided
A Decline in Prophets
Miles Off Course
Paving the New Road
Gentlemen Formerly Dressed
A Murder Unmentioned
Give the Devil His Due
A Dangerous Language
Shanghai Secrets
Where There's a Will

The Hero Trilogy
Chasing Odysseus
Trying War
The Blood of Wolves

Standalone Novel
After She Wrote Him

THE WOMAN IN THE LIBRARY

a novel

SULARI GENTILL

Poisoned Pen
PRESS

Published by Poisoned Pen Press, an imprint of Sourcebooks
P.O. Box 4410, Naperville, Illinois 60567-4410
(630) 961-3900
sourcebooks.com

Library of Congress Cataloging-in-Publication Data

Names: Gentill, Sulari, author.
Title: The woman in the library / Sulari Gentill.
Description: Naperville, Illinois : Poisoned Pen Press, [2022]
Identifiers: LCCN 2021023650 (print) | LCCN 2021023651
(ebook) | (hardback) | (trade paperback) | (epub)
Subjects: GSAFD: Mystery fiction.
Classification: LCC PR9619.4.G46 W66 2022 (print) | LCC PR9619.4.G46
(ebook) | DDC 823/.92--dc23
LC record available at https://lccn.loc.gov/2021023650
LC ebook record available at https://lccn.loc.gov/2021023651

Printed and bound in the United States of America.
VP 10 9 8 7 6 5 4 3 2

For Barbara

"Open me carefully..."
—Emily Dickinson, *"Intimate Letters"*

Dear Hannah,

What are you writing?

I expect you've started something new by now. If not, consider this a nudge from a fan. You have a following, my friend, desperate for the next Hannah Tigone. To paraphrase Spider-Man: With great readership comes great responsibility.

Seriously though, I saw *An Implausible Country* in the bookstore around the corner, yesterday. A place called The Rook...one of those hipster joints where you can get a half-strength turmeric soy latte, and a wheatgrass and birdseed snack with your book. Anyway, the U.S. jacket pops in the wild, in case you were wondering. Photo of it on the new releases shelf attached. I might have bought myself another copy, just so I could brag to the bookseller that I knew the author! I think she was impressed. There was a definite hint of admiration in the way she asked, "Do you need a bag?"

I so regret that I was unable to come to New York when you toured last Fall. We could have met after all these years as colleagues and correspondents. I shall make amends by crossing the seas to you in a few months, unless of course you are coming stateside. Perhaps if you were to set a book here, then a research trip might be justified? Still, there might be something fitting about a friendship based on a common love of words being founded on an exchange of the same.

As for your enquiries about how my own book is coming: Well, I spent Friday at the library. I wrote a thousand words and deleted fifteen hundred. Regardless, the Boston Public Library is a nice spot in which to be stood up by the muse. I'm afraid she's playing hard to get where I'm concerned. I had hoped that the venue might shake loose some inspiration. It's pretty spectacular—the ceiling in the Reading Room is something to behold. I'm afraid I spent rather a lot of time staring at it. I can't help but wonder how many frustrated writers have counted the decorative cornices before me... Perhaps Emerson or Alcott gazed aimlessly at that same plasterwork, or at least its equivalent in the earlier incarnation of the BPL when it was on Boylston Street. It's vaguely comforting to think that they might have.

Anyway, I look forward to hearing about your current project. As always, I'm happy to be a sounding board if you require one—to read chapters as you write, so the feedback is immediate. It'll give me something to do while I'm in this writing slump, and perhaps your productivity will rub off! And eventually, I might have something for you to read and comment on in return.

Regards and so forth,
Leo

CHAPTER ONE

Writing in the Boston Public Library had been a mistake. It was too magnificent. One could spend hours just staring at the ceiling in the Reading Room. Very few books have been written with the writer's eyes cast upwards. It judged you, that ceiling, looked down on you in every way. Mocked you with an architectural perfection that couldn't be achieved by simply placing one word after another until a structure took shape. It made you want to start with grand arcs, to build a magnificent framework into which the artistic detail would be written—a thing of vision and symmetry and cohesion. But that, sadly, isn't the way I write.

I am a bricklayer without drawings, laying words into sentences, sentences into paragraphs, allowing my walls to twist and turn on whim. There is no framework, just bricks interlocked to support each other into a story. I have no idea what I'm actually building, or if it will stand.

Perhaps I should be working on a bus. That would be more consistent with my process such as it is. I'm not totally without direction…there is a route of some sort, but who hops on and who gets off is determined by a balance of habit and timing and random chance. There's always the possibility that the route will be altered at the last minute for weather or accident, some parade or marathon. There's no symmetry, no plan, just the chaotic, unplotted bustle of human life.

Still, ceilings have a wonderful lofty perspective that buses do not. These have gazed down on writers before. Do they see one now? Or just a woman in the library with a blank page before her?

Maybe I should stop looking at the ceiling and write something.

I force my gaze from its elevated angle. Green-shaded lamps cast soft ellipses of light that define boundaries of territory at the communal reading tables. Spread out, by all means, but stay within the light of your own lamp. I sit at the end of one of dozens of tables placed in precise rows within the room. My table is close enough to the centre of the hall that I can see green lamps and heads bent over books in all directions. The young woman next to me has divested her jacket to reveal full-sleeve tattoos on both arms. I've never been inked myself, but I'm fascinated. The story of her life etched on her skin... She's like a walking book. Patterns and portraits and words. Mantras of love and power. I wonder how much of it is fiction. What story would I tell if I had to wear it on my body? The woman is reading Freud. It occurs to me that a psychology student would make an excellent protagonist for a thriller. A student, not an expert. Experts are less relatable, removed from the reader by virtue of their status. I write "psychology student" onto the blank page of my notebook and surround it with a box. And so I hop onto the bus. God knows where it's going—I just grabbed the first one that came along.

Beneath the box I make some notes about her tattoos, being careful not to make it obvious that I am reading her ink.

Across from me sits a young man in a Harvard Law sweatshirt. He cuts a classic figure—broad shoulders, strong jaw, and a cleft chin—like he was drawn as the hero of an old cartoon. He's been staring at the same page of the tome propped before him for at least ten minutes. Perhaps he's committing it to memory...or perhaps he's just trying to keep his eyes down and away from the young woman on my left. I wonder what they are to each other: lovers now estranged, or could it be that he is lovelorn and she indifferent? Or perhaps the other way round—is she stalking him? Watching him over the top of Freud? Might she suspect him of something? He certainly looks tormented... Guilt? He drops his eyes to check his watch—a Rolex, or perhaps a rip-off of the same.

To the left of Heroic Chin is another man, still young but no longer boyish. He wears a sport coat over a collared shirt and jumper. I am more careful about looking at him than I am the others because he is so ludicrously handsome. Dark hair and eyes, strong upswept brows. If he catches my gaze he will assume that is the reason. And it isn't…well, maybe a little. But mostly I am wondering what he might bring to a story.

He's working on a laptop, stopping every now and then to stare at the screen, and then he's off again, typing at speed. Good Lord, could he be a writer?

There are other people in the Reading Room, of course, but they are shadows. Unfocused as yet, while I try to pin a version of these three to my page. I write for a while…scenarios, mainly. How Freud Girl, Heroic Chin, and Handsome Man might be connected. Love triangles, business relationships, childhood friends. Perhaps Handsome Man is a movie star; Heroic Chin, a fan; and Freud Girl, his faithful bodyguard. I smile as the scenarios become increasingly ridiculous and, as I do, I look up to meet Handsome Man's eyes. He looks startled and embarrassed, and I must, too, because that's how I feel. I open my mouth to explain, to assure him that I'm a writer, not a leering harasser, but of course this is the Reading Room, and one does not conduct a defence while people are trying to read. I do attempt to let him know I'm only interested in him as the physical catalyst for a character I'm creating, but that's too complex to convey in mime. He just ends up looking confused.

Freud Girl laughs softly. Now Heroic Chin looks up too, and the four of us are looking at each other silently, unable to rebuke or apologize or explain, lest we incur the wrath of the Reading Room Police.

And then there is a scream. Ragged and terrified. A beat of silence even after it stops, until we all seem to realise that the Reading Room Rules no longer apply.

"Fuck! What was that?" Heroic Chin murmurs.

"Where did it come from?" Freud Girl stands and looks around.

People begin to pack up their belongings to leave. Two security guards stride in and ask everyone to remain calm and in their seats until the problem can be identified. Some idiot law student starts on about illegal detention and false imprisonment, but, for the most part, people sit down and wait.

"It was probably just a spider," Heroic Chin says. "My roommate sounds just like that whenever he sees a spider."

"That was a woman," Freud Girl points out.

"Or a man who's afraid of spiders…" Heroic Chin looks about as if his arachnophobic friend might be lurking somewhere.

"I apologize if I was staring." Handsome Man addresses me tentatively. I have enough of an ear for American accents now to tell he's not from Boston. "My editor wants me to include more physical descriptions in my work." He grimaces. "She says all the women in my manuscript are wearing the same thing, so I thought… Heck, that sounds creepy! I'm sorry. I was trying to describe your jacket."

I smile, relieved. He's volunteering to take the bullet. I'll just be gracious. "It's a herringbone tweed, originally a man's sport coat purchased at a vintage store and retailored so the wearer doesn't look ridiculous." I meet his eye. "I do hope you haven't written down that I look ridiculous."

For a moment, he's flustered. "No, I assure you—" And then he seems to realise I'm kidding and laughs. It's a nice laugh. Deep but not loud. "Cain McLeod."

After a second I register that he's introduced himself. I should too.

"Winifred Kincaid…people call me Freddie."

"She's a writer too." Freud Girl leans over and glances at my notebook. "She's been making notes on all of us."

Damn!

She grins. "I like Freud Girl…I sound like an intellectual superhero. Better than Tattoo Arms or Nose Ring."

I slam my notebook shut.

"Awesome!" Heroic Chin turns to display his profile. "I hope you described my good side and…" he adds, flashing a smile, "I have dimples."

Handsome Man, apparently also known as Cain McLeod, is clearly amused. "What are the chances? You two should be more careful who you sit next to."

"I'm Marigold Anastas," Freud Girl announces. "For your acknowledgements. A-N-A-S-T-A-S."

Not to be outdone, Heroic Chin discloses his name is Whit Metters and promises to sue if either Cain McLeod or I forget to mention his dimples.

We're all laughing when the security guards announce that people may leave if they wish.

"Did you find out who screamed?" Cain asks.

The security guard shrugs. "Probably some asshole who thinks he's a comedian."

Whit nods smugly and mouths "spider."

Cain's brow lifts. "It was a convincing scream," he says quietly.

He's right. There was a ring of real mortal terror in the scream. But that's possibly a writer's fancy. Perhaps someone simply needed to expel a bit of stress. "I need to find coffee."

"The Map Room Tea Lounge is the closest," Cain says. "They make a decent coffee."

"Do you need more material?" Marigold asks. With coat sleeves covering the ink which had held my attention, I notice that she has beautiful eyes, jewel green and sparkling in a frame of smoky kohl and mascara.

"Just coffee," I reply for both Cain and myself, because I'm not sure which one of us she was asking.

"Can I come?"

The childlike guilelessness of the question is disarming. "Of course."

"Me too?" Whit now. "I don't want to be alone. There's a spider somewhere."

And so we go to the Map Room to found a friendship, and I have my first coffee with a killer.

———

Dear Hannah,

Bravo! A sharp and intriguing opening. You have made art out of my complaints. The last line is chilling. An excellent hook. I fear that a publisher will ask you to make it the opening line to ensure you catch the first-page browsers. All I can say is: resist! It is perfect as it is.

That line, though, is as brave as it is brilliant. Bear in mind that you've issued your readers a challenge, declared one of those three (Marigold, Whit, or Cain) will be the killer. They'll watch them closely from now on, read into every passing nuance. It may make it more difficult to distract their attention from clues in the manuscript and keep them guessing. Still, it's kind of delicious—particularly as they each seem so likeable. As I said, brave.

Dare I hope that since your setting is Boston, you'll make a research trip here sometime soon? It would be wonderful to suffer for our art face-to-face over martinis in some bar like real writers! In the meantime, I'd be delighted to assist you with sense of place and so forth. Consider me your scout, your eyes and ears in the U.S.

A couple of points—Americans don't use the term *jumper* (description of Handsome Man). You may want to switch that reference to sweater or pullover. It's also much less common in the U.S. for women to be as heavily inked as women in Australia. I haven't seen any full-sleeve tattoos on women, here. Of course, that doesn't mean Marigold can't have them—perhaps that's why Winifred notices them particularly.

I returned to the Reading Room after I received your email and chapter to check, and I'm afraid there's no explicit rule against talking. It's more a general civility. Easy to fix. Insert a disapproving shushing neighbour or two on the table and the pressure for silence won't be lost. I had lunch in the Map Room, so if you need details, let me know. As an Australian, you'll probably find the coffee appalling out of principle, but since Winifred is American, she is not likely to find it wanting.

Do you need somewhere for Freddie to live? If money is no object, you could put her in Back Bay, right in the BPL neighborhood. Many of the apartments are converted Victorian brownstones, but Freddie would have to be an heiress of some sort to afford one! Is she a struggling hopeful, or an author of international renown? The former would probably live somewhere like Brighton or Alston. Let me know if you'd like me to check some buildings for you.

I received my tenth rejection letter for the opus yesterday. It feels like something which should be marked. Perhaps I shall buy a cake. This one said my writing was elegant but that they felt I was working in the wrong genre...which I suppose is an indirect way of saying they want my protagonist to be a vampire and the climax to involve an alien invasion...and not the kind with which our President seems preoccupied!

I know the repeated rejections are a rite of passage, Hannah, but, honestly, it hurts. I don't know if I'm strong enough for this business. It must be wonderful to be at that stage where you've paid your dues, where you know that whatever you write now, it will at least be seriously considered. This stage just feels like a ritual humiliation.

Yours somewhat despondently,
Leo

CHAPTER TWO

I'm still a little in awe every time I step into the chequerboard foyer of Carrington Square. It's one of those Victorian brownstones for which Back Bay is famous—a magnificent gabled exterior, renovated to perfection within. My one-bedroom apartment looks out over an internal courtyard featuring landscaped gardens and cast-iron fountains. It's beautifully furnished and decorated—an address usually beyond the means of a humble writer. In the sitting room, on either side of the marble fireplace, are built-in bookcases in which are stored the works of each of the previous Sinclair scholarship winners who were writers in residence here. The collection is both inspiring and terrifying. Wonderful novels in almost every genre, crafted in the year during which the writer lived in this apartment. In the fifty or so years the scholarship has been running, the apartment has no doubt been refurbished and redecorated several times, but these bookcases remain untouched, sacrosanct. The heart and purpose of this place—sometimes I fancy I can hear it beating.

Perhaps it was the bookcases that stilled my pen in the beginning. I had thought that the words would come easily here. A time and place to write—a dream bolstered by the endorsement of the award. And yet I'd felt unworthy, uncertain. I'd choked, and in the first month I'd deleted more than I wrote. But not today.

Today I return from the library exhilarated. We had lingered in the Map

Room for hours, Cain, Whit, Marigold, and I. It was bizarre, four strangers who seemed to recognize each other, like we'd been friends before in a life forgotten. We talked about all manner of things, laughed about most of it, and poked fun at each other without restraint. It felt like being at home, and I breathed out completely for the first time since I stepped on that flight from Sydney.

Cain is a published writer—his first book was reviewed by the *New York Times*. He doesn't tell me that last bit; I google him on the way home. The *Washington Post* called him one of America's most promising young novelists, and his first book was something of a sensation. Marigold is in fact studying psychology at Harvard, and Whit is failing law. The failing part doesn't seem to bother him. It is the only way, apparently, that he can avoid being absorbed into the family firm.

And so my attention is initially elsewhere when Leo Johnson crosses my path on the stairs.

"Freddie! Hello."

Leo is also a writer in residence at Carrington Square. He's from Alabama originally, though I think he went to Harvard at some point. He holds a fellowship which seems to be the American equivalent of the Sinclair, and occupies an apartment a few doors away from mine. "How was the library?" he asks. He speaks with a gentle Southern pace that invites you to slow down and chat a while. "Get much work done?"

"How did you know I was at the library?"

"Oh, I saw you at the Map Room." He pushes his glasses back up against the bridge of his nose. "I dropped into the BPL to pick up a book I'd reserved, and then I needed coffee. I just happened to see you there. I waved, but I'm guessing you didn't see me."

"Of course I didn't, or I would have asked you to join us." Leo is the closest thing I have to a colleague. I tell him about the scream.

He laughs. "I expect it was some nutcase, or a club initiation of one sort or another. A number of the Harvard clubs are co-ed now."

I raise my brow, uncertain what that has to do with it.

"It seems like the kind of prank that would be conceived in the brain of an adolescent male," he explains. "But, of course, a woman would be required to execute it."

I smile. "You don't think women might have planned it?"

"I don't think a woman would have found it that funny... A man, however, would be delighted with his extraordinary wit."

"Remember that you said that, not me." I glance up the stairs. "Would you like to come in for a coffee?"

Leo shakes his head. "No, ma'am. There's a story-cooking gleam in your eyes. I'll leave you alone to write. Let's compare notes in the next couple of days."

I agree, relieved. I do feel an urgency to write. And I like Leo even more for the fact that he understands.

I open my laptop as soon as I get into the apartment, slipping off my shoes and nesting into the couch. I begin typing, using the monikers Handsome Man, Heroic Chin, and Freud Girl. They appear on my page like a rubbing taken from life, shape and dimension created with words. I'll give them real names later; for now I don't want to stem the ideas by trying to work out what to call them.

I dwell on the scream. It, too, has a place in this story. The four of us had talked about it at length. How could something like that be unexplained? Someone must have screamed, someone must have had a reason to. Whit brought up spiders again. I think he must have some kind of phobia.

We had all agreed to meet at the BPL tomorrow. Actually, Cain and I had agreed to meet, to form a writers' group of sorts. Marigold and Whit had decided that any group should include them, regardless of its purpose.

"We can be sounding boards," Marigold insisted.

"And inspiration," Whit added. And so it was arranged.

It is exciting to have plans, people to meet.

I turn on the television, initially for background noise. I'm working, so it's only sound. A murmur that connects me to the real world as I create one of my own, an anchor barely noticed. Until I hear the words "Boston Public Library today."

I look up. A reporter talking to a camera. "...the body of a young woman was discovered by cleaning staff in the Boston Public Library."

I close the laptop and turn up the volume, leaning forward towards the television. A body. My God, the scream! The reporter tells me nothing more of any use. I switch to another station, but the report is much the same. The body is not identified beyond being that of a young woman.

My phone rings. It's Marigold. "The news! Did you see the news?"

"Yes."

"That scream!" Marigold sounds more excited than frightened. "That must have been her."

"I wonder why they didn't find her then."

"Maybe whoever killed her hid the body?"

I smile. "They didn't say anything about murder, Marigold. She might have screamed because she fell down the stairs."

"If she'd fallen down the stairs, someone would have found her straight away."

That was true. "Do you think they'll close the library tomorrow?"

"Maybe the room she was found in, but surely not the whole library." Marigold's voice drops into a part whisper. "It must have been close to Bates Hall."

"I did think that too."

"We might have passed him on the way out—the killer, I mean."

I laugh, though it's possible of course. "If this were a book, we would have bumped into him at the very least."

"So we're still meeting tomorrow?"

I don't hesitate. The cleaner employed by the Sinclair Fellowship comes on Tuesdays, and I prefer to avoid the feeling that I'm in the way, or lazy or unclean, that is part and parcel of having someone clean up after you as an adult. "I'll be there. We'll at least find out if the library is closing for any period of time."

We talk for a while longer about other things. Marigold has a paper due on juvenile maternal separation anxiety, which she calls "mommy's boys and the women who create them." I'm laughing aloud by the time we arrange a place to meet in case we are not allowed into the BPL.

But when the call is over, my mind returns to the scream, the fact that I'd heard it. I'd heard someone die, and however it occurred, I was in no doubt she had been in terror. The fact seems to have a weight of its own, and I feel that weight in the pit of my stomach.

The news reports are now labelling the incident a murder. I'm not sure if they have more information or if it is simply an inevitable evolution of sensationalism.

Turning up the television, I return to work, guilty that whatever I feel about this poor woman, it does not curtail or slow the words. They are coming quickly, swirling into sentences that are strong and rhythmic, that surprise me with their clarity. It feels a little indecent to write so well in the wake of tragedy. But I do. The story of strangers bonded by a scream.

Dear Hannah,

Well played, my friend, well played! The Sinclair Fellowship is a terrific idea. You can place Winifred in Back Bay without burdening her with vast wealth. And she can be Australian.

And you put me in the story! With a Southern accent and my own fellowship. I am overwhelmed! You forgot to mention that Leo was tall and devastatingly attractive, but I suppose that's a given. Not only that, you've introduced a sneaky 4th option into your declaration that the perpetrator was present when Freddie had coffee in the Map Room. Was that your intention?

With respect to your first question, yes, I believe Bates Hall would be open the next day. Clearly the murder did not occur there but in one of the surrounding rooms or halls. There are plenty to choose from—I've listed a few suggestions below.

With some of these you might need to consider the volume of the scream. If it was loud enough to be heard within Bates Hall, then it really would have to have occurred in one of the adjoining rooms. I will be intrigued to read how you are going to explain why a search revealed nothing.

I did duck over to the BPL to see if I could spot anything of use. There are some vents that could possibly carry sound from a room farther away, but you would really need some sort of engineering or maintenance plan of the building to be sure. I'm a little wary of asking in case they decide I'm up to no good, but if I get a chance, I'll see what I can find out.

And now the other subject of your email... God, Hannah, thank you. I really did not expect you to offer to take my manuscript to your agent. I'm embarrassed that you might think that I was fishing for that. I assure you I wasn't. And though I'm too proud to accept your help, I'm too desperate to turn it down.

So, my manuscript is attached with the last of my dignity. Bear in mind that if you think it's terrible and never pass it on, I'll never know. And I'll never ask because there must be a way for our friendship to survive my lack of talent. I'm expressing this badly...which I suppose does not bode well for my manuscript, but I am grateful and touched that you would want to help me.

Anyway, I look forward to your next chapter, and I shall see if I can find anything that might be useful in placing your dead body in an appropriate place.

Again, with my thanks and admiration,

Leo

CHAPTER THREE

I spot Cain in the Newsfeed Café just inside the Johnson Building, where we'd arranged to meet, and wave. He smiles when he sees me, and I am reminded that he is very handsome. He's buying coffee and signals madly to see if I want one. I nod, and when I reach him he hands me a macchiato.

"No sugar, right?"

I am impressed he remembered.

We find a table at which to sip coffee and wait for Marigold and Whit. And, of course, we talk about the body found the night before.

"Where do you think they found her?" I ask. I don't really know the library that well. I've only been using it for a few days.

"That's what I can't figure out," he says. "We heard her scream, so she had to be in one of the rooms around Bates Hall…but they were searched."

"Unless the scream had nothing, in fact, to do with the body."

He frowns. "True. The scream might have been what the crime writers call"—he pauses for effect—"a red herring."

I smile. "Still, a heck of a coincidence."

"They do occur in reality, even if they are a bad plot device." Cain rises and excuses himself as he notices a newspaper left on the next table. He returns with the *Boston Globe* and sits beside me holding the paper between us. The account of the body in the public library is plastered across the front page. We pore over it, shoulder to shoulder, sipping coffee while we read.

We learn that the body was found in Chavannes Gallery, which was being prepared for an event the next day. That the woman's name was Caroline Palfrey. The name means little to an Australian like me, of course, but Cain mutters, "Brahmin."

"As in the cow?" I ask, a little confused.

"As in the social class." He explains that the Palfreys are from a long line of Brahmins, members of Boston's traditional upper echelons.

"They're rich?"

"It's more than wealth," he says. "The Brahmins were integral to the East Coast establishment. They're a culture unto themselves. Surely Australians have their equivalent—old family names that are prestigious because they declare themselves to be so?"

I smile, remembering Margaret Winslow, from the board of directors of the Sinclair Fellowship, who was so proud of being a sixth-generation Australian. In the country of the oldest living civilisation in the world, some sixty thousand years of indigenous history, six generations had seemed a pallid boast. And yet she made it, waxing lyrical about the property near Wagga Wagga that her great-great-great-grandfather had claimed in the mid-nineteenth century, the country he'd cleared and cultivated. Country that belonged to the Wiradjuri.

"Probably," I reply. "But I don't move in those circles."

"I believe that's the point of those circles."

"Does it say what was going to take place in the Chavannes Gallery?" I ask as I scour the article myself for the answer.

"Not really." He points to the relevant sentence. "She was found by a cleaner, so the gallery would probably have been otherwise empty."

"I wonder if Marigold or Whit knew her."

"Speak of devils," Cain says as they walk into the Newsfeed. He waves.

Marigold sees him, grabs Whit, and drags him towards us. Her eyes are bright and her cheeks flushed. She glances at the paper. "So you've seen it?"

"Yes, did you know—"

"No. But Whit did."

"I didn't really know her," Whit protests. "She worked on the *Rag*."

"The *Rag*?"

"It's a local tabloid." Whit shrugs. "Arts coverage mostly, with an occasional feature on something or other. I wrote a piece for them when I was a freshman…came across Caroline then."

"You write?" I ask, surprised that he hadn't mentioned that before.

"I tried my hand at a lot of stuff when I was an undergraduate…and it was just an article about football. I wouldn't call it literature."

Still, the connection, however tenuous, makes it all a little more real. I look at Whit and I imagine that he's not as blasé as he appears. "Did you hear anything about what happened?"

He shrugs. "Rumors about ex-boyfriends. Some guy who couldn't let go."

"Who?" Marigold asks. "Do you know his name? Is he a student? Where—"

"Steady on, Sherlock." Whit stems the deluge of questions. "What do you think I am?"

"Well, I thought—"

"That I might go interrogate people at the vigil, so you can rush in and make a citizen's arrest?"

I laugh. Marigold rolls her eyes.

Whit and Marigold decide against coffee. Cain and I finish ours, and we all head into the library only to find that Bates Hall—in fact the entire second floor—is closed. A security guard stationed at the base of the stairs maintains the cordon. The Map Room Tea Lounge is full, occupied by those turned out of Bates Hall, as well as reporters and the odd policeman; and Cain and I have, in any case, already had coffee.

"Did they discover another body?" Whit takes a step or two towards the stairs. The guard tells us in no uncertain terms to move on.

"Looks like today's a bust," I groan.

"But we were going to compare notes on our books today," Marigold protests.

I meet Cain's eye. Were we?

"You and Whit aren't writing books," he reminds her.

"You've inspired us to start," she says, smiling.

I can't help but return it. The look on Whit's face fails to appear particularly inspired.

There's something all-American about Marigold's smile, wide and quick and optimistic. You can imagine the Stars and Stripes fluttering behind her when she smiles, almost smell the apple pie. Whit's is similar. Cain's smile is different. It's slower, a little wry, and reveals less of his teeth. But they all smile while they talk—that's the difference, I think, that's what makes it American. Australians don't seem to be able to smile and talk at the same time—unless we're lying, of course. And then the smile is involuntary, a tell of deceit.

"What are you thinking?" Cain asks, regarding me curiously.

I tell them.

"Wow! That's a bit random!" Marigold is clearly not sure whether she should be offended.

"Sorry—writer's mind."

"That's interesting," Cain's head tilts as he studies me and, immediately, I smile. "So how do you tell when Americans are lying?"

"I don't know. Maybe you can't."

The security guard is glaring at us now. Clearly, we're loitering and possibly he overheard the conversation. In unison we flash him a smile.

"We could head across the square and find someplace to have a burger," Whit suggests. "We can teach Freddie how to smile properly, in case she ever needs to get a job at McDonald's."

"I'm a writer," I say. "It's a distinct possibility."

The Boston Burger Company in Boylston Street is quiet at this time of the day. It's only opened its doors in the last few minutes, and the lunch influx has not yet begun. We claim a table and order onion rings and nachos.

Marigold asks me immediately how Freud Girl is faring. "Have you thought about a love interest for her? Someone incredibly sexy. She wouldn't settle for just any old Joe... He's got to have prospects and a stock portfolio."

"Really?" It seems incongruent that someone so extensively inked and pierced as Marigold would have such traditional, not to mention fiscal, requirements.

She shrugs. "The heart wants what it wants."

I glance at Whit and Cain. Neither is willing to comment.

After a little prompting by Marigold, I tell them about the novel I've started to write. I don't usually share my work at this stage, but as this story begins with a group of people united by a scream, it seems fair, even necessary. And I'm excited. I want to talk about it, discuss the possibilities. Whit and Marigold are immediate with their input. Marigold bubbles enthusiastically; Whit echoes with the odd quip thrown in; and even as they comment on the story, they hand me their own dialogue. Cain is slower, more considered—he asks about points of view, tense, and story arcs. And his questions help give form to the swirling mists I've conjured. He's intrigued by my method, the fact that I don't plot, but there's nothing judgemental in the way he asks, and I try to explain my metaphorical bus without sounding like a lunatic.

Cain shows us his plot, an intricate flowchart created on his laptop, and explains the themes and subplots which radiate from his central premise. There's something beautiful about the chart. It's like a spider's web spun to catch a story. I'm fascinated by it, and a little regretful that my work does not begin with gossamer webs.

Cain's book is the story of a homeless man called Isaac Harmon who takes up residence in and around the Boston Public Library. Threads of backstory, self-discovery, and social commentary radiate from the novel's very human centre. His plan defines links, the points at which one thread meets another and entwines or branches again. I ask him about the story's origins, where he found Isaac Harmon, around whom everything was spun.

"I ran away from home when I was fifteen. Ended up in Boston and lived rough for a couple of weeks."

"You ran away? Why?" I ask.

"Usual teenage melodrama," he replies. "I only lasted two weeks. Would have been much less if I hadn't met Isaac. He kept me out of real trouble and made sure I didn't starve until I was ready to go home."

"You parents must have been insane with worry."

He laughs. "Actually, they thought I'd gone on vacation with a friend, so not so much. They were mad but not worried. As far as grand gestures were concerned, it was less than successful. But I did meet Isaac."

"Are you still in touch?" Marigold asks.

A darkness flashes across Cain's eyes. For a while he keeps his own counsel, before he responds. "He'd ring me every now and then. I'd meet him, take him for a burger. We'd talk. He was killed about five years ago."

"I'm sorry." I know instinctively that he isn't talking about an accidental death.

"How was he killed?" Whit speaks reflexively as if he's asking about where Cain bought his shoes.

"Someone stabbed him."

"Oh, shit!" Whit blurts.

"He was murdered?" Marigold seems more intrigued than shocked.

Cain nods. "The police appear to believe it was an argument over a doorway or something. I only know because Isaac still had a piece of paper with my number and address on it, in his pocket. They found it and thought that I might be a relative."

Whit shakes his head. "That's tough, man."

"So, this is Isaac's story?" I ask, tentatively, because I'm not sure he wants to talk about it. I know he's writing about it, but that's different. Words are put down in solitude; there is a strange privacy to those disclosures. Time to get used to the revelation before readers are necessarily taken into your confidence.

"In a way, I suppose." He heaps refried beans and cheese onto a corn chip that's too small for the purpose. "It's part him, part me, part stuff I just made up."

"The magic formula," I say.

Cain smiles at me, and the fact that he's handsome is again very salient.

"Did they ever find him? The man who killed your friend?" Marigold is still curious.

"No."

"How sad." Marigold looks hard at him. "Does it bother you?"

Cain considers the question. "I guess. But not as much as the fact that he died cold and alone and in pain." He folds his arms across his chest. "Isaac could be...fierce. Whoever killed him might have been scared, or sick, or angry. There are a lot of scared, sick, and angry people sleeping rough."

I wonder what exactly he saw in the two weeks he was on the streets. I don't ask him. Those are stories that should be offered rather than elicited.

"There are a lot of scared, sick, and angry people sleeping in beds every night," Whit observes.

Cain glances at him.

Whit flinches. "Sorry, man; I didn't mean—"

"No, you're right." He taps a note into the laptop. "It's a good line. You don't mind if I use it, do you?"

I laugh.

Cain points at me over the screen. "Don't pretend you're not doing the same thing. At least I ask."

Marigold places her elbows on the table and props her chin on her hands. "So what are we going to do about Caroline Palfrey?"

"What do you mean *do*?" Whit demands.

"We can't just pretend it didn't happen and carry on. Someone was killed mere feet from where we were sitting. It has to change things."

Whit carefully pulls an onion ring from a stack smothered with honey barbeque sauce and cheese. "If anything is going to make us reveal our true identities as avenging superheroes, surely it's that."

"There were a lot of people in Bates Hall that day, Marigold," Cain says more gently.

"It just seems indecent to not do anything. We heard her die." There is an earnestness in Marigold's voice.

"I'm not sure what we can possibly do," Cain admits.

"What if they never find out who killed Caroline?" Marigold's voice trembles. "We heard her scream. A scream is supposed to bring help, and we heard her scream."

Dear Hannah,

It's reading well. I feel like I know them all just better enough to be intrigued by their individual stories. I think you've struck the right balance there. They all seem much more than they present initially. Again, I really like the last line. It's haunting—particularly if you've ever heard anyone scream.

Tiny terminology issue. Americans don't really use "sleeping rough." We'd probably understand it from the context, but it is a little unusual in an American character's dialogue. It is quite a nice term, though, less defeated than homeless, and less permanent.

With respect to your question as to whether the distance between Harvard and the Boston Public Library is walkable—if you're a German hiker, yes. If you're anybody else, you'd catch a cab, an Uber, or a bus. The bus would be a number 57 or 86. The train (subway) would be the Green Line to Park Street, which is the subway stop across the street from the BPL on Boylston and Dartmouth, transferring to the Red Line at Park Street for Harvard Square. That's probably too much detail, but I'd rather give you too much than too little.

Anyway, does this mean you're going to make Copley Square the center of operations for this novel? I do like that you've taken them across to The Burger Company on Boylston, though there are any number of eateries from which you could choose. I've attached a list of places which are not too expensive. You should know that there are two churches in the Square—Trinity and the Old South Church. I imagine there could be vigils for Caroline at either or both of them. I've attached a couple of photographs. Let me know if you'd like me to take some pictures inside.

Depending on the time of year in which you're setting the novel, your foursome could also easily meet at the Copley Square Fountain with packed lunches. There is also the Fairmont Hotel in the Plaza, but it would be very expensive as an ordinary lunch venue.

I do wonder how you're going to move the story on from this point. They don't really have a reason to become involved in the investigation. When I read that Caroline Palfrey worked on a paper, I thought for a moment that Cain might have known her or have been interviewed by her, but you don't seem to be moving that way...or are you? Sorry, I don't mean to be second-guessing where the narrative is going. Take it as a compliment that I already care.

Is there any update on when you might be coming to the U.S.? Not that I mind being your man in Boston—it's a pleasure, and I really am having fun—but being seen with a famous author would do wonders for my reputation!

Now my news: An old friend from my college days happens to play tennis with Alexandra Gainsborough, the agent. Diane's invited us both to dinner in the hope that face-to-face, in a social setting, I might be able to entice Miss Gainsborough to look at the opus. I must admit I'm a little nervous. Perhaps the poor woman is sick to death of being ambushed by desperate writers while she's trying to eat. How does one do this sort of thing with any level of social grace and reserve, when what I really want to do is beg her to give my book a chance? Don't worry, I won't do that...unless I have to. Anyway, keep your fingers crossed for me.

With a cautious spring in my step,

Leo

CHAPTER FOUR

The muse and I have been locked in my apartment for three days. Leo is the only other human I've seen in that time, and even he was warned off by the distracted haze through which I regarded him.

"You're writing?" He looks me up and down. Clearly, I look the part.

"Yes. Would you like to come in for a drink?"

"Are you simply being polite?"

"Yes," I admit.

He smiles. "Then I reckon I'll take a rain check."

I feel my face relax. "Thank you, Leo. I'm sorry—that's the second time I've begged off..."

"Don't fret none, Freddie." He takes off his glasses and squints into the apartment behind me. "I wouldn't have even come to the door. Only hope you haven't let the muse out by doing so."

"I broke her legs...she's not going anywhere."

He stops, a little startled.

I grin. "I kid, I kid. I've bribed her with Tim Tams."

Leo shakes his head. "You Aussies have a dark side."

"Nonsense. We're friendly alcoholics who like to barbeque and swear."

He's already walking away. "I wish your muse the best of luck!"

That was two days ago. The story is still coming in waves, surging ideas crashing onto the page faster than I can type. I've not yet found actual names for Handsome Man, Heroic Chin, and Freud Girl, but it doesn't seem to matter. Perhaps it's because I am not yet ready to diverge them from their inspiration, to stem that momentum of discovery, the excitement of new friendship that seems to form a story of itself. The narrative is strange—unlike anything I've written before. The library takes on a consciousness of its own, watchful, patient, dangerous. The scream becomes a motif, an echo of each character's silent cry for connection and friendship, for help.

Freud Girl is the story's heart, which she wears on sleeves of ink. Forthright, vibrant, and a little romantic, she believes in justice and loyalty and moves through the world with a kind of child-like innocence. But there's some part of her that wants to warn people to stay back, to clothe her natural warmth in signals of street ferocity. For a while I wonder what it is that makes her wary of strangers: a troubled childhood, a lack of stability, even tragedy. Perhaps it's simply a matter of taste. I expect Marigold just likes tattoos and piercings, but Freud Girl will have to be more complex than that.

Heroic Chin is laid back to almost Australian levels, his defiance passive, but effective. A young man trying to prove he is unworthy of his parents' ambitions. His infatuation with Freud Girl possibly has roots in that same impulse to thwart expectations.

For some reason, although I am centering the story on Freud Girl, I write Handsome Man as a hero. I am self-aware enough to recognise a kind of glow to the way I describe him. I laugh at myself, but still, Handsome Man draws me in.

I find myself thinking about the weeks Cain spent on the street, wondering if there was something more than a surge of adolescent temper behind his leaving home. Cain doesn't seem given to grand gestures for no reason, but I've only known him a few days, or perhaps he's changed, grown up.

I scroll down through all the pages I've written in the last few days. The manuscript is a bit wild—I wonder if the bus is going too fast, careening out of control. A fleeting sadness that there is no character to hold my place. I feel somehow left out, even though the decision, the omission, was mine.

My phone rings, and I spend several flustered seconds trying to locate it beneath piles of books and plates which had once held toast. I barely manage to answer it before it goes to voicemail.

It's Cain. "Do you feel like taking a break?"

I hesitate. Not because I don't want to stop, but because I'm not even dressed. "Right now?"

"Oh, sorry, have I caught you in the middle of something? I didn't mean to—"

I come clean because I can't at this moment think of anything aside from the truth. "I'm in my pyjamas…haven't even showered."

He laughs. "How long do you need?"

"At least an hour… We're looking at a major overhaul."

"Okay, do what you can, and meet me in Copley Plaza at one o'clock."

I check the time. An hour and a half. "I can't guarantee the result."

"I'll keep my expectations low," he replies. I can hear the smile in his voice, see it in my mind's eye. "How about I wait for you at the fountain?"

I'm already walking to the bathroom. I must be more beset by cabin fever than I realized because I'm excited about the idea of stepping out, of meeting Cain. Deep down I know this is about Cain, but one should maintain one's dignity even in conversations with oneself. Three days is enough to make anyone stir crazy, and I probably do need to talk to someone, make sure the work is not embarking in a direction that's too implausible. And I'm running out of food anyway—this will be a chance to pick up supplies.

I shower and get dressed, finally draping a woollen scarf around my neck and pulling on gloves. For a moment, I languish in the childish fleeting pleasure of putting on new things for the first time. The scarf and gloves were both purchased last week as autumn set in. It's rarely cold enough for such accessories back home, and so they are yet a novelty. I wave bright yellow gloved hands into the mirror. They make me feel a bit more like I belong in Boston—I guess there's nothing that says "visiting Australian" more than wandering about shivering.

Copley Square is only a brief walk from my building. I take my laptop with me. I don't like it out of reach at this stage, for reasons that have nothing to do with whether I intend or expect to write. When I'm an old lady, one shoulder will probably be lower than the other after a lifetime of lugging laptops like they are some portable life-support system—which perhaps they are.

The fountain in Copley Square is styled on the Roman aqueduct: arches, channels spouting water into a pool. Despite that, it's not old, particularly in amongst the buildings of the historic square. Nor is it spectacular, but the area is pleasant, and the day is beautiful. Sharp and bright, and softened by the warm blaze of an American fall. Cain spots me as I approach and runs over.

"Am I late?" I ask, worrying suddenly that I spent too long fussing over what I was wearing.

"Not at all. Did I interrupt your momentum?"

I shake my head. "No...you saved me from myself. It's nice to walk outside, to be honest."

He looks noticeably relieved. "Shall we go for a stroll before we find somewhere for lunch then? Or have you had enough of walking?"

I haven't.

Though I did join a couple of guided tours of Boston when I first arrived, it's different walking those same streets with Cain. He's not telling old stories attached to landmarks but looking for new ones, places and details which might be spun into the web of Isaac Harmon's story. It's like a game—what might have happened here—and soon I'm playing.

We come to a doorway, the entrance to an antique store, and though he stops and stares at it, he says nothing. I prompt him. Perhaps there is something in the window which is connected to his hero's old life.

He winces. "This is where I tried to sleep that first night after I got off the bus from Charlotte."

"Oh...I see..." The doorway is wide and sheltered, but it smells unsavoury, and even in the day, this part of the street is shaded and cold. "What happened?"

"The junkie who usually slept there came along and beat the hell out of me."

"Oh, my God!"

"Isaac happened to be sleeping over there." Cain points across the road to a gap between two buildings. "He came over, calmed the guy down, gave him a couple of cigarettes, and took me with him."

"You must have been terrified."

"Not terrified enough. Isaac tried to talk me into going home, or at least to a shelter. When I wouldn't, he let me hang around with him." Cain glances at me. "You seem shocked."

"Only that it took you two weeks to go home." I meet his eyes. They're dark, nearly black. "Things must have been bad."

"My stepfather was a..." He shakes his head. "We didn't get on."

"And when you went back?"

"He wasn't around for much after I got back."

"And your mother?"

"Mom got over him. She lives in Minnesota now."

I look back at the doorway. "Are you going to write this into your story?"

"I don't know… I can't write me, but what Isaac did for me is important, I think. He wasn't a saint, Freddie. He didn't help everyone, and I saw him do things that were downright mean, but he chose to save my life. The choosing is interesting. I can't leave it out."

"So don't. Just change who he chose…a girl maybe…or a dog."

"A dog?" He groans. "You want me to cast a dog in the role of myself."

"Make it a nice dog—one without fleas or rabies."

Cain glances at his watch. "There's a really cool vegetarian place around the corner. Will that do for lunch?"

"Yes…sure." I'm surprised that he's noticed that I'm vegetarian. We've shared a couple of meals, but I don't remember announcing the fact, only not ordering meat.

There's a small crowd on the corner watching a street performer, and Cain takes my hand so we don't lose each other as we weave through. The restaurant, a couple of doors down from the corner, is called Karma. It's clearly popular, packed, yet somehow we manage to get at table by the window.

"Are you sure this is okay?" I ask as we peruse menus. "I really don't mind eating in an ordinary restaurant—there's always a vegetarian option."

"And miss out on all this…tofu?" He pulls a face.

The grimace seems to summon a waiter, and we order lentil burgers and fruit smoothies. We fall into conversation again, about our work, Boston, and, inevitably, Caroline Palfrey.

"I've been thinking about that scream," Cain tells me. "We all heard it, and yet she wasn't found right away. I've been wondering how that could happen."

I nod. "It's a bit like a locked room mystery in reverse."

He looks at me quizzically.

"Sorry—I forgot you're not a mystery writer." I try to explain. "A locked room mystery is one in which the victim is found in a room locked from the inside. Where the mystery is really about how the murderer got in and out again."

He frowns. "So when you say it's locked room in reverse—"

"I said *a bit* like," I qualify. "But yes, we heard Caroline scream…as Marigold says, we heard her die. And yet her body wasn't there when the guards searched. And then, a few hours later, there she was. The mystery is about where her body was between the scream and when she was found."

"Perhaps the scream wasn't Caroline's."

"Ah, yes, the coincidence theory."

"What else could it be?"

"Well, you'd have to look at the security guards who checked the surrounding rooms." I'm thinking as I speak. "Maybe Caroline was there all along. Maybe someone had a reason for reporting that the Chavannes Gallery was clear."

We are startled by a tapping at the window against which our table is positioned. We look up to see Marigold and Whit. After a few seconds of frantic signalling and gesticulating, they come in and join us.

"Were we supposed to meet for lunch?" Marigold asks. "I'm so sorry—"

"No…we weren't." I feel vaguely guilty. "Cain and I just caught up to discuss book stuff."

"Oh." Marigold looks a little crestfallen, and I feel terrible.

"I was stuck." Cain volunteers. "I needed to check some locations and thought Freddie might like to come—being an out-of-towner and all. She's now seen some of the seediest parts of Boston."

"Well that's a relief!" Whit intervenes. "I thought for a moment I'd forgotten to pass on a message."

"What are you two up to?" Cain asks.

"I was heading to the library," Marigold says. "I saw Whit from the other side of the road and crossed to say hello."

Whit grins. "I was going to the donut place down the block a ways, when I spotted you guys in the window…and then Marigold came squealing across the street."

"I don't squeal!" Marigold shoves him.

Cain smiles at me. "We'll call it a coincidence then."

———

Dear Hannah,

Dinner was lovely. Diane went all out—served lobster, seated me beside Alex, and raised the opus because I still hadn't summoned the courage to mention it myself by dessert—which was a positively decadent chocolate concoction which you would have loved!

I had taken the time to devise an eloquent way to summarize the opus into a couple of apparently casual sentences...the dreaded elevator pitch. I added a few thoughtful pauses and an "ummm" to make it seem spontaneous.

Diane, bless her, kept asking questions so the conversation didn't move on, and I was able to "reluctantly" talk about my work.

Anyway Alex gave me her card and asked me to send her the manuscript.

So as you can imagine I am so far over the moon I can see Pluto!

I remember you telling me that the first time someone says "yes" is unsurpassable. I can't verify that, but "maybe yes" is pretty mind-blowing. I'm blaming that for the fact I don't have any comments on your last chapter. I'm just too happy to concentrate. I'll read it again tomorrow—I'm sure I will have calmed down a bit by then—and get back to you if I have any comments or suggestions about the Boston bits.

I'm going to check the opus one more time for typos etc before I send it out.

Keep your fingers crossed for me when you're not writing.

In hope,
Leo

CHAPTER FIVE

We end up in my apartment that evening, eating delivered pizza and just hanging. Whit pokes around in my kitchen and cobbles together a massive banana split sundae for dessert, which he serves in a salad bowl with four spoons. I'm surprised by how comfortable I am with these people so recently strangers. Today I'm telling them about my crazy family and old boyfriends, moments of mortification, and assorted personal horror stories I didn't think I'd ever share. It might have something to do with the wine—not that any of us drink a debilitating amount. Only enough to be a little compromised. And in our mutual, if marginal, inebriation there is a demonstration of trust, in each other, and the fledging friendship between us all.

Marigold tells us of the twelve years she spent studying classical ballet and attempts to demonstrate that she can still stand *en pointe*. It turns out she can't—not anymore, or at this moment anyway. She speaks of the dance that she loved, the discipline that she loathed. And through these stories, I glimpse a traditional conservative and highly aspirational upbringing. I see a young woman in the process of redefining herself. Marigold shows us her first tattoo, a ballerina in repose, stretched out across her back.

Whit is the first to respond. "Fuck! Is she dead?"

I gag on my wine. Cain freezes, expecting an explosion.

But Marigold laughs. "She was supposed to be resting, but perhaps she's dead. Perhaps it was an omen."

"Is that Mickey Mouse?" I ask, peering at the image hidden partially by her shirt.

"Yes," she says, removing her shirt entirely so that we can see the tattoos which cover every inch of skin below her collarbone. She places her hands on her hips and turns slowly so that we can see every inking. I am aware of her nakedness but I'm too intrigued by her skin to be shocked. Cain takes a breath, while Whit pours himself another glass of wine. "Donald's there too, above my hip."

"God, I hope you mean the duck," Whit mutters.

Her small breasts are covered with flowers. The tattoos are eclectic, and yet none stand out from the complex cohesive picture. We ask about individual designs, and Marigold explains the circumstances of their acquisition.

Cain questions her about the needles and the level of pain involved with each tattoo.

"The ones around the ribs hurt the most." She touches the area as she speaks. "I screamed like I was being—well, I screamed."

"Where are you going to put the next one?" Whit asks, walking around her in search of un-inked territory.

"I'm pristine below the waist." Marigold pulls up the leg of her jeans to show us the untouched skin. "But I'm not sure I will get any more."

"Why not?" I ask, because I'm curious as to her reasons, not because I think she needs more body art.

"An arbitrary boundary… It means I'll always have space for the perfect tattoo should I ever find it. It means I won't be finished… I don't want to be complete…not yet." She puts her shirt back on. "Aren't you guys inked at all?" She looks at me. "Is it not a thing people do in Australia?"

"Oh, no—they do. A lot of people do. And a lot of people don't. I don't."

Whit flops onto my couch. "The police questioned me."

For a moment we all just stare at him. Marigold speaks first…or shouts. "Why the hell didn't you say?"

"I'm saying now."

"It'd be strange if they didn't talk to you," Cain offers. "They're probably talking to everyone who knew Caroline Palfrey."

"They'll probably talk to the three of you now, too," Whit says apologetically.

Marigold looks at him suspiciously. "Why?"

"To verify that I was in Bates Hall when she died."

"Oh, my God! They asked you for an alibi!"

"Only where I was."

"Are you okay, Whit?" I ask gently. He does look a little shaken.

"Yeah. I'm fine." He winces. "I saw a picture of her body."

"They showed you a picture of her corpse?"

"No...I saw it on the whiteboard as I was going to the interview room."

"Was it really awful?" Marigold asks.

"Not particularly. She must have been hit in the head...there was blood in her hair...but otherwise she looked sort of peaceful. Like she was sleeping."

"Did they say anything about why it took so long to find her?" Marigold tops up his glass of wine.

I'm surprised when Whit answers. "Yeah, apparently the Gallery was being set up for some event the next day. She was under the buffet table—hidden by table linens and rosettes and stuff. They only found her because one of the cleaners was fastidious enough to lift the tablecloth to vacuum."

"Good God! Are you on the case now?" I ask, wondering how he's come to know so much.

He snorts. "No, but my folks are. The Palfreys have been clients of Metters and Putnam for years."

"They told you this?"

"Not directly—that would be unprofessional. And the parental units are nothing if not professional. But you overhear stuff when you drop by." He exhaled. "I expect that me being questioned is a little awkward. If you didn't know them, you'd worry about a conflict of interest."

I'm not sure how to respond, but Marigold, who is possibly a little drunker than the rest of us, embraces him.

Whit looks startled. "What's that for?"

"I just thought you needed a hug."

"I'm fine, Marigold. The police questioned me...they didn't torture me."

Cain returns us to the subject to Caroline Palfrey. "So, whoever killed Caroline managed to hide her beneath a table without anyone seeing? And before the security guards got there?"

"That's the theory."

"Perhaps the murderer was disguised as someone from the catering company," I suggest. "The security guards wouldn't have raised an eyebrow, particularly as the body wasn't found until much later."

"You're right," Cain replies. "Or maybe they weren't disguised at all. Perhaps she was murdered by a caterer."

"Are you making fun of me?"

"Not at all. Murderer isn't a job description, Freddie. It tends to be something you do on the side." He opens another bottle of wine. "Maybe one of the caterers knew Caroline. Maybe he had reason to kill her."

"Or she," Marigold points out. "The murderer might be a woman."

"Or she," Cain concedes as he hands her a glass of wine.

"You would have thought you'd see blood spatter, or something of the sort." I still find it odd that Caroline's body was undetected. "Unless she was under the buffet table when she was killed, you'd expect the security guards to have seen something."

"She could have been under the buffet table," Whit says.

"Why?"

"Looking for a dropped earring, or a bit of privacy." Whit shrugs. "Could be she was trying to avoid someone. I once ran into the ladies' restroom trying to avoid an old girlfriend."

"Would have thought it'd be more sensible to run into the men's room," Cain murmurs.

"Oh, yeah!" Whit exclaims. "I'll do that next time."

"What are you two doing to your exes that you have to hide from them?" Marigold pokes him.

He smiles and raises his brows. "You're not asking a gentleman to kiss and tell, are you, Marigold?"

"You're not a gentleman," she says.

It's well past midnight, and they are probably too drunk to go home safely. They're too drunk to want to go home, anyway. So I gather extra pillows and blankets from the linen closet in the hall and make up beds for Cain and Whit in the sitting room. They toss a coin for the couch. Cain loses and takes the floor.

I bring him extra pillows from my own bed. "Are you sure you'll be all right?"

"I lived on the streets, remember."

Whit snorts. "For two weeks!" He strips down to his underwear without the slightest hint of modesty or self-consciousness.

"Are you sure you don't mind us staying?" Cain asks. "You probably want to get back to work."

I glance at Whit, already stretched out on my couch. It's clear he's not going anywhere. "It's cool," I reply. "You're all material."

Marigold is sharing my bed. It's big enough that it's not awkward. She makes us mugs of tea and closes the door so that we can chat without being overheard.

"Do you like him?" she asks.

"Who?"

"Cain."

"What are we—twelve?"

She giggles. "Whit and I busted you."

I sip my tea. Apparently we're having a slumber party. "Cain and I were talking about our books, Marigold. We figured you and Whit would have better things to do than listen to us blither about subplots and themes, or whether adverbs have been unjustly vilified and metaphors overused."

Marigold considers what I've said. "We don't have better things to do."

"Aren't you both trying to get degrees…or more degrees?"

Marigold wrinkles her nose. "Well, yes, but that's more background noise than something to do."

I laugh. "We all met only a few days ago… How can everything else be background noise?"

"Not everything…just classes." She shrugs. "It doesn't really matter if we attend. Whit wants to fail, and I'm something of a genius."

She smiles as she says it, but I don't for a moment doubt it.

Marigold wraps her arms around her legs and rests her chin on her knees. "But don't you think there's something special about the four of us? I feel like I recognise you all."

It may be that I'm more drunk than I think, because I know what she means. I leave my mug of tea on the bedside table and drop my head back onto the pillow. "Did you and Whit know each other before that first day in the library?"

"No. I had seen him around, but we'd never spoken to each other." She climbs under the covers. "I wonder if any of us would ever have spoken to the others if we hadn't heard Caroline scream."

I think about that. It seems inconceivable now that we might have gone our four different ways.

Marigold's voice is low and melodic, and she is still talking when I drift off, something about Whit and sabotage.

Dear Hannah,

I think I may be in love with Marigold! She'd probably drive me nuts in person, but on the page, she is luminescent. She steals scenes. Not that the others are slouches either...but Marigold!

I wonder if you should give the reader an idea of what Winifred looks like. She's given us descriptions of Handsome Man, Heroic Chin, and Freud Girl, but we have no real sense of what she looks like. And I want to know why Cain is more interested in Freddie than Marigold. Sure, they're both writers, but it's got to be more than that. Of course, it may not be what she looks like, but when you create a character as beguiling as Marigold, the reader will wonder why the guy is choosing her friend. Unless he's not choosing Freddie...(cue dramatic music).

I see on the news that Australia's dealing with wildfires again. They must be pretty severe if we're hearing about them here. We don't really hear much about Australia. This is probably a dumb question which will demonstrate my appalling lack of knowledge with respect to Australia's geography, but are you safe? I have images of you typing just one more paragraph as the flames lick at your door. It started to snow in Boston today...not heavily, but enough to warn us all of what's to come. Big flakes, the kind that grace Christmas cards—does anyone send Christmas cards anymore? I imagine it must be strange to write your gang in a Boston winter when you're living through a heat wave on the other side of the world.

Anyway, I thought of a couple of things Freddie might be dealing with while you swelter. Heat waves in your hemisphere seem to be balanced by ice ages in ours.

A place like Carrington Square is bound to have good heating, so it will be a matter of layering on and off every time she leaves or enters the building. If she's out early, she'll have to be careful of ice on the sidewalks—they're great fun when you're a kid, less so when you break a hip. The scarf and gloves are fine, but most sensible people wear a hat of some sort—remember though that we don't use the term beanie! Freddie doesn't have a car so she won't have any cause to shovel snow...but perhaps Cain will. Or Leo. Because, let's face it, a character that charismatic deserves a bigger part.

I haven't heard anything from Alexandra Gainsborough as yet, but it's probably still too early to expect or even hope for a response. Of course, the dream is that Alex will have been so taken by the manuscript that she reads it in one sitting, forgetting all other demands on her time, and that, on finally putting it down, she rings the genius author immediately to sign him to a contract before anyone else can. As I said, the dream.

Anyway, I better sign off and return to trying not to think about Alex reading the opus.

Yours in eternal and stubborn hope,
Leo

CHAPTER SIX

The gift basket is delivered to the reception in the chequerboard foyer. When I go down to collect it, Mrs. Weinbaum and her sister-in-law, Mrs. Jackson, who share an apartment on the ground floor, are discussing the basket which they apparently saw arrive. They are elegantly dressed in smart coats and jaunty hats. If we were in Sydney, I would assume that they were setting off for a day at the races, but here, they might just be going shopping. They don't notice me come downstairs.

"Yoghurt? What kind of man sends yoghurt...and eggs?" Mrs. Weinbaum's pencilled eyebrows furrow as she *tsks*.

"Perhaps she's ill?" Mrs. Jackson looks closely at the large basket sitting up on the reception desk, taking a careful inventory of its contents. "There's coffee, too. And cheese."

"Good morning," I say.

They show not the slightest embarrassment at being caught examining my mail. "This came for you," Mrs. Jackson says.

"How lovely." I extract the card from the bunch of flowers on the top.

Because we forgot to pick up supplies yesterday and then Whit ate everything you had left. Get back to work. I don't want to be responsible for derailing your masterpiece—Cain.

I must have mentioned needing to restock when I met Cain, or perhaps he noticed I didn't have much by way of food in my kitchen. Whit had fried and devoured the few groceries I had—eggs, potatoes, bread—that morning before Cain marshalled them out so I could get back to writing.

I smile. I've been starving for at least three hours, afraid to ask the muse for time off to buy food. She's fickle and easily offended, likely to sulk if I don't give her my complete attention when she's gracing me with her presence. Perhaps that's why writers starve in garrets—because the literary muse is a sadistic fascist. Mrs. Weinbaum and Mrs. Jackson titter with satisfaction, reading something into my smile. I chat with them for a while, assure them that I'm not ill, despite the yoghurt.

"It's good for stomach upsets," Mrs. Weinbaum tells me, nevertheless.

The doorman carries the box up for me because it's huge and heavy, setting it on the kitchen table and leaving me to unpack its contents. Milk, cereal, eggs, coffee, tomatoes, apples, dried fruit, cheese, almonds, chocolate, three different kinds of cookies, bread, peanut butter, jam, yoghurt, and a posy of yellow hothouse roses. I make myself peanut butter and cheese on rye while I put everything away, savouring both the sandwich and the thoughtfulness of the gesture. I call Cain to thank him, but his phone has been turned off. He's probably working, too. I leave a voice message and then, the moment I hang up, wonder if it's too gushy.

I flick through the other mail which was waiting with the box. A couple of letters to do with the Sinclair scholarship, and a Christmas card from my grandmother. One of those cheap cards you buy in packets of fifty at the supermarket, for less than what it costs to post them—a red background with a silver snowflake. It's barely November, but Nana likes to have her cards be the first of the season. She treats each Yuletide like a race, a demonstration of the efficiency on which she prides herself. A fleeting twinge as I think of home. Nan would have a tree up and her house already decorated with plastic Santa Clauses and reindeer cutouts. There'd be a giant inflatable snowman on her front lawn, misshapen after several seasons in the summer sun, its printed face faded, its seams puckered by the heat. Christmas in Australia is sometimes an exercise in irony.

I return to the laptop with a cup of coffee and cookies. Freud Girl is centre stage, consumed by the scream and now strange memories of a murdered ballerina. Disjointed images she can't explain, but which torment her. I write her terror gently, allowing what is unsaid to carry the narrative, aware that overt emotion could well move the story into melodrama. I'm not yet sure what her memories mean. Actually, I have no idea. The bus is still gathering speed and passengers. For a while I play with the image I see in her mind, explore why it might be there. Was Freud Girl a bystander, a surviving victim, or perhaps a killer?

I don't really consider the last possibility seriously. At this stage I don't want to know, don't want to risk the knowledge seeping into the manuscript too early and undermining the mystery. And so I ride, almost indifferent to where I'm going as I focus on rhythm and momentum, on who boards and where they choose to sit, whether they chat or read or simply stare out the window. The bus driver is a shadow, a practical necessity of transport, and for now I disregard him entirely.

Fortified by Cain's box of supplies, I don't leave the apartment that day or the next. I am vaguely aware that Cain has not returned my call, but maybe it's absurd to expect a call to thank me for calling to thank him. Where would it end? Still, I wonder if I was too gushy with my voicemail… Perhaps he's worried I'm getting the wrong idea. God, how embarrassing! Why couldn't I have left something understated and witty…?

It's quite late when I take a video call on my laptop, expecting it to be someone from home. Cain's face opens on my screen, and I'm startled enough to gasp and pull away. He smiles. "Freddie?" He sounds slightly unsure.

I glance at the box in the lower screen which shows me what he can see. I have the hair of a mad woman, and I'm wearing pyjamas that should have been cut up for rags long ago.

"Sorry." I try to smooth the untamed curls with my hand. "I thought you were my grandmother…"

His right brow moves up, but he doesn't ask. "I was just checking that you got the box I left."

"Oh, yes." I thank him again and mention that I'd left him a voice mail two days ago.

"I seem to have misplaced my phone," he replies grimacing. "In fact, I was hoping you might have come across it at your place."

"No…it can't be here. I would have heard it when I rang you."

He groans. "I might have to bite the bullet and buy another one."

We talk for a while about where else he might have left his phone. He asks me how my manuscript is going, and I tell him that Marigold's ballerina has worked its way into my story. He sits back in his swivel chair as he talks to me. I can see the room behind him. The wall is covered with sticky notes in various colours and pictures. Lengths of string interconnect clusters of notes. Cain's spiderweb.

He notices me squinting at the screen and looks over his shoulder.

"Is that your plot?" I ask. "My God, it looks like you're sitting in a police incident room!"

He laughs and holds up his laptop so I can see that the strings run onto the ceiling, where more notes are tacked to the plasterboard. The lines cross and weave around the entire room. "This," he says, "is what procrastination looks like."

"Well, it's very impressive." I'm fascinated. It's like peeking inside his mind. "Does it help?"

"Sometimes." He shrugs. "Sometimes when I feel like I'm free-falling, I write in here and the story catches me."

"A net beneath the tightrope." I understand free-falling. In a way, my work is all free-falling. But I have no net.

"I don't how you do what you do," he says, turning the camera back to his face.

The admission is admiring, and I can't help but be pleased by the compliment of it.

"I suspect I'd get tangled in a net," I reply. As much as Cain's web is beautiful, I think I'd find it confining. I tell him about my current bus journey.

He listens intently. "That's a brave way of writing, Freddie. I'm not sure I have that kind of courage."

"We're writing stories, Cain," I say smiling. "It's not brain surgery… Nobody's going to live or die because the bus goes nowhere."

"Clearly you have not read *Misery*."

We talk then about Stephen King and his books and the films made from them, what it would be like to be that iconic as a storyteller. He asks me if I'd like to go see the latest King film later in the week. I say sure. For some reason neither of us mentions Whit or Marigold.

When I eventually close the screen, I'm excited—embarrassed that I am, but excited, nonetheless. Though I won't be seeing anyone that night, I clean myself up…tying back my hair and changing into less ragged pyjamas. I'm making scrambled eggs for dinner when my phone rings. I assume Cain's found his phone. Thank goodness! I'm not sure I could cope with the pressure of always being video-chat presentable.

I answer. "Hello again—"

The scream that cuts me off is not a man's. It's female, and terrified, and familiar. The scream is Caroline Palfrey's.

———

Dear Hannah,

Jeepers! That ending sure got my attention!

But first, the fires near Sydney! The reports we're getting look terrifying. But I'm glad to hear you at least, are not on the roof with a garden hose, protecting the homestead from a fire front. I saw images of some Aussies doing just that. It's been a while since I spent a summer in Australia, but I recall how tinder dry the country became in the heat. Even the air seemed combustible. It was threatening in a way that the summers here never are. But perhaps it doesn't seem that way to an Australian.

I'd be lying if I said I wasn't disappointed that your research trip to the U.S. is being postponed, but considering that your country is on fire, I understand, of course. But there's absolutely no need to shelve this manuscript. I am happy to continue as we have been and to help however I can. I'm learning more assisting you than I could at any creative writing course. And between us, we can make sure your story rings true, even if you can't be here.

Now, about your manuscript. I do need to say that I still have no idea what Freddie looks like...aside from disheveled hair. You know in the absence of a description, I can't help but give her your face. Don't say you weren't warned!

Cain's looking seriously dubious at the moment—is that what you intended? No American snags in this chapter except perhaps that she didn't tip the doorman for carrying Cain's box to her apartment. You would tip for that.

I'll send you a list of companies that deliver grocery gift baskets in Boston. That was a nice touch...A basket of groceries is thoughtful but could also be read as overbearing or patronizing.

I knew a guy who used to plot his work like Cain. He was a cop, so that might have had something to do with it. And he was a control freak...planned everything, left nothing to chance. His name was Wil Saunders. You won't have heard of him—he never finished his novel.

So, this scream...I don't want to preempt anything, or be pedantic, but I do wonder if it is possible to recognize a scream. Aside from the difference between genders, don't they pretty much sound the same? Why is Freddie so sure it's Caroline Palfrey?

Anyway, I'm going to go now so you can get back to work. I'm anxious to read what happens next. I'm not going to send you a box of groceries, but I do want you to write!

With bated breath,
Leo

CHAPTER SEVEN

The Boston PD does not offer to send an officer round. A policewoman takes my statement over the phone. She's brusque and bored and mildly contemptuous. I realise as I'm talking to her that I'm calling the police over a nuisance call, and I feel idiotic. I try to explain that I'd been there at the BPL when Caroline Palfrey screamed, and this sounded exactly like that, but I succeed only in sounding more pathetic. In the end I apologise and hang up.

But I'm still shaking and now my phone feels dangerous, a door through which evil could enter my world. I turn it off and tell myself to calm down, to stop being absurd. It was probably some kid.

I open the laptop to write, and I see that Cain is online. The impulse to speak to him nearly overwhelms my resolution to stop being an idiot. But the scream is fresh in my memory, and I can't shake the sense that it was Caroline.

I turn my phone back on and ring Marigold. I'm crying almost before I say hello.

"Freddie, what's wrong?"

I sob out something about screams and phones.

"I'm coming over," she says immediately. "Be there in fifteen."

"No...you don't need to...I'm just being—"

"Fifteen." She hangs up.

I stare at the phone embarrassed, and ashamed that I am relieved. It was just a prank call…but the scream sounded familiar and that unnerves me.

I put on a pot of coffee and tidy up the apartment until the doorman buzzes me that Marigold has arrived. I ask him to send her up. She envelops me in a bear hug as soon as I open the door. "God, Freddie, are you okay?"

"I'm fine, Marigold. I think I must be drinking too much coffee… It's making me stupid and jumpy." Even so, I pour us each a mug and we sit at the small table in the kitchen to talk.

I tell her about the call, the scream. "I don't really know why, Marigold, but some part of me is sure it was Caroline's scream."

"Well, no wonder you're spooked, you poor thing. What happened was bad enough without the fucking spirits learning to use phones."

I look at her blankly for a moment, her beautiful face full of concern and sympathy, and I giggle. And suddenly I'm laughing helplessly, though it's not that funny. Marigold regards me quizzically and then she too laughs, and we disintegrate like children, unable to stop but not quite sure why we're laughing.

Eventually I sober up. My face and sides hurt. "Thank you," I say. "I needed that."

"I wish I'd done it on purpose." She tops up our coffee. "It is probably some brat who heard the news report of the scream and is calling random numbers."

I exhale. "It sounded the same, Marigold."

"All screams sound pretty much the same."

I shake my head. And I tell her about my sister. "She was two years younger than me. At home she was my best friend; at school we barely acknowledged each other. She died when she was eleven."

"Oh, Freddie, I'm so sorry."

"We were on a school excursion to the Blue Mountains. The entire junior school…so about three hundred kids. They separated us into year groups, and so we went up on different buses, and Gerry and I were hanging with our own friends. I really couldn't have told you exactly where she was until she fell." I swallow, wondering if I've ever talked about this before. If I have I can't remember. "There was a loose safety rail on the lookout, and apparently Gerry was leaning out to take a photo when it gave way. The point is, Marigold, that I knew the scream was hers the moment I heard it. I recognised it. And recognised that it was a real scream…not a joke or a prank."

Marigold puts down her coffee and grabs my hand. "God, how awful, Freddie. How truly awful. But she was your sister. You'd probably heard her scream, or shout, or squeal, a hundred times. You've never met Caroline Palfrey."

"It sounded exactly like the scream we heard in the library."

"Are you sure you remember it?"

"How could I forget it?"

She chews the nail of her pinkie finger for a second. "Give me your phone," she says.

"Why?" I turn it on and hand it to her.

"Because the little monster might not have turned their number to private. Or better still, they might have used their mother's phone, in which case it might be interesting to call back and tell the poor woman what her cursed spawn has been up to."

She brings up the call register. "Have you received any other calls this evening?"

"Nope."

She frowns. "When did you get this call?"

"About an hour ago."

"This doesn't make sense."

"What?"

She shows me the phone. "This is the last call you picked up...about an hour ago."

The caller is identified by name. CAIN.

I pull back.

"Are you sure you didn't talk to him tonight?"

"I did." I take my phone from her and stare at the call record. "He called me online—via my laptop. Because he'd lost his phone. He wasn't sure whether he'd left it here."

Marigold blinks, processing. "So whoever has his phone called you?"

"Yes...I guess."

"And screamed?"

I nod.

"Well, maybe that makes sense. If some brat picked up his phone, they may be nuisance-calling his contacts list...or even whoever last called him." Marigold notes on my call register that I had tried to call Cain a few times.

I explain that I had been trying to thank him for a box of groceries. The explanation becomes somewhat convoluted, and I realise I'm blushing.

"Uh huh." Marigold keeps her thoughts on that score to herself. "We could ring this number—perhaps the little thief will pick up."

"He—or she—hasn't before…and presumably my number will be caller identified."

"Yeah, but someone else may hear it ringing…you never know."

I shrug. "Sure—we might as well give it a go."

Marigold turns on the speaker and calls, placing the phone between us on the table.

The call is picked up.

I hold my breath.

Silence.

"All right, you thieving bastard…We're onto you. The police have tracked the GPS on that phone you stole, so you'd better come clean…"

A crackle and then a voice. My voice. The message I'd left for Cain thanking him for the groceries. I was right—it was too effusive. And then the connection is cut.

So Marigold and I stare at each other without speaking.

"Well, that was creepy," she says eventually.

"I was really hungry when the box was delivered," I explain. "I was probably a bit overexcited by the sight of food."

"I meant that the little asshole played back the message, not what you said."

"Oh…yes. It is." I take a breath and stand to get my laptop. "We should let Cain know someone has his phone and all his contacts. Obviously, the phone wasn't password-protected."

Marigold frowns. "Jesus, that was careless."

We call Cain from my computer, sitting beside one another, so he can see us both in the camera's frame. Cain appears on screen without a shirt, and his hair dishevelled. He squints at the screen and checks his watch, and it's only then I realize it's past midnight. "Freddie…and Marigold!" He yawns. "What's up?"

I tell him what's happened.

He leans closer to the camera. "They used my phone?"

"You said you lost it…Whoever it is must have found it."

"Are you all right?"

"Yes, I'm fine." I glance at Marigold, hoping she won't give away how unnerved I'd been.

Marigold says nothing about the tears. "The thing is, Cain, your phone is not password-protected, so they've got in. They have your contacts and—"

"Hang on, my phone's protected by facial recognition."

"With or without a password?" Marigold asks.

"Without—there's no point having both..."

"Facial recognition can be fooled by a photo." Marigold shakes her head disapprovingly. "It's not really all that secure."

"So you're saying whoever has my phone also has a recent photograph of me? That narrows it down to my mother."

"This isn't funny, Cain. Whoever has your phone is using it to stalk Freddie! For all we know, it could be the same person who killed Caroline."

"Whoa!" I try to wind Marigold back a bit. "I know I was scared, but stalking—"

"You were scared?" Cain looks more awake now. "Of course, you were. God, I'm sorry. I'll come over—give me a minute to get dressed."

"You don't need to do that," I say, abashed. "I panicked for a bit, but I'm fine now."

"Yeah, and I'm here," Marigold adds. "We just thought you should know what your phone's been up to."

Cain rubs his eyes with the heels of his hands. "How about I take you both to breakfast tomorrow...as an apology for my delinquent phone? We'll try to get to the bottom of this over pancakes."

Marigold looks to me for approval.

I shrug. "Sure."

I make up the couch for Marigold, who has had the foresight to bring an overnight bag with her.

"Thank you." I check she has enough blankets. "I'm sorry to drag you out here for something so stupid..."

"Don't worry about it, Freddie." She pounds a pillow into shape. "For the record, you're not overreacting. This is weird and a little creepy. And if we ever find the little monster who's got Cain's phone, we should beat the shit out of him."

My dear Hannah,

I'll be quick.

We tend to say "cell phone" here. Americans like to be specific. And we call it "crank calling." "Nuisance calling" is fairly self-explanatory, but it appears in Marigold's dialogue so probably best to use the American.

I do wonder if someone should point out that they only have Cain's word that he's lost his phone...or will that point readers to the killer too early? It's a fine line between giving the reader enough information and telegraphing the climax.

I forgot to mention in my last letter—I was on the subway, and I saw not one but three separate people reading your latest book. On the subway! Photos attached.

Now get back to writing! I need that next chapter as soon as possible!

Impatiently yours,
Leo

CHAPTER EIGHT

Marigold insists we call Whit and tell him we are gathering for breakfast. "He might be hurt if he thought he wasn't invited," she says.

I doubt it, but I still suspect that there is something between Marigold and Whit, whether or not they know it yet, and so I don't object.

"He isn't answering," she says after a minute.

I detect disappointment, and I am faintly smug that I picked up on this attraction that first day in the library. Freud Girl and Heroic Chin. "You can text him when Cain tells us where we're going."

We meet Cain in the foyer. He's talking to Weinbaum and Jackson, or rather they're interrogating him. The wily old biddies have worked out he's behind the box of groceries and are cross-examining him on the yoghurt. I can almost hear him think "thank God" when we arrive. I introduce him and Marigold. They enquire if I'm feeling better, if the yoghurt helped. It's easier to assure them that it did and make a break for it.

Cain whispers an apology as we leave Carrington Square. "I didn't realize yoghurt would be so contentious."

I laugh. "It's nice, actually. They didn't really talk to me before, but now they're so concerned for my health, it's like we're old friends. It makes me feel more like I belong at Carrington Square."

Cain takes us to a creperie in Boylston Street. It's styled after a French café—round tables with red-and-white-checked linen, candles in wine bottles, and a wallpaper mural of the Eiffel Tower. The clientele might also be part of the decor. Apparently this is the kind of place to which you can wear your beret without feeling ridiculous, regardless of how absurd you look. Indeed, I can't help feeling the three of us are underdressed. As we order, Marigold texts Whit.

I hand my phone to Cain so he can look at the call register as we discuss what happened.

"You have a couple of messages," he says.

I hadn't realised. I haven't wanted to touch my phone since the previous evening.

He frowns. "They're from my number."

I take the phone from him. Two unopened messages. I very nearly hand the phone back and ask him to open them, but I pull myself together just in time, remember that I am not the terrified damsel type. I tap the first icon and a photograph opens. I stare for a moment to work out what I'm seeing on the small screen. The picture is dark, and grainy, taken in low light. A door with central brass knocker, a gryphon I think, atop an orb. The second message is also a picture—another door. But I recognise this one immediately. It's my door at Carrington Square.

"Freddie?" Marigold asks as I drop the phone. "What's wrong?"

Cain picks up my phone and looks. "Doors?" He hands the phone to Marigold.

"The second one's mine," I say, trying to keep calm. "I don't recognise the first."

"I do." Marigold makes the image larger on the screen. "That door-knocker...this is Whit's door...at his parents' house."

"You've been to his parents' house?" I ask, surprised.

"Are you sure?" Cain signals for the bill, though our food has not yet arrived.

Marigold nods, standing.

"Where are we going?" I ask, still a little shaken.

"I think we should take this to the police now," Cain replies. "Marigold, try Whit again."

Marigold is already calling. Cain and I watch her as the phone rings. "Hello...Whit? Thank Christ—we've been trying to get hold of you—"

We see her eyes widen. "Oh, my God!" she stutters. "No...we'll be right over." She doesn't wait for us to ask. "Whit's at Mass General."

"What happened?"

Marigold shakes her head as she stands. "I don't know…but—" She glances at my phone as if it is possessed.

"He could be having an ingrown toenail removed," Cain says evenly. "Let's find out before we panic."

"And the police?" I ask.

"We'll go check on Whit first."

Cain's car is parked a little way down the street. An old black Jeep. The back seat is piled with boxes of books and files, which he shoves to one side to make room for Marigold. She is unusually quiet.

"He was outside your door last night," she says finally as Cain drives through Back Bay to Mass General. "And he's put Whit in the hospital."

"We don't know that yet," Cain cautions, though we do.

I twist round to look at Marigold. "Whit spoke to you, right? How did he sound?"

Marigold closes her eyes for a second. "A bit out of it, actually."

Cain glances at me. "Painkillers, maybe."

I flinch.

We enquire at the reception desk and are directed to his room. There are at least a dozen people in the corridor outside it already. A number of students comforting each other, mostly female. Plainclothes policemen asking questions. I recognise the detective dealing with Caroline Palfrey's case from the news reports. Marigold takes my hand. I understand. This looks serious. A uniformed policeman is stationed outside the door, regulating who goes in and out. Someone asks who we are. Cain explains that we are friends of Whit Metters' and that we've come to see him.

Whit's mother introduces herself. Jean Metters. She's very thin, very beautiful, and looks no older than thirty-five. She speaks politely but efficiently and neither her upper lip nor her brow moves at all.

"I'm afraid Whit is not up to visitors."

"What happened to him?" Marigold blurts.

Jean regards her coolly. "The police are still trying to ascertain that."

A man places his hand on her shoulder. He's tall, grey hair and sharp blue eyes. "Let them go in, Jean. You could use a break." He glances over his shoulder through the open door. "Whit invited them, after all."

"Whit appears to have invited half the campus," Jean replies, looking irritably at the concerned students holding hands in the waiting room. "Which half-wit gave him back his phone?"

They argue back and forth for a few moments and then finally, the man, who I presume is Whit's father and may also have been the half-wit to whom she referred, convinces her to accompany him to the cafeteria. "There are no less than five of Boston's finest here, Jean. He'll be perfectly safe."

And so we're allowed into Whit's room. He's hooked up to a saline drip and various monitors, and there are dark circles under his eyes, but otherwise he looks like himself. He smiles when he sees us. "Hello..."

"Jesus at the wheel!" Marigold can't contain herself any longer. "What the hell happened!"

"I got mugged, I think."

"What do you mean you think?"

"He took my phone but he left my wallet...but maybe someone came along..."

"Who—"

"No idea... He stabbed me and I think I blacked out. I don't remember seeing his face."

"He stabbed you? Are you all right? He might have killed you!" Marigold is speaking, or shouting, for all of us. There are tears in her eyes when she grabs his hand.

"Relax, Marigold. I didn't really know anything about it until they brought me out of the anaesthetic a couple of hours ago. It was probably some junkie."

"In Back Bay?" Cain asks sceptically.

"We have junkies," Whit protests. He looks at Cain, frowning. "How did you know I was in Back Bay? Did my mom—?"

Cain tells him about the calls and shows him the images on my cell phone.

Whit sits up, wincing and cursing as he does so. "When was the image of my folks' front door sent?"

Cain checks the message. "Twenty past ten last night."

"I headed out a little before half past. I didn't make it a block."

"You didn't see—"

"Nothing at all." Whit frowns. "Not that I remember anyway."

"We should tell the police." I glance at the people in the corridor. "Whit, why is the detective from Caroline Palfrey's case here?"

"On the off-chance there was some connection... Harvard students being targeted, that sort of thing." He meets Cain's eyes. "Are you sure you want to tell her, man? It was your phone."

"They might be able to use that fact to track him down."

Whit nods, buzzes for a nurse, and asks her if she'd send Detective Kelly in.

Kelly is somewhere between thirty-five and fifty and tall and broad, particularly for a woman. She has a strong face, immaculately made-up, blond hair pulled back in a knot with not a strand out of place. When she smiles, it looks more like a reflex than an emotion.

"You asked to see me, Whit. Have you remembered something?"

Whit introduces us. "I met these guys the day Caroline was killed. We were all in the Reading Room when she screamed."

Kelly nods at each of us in turn. A moment of awkward silence, and then Marigold blurts, "We think the murderer has Cain's phone."

We explain.

Kelly's face is impassive as she listens. I unlock my phone and hand it to her, so she can see the images for herself.

"Did you report the loss of your phone to your service provider, Mr. McLeod?"

Cain shakes his head. "Until last night I was still hoping to find it somewhere."

"I see." She turns to me. "You say the scream you heard in the first call sounded like Caroline Palfrey."

I'm unsure now. Logic and hindsight compromise my previous certainty. "Yes…I mean, it was a scream. It made me think of the scream we'd heard in the BPL but, I suppose, maybe it was just a scream."

"But it unnerved you enough to call the police and then Miss Anastas?"

"Yes, it did."

"How did you know it was not Mr. McLeod making the call?"

"Because he'd told me he'd lost his phone…when we were speaking earlier online."

"Just before you received a call from his phone?"

"Yes." I glance nervously at Cain, unsure where her questions are going.

She turns to Marigold now. "How did you recognise the image of Mr. Metters' door? Had you visited his home?"

Marigold blushes. Whit regards her curiously.

"No…not really," she says. "I dropped by once but I didn't knock."

"Why?"

"Why did I drop by? Or why didn't I knock?"

"Both."

I can see Marigold twisting inside. I want to help her, but I don't know how.

"I just changed my mind. I was going to see if Whit was...I can't remember exactly. Anyway, I changed my mind...but that's when I noticed the doorknocker. And so I recognised it in the photo..."

Even Marigold's ears are pink now. I glance at Kelly, wondering if she finds pleasure in humiliating Marigold.

Whit intervenes. "I keep telling Mom that that fucking knocker makes the place look like Dracula's castle. I would have run for the hills, too."

Marigold is still unable look at him, but I want to hug Whit for that. Of course, I can't, because Kelly is watching us all.

"We'll need to take statements from each of you," Kelly says carefully, hawkish still. "And we will have to take your phone, Miss Kincaid."

I nod. "Of course."

"I'll have one of my officers take your statements and details."

Whit crosses his eyes as the detective walks out of the room.

"How are you really, Whit?" I break the silence in Detective Kelly's wake.

"A bit sore and tired," he admits, "but not bad, all things considered. They're going to let me go home in a couple of days." He shifts in the bed, gritting his teeth as he moves. "The worst part is that Mom's using the incident to get me all sorts of special consideration with my classes, which is going to make it all the harder for me to fail the term."

Cain grins. "You might have to graduate."

"Over my dead body." Whit wrinkles his nose in the uneasy silence which follows. "Bad taste?"

"Is there anything we can bring you?" I ask. Marigold doesn't seem able to say anything.

He looks at Marigold. "Donuts. Marigold knows the ones I like."

"From the place near Copley Square?" Marigold finally shakes off her embarrassment. "Sure, I'll grab a box."

"Do you think this could really be connected to Caroline Palfrey's murder?" Cain asks suddenly.

"Surely it has to be." I think of the scream.

Whit shrugs. "There are probably a dozen little brats ringing random numbers and screaming after the news reports of what happened at the BPL."

"Yes, but these brats stabbed you."

"I haven't forgotten," he promises ruefully. "But I still don't know that the son of a bitch who knifed me had anything to do with Caroline. Rising crime rates and all that…"

"Maybe there is someone targeting students," Cain suggests tentatively.

"Someone who's got your phone," Whit adds sharply.

Cain's right brow shoots up.

Whit groans. "Sorry…that was the morphine talking."

"We should go." I reach over and touch Whit's arm. "You need to rest, and even if you didn't, you have other friends who'll want to see you. We need to buy donuts."

A shadow rises in his eyes. "What about your statements?"

"We'll give them on the way out."

"You'll come back, won't you?" He seems anxious now.

"Would you rather we stayed?" Marigold asks.

Whit smiles weakly. "Nah…I'm not dying and I'm protected by the Boston PD…not to mention my mom. But you will come back tomorrow?"

"Absolutely."

"And you won't forget the donuts?"

Cain shakes his hand. Despite the circumstances, Whit's grip seems strong, his handshake square. "We'll pick them up in the morning, so they're fresh."

Dear Hannah,

While your summer lingers, so too does the glacial period which is passing itself off as winter here. I know you are imagining picture postcards of children playing in the snow, but really, after the first day snow is just work. It's shovelling and scraping, walking carefully, the tedium of layering on and off each time you go in or out a building. It takes hours out of everyone's day. And while fresh snowfall can be pretty, the slushy muddy mush left after a day of two is anything but! I really miss the color green—it's something you don't experience in Australia, I suppose. The complete absence of green.

I will concede, however, that our climate is conducive to keeping a writer on task… It's easier to stay at one's desk than put on four layers of clothing and shovel the driveway so you can leave the house. I took your advice and started something new. Inspired by your descriptions of Cain McLeod's method, I created my own incident room. I've got to admit it was fun. I'm not sure it will actually lead to the production of a novel, but there is a certain satisfaction in being able to see your ideas in three dimensions. I may have gone a bit over-board with the string... I ended up running it between every single character and every single plot point, so the result looked a little like what one would imagine a nuclear fission reaction. Everything's connected after all...but I've come to the conclusion it does not need to be connected by string. I am now being restrained and sparing with the red twine.

There was a murder on Mass Avenue last night. Barely got a mention in the papers here so I'd be surprised if was reported in yours. I happened to be coming back from the library and passed it. It occurred to me that seeing a crime scene would be useful to you, so you could describe the details, cor-dons, police tape, what the coroner's van looks like—that sort of thing. Anyway, I took some quiet photos which I've attached. The body had been removed by then, so don't worry that you're going to open a picture of the deceased... though I suppose that too would have been useful. You mystery writers prac-tice a dark and brutal art, but it's strangely seductive.

It's also occurred to me that Cain needs to have an accomplice—I know, I know, you haven't decided it was him yet, but he's my favorite for the role of serial killer. Unfortunately, he was sitting across from Freddie when Caroline Palfrey screamed, so you will need to explain that. It might be time we learned a little more about him aside from the fact that he's handsome and spent a couple of weeks pouting on the streets as a troubled adolescent. Please for-give me if I'm overstepping with this... It's your book, of course. Please read this as the enthusiasm of a thoroughly engaged fan.

On less important matters, I received a letter from Alexandra, who says that while she enjoyed reading the opus, she regrets that she cannot offer me representation. I'm not sure she actually regrets it, but that's what she wrote. The reality is, I suppose, that I am a straight white man with no diversity or disadvantage to offer as a salve for the fashionable collective guilt that rules publishing. I understand that popular correctness demands that men like me be denied to compensate for all the years in which we were given too much. I just wish I'd had a chance to enjoy a little of that privilege before it became a liability. Anyway, she said no. So there we are.

Yours,

Leo

CHAPTER NINE

Detective Kelly asks us to come into the station to give our statements. We each sit with officers who type our accounts into laptops and then print them for signatures. They separate us for the purpose. For me at least, the interview is emotionless, a simple gathering of facts—dates, times, locations. I'm simply punching in information. I get the feeling that I have become part of a process, absorbed into the machinery of the investigation. It's afternoon by the time we are able to leave.

Cain is the last to be released from the interrogation room. He smiles fleetingly at Marigold and me and shrugs. "Shall we get out of here?"

"Let's."

None of us speaks until we're back in Cain's old Jeep. In fact, even then, we sit there a while in silence.

Marigold's voice trembles at first. "What…" She takes a breath. "What now?"

Cain turns to look at her. "I'm starving. We didn't actually have breakfast, did we?"

"You're hungry?" Marigold doesn't seem able to comprehend how he could be so in the circumstances.

Cain nods.

"I could make us something at home," I suggest.

Cain glances at his watch.

"Unless you have somewhere you need to be?"

"No. It's not that. Just thought that we should probably get new phones while the stores are still open."

"Oh, yes. Of course." I remember that my phone has been retained by the police and Cain's is probably in the hands of the killer. This doesn't feel real. Not entirely.

And so we go to Walmart to purchase cell phones. He chooses a reasonably able smartphone for himself. I go for a more basic model. It only needs to serve until the police return my cell, which I presume they will...hope they will. And though having to memorise a new number is irritating, it does close the door through which this person—thief or killer or jerk—crept into my life.

It's starting to get dark and cold when we return to Carrington Square. Cain pauses outside my door, stepping back and holding up his phone.

"What are you doing?" Marigold demands.

"I'm trying to figure out where exactly the clown who has my phone stood when he took that photo...how close he got."

"Does it matter?" I ask. "We know he had to have been somewhere within a few feet. Does it make any difference where exactly he stood?"

"Probably not."

"He might have been zooming in, anyway," Marigold points out.

Cain concedes. "You're right. Clearly, I'm not a detective."

We go in, and I feel myself relax a little when Cain closes the door behind us. Marigold grabs crackers and cheese from the kitchen which she arranges on a plate with sliced apple to tide us over until I prepare dinner.

Cain helps himself. "I like this cheese."

"You should," I reply, smiling. "You bought it."

He looks at the chunk he's about to put into his mouth. "Oh, yes, I forgot. I've got excellent taste."

I browse the pantry for beans, onions, and tomatoes and begin on a vegetarian spaghetti Bolognese, while apologising for the fact that it will be vegetarian and that my culinary skills are, in any case, fairly rudimentary. Marigold helps Cain set up his new cell phone with both facial recognition and password. There is a hint of disapproval in her voice, which I assume is directed at his failure to install a password on his previous phone.

I hand Cain a bottle of wine and a corkscrew. He opens it and pours me a glass which I stir into the sauce, thinking fleetingly of my dad, who added wine to everything but cereal. For a while they watch me cook, and we talk about food. Clearly, we are all hungry. One of the benefits of vegetarian meals is that they rarely take long to prepare and, motivated by the fact that this will be the first meal of the day we actually eat, I'm ready to serve large bowls of pasta and sauce very quickly. We eat, unsure how to begin talking about what has happened.

Marigold takes the first step. "What do you think he wants? This guy who stabbed Whit."

Cain swallows and wipes his mouth with a napkin before he replies. "You think he wants something?"

"He must. Why else would he do this?"

"Perhaps he's crazy."

"Even if he's crazy, he wants something." Marigold waves her fork as she speaks. "Revenge, sexual gratification, the approval of the voices in his head…"

"Sexual gratification?" I ask. "Caroline wasn't… And Whit—"

"It's hard to know what position they were in when Caroline sustained the injury to her head. He may have been lying on top of her, pounding her head against a hard surface in some kind of thrusting movement. And some-times penetration with a blade is a surrogate of sorts for sexual satisfaction. There are a number of conditions ranging from piquerism to full-blown sadism and lust murder."

I am reminded that Marigold is studying psychology. I try not to look squeamish and nod.

"But Whit—" Cain begins frowning.

"So the killer's not gender specific." Marigold preempts Cain's objec-tion. "Caroline and Whit were both white, the same age, from the same background. They both wrote for the *Rag*… There are plenty of links aside from gender."

Cain seems sceptical.

"It isn't necessarily sexual satisfaction," Marigold says patiently. "But it is possible. It could just as easily be any number of reasons, but there will be a reason. He will be doing this because he wants something."

Cain reframes his original question. "Does it matter what he wants?"

"Knowing what he wants might help us work out who he is," Marigold replies.

"God, how did we wake up in the middle of an episode of *Criminal Minds*?"

Marigold stops. Her eyes well suddenly. "I only meant—"

Cain realises that he's hurt her feelings. "Jeez, Marigold, I'm sorry. I wasn't—I'm tired, that's all. You're right. Working out what this lunatic wants could be the key to stopping him, but maybe we..."

Marigold is crying properly now.

Cain looks at me helplessly.

I get up and grab Marigold a box of tissues while Cain continues to apologise.

"Cain, there's chocolate in the top cupboard," I say as I put my arm around Marigold. "Would you mind grabbing it for me? I think we might need it."

He agrees quickly, a little desperately.

I'm pretty sure that Marigold's tears have been building all day and probably have more to do with Whit and the questioning than anything Cain said. The poor bloke was just the trigger.

"Whit will be okay," I say quietly as I hug her.

"Oh, God, what must he think of me?" she gulps.

"Cain knows it's been a tough day."

"I mean Whit." She wipes her nose and tries to steady her voice. "All that stuff about knowing what his door looks like—he must think I'm some kind of weirdo..."

"Don't be daft. You called by and changed your mind about knocking at the last minute. We've all done it."

"Five times?"

"Oh." I try not to sound too startled. "You went five times?"

She nods.

"You didn't tell the police that?" I don't want to advise Marigold to keep things from the authorities, but this would look odd.

"They knew. Whit's house has CCTV at the front door. Oh, God, I felt so stupid." She stares at her empty plate. "They've probably told Whit...and his folks. They'll think I'm..."

"They might just think you're shy." I'm trying to comfort Marigold, ease her panic. I don't really believe that people whose son has been stabbed a few yards from their doorstep would think anything of the sort.

Cain fills my kettle and places it on the stove to heat. He can hear what we're saying, but clearly he's trying to give us a little time—or he's a coward. But tea isn't a bad idea.

"Did you find the chocolate?" I ask him, unsure what to tell Marigold.

"Yes. There are two bars. Do you want them both?"

"Of course." I signal for him to toss them over, so that we don't starve while he's making tea or doing whatever he's doing to avoid coming back to the table. I pull back the wrapping. "This," I announce, "is Australian chocolate. Unlike American chocolate, it's edible."

"Hey!" Marigold smiles tentatively. "That's offensive."

"But sadly true." I push the block of Cadbury Dairy Milk towards her.

Marigold breaks off a square and pops it into her mouth, tilting her head as she savours it. I notice the slight ecstatic roll of her eyes. "It's okay, I guess." She snaps off another large portion and takes a bite.

I laugh and reach for the remainder of the block.

Marigold reaches it first and clutches it to her heart.

Cain returns to the table with mugs of tea. He is wary. "Is everything all right?"

Marigold groans. "I'm sorry. I didn't mean to lose it."

"I didn't mean to be a jerk, Marigold." Cain sits down and takes the chocolate she offers him.

Marigold studies him. "When your mentor, Isaac, was murdered, didn't you want to find out who killed him?"

I am surprised by the directness of her question, aware that the subject may be a sensitive.

Cain laughs. "I wouldn't call Isaac my mentor."

"Didn't you want to find out?" Marigold persists.

"Yes, of course." Cain chooses his words carefully. "But the police couldn't—"

"So that was it?"

I interrupt but gently. "Marigold, if the police couldn't…"

"No, she's right," Cain says. "I shouldn't have let it go. Isaac had no one else—as far as I know, anyway. I should have done something."

"What do you think we can do, Marigold?" I ask.

"I don't know. But we were there when Caroline screamed, and Whit is our friend, and the murderer has Cain's phone… We're in the middle of this, whether we like it or not."

I exhale. She has a point. "When was the last time you remember having your phone?" I ask Cain. "Perhaps it would be useful to narrow down where he might have gotten hold of it."

He shrugs. "I haven't really got a clue. I thought it was in my pocket, until I tried to call to see if you liked yoghurt."

I meet his eyes and smile.

"So you ordered the basket of groceries for Freddie...?" Marigold begins.

"On the computer—online."

Marigold frowns. "Did you have the cell phone when we were here?"

"Yes, I checked for it when I put my jacket back on. I remember thinking I would have to charge it."

"Where did you go from here?"

"Home."

"Where you realised it was missing."

"I guess so...yes."

"How did you get home, Cain? Did you drive?"

"No. I caught a bus."

"Was it crowded?"

Cain looks at her quizzically. "The bus? Yes, I suppose it was."

"It's easier for someone to pick your pocket if it's crowded," Marigold explains. "Did you notice anyone in particular standing next to you?"

Cain shakes his head slowly. "I was reading," he admits.

"Oh...what were you reading?" I ask.

He fishes a battered copy of *The Great Gatsby* out of his inside pocket and hands it to me.

"*The Great Gatsby?*"

"I reread it every couple of years," he clarifies. "I didn't discover it yesterday."

"Every two years?" I rarely reread books. There are too many wonderful books without retreading old ground.

"Just *Gatsby*," he says. "It reminds me that flawed people can create perfect works of literature."

"And why do you need to be reminded of that?"

"If you were reading"—Marigold is impatient—"then it's conceivable that your pocket was picked without you noticing."

"Yes, it's definitely conceivable."

"Which means the murderer followed you from here."

"Hang on, Marigold." Cain pulls back. "That's a bit of a leap, don't you think?"

Marigold shakes her head. "We know the person who has your phone took photos of Whit's door and Freddie's; that he rang Freddie and either screamed or played her a recording of a scream."

"That still doesn't mean he killed anybody."

"He stabbed Whit."

"*Someone* stabbed Whit. We don't know that it was the guy with my phone."

"But he must have known who stabbed Whit, or was going to stab Whit, at least."

"Maybe he did," Cain says slowly. "Maybe he was trying to warn you, Freddie."

I look up sharply. "Warn me?"

"That there was danger outside your door, I suppose…and Whit's. Maybe that's what the pictures and the recorded scream were about."

"So we're looking for someone who doesn't know how to text. That rules out everyone under sixty I guess."

Cain winces. "I'm just saying that whoever it is might not be trying to scare or threaten you. They might think they're helping."

"Or he could be a sick son of a bitch who gets off on torturing people," Marigold counters.

Cain rubs his brow. "That too."

Dear Hannah,

Finally! I was beginning to fear you'd thrown in the towel and returned to that historical series you were writing. I expect the events of this summer have made it difficult to focus on writing. The coverage of the Australian bushfires here has been horrifying—I've been watching in dismay the reports of the landscape lost. I have been hoping to hear from you on that count if nothing else, to know you're safe.

I do worry you might offend your U.S. readership by slandering our chocolate. We do know that our chocolate is inferior, but there's a kind of national agreement to pretend otherwise. Without it we might have had to invade you.

I'm intrigued as to where you're going with the phone messages. Logic says that Cain is right…they are more likely to be a warning sent by a cryptic good Samaritan. Because why would a murderer show his hand like that? Perhaps because he or she knows that Freddie will talk to Cain about it. Are they trying to warn her without revealing themselves to the murderer?

I don't suppose you've heard from your agent with respect to my manuscript.

I know these things take time, but I wonder if she might have mentioned anything to you. I know I must have sounded quite sour about Alexandra's rejection in my last email. And to be honest, I was. Disappointment is the most caustic emotion. But I have recovered and am more determined than ever to see this dream through, to find my way into print somehow.

I shall be looking for your reply,
Leo

CHAPTER TEN

Whit has sent us to Around the Hole, a buzzing, trendy bakery. Slick and modern, with shiny surfaces and small tables which say *Stop, but don't linger too long.* It serves coffee, but it's clear that its patrons come for the donuts, which they carry out in white cardboard boxes tied with twine. Glass cases display raised donuts and cake donuts—which are apparently different—as well as sourdough, vegan, and gluten-free varieties, all in bizarre flavour combinations, both savoury and sweet. Marigold takes over ordering by the dozen in flavours like lavender and truffle, cream cheese and fried onion, shitake mushroom and clover.

"The poor guy's in the hospital," Cain mutters as Marigold requests a burnt caramel with lemongrass ganache. "Hasn't he suffered enough?"

I laugh.

Marigold is less amused. "So what would you recommend?"

Cain turns to me.

"Chocolate looks good," I offer.

"And there's nothing wrong with jelly," Cain adds, smiling.

The contempt of the young man behind the counter is undisguised. Apparently, this is not the kind of place in which one asks for a jelly donut. Marigold apologises for us, adds a quinoa and liquorice donut and, in a dubious act of compromise, a dark chocolate and jalapeño jelly confection.

We end up leaving with three dozen donuts. Marigold insists upon it and pays for them, but even she realises it's excessive.

"He might need to share," she says in an attempt at justification.

"He's surrounded by cops, I guess." Cain pulls out to drive to the hospital.

I smile. "I'm not sure you should be risking offending the police with tired jokes."

"Tired?" Cain frowns. "I think you mean classic."

"No—I mean tired."

"Why should Cain be worried about the police?" Marigold leans between us from the back seat.

"It was only a joke," I reply hastily. "I didn't mean—"

"No, seriously," Marigold says. "Do you think the police suspect Cain because of the phone?"

"Uh…maybe…I don't know." I feel the colour rising to my face. "I was only kidding around."

"The police wouldn't be doing their jobs if they weren't looking at me," Cain says calmly. "They only have my word for it that I lost my phone and…" He shrugs off the end of his sentence. "Though, after they see these donuts, they're bound to think Marigold is trying to poison Whit."

"Very droll," Marigold flicks his shoulder.

Cain stops his Jeep in the parking garage near Mass General, and we transport three dozen ridiculous donuts to Whit's hospital room. En route, we pass Jean Metters, standing in the visitors' lounge where the use of mobile phones is permitted. Her free arm is folded across her chest, her voice low and sharp. I hear the words "subpoena" and "discovery." We don't interrupt, secretly glad we don't have to face Whit's mom.

The policeman in the corridor recognises us and waves us through. I knock and stick my head in through the doorway.

"Oh, I'm sorry." I bump into Marigold as I pull back. She drops a box of donuts, and matcha, quinoa, and star anise masterpieces scatter and roll onto disinfected floors. The two men by Whit's bed turn. Their eyes move up from the bouncing donuts to my face and then back down to Marigold, who's scrabbling to retrieve the carefully selected items.

"Don't step on my donuts on your way out," Whit says to his guests. The two men are similar to look at, gym stocky, wearing dark suits, closely fitted jackets which strain to button, and monochromatic ties.

"We'll be seeing you, Metters," one replies.

Whit grunts.

They nod as they walk past, making no attempt to hide their scrutiny while their gazes linger on each of us in turn.

Whit beckons, holding his arms out expectantly for the donuts.

"This box is the one I dropped," Marigold says.

Whit takes a donut from it. "If you can't eat off a hospital floor, what can you eat off?"

"There are two other boxes," Marigold tells him, placing said boxes on the table beside Whit's bed.

"I have faith in the cleaners." Whit takes a bite. "They're immigrants. They get the job done."

"That's not less offensive because it's a *Hamilton* quote," I say reprovingly.

"Is it offensive?" Whit is genuinely surprised. "Why?"

"I'm not sure," I admit. "It just sounds reductive."

Whit rolls his eyes.

"Who were those men?" Marigold asks.

"Oaks and McIntyre, I think they said—Feds."

"FBI?" Marigold is startled.

"Where's Cain?" Whit asks.

"I don't know…" I notice his absence for the first time. "Where did he go?"

Cain comes through the door. "Sorry, what did I miss?"

"Where were you?"

Cain hands Whit a slip of paper. "One of the doctors called me over. She wanted me to get that past your mother."

Whit reads the note and smiles. "Molly," he says.

"What does she want?" Marigold asks.

"Nothing. It's her number."

"You don't have a phone."

Whit glances at Marigold. For a moment I fear he's going to say something witty and cutting, but he opts to be kind. "I guess not." He looks for a pocket in his hospital gown and realising that there isn't one, he places the slip of paper under one of the boxes of donuts. "Molly was on my surgical team."

"So the number is for…?" Cain leans on the foot of the bed.

"I promised I'd keep her posted on my recovery."

"Really?"

"It's nice when they care, isn't it?"

Cain's lips quirk. Presumably Molly's interest extends beyond checking Whit's chart.

"You must be better if the doctors are flirting with you," Marigold says, rearranging the donuts that had fallen out of the box.

"Aren't you going to have one?" Whit asks, taking a donut that seems to be growing its own lawn.

Marigold opens one of the other boxes. "I'll leave the ones from the floor for you—you're on antibiotics anyway."

"Cain, Freddie?"

We decline simultaneously, and Marigold explains that Cain and I are both far too lame and conventional to give anything aside from peanut butter and jelly a chance. Cain mutters something about the unfortunate victims of donut scams, and Marigold calls us "old."

It's true in a way. Cain and I are probably five years older than Whit and Marigold, who couldn't be much more than twenty-one or two.

"How old are you?" Marigold asks Cain.

"Thirty."

"Jesus, you're older than I thought!"

Cain shrugs. "I can't be sure about Freddie, but I still have my own teeth."

Whit looks at me. Curiosity struggling against social taboo.

I put him out of his misery. "I'm twenty-seven."

"Well, I suppose you have a couple of good years left," Whit commiserates. "But I can see why you're staying away from the donuts. Blood sugar and all that."

I call him an idiot. Whit winces as he chuckles.

"Are you all right?"

"Yeah. My laughing muscles have stitches in them, is all."

"Have the police got any leads on who might have done this to you?" I ask. "Have they said anything?"

"They've decided it was someone I know…or who knows me."

"Why?"

"They seem to think it was the person who had Cain's phone. And that to send the messages he did to you, he must have known we were friends."

"How many people know we're all friends?" I ask. After all, we've only known each other a couple of weeks.

Whit shrugs. "Not many. But who knows who might have been sitting near us at the library or at lunch somewhere? It's only the police who think there's a homicidal lunatic in my social circle."

"What about the FBI?" Marigold asks.

"They were asking about Cain."

"Cain? What the hell for?"

"It's not surprising, considering what my phone's been up to." Cain doesn't seem nearly as alarmed as I am by the revelation. "What exactly did they ask?"

"How long I'd known you, how I'd met you, what you like to do with your time, whether I'd ever seen you stab anyone…"

Cain laughs.

"That's not funny, Whit." Marigold moves the box of donuts out of his reach.

"Who would have thought you'd meet someone wanted by the FBI in a library?" Whit stretches gingerly.

"Just because they were asking about Cain doesn't mean that he's wanted by them," I point out.

"Oh, yeah." Whit looks at Cain. "They asked if I'd ever known you by any other name."

"Like an alias?" Marigold studies him curiously.

"Like a pen name," Cain says sheepishly. "Actually Cain McLeod is my pen name," he admits. "They're probably talking about my real name."

"Which is?" Marigold demands, exasperated.

Cain folds his arms.

"Come on, whoever-you-are," Whit says, grinning. "Out with it."

After a moment Cain resigns. "Abel Manners."

Marigold gasps. Whit guffaws. I try not to let my feelings show so obviously.

Cain sighs. "You can see why I changed it. One of the perks of writing a book is that you can change your name and pretend the publisher made you do it."

"Abel Manners!" Whit roars laughing, choking on a donut as he does so. "God, that's wicked awful! You sound like a courteous porn star!" He clutches his side and coughs violently, rolling onto his side. "Oh, fuck that hurts."

"I didn't want Abel Manners on the spine of my book, so…" he trails off staring at the expanding spot of crimson on the back of Whit's hospital greens. "Dammit, Whit—you're bleeding."

Whit reaches back to the patch of blood, which is already wet enough for him to feel, and then stares at the blood on his fingers as if it is something incomprehensible.

Marigold runs out of the room to find help, and I press the buzzer to summon nurses, someone, anyone who'll know what to do. Within seconds we are pushed out of the room by the stream of people who pour in. We linger in the hallway, trying to stay out of the way, hoping to catch some fragment of shouted conversation that might tell us what's happening. We hear "haemorrhaging" and something about "vitals." Whit's mother arrives. A doctor speaks with her. She glances at us during the conversation which we cannot hear. Whit is wheeled out to the theatre, and we're politely but firmly asked to decamp to the waiting room.

Dear Hannah,

I must admit this chapter made me hungry for donuts. I note that you didn't use a real shop—there are a few in Boston which offer exotic concoctions. And of course there's Dunkin', which is something of a Boston institution. I've made a list which I've attached in a separate file, along with images of their shop fronts and some notes on nearby alleys or places which are conducive to the illicit.

I expect, however, that you have created a fictional donut shop so that you may use it as a venue for violence of some sort without ruining anyone's business. It's considerate, though to be honest, that type of notoriety might do more to attract customers than repel them...unless, of course, you're planning on poisoning people.

I addressed my own cravings at a bakery in Back Bay. Divine! Honest, their products make you believe in God and willing to forsake him at the same time. The bakery is two miles from my pad so I figure the walk there and back is worth at least two donuts.

Now a couple of little things. If Whit is in the latter stages of a law degree, which over here is a postgraduate course, he would be closer to twenty-five than twenty-one or two, unless he was some kind of child prodigy. The same goes for Marigold.

I do like that Cain's name was once Abel. If it is possible to have a favorite biblical story, mine was that of Cain and Abel, the first murder. It adds a kind of ancient weight and tradition to the petty homicides of today, as though even the most base and inelegant dispatch has an echo in time and is a curse of the ages.

I promise I'm not completely discouraged by your agent's decision to pass on my manuscript. I know that you used all your influence on my behalf and will continue to do so. My time will come. Until then, I will bask in the reflected glory of your success.

Anyway, I look forward to eating donuts with you in person someday soon.

Yours,
Leo

CHAPTER ELEVEN

Whit's father approaches us in the visitors' lounge where we've been for over an hour. He's smiling, and so we are relieved even before he tells us that it was just a burst stitch and that Whit will be okay, though he'll need to rest quietly to make sure it doesn't happen again.

Cain apologises for anything we might have done to make Whit exert himself too soon.

"He said he was laughing." Frank Metters's lips curve to one side. "He wouldn't say why, but clearly it was one helluva punch line."

We say nothing.

Metters loosens his tie. "Look, Whit's not going to be able to see anyone for a while—"

"I thought he was all right," Marigold says.

"Oh, he is. But Jean has swooped in to personally protect her boy. She's going to work from his room." Metters' face is sympathetic. "I wouldn't bother trying to see him for a couple of days at least."

"You're sure he's all right?" Cain asks.

"Whit? Oh, the boy is fine. And believe you me, his mother will make sure he doesn't laugh for a couple of days."

"We'll be on our way then." Cain offers Metters his hand.

Metters accepts the handshake and gives Cain his card. "If you're worried about Whit, please call, and I'll give you the latest."

It's strange leaving without at least seeing Whit to say goodbye, but there's no point setting up residence in the visitors' lounge, and Frank Metters promises to pass on our good wishes.

It's only about a half-hour's walk to Carrington Square from Mass General, and so I decide to send Cain and Marigold off without me. "I'm sick of sitting."

"Are you sure it's safe?" Marigold frowns. "Maybe I should walk with you."

"Don't be silly. It's three in the afternoon. I just want to walk and think about what I'm writing—get my head back in that space."

Cain nods. "Good luck. Hope the bus stops for you."

For a flash, I'm confused, and then I realise that I've told him about my bus. I smile, pleased for some reason I can't quite identify. Perhaps it's merely knowing that he understands. "I'll throw myself under it."

Cain's brow rises. "I don't want to be culturally insensitive, Freddie, but in America we just wait at the bus stop."

I snort and call him a hack.

Marigold still seems troubled. She hugs me farewell as if I'm going to war, and that in itself gives me the giggles, which is a poor way of repaying her concern. Cain starts his Jeep and tells Marigold to get in. "We can follow her at a distance if you want," he says, leaning across and opening the passenger door.

I wait and wave them off if only to make sure he was kidding.

I tell my phone that I want to go home and wait for it to pull up a map. Thirty-four minutes by foot. Perfect.

My mind slips easily into the manuscript as I walk. It feels like breathing out. My footsteps meter my thoughts. I ponder Heroic Chin. There's a privileged confidence about him. He's never failed at anything…unless he's chosen to. I think about Whit's mother. She sits behind him on the bus, watching his every move while she speaks to her cell phone. Occasionally, she reaches out and smooths his hair. He ignores her but doesn't move seats either. He stays within her reach. Frank Metters sits beside his wife, reading through a file. He glances up when she touches Whit. There is a passing disquiet in his eyes, but he does nothing.

I wonder what it is that Whit wants to do. Failing law appears to take effort, and it doesn't seem to me that Whit would expend that effort for no reason. I think he'd be more likely to take the path of least resistance, to become a lawyer and make the best of it...unless there was something else. A passion of some sort that did not fit with being a lawyer. Perhaps Heroic Chin wanted to play a sport of some sort professionally—baseball or football...even basketball. Or perhaps something less conventional... And then it occurs to me. Could Heroic Chin be a dancer? Perhaps that was his connection to Freud Girl, to the dead ballerina who lurked in her past. Could they both have known her, both have loved her? Might one of them have killed her? The last thought jolts me. My characters are too connected to the real people who inspired them, and those real people are my friends. New, but already beloved, wrapped in the excited crush of friendship's beginning, untarnished by the annoyances, disappointments, and minor betrayals which come with the passing of time.

I walk into Copley Square, and for a brief moment I pause to revel in the fact that I am here. In Boston. Despite everything that's happened in the past couple of weeks, I am still aware of the privilege of the Sinclair Fellowship, still thrilled by it. I stand by the fountain and soak in the sounds of the plaza: traffic, people, American accents—some Bostonian, others not.

For a while I meander, happily watching people go about their daily business.

"Freddie!" Leo Johnson runs to catch up with me.

"Hello!" I smile as he removes his baseball cap. His hair is damp and he's breathing heavily. "What are you doing here?"

"They let me out of Carrington Square every now and then. Whew!" He wipes his brow with his sleeve. "I spotted you on the other side of the square...only just caught you, though."

I look at him, bemused. "Where were you when you spotted me? New York?"

"No ma'am, I was..." He stops. "Oh...I see what you mean. I was jogging."

"Jogging?"

"Don't look so horrified. Writers jog."

"If they're being chased."

He laughs. "Are you heading back to the Carrington?"

"Yes, but I'm not going to race you."

"Coward." He twists into a stretch as he's talking to me. "I was thinking we could have that dinner—complain about writers' blocks and words without synonyms."

I check my watch. I can't put Leo off again without it seeming intentional, and I would like to talk to him about my work, the reports on our residencies we would each have to present. "You're on. Where shall we go?"

He scratches his head and replaces the baseball cap. "How's about I order something in and we eat at my place…or yours, if you prefer."

"No, your apartment is fine. My place is a mess…my muse is a bit of a slob."

"They tend to be." He begins running on the spot. "Half past six? That'll give me time to shower."

"Sure, I'll see you then."

I wave as he jogs away, vaguely realising that I have for some reason assumed Leo was much older than he obviously is. Perhaps it's his accent… the Southern drawl which conjures *Gone with the Wind*, or the fact that normally he is quite buttoned down in style. Even now he isn't really wearing jogging gear.

Mrs. Weinbaum is watering plants in the foyer when I get back to Carrington Square. It's the janitor's job, she tells me, but she doesn't think he ever gives them enough. She wonders if I have found the yoghurt is helping, only she might try some for her lumbago. To be honest, I have no idea what lumbago is, aside from it being a condition ascribed to old people in sitcoms. I try to explain that there was never anything wrong with me, that I just like yoghurt, but she will not have it. In the end we agree that yoghurt is worth trying, and she promises to keep me posted on the outcome.

I return to my apartment in a good mood after the encounter, which, though absurd, was warm. Shoes off, then coffee brewing and my laptop out. I'll be able to write for a couple of hours at least. Running into Leo reminds me that I am here to write a novel, regardless of murders and donuts, and I'm grateful that I have a colleague who has no connection with the scream and all it has led to, against whom to pace myself.

It's five to six when I notice the time again. I run into the bathroom and brush my teeth, changing my shirt with the brush still in my mouth. There's no time for makeup, but I wet my hands and use them to tidy the curls into some sort of order. I put my shoes back on and grab a bottle of wine from the cupboard before walking down the hallway to Leo's apartment.

"Door's open," in response to my knock.

Leo's apartment is a mirror image of mine architecturally, though its aesthetic is more modern. The sitting room is dominated by yellow sofas and a swivelling leather egg chair. Immediately, I want to try out the egg chair.

Leo grins knowingly. "Go ahead," he says. "Everybody who walks in here is fixed on taking it for a spin."

And so I do exactly that. The chair spins smoothly with very little effort as its curve cradles me. "Do you write in this?" I ask Leo as he comes in and out of view on my rotation.

He shakes his head. "I prefer to spread out on one of the sofas. I find the movement is a bit distracting."

"I can imagine it would be, but it's fun!"

"I've ordered pizza," Leo says. "I hope you like pepperoni."

I stop the chair and grimace. "I should have mentioned, I'm a vegetarian…"

"Oh, shoot! I should have asked. There's so many of you around nowadays, I should have thought to ask—"

"I can pull the pepperoni off—"

"You'll do nothing of the sort—I'll change the order."

He makes a call and adds a vegetarian pizza. "Now that's sorted, can I offer you a drink?"

I hold out my bottle of wine, and soon we are sitting on the yellow sofas with glasses—Leo having warned me that the egg chair and alcohol are a dangerous combination. I ask him about his novel. I fancy that Leo writes historical fiction, and for some reason I'm convinced his era is the Roman Empire. I have no reason to suppose this…it's just a fancy.

"Romance," he says. "I write romance."

My surprise clearly needs no words because he continues to explain. "My agent will tell you it's a story about passionate friendships and reluctant relationships in modern America, but really it's a romance."

"Oh…set today?" I'm still thinking gladiators.

"Modern America, remember."

"Have you…have you always written romance?"

"Yes, and what's more, so have you. The mystery writers, the historical novelists, the political thriller writers, the science fiction writers…everybody but the people who write instruction manuals is writing romance. We dress our stories up with murders, and discussions about morality and society, but really we just care about relationships."

"You can't be serious. You're saying Stephen King writes romances?"

"Yes, ma'am!" Leo sits back in the sofa. "The killer clown is entertaining and all that, but what we're really interested in is whether the fat kid gets the pretty girl."

"I think that may be a bit simplistic."

A knock on the door heralds the arrival of our pizzas, and we open the boxes between us and arm ourselves with slices before we continue.

"I'm not sure what exactly you'd call what I'm writing, but it's not a romance." I tell him about my work, the story of three people bonded by a scream. He listens carefully.

"Classic love triangle," he says. "It's all about whether Handsome Man or Heroic Chin will win the heart of Freud Girl."

"What about the scream, the murderer?"

"Background colour."

"That's ridiculous. You could use that logic to call any book a romance."

"My point exactly."

I look at him silently.

"What are you thinking?" he asks.

"Whether I know you well enough to call you an idiot while sitting on your couch and eating your pizza."

Leo nods thoughtfully. "Yes, ma'am, I think you do."

"I might wait until I've finished the pizza."

"So these characters of yours, they're based on the people you met in the library?"

"Yes. We were together in the Reading Room when we heard the scream."

"Does Handsome Man know you call him Handsome Man?"

"No…that would be embarrassing for both of us."

"I wouldn't worry about it. Good-looking guys know they're good-looking. We have mirrors, after all."

I look up sharply. Did he just say what I think he said? There's laughter in his eyes, and I realise he's teasing me. "So what do you all do with this knowledge? You and the other guys."

He shrugs. "It's all about distraction."

"You are an idiot."

He laughs out loud now. We talk about my work and then his. He asks me a few hypothetical questions about how I'd react against some very specific situations.

"Leo, are you using me for research?"

"Maybe a little," he admits sheepishly. "I'm having trouble with a scene. Do you mind?"

"Not at all. Do you want to show me the scene? Maybe I could help."

"Sure. Though it's still first-draft rough."

We work on his manuscript while we eat the rest of the pizza. The draft is rough with patches of beauty. Leo's characters are ethereal, a little idealised, which is probably why he wanted help. Well, perhaps not help exactly. Rather a friendly wall against which to bounce his thoughts, and the insight of my gender. The story he's calling a romance is a gothic tale about rejection and obsession, and his prose, haunting. It makes me yearn to be working on my own manuscript.

I glance up at the clock projected onto the ceiling and spin slowly to orient the face. "Is it eleven o'clock?"

Leo nods. "Did you have to be somewhere?"

"No, but it's late. I'd better make tracks."

He offers me coffee.

I shake my head and get up to go. "Thanks for the pizza, Leo."

"Thanks for helping me out. I appreciate it. If you ever need me to do the same—"

"I might just take you up on it if you quit trying to tell me that I'm writing romance,"

"Yes, ma'am!" He walks me to my door and wishes me good night. A moment of awkwardness as we say goodbye. We end up shaking hands, laughing because it's a little weird. We have just shared pizza and talked for hours—but about our work. We're more colleagues than friends, I think. He waits until I've unlocked my door before he leaves me to it—Southern gallantry, possibly. Or perhaps it's the fact that there's a murderer somewhere.

⌇

Dear Hannah,

I can't tell you how thrilling it is to walk into your work. Thank you—this chapter cheered me up no end! I do like Leo. There's a real chemistry between him and Freddie. I promise he and I will be there to console Freddie when she finally discovers the awful truth about Cain.

I love the way you describe Leo's writing. I dare to hope you took that from life as well.

The chapter is perfect. Change nothing.

And thank you. You have done me an honor.

In answer to your question about cinemas, I'd recommend The Brattle. It has an interesting culture of its own.

And, incidentally, by way of interest, I read in the *Globe* yesterday that Alexandra Gainsborough—that agent who turned down the opus—passed away. An accident of some sort. Two days ago she was vibrant and mighty, she had the power to realize or kill dreams, and today she herself is dead. I sent condolences, of course. It's funny how things work out sometimes.

Yours,

Leo

CHAPTER TWELVE

Another box of groceries is delivered the next morning. The doorman brings it up for me.

"Thank you, Joe." I take the box from him and grab ten dollars from my wallet.

"You have a fiver in there, ma'am?"

"Oh, of course, I'm so sorry," I splutter, mortified. I'm never sure how much to tip for things without a bill, and it horrifies me that Joe would think I was mean.

He takes the five and gives me back the ten. "Let's not get carried away—I just brought it up."

"Oh…yes…sorry. We don't really tip in Australia. I'm having a hard time getting used to it."

"No tips, eh? Can't say I understand how that would work."

"I guess we pay people more for the kind of jobs that you tip people for here."

"We?"

"Employers. It's the law."

Joe shakes his head. "I can't see it working…how do you show your appreciation?"

"Generally we say thank you."

Joe laughs. "Well, maybe that's worth something."

"Thank you, Joe."

"I ain't giving you back the tip, you know." His laugh is deep and kind of round. I like Joe. It's taken a little while to be able to kid around with him, but he's always been thoughtful and warm.

"Hey Joe, I don't suppose you noticed anyone who mightn't have been a resident at Carrington or shouldn't have been here last Friday?"

"No." He says absolutely and without hesitation.

"Are you sure?"

"It's my job to stop anyone who isn't a resident or with a resident and ask their business, Miss Kincaid. I haven't stopped anyone aside from your friends and Mrs. Weinbaum's granddaughter for more than a week."

"Oh."

"Is there something wrong, Miss Kincaid?"

"No…well, maybe." I tell him about the photograph of my door without going into the rest. "It's only a picture, but it's freaked me out a little."

"Who sent it—the picture of your door?"

"I don't know. It was sent from Cain's phone. He'd lost it the day before."

Joe frowns. "Well, I reckon it could be one of your friend Cain's buddies. He's found the phone and he's playing a joke."

"Wouldn't a friend have come forward by now?"

"Maybe he intended to fess up but chickened out."

"I guess you're right." I'm not really convinced, but I don't want to go into everything else that had gone on.

"I'll keep an eye out, just in case," he assures me.

Joe leaves me to unpack my box of groceries. Its contents are different from the ones in the last box. The foodstuffs more luxury items than essentials—fine cheeses, Quince paste, wine, and sweets. Definitely no yoghurt.

I call Cain to thank him. "Don't tell me—you're actually the heir to Whole Foods?"

"What do you mean?"

"I mean thank you, Cain. It's so kind, and very generous, but you don't have to send me a box of groceries every time you have a meal at my place."

"You got another box of groceries?"

"Well, more gourmet than groceries—"

"Freddie, I didn't send it."

"Oh."

"Marigold?"

I laugh, a little sheepish. "Probably. I should call her."

"There wasn't a card?"

"No." I peer again into the box in case I missed it. "Just cheese, wine, and chocolate…that sort of thing"

"I guess that beats yoghurt. How's your novel coming?"

"I wrote heaps last night, actually." After returning from Leo's I had worked until three in the morning. "You?"

"I'm not really focusing, to be honest."

"Whit?"

"Probably."

"Is there anything I can do to help?"

"I don't suppose you feel like seeing a movie tonight? *North by Northwest* is playing at The Brattle."

"Cary Grant? Oh, my God, yes, please!"

Cain chuckles. "Don't tell me—he's still a big star in Australia."

"My dad was a classic film buff… I'd watch with him sometimes. Especially if it was a Cary Grant film."

"His real name was Archibald, you know. Archibald Leach."

"I didn't know, but I don't care."

"I'll pick you up at six, then."

I switch off my phone, smiling. Excitement bubbles against my determination not to behave like a giddy teenager. I return to work, telling myself that this will be no different than having dinner with Leo. A meeting of colleagues, nothing more. But I suspect it is more. Regardless, denying the possibility is a necessary defence against disappointment—protection against making a fool of myself.

The words are coming today. Heroic Chin beckons me. His relationship with Freud Girl is tantalising. There's a kindness to the way he treats her, a care, and yet the sexual tension, at least on his part, seems a little cavalier. He is sexually interested in her, but that interest is casual. The care comes from a different place.

Of course that's not so for Freud Girl.

I wonder if Leo might not be right. Am I writing romance?

Even as I focus on Heroic Chin and Freud Girl, thoughts of Cain McLeod come upon unguarded moments. They surprise me. And without knowing where exactly the thought began, I find myself contemplating him. And I feel guilty. Because I should be concentrating on my manuscript.

I call Marigold in the hope the conversation will be a kind of circuit breaker and begin by thanking her for the box of fancy groceries.

"What groceries?"

"You didn't send them either."

"Either?"

"I thought it might have been Cain again, but it wasn't." I stare at the box as I speak.

"What exactly was in it?"

"Chocolates, wine, cheese…"

"Wow! I'm on my way—"

"You can't, I'm going out…"

"Oh. Where?"

"Don't you think it's weird? There was no card."

"No, that's not weird…people forget to include a card all the time."

"I guess."

"You'll probably realise who it is in a couple of days."

I give myself an internal shake. "You're right. It's only that I feel rude not thanking someone… What are you doing?"

"I'm buying donuts." A pause and then Marigold continues hastily. "I've become a little hooked on the chai custard and coffee ones."

I laugh. "I'll keep your secret. At least until you start mugging people to support your habit."

"I can stop anytime…after tomorrow." Another pause. "You haven't heard anything from Whit's dad about how he is, have you?"

"No… He gave Cain his card. Maybe—"

"Oh, yeah… Do you think—?"

"I spoke to Cain a few minutes ago. He didn't mention anything, and I'm sure he would have."

"I might call the hospital."

Cain arrives at ten to six. He's wearing a collared shirt and sports coat, and I am relieved that I decided on a skirt rather than jeans. Perhaps it's because the film is vintage, but it seems appropriate to dress more formally than I would for the latest Marvel Universe offering.

Cain waits while I grab my coat and gloves. He's looking at the old picture in a small silver frame on the mantelpiece, when I emerge from the bedroom ready to go.

"Which one are you?" he asks. There are two barely adolescent girls in the photograph.

"I'm the taller one on the right."

"So this is your little sister?"

"Was my little sister. Gerry died about a month after than photo was taken." I tell him about the accident.

"God, how awful. I'm sorry, Freddie."

I look at the photo, wondering what Geraldine would have thought of Cain. She'd been scathing of most of the boys who had caught my eye back then…but I can't imagine she'd have any objection to Cain. "Do you have any siblings?"

"No." He shakes his head. "I was it."

"Was that lonely?"

"Probably. If I'd stopped to think about it."

I tell him about Gerry on the way out to the car, my tomboyish, smart-aleck sister. "Of course, most of us have changed a bit since we were eleven, so maybe she would have been different if she lived."

"Are you different?"

I think about it for a moment. "I began to write after Gerry died. Letters to her at first—I expect some counsellor suggested it. Then poems and stories as part of those letters. Even now, I think I'm writing for Gerry."

The Brattle Theatre is near Harvard Square and specialises in classic and international films. It's a single-screen repertory theatre, and its runs are short. Cain tells me that *North by Northwest* is showing for one night only.

"Have you come here before?" The Brattle has a kind of hidden feel about it, like a speakeasy known only to trusted patrons. A life-size poster of Alfred Hitchcock with his finger on his lips greets us at the end of the stairs to the main theatre. Murals from *Casablanca* grace the walls.

Cain nods. "Since I came back to Boston—a few times. They had a Bogart marathon here a few weeks ago."

We choose seats. There are a few people there, mostly couples, but it is by no means full. Cain leans in to point out the old signs and other movie paraphernalia around the hall, and I am aware of something fluttering inside me. I nearly laugh out loud at the cliché of me.

Cain notices. "Sorry—I didn't mean to sound like a tour guide. I just love this old place."

I nudge him. "I'm enjoying the tour. Thank you for bringing me here."

He takes my hand. At that moment the house lights dim, and I'm so glad because I'm sure not what my face is doing. My heart is pounding like a schoolgirl's, and I'm afraid to move lest the moment pass. His hand feels large and strong, the pressure is gentle, casual. The opening credits begin and we watch. Occasionally, he leans down to whisper something about a shot, and by the time Cary Grant is clambering around Mount Rushmore, our fingers are interlaced.

When the lights come up, I'm not sure what to do. Do I let go first? Will he?

Cain looks at me. "Are you hungry?"

I nod.

He squeezes my hand before he releases it to retrieve his coat, which he'd left on the empty seat beside him. I calm the flutters. This is silly. I'm twenty-seven, not fourteen.

We walk from The Brattle to an Italian place in Harvard Square. It's called Jake's, which admittedly does not immediately evoke the Mediterranean, but inside the aroma is rich and tantalising. The decor is simple and traditional, small tables draped in checked linen, bentwood chairs, candles in bottles. A basket of bread, still warm from the oven, and a pat of butter are placed on the table as we sit down. I realise I'm starving.

"At the end of the night," Cain says quietly, "Jake's leaves the leftover food in the back alley in takeaway boxes, so you don't have to rummage through the bins. Believe it or not, it's almost as good cold."

"Are there a lot of people sleeping rough in Boston?"

Cain nods. "More than you'd think. Not all of them sleep in the streets—a lot live in their cars or move from shelter to shelter. There are always more than enough people to take what Jake's put out anyway."

"So how does it work?" I ask.

"I can't be certain about now, but back then it wasn't always pleasant—there'd be shoving and pushing, threats, though it stayed basically civilised. We all knew Jake's didn't have to do it…you didn't want them to stop because fights were breaking out in their alley."

I choose vegetarian cannelloni for what I call mains and Cain calls entrée. We both order panna cotta for dessert, committing at the outset to lingering, and when the waiter retreats, we talk about the film, Cary Grant, Eva Marie Saint, James Mason, and Hitchcock, then Weinstein and the revolution and what it's changed. We discuss Tippi Hedren and the problem of loving Hitchcock's work.

"Would my book, my words, be different if I were a murderer, for example?" Cain asks carefully.

I think about it for a moment. "Words have meaning. I suppose who the author is, what he's done might change that meaning."

"Isn't meaning more to do with the reader?"

"No…a story is about leading a reader to meaning. The revelation is theirs, but we show them the way. I suppose the morality of the writer influences whether you can trust what they are showing you."

"Even if you don't know what they've done?"

"Especially if you don't know. If you are aware, then you can account for it in your interpretation of the work. Is it a manipulation, a defence? Is it an expression of guilt?"

Cain's quiet for a moment. "I guess so."

"You don't agree."

"No…you're right. But I still like Hitchcock's work."

I sigh. "Yes, so do I." I ask him to tell me more about himself. "I know you spent time on the streets in Boston, but are you from here?"

"No—it was just where I ran out of bus money. I grew up in Charlotte, North Carolina."

"And you had a stepfather, so your own father—"

"He died." Cain takes a sip from his wineglass. "When I was about six. He had a heart attack."

"I'm so sorry."

"Thank you." He shrugs. "To be honest, I don't remember too much about him. He rooted for the Red Sox, and he liked broccoli…at least he used to tell me he did."

"And your stepfather?"

"Mom married him when I was eight. He was great at first. Took me to games, played ball with me. He wanted a large family—was always telling me what we'd do when my brothers and sisters came along." Cain pauses. "But they didn't come along—he and Mom tried but they couldn't get pregnant. He started to drink. He blamed Mom first and then me."

"Oh, Cain." I want to reach out to him but there's a table between us.

He smiles. "It was a long time ago, Freddie. Isaac used to say, 'Everybody's got a sad story, boy, and yours is a boring one!'"

I can feel my head moving back. "Really?"

Cain's smile broadens. "I told you, he wasn't cast by Disney."

"So, did it change when you went back?"

"No. But I had."

Our meals arrive and the next moments are taken up with welcoming them to our table, thanking the waiter, and comparing dishes. Cain asks about my work and, for a fleeting absurd moment, I think of Leo asking me if Handsome Man realises I'm calling him that. I can feel myself blush for apparently no reason, but if Cain notices he does not mention it. And I talk to him about everything aside from what I've named him. He listens as I describe how the characters in my work are growing and mutating from their real inspiration.

"At what point are you going to untether your characters?" he asks. "When are you going to let them diverge from the people you know?"

"When I know you all enough to know I'm diverging, I suppose. Or when your real stories become boring."

He laughs.

I see his eyes widen suddenly.

"Is something wrong?" I glance over my shoulder.

"No—not wrong," he begins.

I see then what's caught his eye.

Marigold.

———

Dear Hannah,

Some may find a tendency to stalk people a negative trait, but on Marigold it is somehow alluring. Who knew a hint of psychosis could be so attractive?

And we find out just a little bit more about Cain. Not a lot...he remains elusive. But we know now he's from the Tar Heel State! He, too, would have a Southern accent—not as marked as that of my namesake. You may wish to add a bit of dialect. For example, Cain would probably refer to Jake's as a "joint" rather than a "restaurant." He might also use "y'all" and "yonder" occasionally. I must say I do like the sounds of Isaac. It a shame he's already dead.

I read this morning that Australia has now closed its borders to non-citizens, as has the U.S. It's a strange and tedious new world. I suppose this means your postponed trip stateside will not be undertaken in the near future. Fortunately, I remain willing and able to be your American informant.

I am excruciatingly aware of the moments of history through which we are living. It seems to me that we are seeing the dying days of democracy—at least here in America. And perhaps the beginning of a new Dark Age. I find myself more intrigued than despondent about the notion. The world is on the cusp of being overwhelmed by fear and rage, a dystopia beyond any we might have imagined in our writings.

Stay safe.

Yours,
Leo

CHAPTER THIRTEEN

Marigold picks up a bag of takeout and hands over her card. She doesn't appear to have seen us.

My eyes meet Cain's. Guilt, and uncertainty how to proceed.

Cain speaks first. "Should we?"

I nod, swallowing my reluctance.

Cain stands and catches Marigold's attention. She looks at us blankly at first and then with surprise.

He beckons for her to join us, and Marigold makes her way to our table.

"What are you two doing here?" She asks before I can ask her the same.

Cain is unflustered. "There was a film on at The Brattle that I thought Freddie might find useful for her book."

"The Brattle? Was it a documentary?" She groans.

"It wasn't that bad," Cain replies. He pulls a chair out for Marigold. "Are you going to have dessert with us, Marigold?" He glances at her takeout bag. "Unless dessert is preemptive."

Marigold takes a seat. "Eating dessert last is a ridiculous social dictate. Gosh, it's lucky I ran into you."

"A happy coincidence," I say, thinking for the first time that it is, indeed, a coincidence.

Marigold agrees. "I come here all the time. Funny that of all the places in Harvard Square, you'd pick this."

"Clearly, we all have good taste." I change the subject. "Did you get through to the hospital?"

"Yes." Marigold communicates with the waiter on the other side of the room via elaborate charades that she'll have whatever we're having. "They've released him."

"What? Already?"

Marigold thanks the waiter. "Apparently."

"Well, that's terrific, I guess." I am admittedly a little bewildered by this sudden return to health.

"They've probably decided Whit can recuperate at home," Cain suggests. "Between the police and his mother, he was turning the ward into a circus."

Marigold screws up her nose, but she agrees. "I think Whit's mom is suing the hospital for negligence—because the stitch broke."

"Oh." I shake my head slowly. "I suppose we could consider ourselves lucky she's not suing us for making him laugh."

"Us?" Marigold points at Cain. "He told Whit that his name was Abel Manners!"

Cain grimaces. "In hindsight, I agree I should have kept my fool mouth shut. But not because Whit broke a stitch."

"Well, I'm glad Whit's home safe." I take my first bite of panna cotta and savour it unashamedly.

"Oh, he's safe," Marigold says. "There are at least a dozen security guards stationed outside his parents' house."

I swallow. The pause is just a beat too long as both Cain and I process her words.

"Marigold," I put down my spoon and look at her, "did you go to Whit's house?"

She nods, smiling conspiratorially. "Don't worry, I didn't knock or anything. I only walked past a couple of times."

"That mightn't have been the best idea at the moment," Cain says quietly.

Marigold's face falls a bit. "I know. But I needed to see if he was there."

"Why?"

She says nothing for a moment. When she speaks her voice is thick, forced. "I don't know. Sometimes it's like I can't breathe if I don't know where he is."

"Oh, Marigold." There's something so young and confused about her, so fragile, despite everything.

"Does Whit know you feel this way?" Cain asks.

She regards him with horror. "Of course not!"

I wonder. It seems to me that he might have an idea, but I don't raise it.

"Still, maybe you shouldn't be hanging around Whit's house right now," Cain says gently.

Marigold's giggle is nervous. "I wasn't hanging around. Just passing." She shakes her head firmly. "I didn't even pause."

Cain glances at me.

"That might look a bit suspicious, Marigold, if they notice you." I'm worried about her. "Next time, maybe stop and call in. It's not strange that Whit's friends want to know how he is."

Marigold's eyes brighten. "Do you think I should?"

"I think it would be better than lurking on the street outside."

"I wasn't lurking—"

"I know."

"Have you heard anything more about Caroline Palfrey?" Cain asks. He's changing the subject ever so slightly, and both Marigold and I are grateful.

Marigold frowns. "No, not really. There are a lot of reporters asking questions for stories…you know, the 'all-American girl slain' type. They're looking for some kind of double life, I think."

"And was there?" Cain asks. "Did she have a double life?"

"No. Not that I've heard. Unless you count writing for the *Rag* a double life."

We return to our desserts in silence for a while, until Marigold offers a further fact.

"That's where she met Whit. At the *Rag*."

"That's right. Whit wrote once," I remember.

Marigold shrugs. "He reported—and it was more than once."

For a moment I think of Heroic Chin and his secret love of dance.

Cain is looking at Marigold thoughtfully. "Had you and Whit met before that day in the library?"

Marigold hesitates. "We literally bumped into each other once. But he doesn't remember."

It occurs to me that Cain is only this evening fully realising that Marigold is in love with Whit. I'm a little bemused that it has taken him so long.

As we finish dessert and drink coffee, Marigold asks about *The Adventures of Freud Girl*, as she is fond of calling my manuscript. "Will you let me read it when you're finished?"

I'm touched by the way she asks. Like reading the work of a writer is a privilege and not the purpose for which we write. "Yes, if you'd like."

"Of course I'd like! And I promise I won't get upset if it's not all about Freud Girl."

I laugh. "I'll bear that in mind."

She turns to Cain. "I was thinking about your novel."

"You were?"

"I was wondering if it might help to know more about Isaac—where he was from, what he might have done before he was on the streets?"

Cain looks startled. "Yes, I suppose it might."

"Harvard's got some awesome research facilities for students. I could do some research for you if you like—his last name was Harmon, right?"

"Yes...but I've already looked, Marigold. There are no records of Isaac before he died."

"It wouldn't hurt to try. Maybe you need fresh eyes."

Cain's brow furrows. "Thank you, but it's really not necessary. I have everything I need for the book. It's a novel, not an autobiography."

"It'll give me something to do." Marigold is typically difficult to dissuade.

"Don't you have a degree to keep you entertained?"

"Degrees do not entertain, Cain." Marigold sighs. "I don't really sleep well—it means I have extra hours to fill when normal people are asleep."

"To be honest, Marigold, I'd rather you didn't." Cain is blunt.

"Why? I could—"

"This is my novel. I'd rather do it myself."

"Oh." Marigold looks crushed, and I am startled by Cain's words if not his tone.

He is immediately contrite. "I'm sorry, Marigold, I didn't mean to snarl. It's just that I feel like Isaac is entitled to his privacy. He didn't have much else."

Marigold's gaze is searching. Cain holds it. Eventually, she looks away. "Of course; I understand."

Cain relaxes. "Thank you." He offers to drive her home. "My Jeep's parked over yonder, near The Brattle."

Marigold shakes her head. "I'm on Athens Street. I can walk."

"We'll walk you home then and come back for the car," I insist, as Cain signals that we're ready for the bill. "You should be careful, at least until Caroline Palfrey's murderer is found."

Marigold scoffs. "I keep forgetting you're Australian. I'd bet there are probably a dozen unsolved murderers within a block or so of here. They're more common than spiders."

"All the more reason then."

The waitress comes to the table to tell us the bill has been taken care of.

"By whom?" Cain asks perplexed.

The waitress looks down at her digital notebook. "I'm afraid I don't know, sir. It just says here that the bill's been paid."

"Could there be some mistake?"

"Maybe. But the bill has been paid."

"How about I leave you my number?" I'm concerned that if there is a mistake the waitress might end up being asked to pay for any shortfall. "If there is a problem, then you can call me, and we can sort it out."

She takes the number but assures me it will be unnecessary. "Sometimes folks do this sort of thing...pay it forward, or pay for a stranger or whatever meme is doing the rounds. I wouldn't worry about it."

And so we thank her, grab our coats, and leave a generous tip before stepping back out into the square. The cold is immediately invigorating, and I'm glad we have reason to walk somewhere. Marigold directs our path to her apartment on Athens Street off Mass Avenue, and we talk about the stars as we walk the well-lit streets, which make seeing them here impossible. I tell Cain and Marigold about the blazing night skies out west in Australia, under which you can truly feel the immensity of the universe. A prick of homesickness as I remember locking my eyes on the Southern Cross to reorient myself among the stars.

Marigold leads us to an elegant, old weatherboard building sporting large bays on either end, so that it's shaped a little like a bone. This is a nice part of town, and the buildings here all have a similar old world charm. Marigold's apartment is on the second floor. We can hear music as we climb the stairs.

"That'll be Lucas," Marigold says.

"Lucas?"

"My flatmate. Come on, I'll introduce you." She unlocks the door and waves us into the apartment which is pulsing with heavy metal played at a thousand decibels. We walk into a living room decorated in a kind of edgy urban chic. The couches are large, worn leather pieces. One wall is lined with what appear to be lockers. The television is massive and sits above the mantel of the fireplace, which defies its industrial surrounds with delicate craftsmen details. Marigold grabs a remote control from the arm of the couch and turns off the music.

"Hey, what the fuck—" A man emerges from one of the other rooms protesting. He's huge, at least six and half feet. His hair is long and dread-locked, and various parts of him are pierced. He's wearing nothing but boxer shorts.

For a moment we all just stare at each other.

Then Marigold groans. "For Chrissake, Lucas, put on some pants, at least."

"Not on our account," I say quickly. "I mean, we aren't staying—we were only seeing Marigold home."

Lucas nods. In greeting or perhaps agreement that he will not be putting on pants.

Marigold rolls her eyes. "This is Lucas, my flatmate. Lucas, my friends Cain and Freddie."

"Pleasure," Lucas grunts. He eyes the bag of takeout. "What took you so long? I'm starving."

She holds out the bag to him. "Go on, then. Don't forget to say grace."

Lucas smiles. "You're real funny, Anastas." His face falls. "It's cold!"

"I was a little longer getting home than I expected." Marigold wrinkles her nose. "It'll be all right cold."

"We're not savages," Lucas mutters. "I'll heat it. You better set the table."

"That might be our cue to go," Cain whispers.

We wish Marigold good night and call a tentative farewell to Lucas as he bustles in the kitchen.

"Are you sure you don't want to stay for something to eat?" Marigold asks.

"We've barely finished dinner," Cain reminds her. He lowers his voice. "Unless you're fixing to tell us that Lucas is dangerous—which I could believe—we'd better go."

Marigold smiles. "Lucas can't even dress himself—he's not dangerous."

We wave as we descend the stairs and set out into the evening, and for a while we stroll in silence.

"Did you know Marigold had a housemate?" Cain asks eventually.

"No, she's never mentioned him."

"Do you think they're—"

"Of course not."

"Because she's in love with Whit?"

"Yes."

He looks at me. "Why do you think she's so hooked on Whit?"

I think about it. "I don't know. Marigold said it herself, I suppose—the heart wants what it wants." I shrug. "And Whit's very boyishly charming..."

Cain laughs softly. "Was it the gender or the age aspect of boyish that made your nose wrinkle when you said it?"

"How could you possibly see what my nose was doing?" It is dark, after all.

"I heard it in your voice."

"I really like Whit," I hedge. "But here is something very Dennis the Menace about him."

"Which bugs you?"

"No—not at all. But I'm a little surprised Marigold is so attracted to it."

"Do you think it was a coincidence that Marigold walked into Jake's?"

"Don't you?"

Cain doesn't reply, curses, and breaks into a run as we approach the Jeep. "Hey, what are you doing?"

There's a man bent near the rear passenger-side of the jeep. He's tall, wearing a knit cap pulled down over his brow, and he reeks.

Cain stops. "Boo?"

The man straightens. "I reckoned it was your car. That's Abel's jalopy, I thought."

"What are you doing here, Boo?"

"Looks like someone stuck a knife into your tyre. A big knife. Maybe they twisted it."

Dear Hannah,

Of course Marigold would keep a naked man in her apartment! I fall more deeply in love with each chapter!

The mystery benefactor at the restaurant was a master stroke. Could be they're being followed, could be nothing. It's unsettling but does not take over the narrative.

The term weatherboard is an Australian one, I believe. I can't think of an

American equivalent. It's not used in an American's dialogue, so you can probably get away with it, or you could just change the reference to "wooden."

I made face masks today. Anonymous black. I know the trend is to make some kind of statement with fabric, but I have no desire to bring attention to myself. Perhaps that's my statement. I am no one and everyone.

I am no longer going to tell you to stay safe, because staying safe does not make great writing. So take risks, my friend!

Yours,
Leo

CHAPTER FOURTEEN

Cain moves closer to have a look at the tyre, Boo explodes, slamming Cain hard into the side of the Jeep and pinning him.

I try to help, but Cain signals me to stay back.

"How many times I gotta tell you, Abel, you don't approach a man from the left. Murderers jump you from the left. I won't always be around to protect you."

"Sorry, Boo," Cain says evenly. "I forgot. I was just fixing to look at the tyre."

"It's cut up, and if you come from the left again, you will be too, you understand?"

"Yes, I do. I'm sorry."

"Do you have any money? I'm hungry."

"Let me up."

Boo backs off.

Cain takes a note out of his wallet and hands it to him. "I'll see you at the library tomorrow, okay."

"Outside. I'm not going into that place no more." Boo clenches the money in his fist and walks away.

I stare after him, horrified and confused, before I turn my attention to Cain, who is standing with his hands in his pockets as if being attacked by a large, smelly man was the most ordinary thing in the world. "God, Cain, are you…"

"I'm fine. Boo has a few quirks."

"He's a friend of yours?"

"He was a friend of Isaac's. I tracked him down when I came back—thought he might be able to tell me something."

"And he slashed your tyre?"

"He didn't say that. But someone did." Cain removes his coat and rolls up his sleeves.

"Who else would slash your tyre?"

"Who knows?" He kicks the tyre and pulls a jack from the boot. "Drunks, kids...some moron who doesn't like Jeeps." He exhales. "Or it might have been Boo. I couldn't tell you."

I open the door and toss his coat and mine into the back seat so I can help, but to be honest, I'm wearing a skirt so I really just stand there, holding the lug nuts he hands me, and watching in case Boo returns. I could put my coat back on since divesting myself of it serves no purpose beyond being an act of solidarity, but already embarrassed by the fact that I'm not doing much of use, I tough it out. By the time the tyre's changed, Cain is warm with the exertion, and I'm shivering.

"What happened to your coat?" Cain asks as he returns the jack and lug wrench to the boot and wipes the grease off his hands with what appears to be an old bandana. "You look frozen."

He fetches my coat from the back seat, and once I've put it on and climbed back into the car, he places his coat over my knees. "I'm sorry about all that, Freddie. I'm pretty sure Boo is harmless; he's just angry with me at the moment."

"Why?"

"He blames me for Isaac dying." Cain rubs his jaw. "He's not—Isaac used to say Boo was troubled."

"Are you okay?" I ask gently. "He nearly pushed you through the door."

Cain grins. "Gimme a break, I was letting him win."

"Cain..."

"I really am fine, Freddie."

"You're meeting him at the library?"

Cain starts the Jeep and turns up the heat. "He sleeps near the library. I sit on the steps outside and he finds me sometimes...if he's hungry, or wants to talk."

"What do you talk about?"

"You name it. The government agents following him, the French Mafia, the conspiracy to sedate Americans by way of subliminal messages in reality television—he may be right about that one—but sometimes he'll talk to me about Isaac."

"Do you have any idea who Isaac was before he was on the streets?"

Cain shakes his head. "Boo says he was an important man, but what that means…"

"Does it matter for your story?" I place my hands beneath the coat on my knees. "Will what Isaac was change it?"

"No. It won't." He smiles faintly. "It isn't about the book anymore. I do want to know more about Isaac, who might have killed him, even if it was only some other poor disturbed vagrant who wanted his coat, or his sandwich or his doorway."

I take Cain's hand. It's impulsive, unthinking, but once it's done I can't really take it back. And so I just sit there holding his hand, a little shocked by what I've done and not sure what to do next. If Cain is startled, he doesn't show it.

"I'm hoping that in a more lucid moment, Boo might give me a clue to Isaac's past…maybe his family."

"Did Isaac never hint at anything himself?"

"I got the feeling that he was from Boston, but I'm not sure there's a sensible reason for that. It might simply have been that I was lost, and he knew his way around the streets here."

The bang on the window jolts the both of us. It's Boo back again. He's agitated, angry.

Cain winds down the window. "Boo—"

"Does she know?" Boo pounds on the Jeep as he shouts into the window. "Does she know what you did? Bet you didn't tell her. Does she know what you did, Abel?"

"Boo, calm down, man."

"You'll do it again. He paid me to do it again…and I did. Below the ribs and towards the spine."

"Stay here," Cain says quietly as he winds up the window and moves to get out of the car.

"Cain—"

"I'll be all right—I just need to calm him down. But don't get out." He opens the door, pushing Boo back as he does so, steps out, and slams the door shut behind him. Boo is still shouting and gesticulating as he follows Cain away from the car. I can see them in the headlights and though I can no longer hear what they're saying, it's clear they are arguing. Boo points at me. Cain hands him something. Boo takes it and then, without warning, he swings at Cain, catching him on the side of the head. Cain goes down.

I grab my phone to call the police, and as I open my door and jump out, Boo looks up. For a moment I'm sure he's about to come for me. "You don't know what he did," he says feverishly. "I saw it. I couldn't stop it, but there is always a reckoning, a punishment." I step slowly towards Cain, and Boo turns and runs.

"Cain?" I kneel beside him. It's only then I see the shattered glass, and the blood on the side of Cain's head. Cain groans and touches the gash above his temple. I begin to dial for an ambulance while trying to talk to Cain. I should keep him conscious, I think. Pop culture medicine. Anyone who's ever watched television knows that keeping an injured person conscious is imperative. "Cain, speak to me!"

"Who are you calling?" Cain sits up slowly. He's still dazed and bleeding quite profusely.

"An ambulance…the police."

"Don't."

"You're bleeding!"

"Really, Freddie, don't." He staggers to his feet.

I forget phoning anybody so that I can help him. His hand is heavy on my shoulder, but he's standing. "He won't come back," Cain says as I look behind us for Boo.

"You said he wasn't dangerous," I mutter as we move back to the Jeep. I manoeuvre him into the passenger seat. He protests weakly.

"You're in no condition to drive."

"There're some cloths in the glove box," he says, still trying to staunch the bleeding with his hand.

I look. A bunch of rags he's obviously being using to work on the Jeep. "You can't use these, Cain; they're covered in grease." I rummage in my bag and find a near full purse pack of clean tissues. "Pull your hand away for a second?"

He does as I ask. The wound is about two inches long and deep enough to make me feel light-headed just looking at it. I press the wad of tissues against it and then get Cain to replace his hand and apply pressure. "I think this will need stitches, Cain."

He winces. "I'll see a doctor in the morning."

I shut the passenger door and run around the car to climb in behind the wheel. "I think I should drive you to the Emergency Room, Cain."

"I have a first aid kit at home—are you okay?"

"You're the one that's bleeding!"

He almost smiles. "You clearly don't like blood?"

"Not this much blood." I reach over and secure his seat belt. "I really think I should take you to the hospital."

"Freddie, I'm not insured. Believe me, this is not serious enough to warrant going to the ER and into bankruptcy."

"Oh." The Sinclair Fellowship came with medical insurance, and so I am woefully ignorant of how the American system works, but Australian travellers have long been warned about the danger of entering the United States without insurance. I slip the Jeep into gear and close my eyes briefly to visualise driving on the opposite side of the road before pulling out. "I'm taking you back to the Carrington so that we can at least see how bad it is."

Cain does not reply. But he is still conscious. I check. Then, and several times on the way to the Carrington.

Joe looks up from his desk as we walk into the chequerboard foyer. He puts down his book and stands up. "I'll call an ambulance—"

"That's okay, Joe." I glance dubiously at Cain, who, despite the blood, seems steady on his feet. "Mr. McLeod insists it's not that bad."

"Okay." Joe shakes his head as he looks at Cain. "You let me know if you change your mind."

Leo is leaving his apartment as I open my door. He looks startled. I mouth *"It's all right"* before he says anything. He hesitates for a moment. I smile to reassure him without explanation, though I suppose the explanation itself is not all that reassuring.

I sit Cain on a stool in the kitchen and fetch some towels to replace the tissues which have long since soaked and disintegrated. The bleeding seems to have slowed, though. I grab the first aid kit from under the sink and inspect its contents for the first time.

"Is there any Tylenol in there?" Cain asks.

"Yes."

"Let's start with that."

I hand him the bottle and get him a glass of water. He puts down the towel and takes a couple of tablets while I find antiseptic and a packet of steristrips. Thankfully, there are instructions on the packet.

I check the wound carefully for any remnant glass, but it seems clean. Cain tenses as I apply the antiseptic.

There's a knock at the door. I answer with the intention of sending whoever it is on their way as soon as possible. It's one of the old ladies from downstairs. She's holding a doctor's bag.

"Mrs. Weinbaum."

"Actually it's Dr. Weinbaum…but since Jerry died, I like to be Mrs. He always wanted me to be Mrs… He didn't harp on about it, but when you're married to a man for fifty-three years, you know." She smiles sadly. "Gladys Jackson says she saw you walking in with a gentleman who might be in need of sutures."

"Yes…but…"

"Well, lead the way; let's have a look at him."

I take her into the kitchen.

Cain looks at me questioningly.

"This is Mrs…Dr. Weinbaum."

Dr. Weinbaum, as she now declares herself to be, waits expectantly until I realise she wants me to finish the introduction.

"This is my friend Cain McLeod."

"Let's have a look at you, young man." Dr. Weinbaum sidesteps me to examine both Cain and the contents of the first aid kit. "You could use steristrips," she says approvingly, "but it will heal quicker and leave less of a scar if I stitch it." She looks closely at the wound. "You really don't want to risk spoiling that face. I'd better sew it." She motions towards the living room. "Sit in that armchair, Mr. McLeod—the stool's too high. Winifred, fetch a lamp over here so I can see properly."

I glance at Cain. He shrugs and does as she asks. So I fetch the lamp and plug it in near the armchair. Dr. Weinbaum pulls on a pair of latex gloves and opens a sealed packet which contains a sterile suture needle and thread. She has me hold the lamp, tells Cain not to move, and then brings the edges of the wound together and stitches it. I can see Cain's grip tighten on the arm of the chair, but otherwise you wouldn't know someone was sewing his head without anaesthetic. It all takes just a few minutes. She raises the yoghurt issue again as she ties off and snips the sutures. "I was thinking, Winifred, that your problem might be lactose intolerance, in which case yoghurt would exacerbate it. Perhaps you should give it up."

"Okay…I'll try."

She removes the gloves and places them with the needle in a zip-lock bag, which she returns to her medical bag. "Just take the usual precautions— keep the wound clean and dry. Come and see me if there are any problems. Winifred, make him a cup of tea. Now I really must go."

She waves away our thanks and is on her way with a reminder to avoid yoghurt until I know for sure about the lactose intolerance. I close the door behind her and return to Cain in the living room. I sit on the coffee table opposite him.

He looks at me. "I suppose you want to talk about what happened."

—

Dear Hannah,

Interesting thing. Generally speaking, Americans say trunk rather than boot, but it is a North Carolinian quirk to say boot as well, and since it's in the narrative, not dialogue, you could probably leave it.

Why on earth is Cain not insured? Is he crazy? I know many self-employed people are not insured, but there are writers' associations and the like that offer insurance. It's possible he simply let it lapse, I suppose, or he has some preexisting condition that means they won't cover him, or he's broke. Are you trying to let the reader know he's broke? Maybe you are. I suppose he's a writer…most of us are broke for large periods of our lives.

That said, I do like Dr. Weinbaum, and it does make sense that a place like Carrington Square would have at least one retired doctor in residence. Certainly, Boston could use all the doctors it can get right now—retired or not. We are not faring as badly as New York, but we are well up there on the pandemic league tables, and I think there is a sense of doom about the place. The schools have been closed, of course, and Copley Plaza seems to have an echo about it nowadays. Still, there's a kind of eerie beauty to abandoned streets and public places.

I am writing more fluidly than ever. Perhaps my muse is fear.

Yours,

Leo

CHAPTER FIFTEEN

"How are you feeling?" I ask. Dr. Weinbaum's sutures are neat, evenly spaced on a bruised canvas. Cain's eye is beginning to blacken, and the upper arm of his shirt is torn where I presume he hit the ground.

"A little embarrassed, to be honest."

"Because you *let* Boo win twice in one night?"

He smiles.

"What did he hit you with, Cain?"

"He was holding a bottle, I think."

"You do realise he might have killed you?"

"If he had, he wouldn't have meant to, Freddie. Boo lashes out when he's frustrated or scared."

"What does he think you've done?" I ask, recalling the man's demands as to whether *I knew*.

"Nothing…everything." Cain flinches. "I should get going."

"Do you have a pet?"

"A pet?"

"You know…a dog, a cat, an iguana…"

"No."

"Then no one's going to starve if you don't go home tonight. You can have my bed. I'll take the couch."

"That's not necessary."

"It is, for my peace of mind." I'm trying not to bully him, but I'm firm. "I don't think you should drive just yet."

"I can't turn you out of your bed."

"I'll be fine on the couch."

"How about I take the couch?"

"You're taller than me. For you, the couch won't be comfortable." I wear him down. The aftereffects of his injury are clearly worse than he's letting on, and in the end, Cain gives in. I direct him to the bedroom and make tea as instructed. It was probably not a prescription, but I prefer to be safe. If not for the transformation of one of my neighbours into Dr. Weinbaum, I might have insisted upon taking Cain to the hospital.

I take the tea in to Cain. He's already under the covers, his jeans and bloody shirt folded over the end of the bed. I grab my laptop from its place by him on the bedside table.

He apologises again for taking my bed and for Boo.

"We probably should report this to the police." I sit on the bed as I talk to him. "Boo is violent, volatile. He might hurt someone…else."

Cain is quiet for a moment. "I'll try and find him tomorrow. See if I can talk him into turning himself in. Maybe there's some kind of program he—"

"What?"

"Freddie," Cain reaches for my hand, "what happened was not entirely Boo's fault. I should have known not to give him money. I should have bought him a meal, but I was with you, and I just wanted him to go away. I should have realised he'd score within seconds." Cain's eyes are piercing. "I know Boo. He'll go somewhere now, hide and sleep it off. I'll find him tomorrow."

I sit there for a while, studying the beautiful man in my bed. I know there is something he's not telling me. I'm not so dazzled by him not to recognise that. But we are all still new friends and there is probably a great deal we have not yet told each other.

He sits up, leans over, and kisses me on the lips, gently. I'm so surprised I stare at him mutely. I'm pretty sure my mouth is hanging open. It feels like it is, but I'm not yet capable of closing it.

"Thank you for tonight," he says. "I'm sorry it derailed a bit."

I pull myself together. "I should let you get some sleep."

Cain looks unsure now. Uncertain. "God, Freddie, I'm sorry. I didn't mean to—"

"Kiss me?" I try not to sound too dismayed by the change of heart.
"To take advantage of the situation."

I smile. "You're the one with a head injury."

"I've been wanting to kiss you since well before Boo hit me on the head."

"You have?" I'm aware I sound like a doe-eyed teenager. I take a breath and remind myself that I'm twenty-seven. "I'm glad. And I don't object. Far from it…I'm a little worried that you may be concussed."

He laughs.

Oh, what the hell—I kiss him now. And we linger in the tingling discovery of it. And then I am staring at him again and he at me, like we're locked into each other. I break the spell, pulling away and standing up. "Get some sleep, Cain. But tell me if you feel nauseous and/or if the headache gets worse or if you lose consciousness."

"Losing consciousness is the point of sleep, I would have thought. You still think I'm concussed?"

"I hope not." I grab my pyjamas from the dresser and pick up his shirt from the end of the bed. "I'll throw this in the washing machine before the blood stains set."

I write. I'm not going to sleep anyway. There's too much to think about, to roll over in my mind. Working is both a distraction and a way to focus. Boo looms in my thoughts, his volatility, his anger. I remember that Cain gave him something. I wonder what—more money? And what was it Boo thought I should know? And should I have kissed Cain?

Eventually I allow myself to think about Cain alone. The way he laughs. The pressure of his lips against mine. And the scars on his chest and back— more than the usual signs of unremarkable surgery. I had noticed them silently. I want to ask him about them, but I don't know that a kiss entitles me to his medical history. I am aware that I am falling in love with Cain McLeod. That I have been falling since that first day in the Reading Room. I cringe a little at the idea. Marigold's guileless obsession with Whit has made me a little shy of admitting to anything similar. And yet I cannot deny I am drawn to Cain, intrigued by him. Boo called him Abel—knew him when he was Abel Manners. Cain killed Abel. Had Cain done that? Had he eradicated his former self? If so, why? I could understand changing Manners, but he'd removed Abel too. I think about what it would be like to be called something other than Winifred—being Freddie is being me… But maybe I could be someone else… I've always like the name Madeleine…perhaps I could be Madeleine…

I am woken by a knock on my door. I check my watch. It's nine in the morning. My first thought is that I haven't checked on Cain. He might have died in the night, for all I know.

Another knock.

I stumble off the couch and answer the door in my pyjamas. There are two gentlemen outside. They wear sharp dark suits and carry briefcases.

"Good morning. Can I help you?"

"Are you Winifred Kincaid?"

"Yes, I am."

"Is there a Mr. McLeod here?"

Now I'm alarmed. "Yes. Who are you gentlemen?"

"Jarod Stills and Liam McKenny from Zackheim and Associates."

"You're solicitors?"

"Attorneys. We'd like to speak with Mr. McLeod if that's possible."

Lawyers. Maybe they're Cain's lawyers. How else would they know he was here? "Why don't you come in? I'll fetch Mr. McLeod." I bring them into the living room, snatching up the sheet and pillows from the couch as I do so and trying not to wonder what they think of it or me. I walk into the bedroom. Cain is still asleep, but breathing.

I place my hand on his shoulder. "Cain. Wake up."

He smiles when he opens his eyes. "Freddie…hello."

"There are lawyers here to see you," I whisper. "Zackheim and Associates."

He squints at me. "Lawyers?"

"Yes. They're waiting on the couch."

He sits up. "How did they know I was here?"

"I don't know. I'll get your shirt out of the dryer…while you get the rest of yourself dressed."

He nods vaguely. "Sure. Did you say lawyers?"

I run into the bathroom which houses a little built-in laundry and pull his shirt out of the dryer. He has his jeans and shoes on by the time I return. Again I notice the scars, several on his back and one beneath his ribs.

"Thank you." He buttons and tucks in the fresh shirt, and we return to the living room. I'm still in my pyjamas, but we can't leave two lawyers unattended in my living room for any longer.

They stand and introduce themselves to Cain. "We have been retained by the estate of Dr. Elias Weinbaum to represent Mrs. Irma Weinbaum from time to time as the need arises," Jarod Stills informs us.

I look at Cain, not sure what's going on. He seems equally bewildered.

"We are given to understand that Mrs. Weinbaum was here last night. That she might have rendered certain assistance?"

"How did you know—"

"Joe—your doorman called us this morning. Our client mentioned it to him. He understands the situation."

"What situation?" I demand. "Dr. Weinbaum sutured a wound on Cain's brow." Wait, are these men delivering a bill for services?

Liam McKenny points at the stitches. "She did that?"

"Yes?"

"How do you feel, Mr. McLeod?"

"Fine. What is this about, Mr. McKenny?"

The lawyers glance at each other.

"To put it frankly, Mr. McLeod, we're here to ask you if you are going to take action, and perhaps to persuade you to deal with the matter via settlement instead."

"Take action? Why would I? Dr. Weinbaum helped me."

Jarod Stills sighs. "I'm afraid, Mr. McLeod, that Irma Weinbaum is not, nor has ever been, a doctor."

"But she said—" I begin incredulously.

"I'm afraid our client is occasionally subject to the delusion that she is a medical practitioner. It's generally not dangerous, but she is neither trained nor qualified to be suturing anyone."

"I see."

"Our client will, of course, bear the expense of any and all remedial medical work required as a result of her well-meaning but misguided intervention."

Cain turns to me, his eyes wide. "Remedial? What exactly has she done to me?"

I can feel my mouth twitch. "I didn't want to tell you. You're hideous!"

"I wondered why you covered up all the mirrors." He cackles in a terrible impersonation of Jack Nicholson's Joker. I get the giggles. The lawyers seem confounded, and to be honest I can't blame them. We should be appalled.

McKenny clears his throat. He pulls some papers from his briefcase and pushes them across the coffee table to Cain.

Cain scans the document. I read over his shoulder. It's a legal waiver that precludes Cain McLeod from taking any further action again Mrs. Irma Weinbaum in respect of anything she might have or might not have done on the named date.

Stills pushes over a business card. Dr. Lemarr. A downtown address and a phone number.

"As I said, all your medical expenses will be met by our client, including any cosmetic procedures which may be required. We are further authorised to offer you the sum of—"

"Do you have a pen, Mr. McKenny?" Cain puts the documents down on the coffee table.

McKenny obliges.

Cain signs. "Wherever your client learned her needlework skills, she did employ them in my aid. I have no intention of pursuing her on that count."

McKenny nods happily, but Stills is at pains to point out, "Mrs. Weinbaum has no medical training, sir. In fact, I doubt very much that our client has ever even had cause to darn a sock."

McKenny casts a dark look in his colleague's direction and takes the documents in case Cain should change his mind.

"I'll keep Dr. Lemarr's card in case my head becomes septic," Cain concedes. "But I think I'm okay." He pauses. "Would you mind telling me where Mrs. Weinbaum acquired her doctor's bag…the needle and suture thread… It was suture thread, wasn't it?"

Jarod Stills' eyes go to the stitches before he confirms, "Yes. She acquired the items on eBay, I believe."

Cain begins to laugh.

McKenny grins now, but Stills remains appropriately concerned. "We will all feel better if you would allow Dr. Lemarr to check you over, Mr. McLeod, whether or not your head becomes septic."

"Rest assured, Mr. Stills. The stitches will have to come out at some point, and since I presume you won't be allowing Mrs. Weinbaum to make house calls again, I will need to see Dr. Lemarr for that purpose."

"You've been very understanding, Mr. McLeod," McKenny cuts in before Stills can advise further caution.

Cain takes advantage of the goodwill. "Can I ask you, Mr. McKenny, are Mrs. Weinbaum's delusions only about being a doctor?"

"I'm not sure what you mean?"

"Does she ever become a lawyer, for example?"

"Occasionally she imagines she is a plumber."

"And does she have plumbers' tools as well?"

"She does."

"A plunger? A wrench?"

"And various brushes, clamps, and washers."

Cain nods thoughtfully. "And people allow her to come in and fix their pipes?"

"Less often than they allow her to conduct medical procedures." McKenny glances at Stills, who is obviously unhappy by his lack of discretion with respect to Mrs. Weinbaum. "Can I ask why you wish to know, Mr. McLeod?"

"Professional interest."

"You are a psychologist?"

"A writer."

Both lawyers react, tensing immediately. "There is a confidentiality clause in that document you just signed, Mr. McLeod."

"I'm a novelist, Mr. Stills, not a reporter. Your confidentiality clause does not preclude me using your client as inspiration."

———

My dear Hannah,

It's like an old-fashioned melodrama! I want to shout at Freddie—look behind you! The villain's in your bed!

As for Mrs. Weinbaum—I love it! I really want her to attempt an appendectomy!

I took myself to a dive bar last night, to absorb the atmosphere while I wrote. Made me feel like Hemingway. Ordered a mojito and took a seat at the bar. It was, to be honest, a little more divey than I had anticipated. There was a fight during which one thug hit another thug over the head with a beer bottle—knocked him unconscious and then left. The barman called an ambulance and the other patrons just kept on drinking. Some of them had masks—they were wearing them like bandanas around their necks and foreheads. Anyway, I took a couple of photos of the unconscious guy's head, in case you wanted to describe Cain's wound in more detail. There were bits of glass embedded in the wound...I don't think you mentioned that in your description. The shards caught the light and glinted in the blood.

In case it isn't obvious, I'm really enjoying watching this story unfold, and maybe helping just a little.

Yours,

Leo

Chapter Sixteen

"I saw her first! In fact, I've known her for weeks!"

"If I recall accurately, it was my head she stitched. I think that gives me a prior claim."

"Rubbish!" I count off my points. "I let her in, the procedure was conducted in my living room, and I held the lamp! You just sat there."

"That's right," Cain agrees. "I am her victim. Victims have rights."

We continue to bicker over which of us gets to write Mrs. Weinbaum into our work, while we make toast and coffee.

"How are you, really?" I ask as he spreads peanut butter on his toast.

"Fine. It hurts a bit if I frown, but otherwise I barely feel it at all."

Another knock on the door.

"What now?"

Cain sips his coffee. "Mrs. Weinbaum to fix that dripping tap?"

More knocking. Then Marigold's voice. "Freddie...Cain! It's me!"

I let her in.

"Hello. I thought that was Cain's Jeep outside...Christ on a bike!" Marigold catches sight of Cain.

I offer her a cup of coffee.

She sits down opposite Cain and scrutinises his face. "Fuck. What happened?"

"I got hit in the head with a bottle. One of Freddie's neighbours put in the stitches."

"Who hit you?"

"Someone I once knew. He was bearing a grudge."

"Did you call the police?"

"I haven't yet."

"Why?"

"Not really sure."

"It's probably best not to...with the FBI looking into you."

I hand Marigold a cup of coffee and a plate of toast. "What are you doing here?"

She looks me up and down and smiles. "Am I interrupting something?"

"I slept late," I murmur.

Marigold grins.

Cain stands. "I'd better get going." He takes his car keys from where I left them last night on the kitchen bench and smiles at me. "As long as you're satisfied that I'm not concussed, of course."

"You seem well enough, but then, I'm not a doctor."

"No, there's a bit of that going around."

I grin, and Marigold demands to know what we're talking about.

"You tell her." Cain rubs my arm. A warmth that might be more than friendly. Or perhaps he's still hoping I'll give him Mrs. Weinbaum. "I had better go."

"So?" Marigold asks once he's gone. "What's going on?"

I hesitate, unsure as to what I have permission to tell. I start with the slashed tyre and tell Marigold about Boo, his accusations, and what he did.

Marigold listens agape. "Jesus Hopping Christ! You got out of the car? Are you out of your mind?"

"Cain was on the ground. What else could I do?"

"You could have screamed! Why didn't you scream?"

"I don't know." I wonder about that for the first time. Why didn't I scream? "I don't scream," I say in the end. "I honestly don't remember ever screaming. It's just not something I do."

Marigold is interested in that. "Never?"

"That I can remember."

"I scream all the time...when I'm scared, or happy or frustrated."

I clear my throat and test my vocal cords. "I'm not sure I know how."

"I can give you lessons," Marigold assures me.

I laugh. "I'm not sure it's an education I require."

"What do you mean? Of course it is!" Marigold is aghast at my suggestion. "A scream is the most human and primal of things, a siren call which binds all those in hearing to help, as it did us to each other and to Caroline."

I stop laughing and smile at the poetry in Marigold's conviction. Her need to link us all by a greater power and cause, to somehow believe that our coming together was more than mere coincidence. I am the writer, but it is she who seeks theme and motif in life, and I am captivated by the earnestness with which she regards the world. "You're right. But perhaps we could conduct lessons somewhere more soundproof than here."

Marigold's smile is guileless and beautiful.

"So...you and Cain?"

"I couldn't let him drive home with a head injury, Marigold. I was worried that he might have been concussed. It seemed easier for him to stay here, to make sure."

She nods. "I'm glad you took him to a doctor at least."

"I didn't, exactly." I tell her about Mrs. Weinbaum and her ministrations and the gentlemen of Zackheim and Associates.

"Jesus H! I take my eyes off you two for a moment..." She becomes serious again. "You know, I did some research on Isaac Harmon."

"When?"

"Last night, online. You can find out quite a lot if you know how to look."

"Marigold, I think Cain would prefer if we—"

"Isaac Harmon was wanted for murder."

"I beg your pardon?"

"Isaac Harmon was wanted for the murder of a young woman in Virginia about twenty years ago. He disappeared before the police could apprehend him and remained on America's most wanted list until the body of a homeless man found on the banks of the Charles River was identified as him."

"You found this online?"

"Relatively easily."

"So Cain probably already knows this."

"He has to."

"Good."

"Why?"

"Then we don't need to tell him."

"But don't you think it odd he didn't tell us?"

I pour another cup of coffee. "He did tell us most of it. And being wanted for murder doesn't mean you're guilty."

Marigold is already following another thread. "Perhaps his man Boo killed Isaac Harmon. Oh, fuck! Maybe he's come back for Cain. Does he know where Cain lives?"

"Not as far as I know." I'm uneasy now. Cain was going to try to find Boo. I pick up my phone to call Cain, but I stop before I dial. What would I tell him that he doesn't know already? How could I call and suggest that Boo might have killed Isaac Harmon and was now after him? It would sound absurd. It was absurd.

I breathe and caution myself against being caught up in Marigold's enthusiasms. Nothing she says is untrue or impossible, but still, she has a way of igniting into action without pause, of taking the wheel of the bus and slamming the accelerator to the floor. I text Cain instead: Be careful.

The answer is almost immediate: Always.

And I decide that's enough.

I shower and change while Marigold cleans up my kitchen. She shouts conversation at me from the other room—general observations about current affairs, things she's read about Australia, the latest gaffes of the American president.

"Do you think it's too early to see if Whit wants to have lunch?" she says as I pull on my socks. "He's been recuperating at home for three days now."

"Would you like me to call him and ask?"

"Would you?"

We're still in different rooms, so I smile without fear of offending her. Marigold is no poker player. The relief and elation in her voice are obvious.

"I'd ring myself, but you know, I don't want Whit to think..."

"No, it would be terrible if Whit were to think."

Marigold looks at me hopefully, pleadingly.

"Shall we make it a spur-of-the-moment invitation?" I walk back into the kitchen, looking for my yellow scarf. It's on top of the refrigerator. "We could find somewhere and call from there."

"Do you think we should?"

"It might seem less orchestrated. And if he can't come, the two of us can still have lunch."

Marigold nods. "Okay."

"Have you tried calling him?" I ask.

"A few times. His mother answered the first time. She said he was rest-ing. After that I couldn't get through... The service was unavailable."

I say nothing. We both know it means her number was blocked. I hope it was by Whit's mother.

"Let's find somewhere close to Whit's place, so he can sneak out easily. What's his address?" I type it in and use an app to find restaurants nearby. "This place sounds good... It's called Oh My Cod! and it's only a few hun-dred yards from Whit's gate."

We decide to walk to the restaurant in preparation for an indulgent lunch, whether or not Whit joins us. On the way we discuss whether Oh My Cod! is a play on piety or pleasure. When we arrive, the decor speaks to the latter. The restaurant is fitted out like a luxurious bordello—each table sits between chaise lounges and is curtained into privacy with fringed velvet drapery. The candelabras feature entwined people with their backs arched in ecstasy, and the menu is titled "Selection de Aphrodisiac."

I get the giggles. Marigold too. Thank goodness for the chaises and the curtains, because in the end we are rolling round cackling like children. Perhaps this is not an unusual reaction, because the waiters allow us to get over the worst of it before peeking through the curtain to take our drink orders. We both request Virgin Ambrosias.

"Christ!" Marigold whispers when the curtain closes behind the leather-clad waiter. "We're asking Whit to have lunch with us in the sex shop!"

"Are you sure we should still..."

"Yes. We can't chicken out now."

I call Whit's number.

He answers. "Freddie! I was beginning to think you guys had forgotten about me."

I issue the invitation and tell him where we are.

He obviously knows the place, because he laughs loud and long.

"Stop it—you'll burst another stitch," I warn, concerned that he might indeed. "Can you come?"

He breaks up again and I flinch as I realise what I just said.

"I'll be about twenty minutes," he promises.

We drink our Virgins and amuse ourselves by reading out items from the menu. It's silly, but there is a relief in the juvenile nonsense of it. A comfort in childish things.

When Whit comes through the curtain, he regards us, amused. "I didn't have to ask for your table…I merely followed the screeching."

"Whit!" Marigold stands up. "How are you? We've been so worried about you."

"I could hear you worrying." Taking a seat beside Marigold, he summons a waiter and orders a Forbidden Apple without so much as looking at the drinks menu.

"You've been here before," I accuse.

"Of course I have. All the cool kids used to come here once. They have a great baked cod with pepper sauce…it's called a Multiple Orgasm. You should try it."

I shrug. "I'm a vegetarian."

Marigold finds that hysterical.

Somehow we manage to order from the ridiculous menu and sit eating surprisingly decent food within our velvet enclave. Whit complains about his mother, the lockdown she's instigated. "She's personally—no, *professionally*—offended by whoever stabbed me. You'd think she lost a case or something."

"She nearly lost a son," I remind him. "Cut her a bit of slack."

"Mom's in court today. She delegated my incarceration to my dad, who is rather more reasonable…and he might be a bit drunk."

Marigold raises her glass. "To your dad!"

"Where's Cain?" Whit clinks his glass against Marigold's. "Did he turn up his nose at this fine establishment?"

Marigold tells him about the previous evening's events as I had told them to her.

Whit is shocked, perhaps excessively so for someone who had himself been stabbed. "Get outta town! Who is this guy? Did you say his name was Boo?"

"Cain called him Boo," I say. "I assume it's a nickname of some sort."

"And he just walked up and hit Cain on the head with a bottle."

"Not initially. He came back. Cain tried to talk to him and Boo hit him."

"And then what did he do?"

"Boo or Cain? Boo ran away…"

"So now Cain's trying to find him? Man!" Whit shakes his head. "Is he trying to get himself killed?"

"That's not the half of it!" Marigold pipes in now with what she's discovered online about Isaac Harmon.

"He was a murderer?" Whit's brow rises. "And Cain knew this?"

"He was wanted for murder. It's not the same thing." The conversation makes me feel vaguely disloyal. "I doubt Cain knew when he first met him—how would he?"

"But he'd know now?"

"Unless his research skills aren't as good as Marigold's."

"They probably aren't." Marigold is reflective rather than arrogant. "But he would have found this."

"Maybe we should find Cain," Whit suggests. "It sounds like he could be in trouble."

"In trouble?"

"He's hanging out with junkies and—"

"Hold on a minute." I stop Whit before he gets too far ahead of himself. "Cain's not hanging out with them…and even if he was, he's not a child."

"But he clearly—" His eyes widen suddenly and he chokes.

Marigold pours him a glass of water. "Whit? What's wrong?"

He looks stricken. I stand ready to call for help.

Whit pats his chest and clears his throat. "I nearly said *Cain doesn't know what's good for him*. I have officially become my mom. I'd better have a drink." He summons a waiter and orders something called Carnal Knowledge with a wedge of lime.

"Aren't you even a little bit worried about Cain?" Marigold asks me as Whit treats the momentary possession by his mother with alcohol.

I am. I have been since he left to find Boo. Worried that he might find him still high or deranged or both. Worried that perhaps we should have taken the advice of Mrs. Weinbaum's lawyer more seriously. But short of calling the police, there isn't a lot any of us can do.

"Freddie?"

"No. I'm not worried."

———

Dear Hannah,

I love that Marigold checks out whose car is parked out front. I do that. So many people nowadays pretend they aren't in.

I dearly wish that Oh My Cod! was not a product of your imagination. I would dine there tonight! In fact, once this book becomes a bestseller, I wouldn't be surprised if someone opens a restaurant along those lines!

I haven't quite decided if Whit is a player or a complete nerd. He does have mommy issues, though to be fair his mother does seem to be some kind of dragon. And though he doesn't appear to be coming on to either Marigold or Freddie, there's a kind of sexual confidence about him that makes me wonder.

I've attached a map of downtown Boston and the surrounding areas, where I've marked alleys and places hidden from passing view in which one might kill someone without risk of witnesses. I thought since Cain is "at large" this might be a good time for another body to be found.

I have finally been able to bring myself to look at the opus again without heartbreak. And I can see places where I might have pulled my punches, and bits that could be cut. Should be cut. It may be time to sharpen my knife again.

Yours,
Leo

CHAPTER SEVENTEEN

Cain calls in the evening. He sounds tired. I don't know how I sound, but I am relieved.

"Where are you? Are you all right?"

"I'm fine… Mrs. Weinbaum's needlework held."

"You probably should have yourself checked anyway."

"I'll see her doctor when I have the stitches out."

"Have you eaten?" I glance at my watch. It's only half past seven. "Do you want to come over? I could cook something…I think…" I survey my pantry for anything which could become a meal.

"I'd love to, Freddie, but I've got a bit of work to do…and I'm beat. Rain check?"

"Sure." I'm both disappointed and mildly relieved that I don't have to make good on my offer to cook. "Are you sure you're okay?"

"Yes. Just frustrated. I couldn't find Boo. He's made himself scarce—probably thinks I'm looking for him to get even."

"Does he have anyone else he can go to for help?"

"Not that I know of."

"Cain…" I broach the subject hesitantly. "Marigold did some research on Isaac Harmon."

"Did she?" Immediately his voice is hard.

I'm unsure now if I should have brought this up. But it's too late. "She found out that Isaac Harmon was wanted for murder in Virginia."

Silence.

"Look, Cain, I know you probably already know. I just thought you should know that we do."

I can hear him exhale. "Yes, I knew. The police told me after he died."

"I absolutely understand that this is none of our business, Cain. But you know Marigold—she really wants to help. She doesn't mean any harm."

"Yes, I know." His voice is still tense. "What else did Nancy Drew find out?"

"Nothing really. She speculates that Boo might have killed Isaac and come back for you."

Cain laughs now. It sounds different from the one I've come to know. Cut bitter with regret. "Boo was Isaac's best friend. He would never have hurt him. And I went looking for him—not the other way round."

I don't argue. "Marigold wants to help, Cain. I guess after seeing you this morning—"

"I know." His voice relaxes. "I'm only surprised Marigold didn't conclude I'd crossed the mob."

"Well, she hasn't yet."

His laugh is more recognisable now. "I'm sorry I was snappy, Freddie. It must seem weird that I didn't mention that the hero of my story was wanted for murder."

I don't actually think it's weird at all. But I don't get a chance to say that before he continues.

"I never believed he was guilty, so it didn't seem like I was leaving out anything important."

"Cain, you don't owe any of us the details of your life or Isaac's."

"I know… I want you to understand that I'm not trying to mislead you."

"You haven't—"

"I left the past behind a while ago."

"Can you do that?"

"Apparently not. I was probably tempting fate writing about Isaac."

"The good news is we all have pasts."

Two days later the body of Shaun Jacobs, sometimes known as Boo, is found on the banks of the Charles River. His throat had been cut. I read about it in the *Boston Globe* on a Thursday morning. I call Cain's number with my eyes still glued to the article. He doesn't pick up, and I leave a message.

"Cain, I've just read the paper. Are you okay? Call me, please."

I read the article again, not sure quite what to do or to think. I'm horrified and strangely grieved for this man I encountered only fleetingly. And for some reason I can't explain, I'm in tears. The picture printed with the article is a mug shot, apparently taken a couple of years before when he was picked up for a misdemeanour of some sort. The man who stood by Cain's Jeep, shouting, accusing, stares out at me from the paper with that same wide-eyed confusion. And I wonder if that is how he died—in bewilderment with the world, confused by its violence and his own.

I try Cain again, and this time there are tears in my message. "Please call me, Cain. I really need to talk to you."

There's a knock at my door. I answer it hoping to see Cain—perhaps he thought to come to me before I even called.

It's Leo. "Freddie? Is this a bad time?"

I wipe my sleeve across my face. "No…not at all."

"You look upset. Does it have anything to do with the bleeding man you were with a couple of days ago?"

I step aside and sweep my arm into the apartment. "Come in. Would you like a cup of coffee?"

"Yes, ma'am."

I pour him a cup from the pot already made, and another for myself. I had been meaning to explain about that night, but somehow the last few days have slipped away. I've been working intensely on the manuscript and have seen no one but Marigold, who finds a reason to drop by each day.

Over coffee and the last of the fancy chocolates that came in the gourmet hamper, I tell him that Cain had been hit on the head with a bottle on the night Leo saw us at my door.

"Dang! Was it a bar fight? Why didn't you take him to the hospital?"

"No. It wasn't a bar fight. And Cain didn't want to go to the emergency room. Mrs. Weinbaum patched him up."

Leo smiles. "Did she tell you she was a doctor?"

"Yes."

"She isn't, you know."

"I do now. How did you…?"

"The first week I was here, I tried to pet a squirrel. It bit me. Mrs.

Weinbaum treated the wound and made sure it didn't give me rabies or plague or whatever it is that squirrels carry these days. The next morning I get a visit from her lawyers, who make a contribution towards my student loans."

"She did suture Cain's head very well," I offer.

"And I have neither rabies nor the plague." He helps himself from the plate of cookies I've placed between us. "So since your buddy Cain has not died of septic shock, why were you crying?"

"I'm just feeling a little homesick today." It's not a complete lie. With Thanksgiving coming up it makes me very aware that I am here and not at home. Not that Thanksgiving means anything in Australia, but the gathering of clans here does make me feel the absence of my own.

"Well, I'm sorry to hear that. Is there anything I can do?"

His concern makes me feel guilty that I am at least inflating my homesickness. "You're doing it. It's nice to have a neighbour to have coffee with."

He glances at the *Globe* I've left on the bench. "Did you read about that poor guy they found by the river? I jog past there every morning. I wondered what was going on."

"You saw him?"

"No, ma'am. I would have had no cause to wonder if I'd actually seen a body. I only saw police, crime scene tape, reporters—I assumed it was more than a cat up a tree, but I didn't know for sure until I read the paper."

"Have you ever seen him on another morning?" I push the *Globe* towards him.

Leo looks closely at the mug shot. "I can't imagine there are many places to sleep on the riverbank in winter—mostly I see other joggers or people walking their dogs. He doesn't look familiar." He looks at me sharply. "Do you know him?"

"No," I reply perhaps a half beat too quickly.

"Of course you wouldn't. Sorry—stupid question."

I laugh. "I pretty much asked it first."

"I'm going to drive up to Rockport this weekend. I don't suppose you'd like to come?"

"Rockport?"

"It's about an hour's drive," he says apologetically.

"That's not really an issue for an Australian," I assure him. "Everything at home seems to be at least an hour away. But why are you going?"

"Research. I'm setting a scene outside its famous fish shack—thought I should check it out myself so I get the details right. Authenticity and all that." Leo picks through the chocolates. "I've organised a car for the purpose. I thought I'd ask all the other residential fellows if they'd like to come, do a bit of sightseeing...so I can add collegiate collaboration to my acquittal report."

I laugh. Leo is ever strategic. "I thought you and I were the only fellows here."

"No, there are two others. From Europe and Africa."

I'm embarrassed that I don't know that, that I've been here for two months and not come across my counterparts. "Sure, I'll come. A road trip to see a fish shack in the winter is too absurd to turn down."

Leo nods. "It's a date, then."

"Leo, where exactly did you come across the crime scene?"

"What—oh, you mean this?" He picks up the paper. "Why do you ask?"

"Because I walk along the river all the time. I feel like I shouldn't walk past somewhere where a man died without knowing or thinking about it."

Leo pulls up a map on his phone and points to a place on the bank in Cambridge. "I expect it will be cordoned off for a while, so I don't think you'll be able to walk past it without knowing for the next few days, at least." He squints at me thoughtfully. "I could show you."

"Now?"

"Sure. If you'd like to stretch your legs. It's a couple of miles from here."

For some reason I say yes. I'm not sure why. Perhaps it's a need to orient myself in what is occurring, to slap myself with the reality of it, and accept that it is really happening. Caroline, then Whit, and now this. Could it be that they are unconnected—random acts which have nothing to do with each other or me? I want them to be that, an accidental confluence in a dangerous city, because the alternative is terrifying.

I set out with Leo, who, though he has been in Boston only as long as I, has learned the city by jogging it. We cross the river at Harvard Bridge and walk through the parklands of Magazine Beach. Even now, closer to the middle of the day, there are joggers and people using the outdoor gym. The park is beautiful, though the best of the fall has long passed. Defoliated trees are a quiet, stark backdrop to the focussed activity of exercise. Near the boathouse, police officers move on the curious from a section of the beach which has been sectioned off with police tape. A young woman with a camera waves at Leo and beckons him over. I hang back, taking in the area as he runs over to talk to her. They chat for a minute or two, and then she returns to taking photographs, and he to me.

"Lauren's with the *Rag*," he says by way of explanation. "This is her current assignment apparently."

"Caroline Palfrey worked for the *Rag*," I say, distracted momentarily by the fact.

"When I was here this morning there was a kind of a tent over there… over the body, maybe." Leo points. "I expect he was either trying to sleep in the boathouse or his body was washed up on the beach here after being dumped upstream." He turns to look at me. "Are you sure you didn't know him, Freddie?"

"I ran into him once," I admit.

"Ran into?"

"I was with someone who knew him, who talked to him."

Leo studies me. "You don't mean the night I saw you with Cain. God, Freddie, was it the dead guy that hit Cain with a bottle?"

"Yes."

"Why?"

"I don't know—I think he was high."

"Have you told the police?"

"No—Cain didn't want to have him arrested,"

"I don't mean then…I mean now. The man was murdered, Freddie. They're probably trying to retrace his last hours."

I know he's right. I should call the police and tell them. "I'm just waiting until I can get hold of Cain so that we can go in together. He'll be able to tell them more than I will."

"You can't get hold of Cain?" Leo frowns.

"He didn't pick up when I called this morning, that's all," I reply firmly. "He probably turned his phone off so he could get some work done."

Leo shrugs. "Or he's already talking to the police."

"In which case, I suppose the police will get in touch with me."

Leo pauses. "Fair enough." He motions me towards a pretzel cart. "Let's get some supplies for the walk home." We purchase warm pretzels drizzled with mustard, which we eat on the way back to Carrington Square.

"If you do decide you want to go into the police station," he says almost shyly as he drops me outside my door, "I'd be happy to come with you…for moral support or as a character witness…or whatever you need."

I dust the pretzel crumbs off my lapel. "Thank you, Leo. I'm sure it will be fine, though. I'll find out what Cain's doing or what he's done and then do my bit. I'm sure Boo talked to dozens of people in the couple of days before he died."

———

Dear Hannah,

I sense my Marigold is in danger. Killing her would certainly enhance the sense of tragedy and tension, but it does run the risk of feeding into the cliché that the quirky best friend is there to be killed off. If you are going to take her (and I will mourn that), make sure you don't waste the opportunity to tear the reader apart with the horror of it. Marigold should not go quietly. For example, Cain might violate her sexually. It'll be a poignant contrast to the gallant manner in which he is dealing with Freddie. Marigold's death scene should be brutal and extended, she should fight, and do her own damage before she goes. Cain should not be able to snuff out her life unscathed, as he did Caroline's.

But what am I writing?—I forget the master to whom I speak. You will write a death scene that is worthy of her, I know.

I went down to Magazine Beach to take some photos for you, in case you want to describe the crime scene in more detail. Coincidentally, there was a man passed out on the bank. I took a picture of that too in case it helps you visualize the scene. Of course this man wasn't dead, merely sleeping off whatever he'd been taking. He might have died of hypothermia since, of course.

Must say I love the way you are underplaying Cain's fury. There's a visceral restraint about the man that is so exciting!

Yours,
Leo

CHAPTER EIGHTEEN

Marigold and Whit arrive about half an hour before the police.

Marigold's eyes are bright and excited. She has the paper. "This is your Boo, isn't it?" She points to the article. "This is the guy who attacked Cain."

I nod.

Whit puts his arm around me. "You okay? It must be a bit unsettling."

"It is."

"What does Cain say about it?"

"I haven't been able to reach him."

"What do you mean?" Marigold's brow furrows. "Didn't you say he was looking for this dead guy? You don't think…maybe we should try to find him?"

I stay outwardly calm. "I think we should at least give Cain a chance to answer his phone before we panic."

"How long's it been?" Whit asks.

"A couple of hours since I left my last message."

"Do you know where Cain lives?"

"In Roxbury somewhere. I'm not sure exactly."

The internal phone from the doorman's desk buzzes. I pick it up, and Joe informs me that two detectives are asking for me.

"I'll come down." I shudder to imagine what the other residents of the Carrington will think about a police visit. I expect they're here to verify

Cain's story about the other night, and I'm relieved that he's not missing, though a little hurt that he didn't call me before he went in.

I tell Whit and Marigold to make themselves comfortable. "I should be only a couple of minutes."

Whit already has his head in my refrigerator. "Ask them what they did with Cain."

"Are you sure you don't want me to come down with you?" Marigold follows me to the door.

"I don't think you're allowed to bring friends to a police interview."

"What about Whit—he's Harvard Law."

Whit sticks his head up over my refrigerator door to indicate he's willing.

"It's a few routine questions, Marigold. If I start bringing lawyers—or law students—I'll look suspicious or at least ridiculous."

Marigold pulls a face. "Fine, but if you're not back in fifteen, we're coming down."

The detectives are standing by Joe's desk when I arrive in the foyer. They begin by flashing their badges, introducing themselves as Detectives David Walker and Justine Dwyer. Walker is about fifty, buzz-cut grey hair, tall, broad, and bearded. Even in plainclothes he looks like he's wearing a uniform. His partner is a brunette, and there's an edge of style to the practicality of her pantsuit and low-heeled shoes. She smiles when she says hello, and I can feel the knot in the pit of my stomach loosen a little.

They are, as I suspected, here to ask me about the night Cain and I encountered Shaun Jacobs. I confirm locations and times, that I saw Boo attack Cain, and that Cain did not retaliate. I worry that they'll ask who treated Cain's wound, which will mean trouble for Mrs. Weinbaum, but they do not. They ask how long I've known Cain and the nature of our relationship.

"I met Cain about a month ago at the library. We're friends."

"And you were with Mr. McLeod until what time, Ms. Kincaid?"

"He left at about half past ten the next morning." I glance at Walker and read what he thinks in his face. "I didn't want Cain to drive while there was a chance he might be concussed, so he stayed here the night. I slept on the couch."

Detective Dwyer nods. "A sensible precaution."

"Mr. McLeod is a lucky man to have such thoughtful friends," Walker says tersely.

"Isn't he?" I'm annoyed.

Walker's smile is not quite hidden by his facial hair. "I mean, there are not many folks who'd be comfortable having a man like Cain McLeod spending the night, whether or not he was concussed."

I assume he's trying to goad me, so I don't give him the satisfaction of a response.

Walker continues. "I mean, you've only known him a month, and the man did serve seven years."

"Serve?" I'm confused now.

Dwyer glances sideways at her partner. I know they are noting my reaction. "Cain McLeod served seven years for murder."

I feel cold inside, and hot and flushed at the same time. "Are you sure?" It's a ridiculous question to ask of the police, and I'm not even sure I'm asking anything. It's more an expression of shock and disbelief. And then I remember that Cain changed his name. Perhaps this is some kind of misunderstanding. "You know Cain McLeod is not his real name—"

"Yes, we do. Abel Manners changed his name to Cain McLeod when he was released."

"You didn't know?" Detective Dwyer sounds almost sympathetic.

I pull myself together. "It didn't come up."

"Uh huh." Walker is sceptical. "So is there anything you wish to change about your statement with respect to the evening of 18 November?"

Somewhere in the distance, behind the feeling that I'm reeling, comes a realisation that they think I'm lying to protect Cain. About what, I'm not sure. "No. That's what happened."

Dwyer hands me her card. "I know this is a lot to take in. We'll be in touch, but in the meantime, if you remember anything at all, just call."

I stand in the foyer for a few minutes after they leave. Joe asks me if I'm all right, and his voice shakes me back.

"Yes, thank you, Joe. They just needed to ask me a few questions."

"About what happened to your friend the other night?"

"Yes." I remember then that he saw Cain and me come in.

"Have they arrested someone?"

"Not yet." I force a smile. "Did they ask you about that night?"

"Yes, ma'am. I told them you and your friend came in at about eleven. That he was bleeding and you were taking care of him." Joe lowers his voice. "I mentioned Mrs. Weinbaum may have called on you, but I didn't say why."

Whit and Marigold are lingering in the stairwell just above the foyer. They walk with me back to the apartment.

"So what happened?" Marigold demands when I close the door.

"Didn't you hear?"

"Nope. Couldn't hear a thing," Whit says unashamedly.

I falter. I don't want to keep anything from them, but telling them what the detectives revealed feels like talking behind Cain's back...I want to speak to him first. "They're corroborating Cain's account of what happened, that's all."

Marigold frowns. "Are you sure? You look like you've seen a ghost."

I shake my head. "It's just a bit weird talking to the police... I need a cup of tea."

"You sound like you could use something stronger," Whit says.

"It's not even midday."

He sighs. "I'm very disappointed in you, Freddie."

Marigold continues to look at me. She knows there's something I'm not saying. "What's going on, Freddie?"

I pick up my phone. "I'm going to try Cain."

They both watch as I dial. Again there's no answer and I leave a message. "Cain, the police have just been here. Please call me."

"Where do you think he is?" Marigold asks.

"He might still be with the police."

"Freddie, what did the police say that's got you so shook up?"

Whit answers for me. "They told her that Cain's been in prison. That he's a murderer."

Both Marigold and I turn to Whit aghast.

"What?" Marigold speaks first. "That's not funny, Whit."

"You knew?" I gasp. "How?"

"One of the FBI guys told me after I was stabbed... They have some crazy theory that Cain killed Caroline and then came after me."

"We were all together, sitting across from one another when Caroline screamed."

"Which is why I told them they were on a bad trip."

"You didn't say anything..."

"You weren't going to, either." Whit shrugs. "Anyway, he's served his time."

I sit down. "What exactly did the FBI tell you, Whit?"

Whit falls onto the couch beside me. "Cain was convicted of murder in the first degree. He served nearly eight years. Got out about seven years ago, changed his name, and wrote a novel."

"And you didn't think this was something Freddie and I needed to know?" Marigold has recovered enough from the shock of the news to shout at Whit.

I interrupt. "If he got out seven years ago, and he served nearly eight, he must have been very young when this happened."

"Unless he lied to us about his age, along with everything else." Marigold folds her arms.

"We don't know that he's ever lied to us," I protest.

"He didn't tell us anything about prison!"

"That's not the same thing as lying. None of us has told each other everything."

Marigold studies me. "It's a big thing to leave out, Freddie."

"It's also a big thing to confide."

"Freddie's right," Whit says. "If Cain's thirty, he must have gone away when he was sixteen."

"Can you even go to prison when you're sixteen?" Marigold asks.

"For murder you can."

"So Cain killed someone when he was around sixteen," I say almost to myself. It sounds ludicrous. Of all of us, Cain always seemed the most sane—the least felonious.

"I wonder if that was why he ran away?" Whit says.

"Poor Cain." Marigold is back to her dogged loyalty. "Did the police say where he was, Freddie? Have they arrested him?"

"No, they didn't say, but they must have talked to him."

"So what do we do?" Marigold asks.

I shake my head. I feel loss and lost, a hole in the place of what I believed, what I should believe.

Marigold checks her phone for the time. "I'd better get Whit back before his mom realizes he's gone."

I turn to Whit. "Still?"

"Yes." He makes his disgust plain as he stands up to go. "Luckily, she goes to work for a few hours every day, and Dad covers for me."

"How are you, anyway?" I forced my thoughts away from Cain.

Whit pulls up his sweater and T-shirt to show me the scar. "They took the last stitches out this morning. I can go back to the gym next week."

"Is it sore?"

"No. Not anymore."

"Well, that's good news at least."

He hugs me. "Don't worry about Cain. There'll be an explanation."

"For going to jail?"

He pulls on his jacket. "You never know, Freddie. Our Cain could be the mythical innocent man."

___

My dear Hannah,

What a beautiful reveal! It becomes clear now why Cain seems not to be disturbed by the fact that Isaac Harmon was wanted for murder. You've upped the ante magnificently!

Talking of which, I came across another crime scene yesterday. I don't know if it was the mask and anonymity it affords, but I was feeling bold, and so I grabbed some pictures of the body for you. I must have got there only moments after the police—they hadn't even got the crime scene tape up. Anyway, the victim seems to have been partially disemboweled. All that dark area is blood. I imagine it took him a few minutes to die, and judging by the smearing in the blood, he struggled. I know you don't generally write such graphic scenes, but this novel might call for a little extra realism...and this could be your inspiration.

I'll keep my eye out for more.

Waiting anxiously for your next installment.

Yours,

Leo

___

Dear Miss Tigone,

Thank you for contacting the authorities with your concerns regarding the man you know as Leo Johnson with whom you have been corresponding, and who has been progressively commenting and advising on the manuscript of your novel.

The images you attached, which you say Leo Johnson sent you yesterday, do indeed evidence an unusual and alarming access to a real and recent victim, whose body, according to our forensic experts, seems to have been reported to police only after these images were taken. The older images you sent of other crime scenes also relate to recent unsolved murders. The matter has been referred to the Federal Bureau of Investigation as possibly pertaining to a number of cases currently under investigation.

We have dispatched our agents in Sydney who, with our colleagues in the Australian Federal Police, will make contact directly, if they have not done so already. Please do not have any further communication with Leo Johnson until you have been briefed.

Sincerely,
Special Agent Michael Smith
Federal Bureau of Investigation

ABERCROMBIE, KENT
AND ASSOCIATES

Dear Sir/Madame,

We represent Ms. Hannah Tigone, who contacted you about correspondence from a party she knows as Mr. Leo Johnson.

Whereas the FBI has requested Ms. Tigone's assistance in the apprehension of Leo Johnson, whom you believe to be responsible for a number of homicides in and around Boston, Massachusetts, and perhaps further afield, but about whom you have little or no information, and with a view to the urgency of establishing the parameters of Ms. Tigone's cooperation, to enable you to identify and locate Leo Johnson, we confirm the following agreements and arrangements arising out of the meeting between your agents and our client.

Ms. Tigone will continue to correspond with Leo Johnson, with the aim of establishing his identity and location without revealing that he is under suspicion for any criminal act. She will attempt to obtain from Leo Johnson an image of himself as well as a physical address.

To this end Ms. Tigone will continue to send Leo Johnson chapters of her manuscript so as not to arouse his suspicions.

Ms. Tigone will give your agents immediate access to any and all such correspondence.

Ms. Tigone will make you immediately aware of any impressions she may have gained through her contact with Leo Johnson as to his location, true identity, or any future criminal acts or intentions.

You will indemnify Ms. Tigone and ensure that she is held harmless against any action, criminal or civil, which arises out of her continued correspondence with Leo Johnson regardless of whether that action is initiated in Australia or the United States.

You will use your best endeavours to ensure Ms. Tigone's physical safety and also the commercial confidentiality of her manuscript.

Yours faithfully,
Peter Kent
Abercrombie, Kent and Associates

Chapter Nineteen

The decision to return to the library early the next morning is made in desperation and frustration. I need to work. Cain is still not picking up and, in the apartment, I'm tempted to try again repeatedly, to think about him and nothing else.

When things get stuck, change the scene.

And so I go back to where it all began, reset to a time before I met Whit and Marigold and Cain, before we heard a young woman die. I cast my eyes upwards and anchor myself in the magnificent vaulted ceiling of the Reading Room, determined to make that my memory of this place.

But Heroic Chin, Freud Girl, and Handsome Man look out at me from my own manuscript. Most of all Handsome Man. The bus is crowded now, so much so that I can't see who's driving it. Handsome Man sits in the back, behind Shaun Jacobs. Perhaps he is, as Whit says, innocent. Wrongly accused, wrongly convicted. God, I hope so. I remember what it was like to kiss him and, when I think about it, I believe completely that he is innocent. And in my manuscript he can be. Perhaps it's time for my Handsome Man to diverge from his inspiration.

And yet I'm not ready to leave Cain behind, to remove him from my manuscript or my story.

I step out at midday because I'm vexed and hungry. I don't feel like going to the Map Room on my own, and so I head out in search of a pretzel vendor. The cold hits me like a wall the moment I leave the building. The temperature has plummeted in the time I've been inside. The clouds are a vague green colour.

"It's going to snow."

I turn sharply. Cain.

"Hello, Freddie."

My voice comes on the second attempt. "How did you know where I was?"

"I went by your place first, and since then I've been looking for you. This was my third guess."

"You've just got here?"

"No, I saw that you were in the Reading Room. I was waiting for you to come out."

"Why? Why didn't you simply come in?"

"I thought we should talk... We can't really do that in the Reading Room."

I say nothing.

"Freddie...you're not afraid of me, are you?"

I'm not sure what to say, or how I feel.

"Should I be?"

The first flakes of snow fall, large and soft and wet. I begin to shiver.

He raises his hand and then pulls back without touching me. I am relieved and disappointed.

"How about we go and have lunch...somewhere warm...and public? And I can explain."

I nod. "Somewhere close; I'm freezing."

We find a diner in Copley Place and take a booth. We order hot chocolate and pancakes like any other couple. And we eat and drink and talk about the snow. I am aware that despite everything, I am happy to be with him.

"I've been calling you," I say.

"They police took my phone again, Freddie. They let me go at midnight."

"They arrested you?"

"No. They just held me for questioning."

"Why?"

"I found Boo's body."

"And you have a history." I take a deep breath. We can't avoid talking about this.

"A record—they call it a record." He stops and looks as me silently as if he's trying to see something in my face. "Freddie, when I was fifteen, I killed my stepfather."

I notice a head turn in the neighbouring booth.

He waits until I'm ready.

"Why?" I ask eventually.

His eyes flicker. "It was self-defence, Freddie. They didn't believe me, but it was."

"Was this why you ran away?"

"No. This was after I came back."

"Why didn't they believe you?"

"My stepfather was a policeman. I was a delinquent kid."

Two heads now, and a whisper between them.

I stand.

Cain looks down and exhales. "I understand—"

I lean across to him and whisper. "Let's go back to my place. We can talk without being overheard."

He looks surprised. "Are you sure?"

"Don't ask me that, Cain. Just come."

Joe opens the door of the Carrington foyer and welcomes us in. "I wondered if you'd get caught in this storm when you went out, Miss Kincaid. I'm glad Mr. McLeod found you."

Joe hands me a cake box which was reportedly delivered a few minutes before. It's full of beautifully decorated cupcakes. But again there's no card or any indication who might have sent it. Joe volunteers to contact the bakery with which the box is branded, to check, assuring me that couriers are always losing the card. I leave two cupcakes for him to have with his coffee, and Cain and I take the rest of the box up. On another day I would have wondered more about my mysterious benefactor, but today they're only cakes.

I shut the door to the apartment and listen to the lock click into place. So now I'm alone with a murderer. But then, it's not the first time.

Cain puts the box down on the coffee table. I curl up on the couch. "Okay, let's do this."

He sits on the other end of the couch. "What do you want to know, Freddie? I'll tell you anything."

I choose my words carefully. "Why did you kill your stepfather, Cain? I know you say you were defending yourself, but I'm not sure I understand how a boy of fifteen finds himself in a place where his only option is to kill a man."

Cain frowns. "It didn't begin that night. In a way, it was years in the making. My stepfather had, as I told you, always wanted a large family. When he realised that wasn't going to happen—that I was it—things changed. He became mean, brutal. By the time I was fourteen, I'd become the proverbial 'clumsy kid' who was always walking into doors and falling down stairs." He swallows. "I still loved him for the longest time. I tried, I really did. And then one day I couldn't take any more, and I hit back. It was the world's luckiest punch...or maybe the unluckiest, because it landed, and then..." He shakes his head. "I panicked. That's when I ran."

"I don't understand. You didn't kill him?" I move closer to Cain.

"Not then. Isaac convinced me to go back eventually." Cain smiles faintly. "Said he couldn't nursemaid me forever, and I'd never survive without him. And so I went home."

"And your stepfather..."

"Said he was glad I was back. That all was forgiven and that we would make a new start as a family." He shakes his head. "God, I wanted to believe it."

"What happened?"

Cain's face clouds, and for the first time I can see that however much he doesn't want to scare me, he's not calm. That this isn't without pain. I reach out and take his hand and hold it tightly.

Cain looks at my hand in his, focuses on it as he continues. "He misses dinner one night and calls to say he's at a bar. But he's coming home because he and I need to have a man-to-man. And I know...and I should have run again but...my mom... Anyway, I stayed."

He doesn't take his eyes off my hand.

"He gets back, liquored up and angry. And immediately he drags me off to my bedroom. I should have known then. He would normally have belted me right where I stood. He's screaming about me running away, what a disgrace I am, how the whole force knows his son had been selling his ass all over Boston." Cain tries to laugh, but he doesn't quite. "It had never occurred to me that he thought that was how I'd survived. I'm too surprised to deny it...though I don't know if it would have helped at that stage. He starts slapping me around. I'm expecting that."

Cain's hand is cold in mine. I hold on tighter trying to warm it somehow.

"He knocks me onto my bed facedown and pins me with my left arm twisted behind my back. I hear him slide his belt out of the loops, and I think he's going to use it to hit me. He's done that before—I could have endured that. It's not until he starts fumbling with my jeans that I realise what he actually intends to do."

A strange, strangled sound leaves my throat. I feel sick.

He looks up at me now, and it's only when he wipes the tears from my cheek that I know that I'm crying. "I fight, but he's got at least a hundred pounds on me." Cain stops to breathe. "Isaac taught me to sleep with a knife under whatever I was using as a pillow. He called it a 'teddy bear'—said it was the only thing that would keep away anything that went bump in the night. I didn't stop sleeping with a teddy bear when I got home. I feel my stepfather's grip loosen as he tries to pull down my jeans, and I remember the knife. I can reach it with my free hand. I twist and swing." Cain shifts slightly, flinching unconsciously as it replays. "He pulls back…makes a kind of gurgling sound. And I don't know where the knife has gone. And then he falls, and I see that the knife is in his neck and there's blood everywhere."

"He's dead?"

Cain nods. "And then the police arrive."

"How could anyone think it was not self-defence?"

"Because I'd hidden a knife under my pillow. And he was a decorated cop." The darkness has lifted a little from Cain's face. His hand feels warm again. "I was sixteen by the time it all got to trial. I was convicted—served two years in a juvenile facility and was transferred to adult prison on my eighteenth birthday."

I must be gazing at him in horror…I feel completely in horror.

"I served another five years before I was paroled. In that time, I finished school and studied literature through UNC. When I got out, I worked whatever job I could get and wrote a novel." He holds my gaze as well as my hand. "Freddie, I didn't mean to deceive you, any of you, but this is not the kind of thing you tell people if you can avoid it."

"Would you ever have told us?"

Cain considers it. "I don't know. Maybe eventually. I'm not sure I regret what I did, but I am ashamed of it. I don't expect people to understand. Whit's biggest problem is how to actually avoid graduating from Harvard Law, and Marigold thinks expensive tattoos make her street."

"And me."

"You?" His smiles ruefully. "You, I might be trying to impress."

"How did you find Mr. Jacobs?"

"I asked around his old haunts. One of the old men he drank with told me that Boo sometimes sleeps in the boathouse on Magazine Beach. I went over there looking for him." Cain exhales. "I get there and find him facedown on the bank. I assume he's just passed out until I turn him over and see that his throat has been cut."

"Bloody hell!"

"He didn't deserve that, Freddie. He was a junkie and a drunk but…" He stops and shrugs. "I called the police."

"And they kept you for questioning?"

"Yes. Given my record, it follows."

"But they let you go, so they realise you had nothing to do with it."

"They didn't have enough to arrest me, and there's a limit to how long you can question people without actually arresting them, so yes, they let me go."

My phone rings. I can see it's Marigold. I decline the call, but I send her a text to say I am writing and will call when I take a break. "In case she decides to come over here to see why I'm not answering my phone."

Cain smiles. "No *in case* about it." He closes his eyes and opens them again. I can see the shadows beneath them. "I suppose the police told Whit and Marigold too," he says, yawning.

"Whit's known for a while." I slide off the couch and fetch one of the blankets folded neatly on the bentwood chair by the heater.

"He didn't say anything."

"No, he's inclined to believe you've paid your debt."

"I like Whit."

I laugh and pull the blanket over him.

"What are you doing?" he murmurs.

"You're exhausted. Close your eyes for a while."

"Don't you need your couch?"

"Not for a couple of hours. Sleep. We can decide what to do later."

⌒⌒⌒

Dear Hannah,

I can't tell you how happy I was to hear from you again. I know it was only a couple of weeks, but I'd begun to fear I'd offended you somehow. I hope you know I wouldn't do that for the world. I so value our friendship, our shared vision and craft—I was bereft with the idea that I would not hear from you again, and frantic with the thought that I had inadvertently insulted or upset you. If not for global lockdown, I might have flown to Sydney to make amends for any transgression.

I did fear that perhaps I had become too strident in my interest in the lives of your characters, too enthusiastic in my suggestions. But you assure me that your absence was simply the result of a computer crash. So I am relieved that we are still as we were and that you managed to retrieve your precious manuscript from the abyss of cyberspace. It surprises me that you don't back up to the cloud, but you wouldn't be the first to distrust it. But perhaps now that you have come so close to losing your novel entirely you might consider an online depository of some sort.

Now, Chapter 19! I think Americans are more likely to say police officer than policeman. It's just a small thing.

I do like that you are not painting Cain McLeod as a simple monster. Of course they do exist, but understandable damage is much more interesting as a motive for murder. As Marigold said earlier, even the monsters have a reason. Anyway, making him sympathetic will make his actions all the more shocking.

There was a march through Boston yesterday. I thought about joining it just to get out. The most trying thing about the pandemic is that it's boring. If not for your chapters, I would have little to look forward to.

Already watching my inbox for your next.

Yours,

Leo

CHAPTER TWENTY

Cain sleeps for most of the afternoon. On his stomach, one hand under the cushion he uses as a pillow, as if even now he's reaching for a knife. I sit in the armchair opposite, pretending to read and watching. My vigilance is not based on fear of him, but for him. The horror of what happened is difficult to take in, and I wonder how he could be so calm, so reasonable, so *not* bitter. If it had been me, I would never have stopped screaming. And yet he sleeps so soundly.

I wonder if he's forgotten that he kissed me and that I kissed him.

I hate myself for thinking about that moment after everything that's happened since. It seems selfish.

A text from Marigold: Are you still writing?

I message back. Give me another couple of hours.

I open my laptop in a vague attempt to not be a complete liar. The words take me by surprise. I don't expect to do any more than stare at the text I've written, a story faded and made trivial by unfolding reality, but suddenly my Handsome Man speaks to me of secrets, of pain and injustice. The scream that connects him to Freud Girl and Heroic Chin echoes the silent one in his head. I understand his need to link every thread into a web of story, his distrust of letting things unfold. He understands, probably better than I, that a story can turn on you.

When I look up again, Cain's eyes are open, watching me.

I smile. "Hello. Do you feel any better?"

He nods slowly. "What time is it?"

I glance back at the laptop screen. "About five."

He sits up. "I'm so sorry, Freddie. I only meant to close my eyes for a few minutes."

I move because he seems too far away. Because I want to be closer. And as I sit beside him he turns and kisses me. I'm surprised and then consumed by it. And exhilarated. I respond so completely, so intensely that I am shaking. And then he pulls away, his breath ragged, and I hear myself gasp in protest.

He stares at me. "Are you sure?"

I pull him back towards me. I'm not sure about anything except that certainty is overrated.

But Cain is afraid I will be caught in the web around him.

I reach out and touch his face, trying to think of some way to reassure him that I am choosing this with full knowledge of what he did. In the end, I just kiss him honestly, and I trust the act to say all those things for which words are tricky and inadequate. The moment extends into forever, deepening with the quickening of our pulses. He fumbles with the tiny buttons on my shirt and manages in frustration to tear off a couple.

"You'd better be handy with a needle and thread," I warn as a spinning button rattles to rest on the floorboards.

"For you, I'll learn," he murmurs into my neck.

I unbutton Cain's shirt with less haste and slightly more care for the fastenings. My fingers linger on a scar above his hip. "How did you get this?"

He seems amused that I would ask this now. "That's an appendicitis scar."

"And this one." I can feel a raised scar on his lower back.

"Are you trying to change the subject?" He kisses me before I can deny it. I stop asking questions. And we lose ourselves to feeling—skin and warmth, breath and heartbeat. Discovery and pleasure and all the searing urgency of new love.

And afterwards I lead him to my bed and we make love there as well, taking our time, coming to know each other's bodies. I am kissing the scar on his back when I ask about it again. "This is not the appendicitis scar, is it?"

"Freddie, I really can't answer questions while you're doing that," he says, pulling me round and against his chest.

"You don't like my interrogation methods?"

"Oh, I like them… They are, however, somewhat counterproductive." He kisses the undersides of my breasts. "It would be like asking you why you were so interested in that scar while doing this."

I wait until he's finished. "Point taken. It's in the exact same place Whit's scar is."

"Is it?" He stops what he's doing. "I was stabbed when I was in prison… with a knife fashioned out of a part of a bed frame."

"One of the other inmates tried to kill you?"

"Not on that occasion." He pulls me closer into his arms. "It was a punishment…a fairly minor one. They stabbed me in a safe place."

"Is there such a thing?"

"If the man doing the stabbing was once a surgeon, there is. No organ damage or permanent injury, and they called the guards and had me taken to the infirmary when they were done."

"Why were you being punished?"

"You know, I'm not entirely sure. Sometimes the smartest thing to do is accept and keep your eyes down."

"They could have killed you!"

"No, they knew what they were doing. As I said, the guy who used the knife was a surgeon—if you didn't move, you'd live. If you struggled—"

"Oh, God."

He kisses the top of my head. "Before you start imagining the worst, the correctional facility in which I served adult time was on the whole quite progressive. It wasn't summer camp, but neither was it Alcatraz."

"But they stabbed you when you stepped out of line?"

He laughs. Pressed against his chest, I can feel it more than hear it. "It was not an official reprimand, Freddie."

"But it happened."

"Even progressive prisons have their own societal rules, their own hierarchy. And men in prison are not necessarily fair or reasonable."

"So nothing happened to them…there was no action?"

"The official version was that I slipped and injured myself in the kitchens."

"But you knew who stabbed you?"

"Yes, but I didn't remember."

"But—"

His lips are on mine. It is a gentle but effective way of cutting short my outrage. "I appreciate that you care, Freddie." He laces his fingers with mine. "It means a lot that you do. But it was a long time ago now. I made the best decision I knew how...and in the end I got by."

I settle against his shoulder, content to enjoy the moment, the feeling of him, for now. Cain tells me about the germination of his first novel while he was still in prison. The idea that lingered with no reason for existing until he found that very few people wanted to employ an ex-con. The book he wrote while he was trying to work out how to be in the free world. I may have remained there in his arms forever, or at least until we got hungry, if someone hadn't pounded on the door.

Even before she calls my name, I know it's Marigold.

I groan. "I told her I'd call. You distracted me."

Cain grins. "I'm glad."

By the time Cain and I have scrabbled into our clothes and answered the door, a few of my neighbours have responded to Marigold's pounding by peeking out to see what's going on. Marigold embraces me the moment I open the door.

"When you didn't call and stopped responding I thought something might have happened—"

"I'm fine, Marigold. I'm sorry... I turned off my phone."

"Why?" She tenses when she sees him. "Cain!"

"Hello, Marigold." Cain greets her from the living room, where he has very recently found and pulled on his clothes.

"You didn't mention Cain was here," she says accusingly.

"I haven't had a chance..."

"You said you were writing."

I hesitate, unsure what to say. "I wasn't."

Cain resolves it all by taking my hand. "That was my fault."

Marigold gapes at us. "Really?"

To be honest, I feel a bit ridiculous. We're all adults, for God's sake, but Marigold has raced over here to check on me out of genuine if misplaced concern. "How did you get here? Tell me you didn't walk?"

"Of course not. We have these things called Ubers." Marigold hasn't taken her eyes from Cain. "I take it the police had their wires crossed...I knew it!"

I glance at Cain.

Cain sighs. "If they are alleging I've killed anyone recently, then yes, they have their wires crossed."

"Recently?"

I announce that I'm going to make coffee.

Cain and Marigold sit in my kitchen, and he tells her more or less what he told me. Marigold is quiet for a while. "You didn't intend to kill him," she says. "Your stepfather?"

Cain pauses before he replies. "No, but I didn't intend not to. I just wanted to get him off me."

She throws her arms around him. "I'm so sorry, Cain."

Cain barely manages to save his coffee from being sent flying.

"Who the fuck were your lawyers?" she demands without letting go. "What kind of dumbass lawyers would let you go to jail for that?"

"I had a few lawyers. I barely saw any of them, to be honest." I notice a shadow cross his face. "My stepfather was a cop, Marigold. It was bad enough that I killed him; they were not going to let me smear his good name."

Marigold shakes her head. "You should sue! It's preposterous!"

"Maybe, but I'd rather just move on."

"But—"

"Do me a favour, Marigold. Would you tell Whit? If I have to go through it again, I'm going to feel like the Ancient Mariner."

Marigold nods. "Yes, of course." She looks at me. "Can I tell him about you two as well?"

Cain looks bemused, but he leaves the reply to me.

I open my last packet of Tim Tams and sit down. "Sure, but don't embroider it."

"Embroider it!" Marigold is indignant. "You two are the writers!" Her eyes well up. "I'm very happy for you both."

I hand around my precious chocolate biscuits, trying to make the moment a little less awkward.

We work our way through the packet. I show Marigold and Cain how to suck coffee through a Tim Tam, a practice which many Australians consider perhaps our greatest contribution to culinary culture. But there's a skill to completing the draw before the biscuit disintegrates, and Marigold and Cain are both novices to the art of the Tim Tam Slam.

The instruction at least alleviates the gravity of the conversation. It's not quite a celebration, but there is joy in chocolate, coffee, and absurd modes of consumption.

"Would you like a ride home, Marigold?" Cain takes my hand as he stands up. "I probably should get going and put my apartment back together."

"What's wrong with your apartment?"

"The police searched it. I think Boston's finest had a competition to see who could make the biggest pile of my stuff."

"That's awful—can they do that?"

"Yep." Cain nods regretfully. "They can. And they are nothing if not thorough."

"We'll help you clean up!" Marigold declares.

"Thank you." Cain picks up the used coffee mugs and takes them to my sink. "But I'll be fine."

"No, you won't be," Marigold is adamant. "You shouldn't have to be. Come on...many hands and all that."

Cain is beginning to look a bit trapped.

I suggest that we give him a bit of space. "He can call if he needs us."

But Marigold will not be deterred. "Neither Freddie nor I will be able to sleep with the thought of you cleaning up that mess on your own."

"This is really something I need to do on my own, Marigold."

"No, you don't. This is when you need your friends!" Again Marigold's eyes well up. And again I am struck by the fragility that lurks just below.

Perhaps Cain sees it too because he gives in to Marigold's determined camaraderie. "Sure. Thank you."

I grab my coat and change into a shirt that is not missing buttons, and we head out to Cain's old Jeep. "I'm sorry," I whisper as soon as Marigold is out of earshot. "Do you want me to tell her to—"

"No, it's fine. My biggest secret is already out."

―――――

Dear Hannah,

I hope you're okay. I caught a story on CNN that Australia was flooding now. Weren't you on fire yesterday? Anyway, I hope that you remain undefeated if not unaffected by the natural disasters assailing your fair nation.

So, our heroine beds the villain. A classic trope! Classic because it works. Her eventual disillusionment will be all the more powerful. And so too, I suspect, will be the disillusionment of Marigold and Whit. Well, maybe not Marigold—she seems to be on to him, but Whit will be shattered. With respect to the scene in which Freddie and Cain become intimate: I wonder if it might be better to have it not go so well. Perhaps Cain is impotent—a symptom or the cause of his homicidal rage—or perhaps he has a sexual need to humiliate or be humiliated. I think a scene along those lines could add a certain raw intensity to the plot.

Re: my address. I am so touched that you would want to send me some-thing, but honestly Hannah, I have an idea of what postage costs between Australia and the U.S., and I cannot in good conscience allow you to go to such expense. Whatever it is, hang on to it, and I will collect it in person one day.

Fondly yours,

Leo

CHAPTER TWENTY-ONE

Cain's apartment is in Roxbury, in an old building, which, if renovated, might be lovely. Several young men linger on the sidewalk outside the entry. A couple of them greet Cain as we pass. They speak loudly, with casual and entirely unaggressive profanity. His response is friendly, but he doesn't stop or introduce us. The inside of the building is crumbling and faded but clean. The elevator clunks up to the third floor and Cain opens the door to 319.

If we hadn't known the police had done this, we might have called them. The apartment is trashed. Every shelf cleared, every drawer upturned, every cushion removed. The items are all heaped in a pile in the centre of the room. For a while, all we can do is stare at the mess.

"We'll begin with the books." I choose a place to start. "Let's get them back onto the bookcases. Cain, how were they shelved?"

"What do you mean?"

"Alphabetically?"

"Novels and poetry there, and nonfiction and research materials there." He points out the relevant bookcases. "And, yes, alphabetically by author."

I smile. My books are shoved wherever they fit. They're quick to put away, less quick to find.

"What about your plotting room?" I ask suddenly. "God! Did they take that apart too?"

"They took most of that with them. My computer, too." His voice is controlled, but I can hear the frustration, the anger. "They're looking for some kind of manifesto, I expect."

The horror must be apparent on my face. He puts his arm around me. "It not as bad as all that," he whispers. "I backed up the manuscript and photos of the plot diagrams and emailed them all to myself."

I lean into him. His eyes meet mine, and for a moment we are lost in each other.

"Hey, you two—get back to work!" Marigold takes a stack of novels to the appropriate shelf.

Between the three of us, we return the living room to some semblance of order. I savour Cain's taste in books as I slide each into alphabetical place. Intelligent, diverse, eclectic. Battered classics with notes in the margins. Recent releases. Prize-winners and pulp. The occasional graphic novel. A thesaurus and a couple of books on grammar.

"Fuck!" Marigold stands at the bedroom door.

I leave the bookcase to see what's wrong. The bedroom, too, is in disarray, clothes and bedding, shoes and more books in a heap by a stripped bed. The mattress had been slashed, foam and fabric pulled away from exposed springs.

"One of the officers thought he saw a tear in the cover." Cain sighs. "Apparently people often hide things in mattresses."

"And they just left it like this?" Marigold is livid. "Where do they expect you to sleep?"

"I think they were hoping it would be a cell."

"But surely they can't do this—"

"They left me some paperwork to fill in—"

"You can't sleep on paperwork, Cain." Marigold's outrage is rising exponentially. "You need to speak to your lawyer about this… You do have a lawyer, don't you?"

"I'm starving." Cain squeezes my hand. "Is anybody hungry? We could order a pizza."

"I am," I volunteer, to help him change the subject and because, now that it's been mentioned, I am actually ravenous. "Do you have a favourite pizza place?"

"There's a place a couple of blocks away that delivers." He reaches into his pocket and then grimaces as he realises. "Damn… Freddie, can I borrow your phone? They took mine again."

I hand him my phone and he dials. "Tell me what you want, Marigold, or we're all going to be eating vegetarian."

Marigold asks for pepperoni with anchovies. I request pineapple and jalapeños on the vegetarian.

"You want me to ask for fruit on pizza?" Cain whispers.

"Trust me, it's delicious," I assure him.

He makes the order, albeit sceptically. In the meantime, we begin work on Cain's galley kitchen in case we need plates. Cain seems to own a minimum of cooking implements, and so it does not take long. By the time the pizzas arrive, the kitchen is nearly sorted.

We sit on the floor in the living room and eat straight out of the boxes. I make Marigold and Cain try the vegetarian pizza to demonstrate the virtue of pineapples. Marigold is revolted. Cain eats a slice, though I'm not sure he's entirely convinced.

"Whit might like it," he offers. "It's a bit like one of his weird donuts."

I laugh at their poor American taste buds and tell them about the perfection of beetroot and fried egg on a hamburger.

For a while we all valiantly ignore the fact that we are here to tidy up a house that has been taken apart by police searching for a murder weapon. But, inevitably, the conversation reverts to this.

"I don't understand why they think you'd want to kill Shaun Jacobs," Marigold says as she picks the pineapple off a slice of pizza. "It doesn't make any sense."

Cain shrugs. "They think I might have wanted revenge for him slugging me with that bottle, I guess."

"Did you?" Marigold asks.

"What?" I'm incredulous that she would ask or even think such a thing. Cain simply looks at her.

"I mean, weren't you even the littlest bit angry with him?" she clarifies. "I know you didn't kill him, but weren't you angry? It would be natural to be angry."

I remember that Marigold is a Psych postgrad—Freud Girl in the flesh.

"He was high," Cain replies. "I'm angry at myself for getting into that situation. I should have been watching for it—I should have at least ducked." He shakes his head, leaning back against the bookcase. "If I'd called the police when you told me to, Freddie, he might have been in prison, but he wouldn't be dead."

"You don't know that." I slide over to sit beside him.

Marigold agrees. "There must be dozens of fights and assaults in Boston every night. It wouldn't rate to get the Boston PD to look up from their Dunkin' glazed jellies."

I glance around the wrecked apartment. "They're looking now."

Marigold frowns thoughtfully. "It's a murder now."

Cain drops Marigold off at her place on Athens Street first.

"You're not going to let him go back to his place, are you?" Marigold whispers to me as she gets out of the Jeep. "That bed…"

I laugh. "I'll offer him my couch."

She opens her mouth, thinks better of it, and turns to go. But she pivots back to kiss my cheek and whisper in my ear, "Be careful."

I watch after her, bemused, yet also a little startled by the warning.

"Is everything okay?" Cain asks.

"Marigold is concerned about where you'll sleep tonight."

"Oh, I see." He glances at the backpack in which he had hastily stuffed a change of clothes when I quietly suggested he sleep at my apartment earlier. "Where exactly is she afraid of me sleeping?"

"She's worried about the violence done to your mattress." I don't mention her last fleeting counsel—I don't quite know what that meant myself.

"Are you sure about this, Freddie?"

I nudge him. "Have you forgotten how we spent the afternoon?"

He smiles. "I haven't forgotten. But I don't want to presume." He shifts. "I am aware that I haven't given you any time to think about what you now know about me, to decide how you feel about what I did."

It occurs to me at that moment. "Is that what Boo meant when he said 'Does she know what you did?'"

Cain's knuckles whiten on the steering wheel. "He said that? Yes, I guess that's what he meant."

"Why did he care?"

"I'm sorry?"

"He seemed outraged."

Cain shrugs. "That may have been more to do with whatever he was on." He pulls into the visitors' carpark at Carrington Square. "I mean it, Freddie. If you need more time to think about getting involved with me, I understand."

I don't look at him, aware that doing so is going to compromise the cautious, rational part of me. I can almost hear his heart pounding as he waits, or perhaps that's mine. I exhale and look up. "Okay, I've thought about it. I'm fine with it."

His smile is surprised. A little puzzled. "Freddie—"

"I'm already involved with you, whether or not we're lovers." I gather my courage and ask. "Are you having second thoughts?"

His eyes widen. "No!" He takes my hand firmly. "Not about being with you. But, Freddie, I've been through this before. I'm a convicted felon. The police are going to make my life hell for a while, and I don't want you to be caught in the damage."

I nod, moved that he wants to protect me. "I understand. But I believe you, and I trust you. At the risk of being too honest, I think I'm falling in love with you. The point of no damage is already passed. So let's just be what we are to each other, and we'll deal with the rest when it happens."

He kisses me then, fiercely, and I am awash with the intensity of what he feels, and what I feel in return. We linger in the Jeep for a few moments before we head in because we're too old to be making out in a car.

As we pass his station, Joe flags me down and thanks me again for the cupcakes.

"I'll bring another couple down." I had until that moment forgotten about the cupcakes. They are, as far as I know, still on the coffee table.

"Oh, no, Miss Kincaid. You enjoy them. I could do with a few less cakes." He pats his ample belly. "My shift's finished now anyway." He picks up a business card from his desk and hands it to me. "That policewoman came back while you were out. Said she'd like you to call her."

I slip the card into my pocket and glance at my watch. It's almost midnight. Joe did say "like"—a request, not a demand. Surely it is not urgent enough to call at this hour. "I'll ring her in the morning."

Cain and I sit up eating cupcakes and talking. There are so many things I want to ask, but I don't wish to interrogate him...or seem like I'm interrogating him. I'm curious about the civility of Cain McLeod. He's not loud, or brutish, or cynical, and yet he survived years in an adult prison. How did he do that?

"I was released over seven years ago," he reminds me. "Jail wasn't the only influence on my life."

"Even so, it doesn't seem to have marked you at all. I went to yoga for a few months five years ago and I'm still traumatised..."

He laughs softly. I savour the sound. There's a trust, an intimacy in it. "You haven't read my first novel, have you?"

Immediately, I'm mortified. I can't believe I didn't think to get hold of a copy. "I haven't yet, but—oh, God, there's no excuse..."

"Don't be absurd, Freddie." He wraps his arms around me. "If reading a writer's books was a requirement, none of us would ever have any friends."

"No...it is a requirement. When I have a book, it will be a requirement."

He smiles. "Actually, I'm glad you haven't read it. It may have scared you away."

"Why?"

"Because it's not civil. It's angry and hurt and hard. It sounds like it was written by an ex-con."

"But the *New York Times* called it a brilliant debut," I remind him.

He shrugs. "People liked it...or hated it enough to make it a success. Believe me, I was as surprised as anyone."

"But you don't want to write like that anymore?"

"I've told that story—I can't tell it again."

"I'd better read it," I say almost to myself. I look at him. "Unless you'd rather I didn't."

"Go ahead. Just don't let it give you nightmares."

I study him gently, certain of him, despite what he has done. "How could it?"

Dear Hannah,

Ah, yes, the autobiographical first novel! Mine, thankfully, is still in a drawer. It served its purpose, expelled the demons, said all those things I felt I had to shout rather than say. The first book is something of a literary tantrum. Anyway, I'm glad I had the good sense to never show it to anyone—they'd probably have had me arrested or committed.

I give you, it's a stroke of genius to publish one's darkest secrets as a novel. Hide in plain sight, if you like. And it makes sense. While killers do not wish to be caught, they must yearn for some recognition of what they did, what they got away with. Having your deeds detailed in a novel would be perfect.

I wouldn't mind reading Cain's novel myself!

Now a couple of chapters ago we were talking about another murder. You may have forgotten or been distracted when you had that computer crash. I know I've sent you some images of a crime scene, but I've attached another set from a different incident to this email. I've become quite good at finding and photographing crime scenes unnoticed.

As you'll see this victim is a woman. She died of a head injury, probably beaten with a blunt object of some sort—something like a brick or a hammer. I wondered if a victim similar to Caroline, and murdered in the same manner, might help connect the crimes and perhaps show the evolution of Cain from a man who initially murdered out of necessity and then simply discovered he liked it. I'm sure it must happen. After all, how are you to know you like killing people until you have taken a life and in doing so discovered the incomparable thrill of holding existence in your hands and snuffing it out? I'm projecting, of course.

Anyway, have a look at the images and let me know what you think.

I must say this is getting very exciting.

Yours,

Leo

CHAPTER TWENTY-TWO

I call Detective Justine Dwyer at nine. "Detective Dwyer? I was told you wished to speak to me. Would you like me to come in?"

"Oh, no—that won't be necessary. There are a couple of things I need to clarify. Are you at home, Winifred?"

"Yes…"

"I have to pass by there on my way to court. I could stop by…in, say, half an hour?"

I hesitate. Cain is still in my bed. "I'm not sure—"

"It'll only take a couple of minutes. I could meet you in the foyer, if you prefer."

"Yes, okay, I suppose that would be all right."

I place my phone on the bedside table, and Cain pulls me drowsily into his arms.

"I've got to get dressed," I moan. "Detective Dwyer is coming by to speak to me."

"Why?"

"I don't know…I'm meeting her in the foyer."

He rubs his face. "I should make tracks," he says. "I have to talk to my agent about what's happening, call my mother, and buy another phone…not in that order obviously…"

I make coffee while he showers, and he makes toast while I do the same. A couple of sips in, it's nine thirty, and we abandon the attempt at breakfast.

"I'll walk you down to the foyer," Cain volunteers as he pulls on his jacket.

I grab a notebook, write my phone number on a clean page, and hand it to Cain. "Call me when you get a new phone, so I have your number." I hesitate a moment before blurting out, "Cain, I really think you should also call a lawyer."

His face clouds a little. "I had lawyers last time, Freddie. Good ones. My mother sold her house to pay for them. And I was still put away for seven years."

I pull him towards me. "That doesn't mean lawyers couldn't help now." I lock my arms around him. "Just think about it."

He kisses my brow. "Okay."

"Okay, you'll call a lawyer?"

"Okay, I'll think about it."

"You could talk to Whit—"

"If I were to retain a lawyer," he says sharply, "I wouldn't involve Whit in the circus. Now I really should get going."

"But I'll see you tonight?" I add, hoping it doesn't sound too clingy.

"That depends."

"On what?"

"On whether you still want to."

Detective Dwyer is climbing the stairs as Cain and I are about to go down. She looks startled.

"I was coming up to see if you'd forgotten our appointment." She glances at her watch. "We did say half past nine?"

"Yes, we did. I'm sorry—I'm running late."

Cain presses my hand. "I'll leave you to it."

He nods at Dwyer as he passes her on the stairs and then waves at me from the bottom tread.

I return my gaze to the detective. "Shall we go down?"

"Actually, it might be better if we go up to your apartment. It'll be more private."

I think about asking her why a few questions need to be private, but in the end I just invite her in.

She looks around, assessing my circumstances.

Nervously, I tell her about the Sinclair Fellowship. "I could never afford an address like this if not for the trust."

She smiles. "I did wonder if you were an heiress of some sort."

"I wish!" I offer her a cup of coffee which she accepts, insisting I call her Justine rather that Detective Dwyer.

"I always thought Australians drank tea," she says as I duck into the kitchen.

"We can drink tea and coffee—we're fickle when it comes to beverages. How do you take it?"

"Black and strong."

I bring two mugs of coffee into the living room and set the black one before her. She picks it up with both hands and sips. "Christ, I need this. It's been one of those mornings."

I say nothing, but I'm aware of a sense of relief that has no cause except perhaps that the detective seems so human—an ordinary person despite the fact that she wields the authority of the Boston PD.

"It must be hard sometimes, even living here," she says. "You must get homesick."

"Occasionally," I admit. "But less than I expected."

She nods. "Did Cain McLeod spend the night here?"

I am momentarily wrong-footed by the question. "Yes."

She doesn't react particularly. "You said you were just friends."

"We are…were—"

"But now you're involved?"

"I guess so."

"Despite his past?"

"Yes."

"He committed cold-blooded murder."

"He was defending himself."

"Is that what he told you?" Justine shakes her head.

"He was fifteen and that man was trying to—" I stop.

"*That man* was a decorated policeman who was doing everything he could to be a good father." She speaks slowly, with conviction. "Abel Manners waited until he came in to say good night and then stabbed him in the neck."

"Cain was fighting him off. He didn't ever intend—"

"If he didn't intend to kill his stepfather, if he hadn't planned it, why was the knife under his pillow?"

My voice rises. I can't believe it isn't obvious. "Because he didn't feel safe! He kept it there for protection."

"Oh, Winifred." Justine's voice is sympathetic. "If that's true, why did Abel lock his mother in her room until after he'd killed his stepfather?"

I stare at her. "What?"

"Abel locked his mother in her room before his stepfather returned. To make sure she couldn't interfere with his plan to murder the man. To make sure she couldn't stop him."

"That's not true."

"Winifred, she called the police."

For a few breaths I'm speechless as I try to think. Did Cain lie to me? I drag myself back from panic, from the doubt that accompanies it. "If Cain's mother was locked in her room, she couldn't possibly have seen what happened." I'm surprised by how confident I sound. I fix my gaze on the detective. "What was it you needed to clarify with me, Justine?"

Justine exhales. "I got the distinct impression that you were completely unaware of who the man who calls himself Cain McLeod actually was, and I wanted to warn you—"

"I'm sorry you got that impression. It's not the case. You don't need to warn me."

Justine's head tilts to one side. "You're aware that Cain McLeod is a dangerous man, that he's a person of interest in the deaths of Caroline Palfrey and Shaun Jacobs?"

"I was sitting across a table from Cain McLeod when Caroline was killed, and as for Shaun Jacobs, Cain didn't even want to call the police when Shaun attacked him." Once more I sound deceptively calm—to myself, anyway. It's possible I'm not fooling Justine at all. "Why would he then kill him?"

"Maybe he had a reason for not wanting the police involved that had nothing to do with protecting Mr. Jacobs."

"Cain has been out of prison for seven years, Justine. Why would he suddenly decide to start killing random people?"

"You're assuming he hasn't killed anyone before Caroline Palfrey."

"He didn't kill Caroline Palfrey. He didn't even know her."

"So it's just a coincidence that her grandfather was the trial judge who sentenced Abel Manners?"

"I...what?" My voice sounds squeaky.

"Caroline Palfrey's grandfather was Judge Andrew Keaton, who sentenced Abel Manners to ten years—seven without parole." Justine's eyes are fixed on me as she watches intently for my reaction.

"Did Cain know that?" I ask when I can make my voice work again.

"We think he did. We think that's why he organised for her to be killed while he made sure he had an irrefutable alibi."

"That alibi being us—Whit and Marigold and me?"

"Yes."

"But you have no evidence of that—or else you would have arrested him already." I exhale.

"I want you to be safe. I don't want you to get in over your head." She folds her arms and rests them on her knees, leaning forward. "Whatever sob story he's told you about why he killed his stepfather, he did kill him. The man who now calls himself Cain McLeod is dangerous."

I shake my head. "I don't see it."

Justine is clearly frustrated. "Have you read his novel?"

This again. "No. Not yet."

"I have, and you might want to before you decide whether or not you want to continue your friendship with Mr. McLeod."

I roll my eyes. "Cain already told me it's—"

"It's about an ex-con who exacts revenge on those who sent him away— the jury, his lawyers, the DA, the witnesses."

"Oh…really?"

"You're surprised?" There's only the tiniest hint of triumph in her voice.

I shrug. "Well, it's such a tired old trope and I know it was a bestseller…"

"Winifred—this is not a joke."

"I know, but you can't seriously be telling me you think Cain is acting out his novel. Novelists make stuff up—that's what we do." I place my mug on the coffee table, still full, now cold. "Just what is it you want from me, Detective?"

Justine swallows. "You have my number. If Mr. McLeod says or does anything that changes your mind about his innocence, I'd like you to call me."

"You want me to spy on Cain?"

"I want you to not become his next victim."

For several beats we face each other in silence. "Okay," I say in the end.

"Really?" Justine seems surprised.

"If I change my mind about Cain's innocence, I will call you." The promise costs me nothing. If I ever came to believe Cain had killed someone, aside from his stepfather, of course I'd call the police. It's not as if I'm some kind of gangster's moll.

The undertaking seems to satisfy—or at least mollify—Dwyer. She remembers she has to get to court, and after ensuring I have her number and know that I can call her any time of the day or night, she takes her leave.

Afterwards I don't move for a while. I'm just not sure what to do. In the end, I elect to clean up the remnants of our aborted breakfast. I feel unfairly wrenched from a morning in which I woke in Cain McLeod's arms. It is not until I've wiped down the bench and washed all the dishes that I am ready to think about what Dwyer told me.

I had not thought to ask Cain where his mother was the night he'd killed his stepfather. I suppose I'd assumed she'd gone out.

My phone rings and I answer, hoping it's Cain.

"Hey, Freddie!"

"Whit, how are you?"

"I'm good. Doc's given me the all clear—I was looking for Cain."

"Then why are you ringing me?"

"'Cause his phone is being answered by some police officer, and I thought he might be with you. Marigold said you two were…you know…"

"What are you—fourteen?"

"Then you are?"

I sigh. "Cain isn't here. He left this morning to buy a phone and see some people."

"What people?"

"I think he said his agent, but I'm hoping he sees a lawyer too. Why are you trying to track him down?"

"Guy stuff."

"What?"

"You heard me."

I can tell he's kidding but also that he does want to speak to Cain.

"He's buying another cell phone today—he said he'd call me with the number," I offer. "I could text it to you. Failing that, he'll probably come back here tonight."

Whit thanks me. He sounds a little agitated.

"Is something wrong?" I venture carefully. He's already told me to mind my own business—albeit in not so many words.

"Nah…just been under house arrest for too long. Getting a little stir crazy is all."

"If it's company you're after—"

"Thanks, but that's okay."

"Only Cain will do?" I ask, bemused.

"Yes." He hangs up.

I don't remember that I am supposed to be driving up to Rockport with Leo and the other Fellows until Leo knocks on my door. He holds up a picnic basket. "Don't worry—I realise it's snowing. These are snacks for the drive."

"Oh, God, Leo, I'm so sorry—I forgot."

He shrugs. "I'm five minutes early, so no damage. Grab your coat."

I shake my head. "I can't go."

His face falls. "Why not?"

"There's so much going on—I have to be here in case Cain—"

"But we've just been invited to luncheon by one the Sinclair Fellowship board members. You can't not go!"

"You'll have to take my regrets—"

"The others are waiting downstairs, Freddie. They were looking forward to meeting you."

"I'll come down and meet them—I can apologise in person." I feel dreadful. I don't want to stand Leo up, but how can I go out of town today? What if Cain called and—I catch myself. Realise I'm being pathetic. Waiting around in case someone needs me is not how I've ever lived my life. "We'll be back today, right?"

"Sure. Rockport is only an hour's drive. We'll be back before dinner."

I waiver for a moment.

"Honestly, Freddie. You'll be back by five—basically a day at the office." He opens the basket so I can peer in. "I made cookies."

I can smell the veracity of his claim…or at least that there are cookies. I relent. "I'll fetch my coat."

———

My dearest Hannah,

What a splendid fellow Leo is! I am very pleased to give him my name.

First the little things. In the States you'd "wipe down a counter" rather than a bench.

So, our Cain is not just an ex-con, but he has a motive for killing Caroline Palfrey as well as Shaun Jacobs! Of course he would have required an accomplice to pull it off, but accomplices are not impossible to acquire. One wonders why he was at the library at all...surely it would have been better to be alibied in a bar across town? But then I suppose, if he'd not been in the BPL, he would not have been able to at least hear his victim scream. And there is satisfaction in that...though I imagine it would not come close to the completion of taking her life himself. Perhaps that's why he needed to stab Whit? So now the question is the identity of the accomplice. It has to be someone introduced at the outset. One of the security guards possibly or...OH MY GOD—LEO!

I'm not sure if I should be offended...but I'm not. I'm delighted. And what a wonderful twist! But why should I be surprised. You are, after all, Hannah Tigone and I am

Your
Leo

Chapter Twenty-Three

Katerina Wolanski is from London, about fifty, tall, slim, and dressed entirely in black. She embraces me in greeting, kissing each cheek—the left twice. She smells like gardenias. Dr. Briton Ibe is from Somalia. He's small, walks with a limp, and wears a bright yellow puffer jacket and a Cossack hat. His smile is broad and easy, his teeth incandescently white.

I like them both immediately.

Leo introduces us, by name and a sentence or two on our work. Katerina is writing a speculative novel set a thousand years in the future, and Briton, a political satire which comments on the hypocrisy of post-colonial diplomacy. They both seem excited to meet a mystery writer.

Leo directs us to the car he's borrowed from one of the other residents of Carrington Square—a Mercedes SUV with heated seats that recline electronically.

"Someone lent you this?" I gaze at the buttons on the console in the passenger door which control the precise height, angle, and temperature of the seat.

"Mrs. Weinbaum," Leo confirms, grinning.

"She drives this?" The SUV is huge and Mrs. Weinbaum is tiny.

Leo shrugs. "Apparently."

Briton and Katerina have claimed the back seats. I climb into the front beside Leo and check my phone in case Cain has sent through a number.

Leo waits until I put the phone back into my pocket. "Everything okay?"

I nod, deciding to stop fretting. There will be time enough to talk to Cain, to ask him about Justine Dwyer's allegations. I don't doubt him, but I wonder. And I wish I could speak to him now, wish I'd asked more, so that I had an answer for the detective.

Leo marshals the conversation, subtly drawing out similarities between us in our work and our lives. Talking is easy and listening easier, and while I do not quite put Cain out of my mind, I am able to maintain enough social function to uphold my share of the exchange.

As Leo promised, Rockport is about an hour from Boston. A little longer because the road is covered in snow and the journey is broken by a stop at Smith's Point to lunch with Chase Perkins, who is on the board of the Sinclair Fellowship, and his wife, Becca. We might in fact have lingered longer at the beautifully catered affair, chatting with our benefactors over delicious finger food, if Chase's golden retriever had not demolished the immaculately laid out meal while we were taking a tour of his house.

We leave hungry but determined to write that overfed golden retriever into our manuscripts. Indeed, we make a pact to do so—the shared motif of this year's Fellowship holders.

We're still laughing about it when we arrive in Rockport. I take a photo of my companions in front of the famous red fish shack on the wharf. The cold has deterred enough tourists that it's not a picture of three people in a crowd. I laugh at Briton, who is jumping up and down to warm himself. Katerina does not feel the cold in the same way, but neither is she as taken with the winter townscape as I am. I have seen snow before, but on ski fields. There's a special magic to the way snow settles on the sail lofts and fish shacks of Artists' Row. Picture postcard and frozen in time. I am overwhelmed with a reminder that I am living in the U.S., writing, and I am amazed anew that this is my life.

I won the fellowship with a story about Geraldine, and the kind of destructive grief left in the wake of shock, the long road to rebuilding family without her, the inconsolable rage of my mother, the withdrawal of my father, my determination to find sense and purpose where there was none. The resultant novella had been a kind of scream, pain and guilt and hope with a denouement of desperate and exhausted hope. That it had won the Sinclair had stunned me as much as anyone, and now, if I allow myself to think about it, I worry that it was all I had. There is no more pain to draw upon. Perhaps that's what Cain meant about his first novel. Though, clearly, what he expended was not something he wished to reharness.

I loiter outside taking it all in while Leo leads Katerina and Briton into the gift shop. He doesn't try to persuade me to come with them into the warmth, whispering, "If I had my druthers, I'd stay out here with you, but Briton's going to do himself a spinal injury if he keeps jumping around like that."

"You go ahead," I tell him. "I want to try and describe this to myself… so I remember."

He nods, understanding my need to lock the images in words, and escorts Briton and Katerina into the storefront. I walk down a driveway behind the building and onto the wharf. Someone has salted the ice on its surface so walking is not as treacherous as it might have been. The wind which blows in off the water is bitter and gusty. I can almost believe Gerry's standing beside me, seeing what I see, feeling the cold and tasting the faint salt in the air. I've felt her presence often since I came to the U.S.—it's almost as if she gave me the story that won the Sinclair so she could see this through my eyes. I can hear her laughing at me, mocking the fanciful need to conjure her, to find meaning in luck and fate.

My phone rings, and I see Cain's name. I assume he has finally procured a new phone and am relieved at the luck of being alone to receive his call. Hastily, I pull off my glove and answer.

"Hello—Cain?"

A scream. Caroline's scream…or Gerry's. I don't know anymore.

"Who are you?" I shout into the phone. "What do you want?"

Three, four, five beats and I begin to think the caller might speak, and I'm terrified. And the call is ended.

The ding of a text arriving. Again it tells me it's from Cain. A photograph of my door at Carrington Square. I stand there staring, horrified and angry and unsure what to do next. A second message alert. Cain's door now…maybe. The same style and colour, but nothing about Cain's door is particularly distinctive. But it could be his.

Distracted, I don't look up to see Leo approach, and so he is standing beside me with hot chocolate before I realise he's there.

"Freddie? I thought you might like—is something wrong?"

I don't know what to say to him. I show him the texted images. I tell him about the scream, what had happened on the other occasions I'd heard it. "Leo, I think I need to go back…now."

Leo swallows. "I had a few things planned for today…"

"Maybe there's a bus I could catch?"

He glances at his watch. "Not for a couple of hours… You might as well—"

"I really have to get back." I suddenly feel trapped, forced to sightsee in Rockport while some lunatic stalks Cain. And irrationally, unfairly, I'm angry with Leo for bringing me here.

"I promised Briton and Katerina a clam chowder lunch—"

I snap. "For God's sake, Leo!" Furious tears threaten to make me lose my grip entirely. "Please. I know I'm ruining things, but if our places were reversed, I would help you!"

He looks down at me and nods slowly. "Yes, ma'am, I reckon you would." He put the hot chocolate into my hand. "You drink this. I'll get Briton and Kat. You can ring the police on the way."

I am utterly ashamed now that I shouted at him. I use the moments he's away to wipe away tears, to pull myself together.

I'm not sure what Leo's told Briton and Katerina, but they don't seem resentful or put out that I am cutting our excursion short. They emerge with souvenir red fish-shack T-shirts and novelty pens and floating crabs in snow globes. They look at me sympathetically.

Leo suggests very tentatively that we grab sandwiches for the drive back since we won't be stopping for lunch, and I feel like the biggest jerk.

"Let me grab them," I plead. "An apology for wrecking the day. Does anyone have anything they don't eat?"

It turns out Briton is a vegetarian too, and Kat doesn't like eggs. I run into the diner on the corner and order two fried clam sandwiches, two egg salads on rye, and four servings of hand-cut fries to go before returning to the Mercedes.

As we leave Rockport, I call Justine Dwyer and explain what has happened. I tell her what happened the last time I received similar messages and phone calls.

She asks me for specifics. "Did the scream sound like the last time?"

"Yes, exactly like the last scream. A woman's scream."

"And you're sure the second door is Mr. McLeod's?"

"No," I admit. "But it could be his. To be honest I didn't really pay much attention to Cain's door, and there was nothing particularly memorable about it. It's just a door."

"Okay. Bring your phone in as soon as you get back to Boston. I'll send a car round to check on Mr. McLeod as a precaution."

When I hang up there is an awkward silence in the car, and I realise that of course my companions all heard at least my side of the conversation. Briton and Katerina must be wondering what on earth I'm involved in. And so I explain briefly…about Caroline, the strange calls, and Whit being stabbed.

Briton and Katerina listen, gasping and *tsk*ing occasionally. For some reason, I want to leave Cain out of it as much as possible, and so I don't mention Boo. Leo meets my eye, brow raised. He has an idea of what I have failed to mention. The moment disappears and Briton and Katerina ask questions and express concern about the rest, but I am aware that he knows. Regardless, he keeps his own counsel.

Leo drives straight to the police station and runs around to open my door as I say goodbye to the others. "I'll walk you inside," he says as I get out.

"Thank you, but it's okay." I smile. "It's a police station…I couldn't possibly be safer."

Leo's sigh is uncommitted. "I'll take these guys home and come back for you…or what's left of you."

I laugh. "I'm going in to make a complaint, not to turn myself in." I embrace him. "Thank you for today…I am sorry I ruined it. Don't come back for me. I have no idea how long this will take, and I can take a train or catch an Uber home if Justine can't give me a ride."

He frowns. "Justine?"

"Detective Dwyer."

"I didn't realise you were friends."

"We're not. Barely first-name acquaintances."

He relents. "If you need me to come get you, just call."

"Thank you, Leo."

The officer at the front desk takes me to an interview room and asks me to wait. Detective Dwyer comes in about five minutes later. "Is Cain okay?" I blurt as she walks in.

"I sent a car around to his apartment to wait for him. But there's been no sign of him."

I'm relieved…I think…

"Do you have any idea where he might be, Winifred?"

"He was going to buy a new phone and call his mother and his agent… or maybe he was going to see his agent. Perhaps that's where he is."

"Do you have a name for this agent?"

"No, but I expect his publishers would know."

I show her the text images of the doors, and she takes the phone.

I plead with her to copy the texts and return the cell. "All my friends and family have that number, and I've already had to change it once."

Justine has a word with a colleague before informing me that my request will be granted. I wait for about an hour while they do whatever it is they need to do, and my phone is returned.

"Look, Winifred, all we can determine is that the texts and the phone call were made from the cell that Cain McLeod claims to have lost."

"That makes sense," I reply carefully. "Whoever took the phone and sent me the warning last time…"

"Warning? You see it as a warning?"

I shrug. "What else would it be?"

"A threat."

I concede. I don't want to argue about semantics.

"The thing is, Winifred, you've changed your number." Justine watches me carefully as she speaks. "That rules out any notion that this might be kids or pranksters."

"I never thought it was."

"Whoever made the calls had your number both times. The first time it would have been saved on McLeod's cell, but this time that's not the case. The call was made by someone who knew your number."

I nod slowly. The logic is undeniable, the conclusion sickening.

She places a notepad and pen before me. "Winifred, I want you to write down everybody who has your new number. Don't leave anyone out, no matter how absurd you may think they may be as a potential suspect."

I comply. The length of the list surprises me. It doesn't seem possible to give out your number so many times in a couple of weeks, but I have. To my family, naturally, and several people back home. Whit, Marigold, and Cain, of course, but also to Whit's father, Leo, the trustees of my fellowship, Joe, and the custodian at the Carrington, and several of my neighbours including Mrs. Weinbaum and her lawyers, the Boston Public Library, two different pizza delivery places, the Australian Embassy, and the Consulate. Finally, the Boston PD and Detective Justine Dwyer.

Justine glances at the list. "If you think of anyone else—"

"I'll let you know immediately."

Justine stands. "I'll drive you home, check your apartment to be on the safe side, and have a word with your security man."

I get to my feet, pleased the interview is finally over. I need to think, and I can't do that under the scrutiny of a detective.

"I'll make sure a patrol car keeps an eye on your building," Justine continues. "And should Mr. McLeod get in touch, we would like to know immediately for the sake of his own safety."

"I'm not sure—"

"If these images are to be read as a warning or a threat, and given what happened to Mr. Metters on the last occasion, then Mr. McLeod could be in danger."

Dear Hannah,

I notice that you have not once in this novel made any reference to the global pandemic. I understand of course. We're all sick of it and all it entails. But I think it is the responsibility of writers to bear witness to the darkness as well as the light. Without any mention of the virus, your novel risks being dated before it's released.

You could of course be setting this novel in the future, at a time when all this is behind us. But if you don't mind me saying so, that's exceedingly optimistic. I suspect that a world without disease will need to feature flying cars and victims dispatched by laser guns. Writing a contemporary novel without the pandemic is surely more fantasy than mystery.

I'm not suggesting you rewrite the entire book, just make an occasional nod to the fact that the world does not look like it did. In this last chapter, for example, Freddie and her colleagues would be careful to mask up. Freddie might choose between styles of masks rather than jackets. And you could illustrate the rising tensions between maskers and anti-maskers by having them witness an altercation between the two groups. In fact, pursuant to the suggestions in my last letter, the altercation could become fatal. I promise you it's not beyond the realms of plausibility that a masker would end being garroted with their own mask by someone from the opposite camp.

Witnessing that level of violence might also bring home to Freddie the kind of man with whom she has become involved. It might give her a comparison as she runs over in her imagination the scene in which Cain thrust a knife into his stepfather's jugular. That must play over in her mind. Surely, she must think about that. Does it terrify her, or does she find it strangely exciting, erotic even? I think we need more of that in her internal monologue.

Do not be afraid of taking your writing to dark places, my dear. The world is getting darker, and murder now needs to compete with disease, neglect, and the inherent selfishness of man.

Yours,
Leo

Chapter Twenty-Four

The search of my apartment does not leave the same upheaval it did at Cain's, but it is thorough. All rooms and closets, anywhere an intruder might be hiding. Leo ducks his head in, and I introduce him to Justine Dwyer. He doesn't stay long, or say anything, beyond bracing my shoulder and asking if I'm okay.

Justine speaks to the doorman on duty, who is not Joe today, warns him to be vigilant for any unauthorised visitors to Carrington Square, and asks him to ring her if he encounters anyone acting suspiciously. The man, whose name I can't remember, seems a little affronted by the idea that any undesirable would get past him.

Once Justine has gone, I return to my apartment and bolt the door behind me. I'm trying not to be too alarmed by the fact that Cain has not yet called. I think of all the reasons that he might not have done so, why he might have been delayed. I curl up on my couch and try to sort the befuddled, slightly panicked state of my mind. I woke up this morning with Cain. I remember the weight of his left arm resting across my shoulder, his right under the pillow, the contours of his face boyish in sleep. My thoughts linger on the scars on his body, punishment, violence, and an operation for appendicitis. And yet I am in awe that he is so undamaged. Not bitter or resentful.

I rub my face and shake myself out of contemplation, aware I could spend the rest of the day thinking about Cain if I allowed myself to do so.

I open my laptop and force my attention back to my manuscript. I write Justine Dwyer into the narrative. I had been planning to avoid reference to the police because it requires specialist knowledge about how they do things. But I suppose, now, I'm acquiring that expertise, whether I like it or not. I sketch out my policewoman, ambitious, dedicated, by-the-book, but human. Her face is, despite the training, open and animated. She smiles when she says hello. She has a husband who likes to paint fantasy figurines, and three Siamese cats.

The afternoon crawls into evening with me listening for Cain's call. My pulse jumps when the doorman's buzzer goes off. "There are two people for you, Miss Kincaid. They claim to be friends of yours. A Mr. Whit Metters and Ms. Marigold Anastas. Shall I send them up or call the police?"

"Please send them up…Chris." I finally remember the occasional doorman's name. It comes out a little too loud as it breaks through the failure in my memory. I grimace, hoping it isn't too blatantly obvious.

"What's going on?" Marigold asks as I open the door. "Why is the Gestapo checking everyone who comes into the Carrington?"

I bring them in and tell them about the call, and the text messages sent from Cain's old phone.

Whit puts his arm around me. "Are you all right?"

I nod. "The last time this happened, it was your door, and then you were attacked—"

"Where is Cain?" Marigold asks.

"I don't know. He was going to call me as soon as he'd bought a new phone, but I haven't heard from him."

Whit and Marigold glance at each other, and I see something unspoken and tentative pass between them.

"Perhaps he just lost your number," Whit says vaguely.

"I wonder why Cain didn't mention it was his mother who called the police," Marigold says slowly, "why he didn't mention that she was there?"

"How did you know that?" I ask sharply. I have not yet mentioned what Justine Dwyer told me.

"Marigold looked up the court records and read them," Whit says wearily. I can't tell if it is the reading of legal records per se, or their subject, about which he most disapproves.

I stare at her.

"Don't look at me like that," she says. "I couldn't understand how he could go to jail for defending himself—I thought I might find something that might help him."

"Something that his lawyers missed?" I challenge.

Marigold smiles faintly. "Have I mentioned that I am something of a genius?"

I refuse to allow her to lighten the discussion. "Cain's mother locked herself in her room while he was being attacked—perhaps he didn't want us to think badly of her."

"No, he locked her in and hid the key before his stepfather got home," Marigold says calmly. "He said he knew the mood his stepfather was in and was afraid his mother would try to protect him and take the brunt of it herself. They both claimed that Officer Manners was violent."

"What do you mean *claimed*?" I'm getting angry now. "Of course he was violent."

Marigold grabs my hand. "Of course. I didn't mean..." She takes a deep breath. "Look, Freddie, I decided to look up Cain's defence attorney in the hope they might be able to tell us why he was dealt with so harshly. According to the records, his attorney was Jean Le Marque from a firm called Hockey Cole."

"So did you find her?"

Again Marigold's eyes meet Whit's. "Eventually. It took a bit of digging."

"Well."

"Jean Le Marque still practises law, but she married and took her husband's name. She's now Jean Metters."

I choke, turning immediately to Whit. "Your mother? Cain's lawyer was your mother?" I stand up, too agitated to remain still.

Whit doesn't say anything.

"Yes, Whit's mom." Marigold answers for him. "It's another thing Cain didn't mention."

"Neither did Whit's mom."

Again it's Marigold, not Whit, who responds. "It was fifteen years ago, Freddie. He was one of thousands of cases she's defended, and Cain's changed his name. It's understandable she might not recognise him. It's a little harder to believe he'd have no idea who she was."

"What are you saying?"

Marigold looks up at me as I pace. "It makes you wonder if us all meeting in the BPL the way we did—Cain and Whit anyway—whether it was really just a coincidence."

I feel like I'm reeling. The bus has crashed.

"Did you speak to Whit's mom?" I ask finally.

Whit shakes his head. "No. If she gets a sniff of who Cain is, she'll have him arrested for stabbing me."

"He didn't—"

"I know. I don't think he did," Whit says firmly. Too firmly. He's telling Marigold, who is obviously not so sure. I am outraged by her inconstancy.

"Don't hate me, Freddie," she pleads. "I love Cain, you know I do. I simply don't understand why he didn't tell us any of this. Whit's mom was his lawyer, for fuck's sake! But he didn't say a thing."

I sit down and, for a moment, struggle for reasons. In the end I shrug. "I don't know. Cain wanted to put that part of his life behind him. Perhaps he thought that since Whit's mom didn't recognise him, there was no point raising it. Or maybe he didn't recognise her either."

Whit comes to my aid. "Mom's had a bit of work done in the last five years. I've heard Dad say she looks more like the cat than the woman he married."

I smile faintly, gratefully. Whit is still on Cain's side. It settles me a little and I think more clearly. Justine had not mentioned this. She'd told me about the connection between Caroline Palfrey and Cain but not this. "Do the police know?"

"Not as far as we know," Marigold says. "They would presumably be protecting Whit's mom if they'd worked it out." She swallows. "We haven't mentioned it."

"Why?"

"Honestly," Marigold says, rubbing a hand through the razor cut of her hair, "because Whit won't let me."

"I think we should speak to Cain first." Whit sits back, relaxed. "Maybe this is a coincidence. They do happen."

"They do," I say uncertainly.

"You hear about it all the time," Whit continues. "Twins separated at birth who end up living on the same street."

Marigold regards us both dubiously. "You're not helping Cain by refusing to acknowledge the obvious, you know."

"I'm not denying the facts, just the conclusion." I appeal to the Marigold who was sure that the four of us were special, that our friendship was one for the ages, a destiny in itself. "You can't think that Cain is capable of murder."

"No, I don't," she replies urgently. "But I also know my judgement is not infallible. Cain is charming and funny and handsome, but so was Ted Bundy."

"Bundy!" I am shocked by the comparison. "You think Cain is a serial killer?"

Marigold sighs. "No," she says patiently. "Not necessarily. I only mean that you can't judge guilt or innocence by whether a person is likeable or not. Sociopaths are often charming; they know how to make you love them. But they don't operate by the same rules—they don't feel remorse or guilt, they know how to manipulate people and situations."

I groan. This is ridiculous. "Cain spent seven years in jail for defending himself. That hardly seems to be the result of a master manipulation!"

"What do you want us to do?" Whit asks me quietly. "I'm happy to go with your instincts on this, Freddie."

I shake my head. "I know that this doesn't look good, but there will be an explanation. Whatever's going on, it's not Cain." My voice sounds loud, even to me. I recognise an underlying uncertainty in the volume, in the intractability of my declaration. And it terrifies me that I might be beginning to doubt Cain, and yet, I know I'm in love with him.

It's Marigold who breaks the silence that follows. "Okay," she says. "That's how we'll proceed." She smiles, loyal and warm again. "I'm starving. Have you eaten?"

I shake my head, set off-balance by her sudden retreat.

"I'll fix us something. Do you mind if I poke about in your kitchen?"

"No, of course not. Can I help—"

She shakes her head. "You don't want to be in the same room when I cook. It's not pretty."

And so Marigold thumps around my kitchen while Whit and I sit in the living room. I direct him to the bottle of port on my bookshelf, and he distributes drinks. Marigold hums as she continues to clatter and thump.

"Where do you think Cain is?" Whit asks me. "Do you want to go look for him?"

"I'd have no idea where to start," I reply, realising that above everything I am worried about Cain. His physical safety rather than any threat of prosecution. I have no right to expect he would call, except that he said he would. I smile at Whit, still grateful for his support, his trust in Cain. "I think I'm better waiting here for him."

Whit nods. "What about if I drive to his place after dinner? Have a look around for any sign of him. I'll call if I find him."

I reach out and grab his hand. "Thank you."

———

Dear Hannah,

Are you setting up for Whit to pick up the pieces of Freddie's broken heart? But what about Marigold! Say it isn't so!

Seriously, my friend, crime novels should observe a general morality. Characters should reap what they sow. Freddie has chosen to fall in love with a murderer—she's done this knowingly. She should suffer the consequences. I can't help thinking that having Whit waiting in the wings is cheating. Perhaps my namesake is right and we are all writing romance. All the rules of fair play in love tell me that Freddie should not be able to be saved from her own choice.

There's an increased police presence in the streets over here at the moment—in response to the protests, I think, rather than the recent spate of murders by people other than the police. Tedious outrage about the natural order of things. Citizens in masks and police in number. It's a very strange new world. It makes me melancholy at times and, at others, exhilarated.

I understand that it's still before Christmas for Freddie and co, Virus Eve, if you like, but I really think you're making a mistake. Although you started this story before the end game began, it seems such a waste not to take inspiration from the new order, not to have this book take place a little later so that you can bring in the ambient fear and the denial of our times. If you ask me, the current state of the world is the ideal cloak for a man of Cain's proclivities, the perfect cover for death delivered in other ways. And perhaps it will make Freddie's complicity more relatable—after all what are a couple more bodies? I know you want to tell a story about friendship, love, and suspicion, that you don't want Freddie's bus to stop for the pandemic, but I say let the virus drive!

And tell Freddie to stop flirting with Whit!

Yours,

Leo

CHAPTER TWENTY-FIVE

Marigold serves up pizza made with flatbread rather than dough. Unable to find a pizza tray, she uses an ordinary oven tray and so the pie is rectangular, but it is delicious. We eat it with salad and wine, talking about ordinary things and feeling the absence of Cain's voice in our party... We are, as a group, off-kilter, out of balance. As we wash up, Whit mentions that he's going to look for Cain.

I can see that Marigold wants to go with him.

"Take Marigold with you," I suggest. "You've only just recovered. I'd feel better knowing she was with you."

"What about you?" Marigold asks.

"I'll be fine. I'm going to work and wait for Cain to call."

Marigold wavers, but I insist. "Go."

"You know that what I said before doesn't mean I don't care about—"

"Of course I know. Now go away and let me get back to work."

"We'll find him," Marigold says earnestly. I embrace her because she needs to know that there are no hard feelings.

And there aren't. Everything Marigold said was rational and sensible and well meant. I may have lost my heart to Cain, but I haven't lost my mind.

I get back to work and try to get my bus back onto the road. My concentration is ragged, and now, alone in the quiet, I am able to at least acknowledge the fear that I have been taken for a ride, that I've been an infatuated fool. For a while I cry, frustrated, humiliated, and scared that it doesn't change how much I still long for Cain.

Preoccupied with my own misery, I barely register the call alert on my computer at first. I'm not sure why I check it—the last thing I want to do is to speak to someone, but I do open the app. The profile has no name or picture, but I can see now that the same number has attempted to connect with me three times. I accept the call and Cain's face appears on screen. He's outside. Somewhere reasonably well-lit because I can see him, the tree behind him, the people in the distant background.

"Freddie! Thank God." His expression changes. "You're crying. Oh, Freddie, I'm so sorry."

"You didn't call," I blurt, aware of how pathetic the words sound.

"Freddie, listen to me. The police tried to arrest me this morning after I left your place."

"What do you mean *tried*?"

"I guess I'm a fugitive. I couldn't call you in case they'd bugged your phone."

"Why are they trying to arrest you?"

"They think I killed Caroline Palfrey and stabbed Whit." He takes a deep breath. "Apparently, Caroline was the granddaughter of the judge who sentenced me. I didn't know that, Freddie. I swear I didn't know."

"And Whit's mother?"

He's clearly startled. "I recognised her at the hospital, but she didn't seem to know me. I couldn't say anything without telling you all everything, and so I said nothing." He closes his eyes. "That was a mistake."

"Cain, what are you doing? You can't run from the police."

"I need to figure out what's going on, Freddie. Someone's setting me up—as soon as I figure out who, and why, I promise, I'll turn myself in."

I need to ask. "Cain, why did you lock your mother in her room?"

He blinks. "Because I expected my stepfather to give me a hiding that night, and I knew she would try to stop him, and then he'd beat the hell out of her. I was trying to protect her."

"She called the police."

"To save me, not him."

I pull myself together. "What can I do?"

He smiles wearily. "I don't know. I don't know what *I* can do."

"Who would want to do this to you Cain? Someone from when you were in prison?"

"As far as I know, I didn't make any enemies. I kept my head down for the most part."

"What about the man who stabbed you?"

"He's dead, Freddie."

I don't ask Cain where he is, but I tell him that Whit and Marigold are out looking for him.

"They know about all this?" he asks.

"Yes. They were just here…Whit's completely on your side."

"But not Marigold?"

"She thinks that you and Whit happening to meet on the day Caroline Palfrey was killed is too much of a coincidence."

Cain says nothing for several beats and then, "She's right." He looks directly at the camera so I can see his eyes. "Freddie, I swear, I didn't know who Whit was until I met his mother at the hospital."

And I believe him. Because I'm in love with him, and I don't want to believe I could love a murderer, but mostly just because I believe him.

I'm crying again because this is so impossible. "My God, Cain, what are we going to do?"

Cain waits for me to be ready. "Do you think you could find out what you can about Caroline Palfrey?" he asks in the end. "This all began with her…with her scream. If we can figure about who might want to kill her, perhaps—"

"Of course. I'll find out what I can." I have no idea how, but that's irrelevant. I'll work it out. "That day when we all heard Caroline scream, did you just happen to go to the library?"

"I use the library fairly regularly." He frowns as he tries to recall. "That day, I came in particularly to look through a book they'd sourced for me. One of the librarians had called me that morning to say it was in."

"And was it?"

"No, actually. When I came in they couldn't find it. I went to the Reading Room while they tried to track it down. What are you thinking?"

"If the fact that you and Whit were in the Reading Room when Caroline screamed was not a coincidence, then someone must have organised for you both to be there."

Cain exhales. "You're right. Maybe someone brought Whit to the BPL too."

"Where are you going to sleep tonight, Cain?"

He smiles. "I have somewhere to sleep, Freddie. Don't worry about me...I'll be fine."

I don't ask him where. I need to be able to say I don't know where he is.

"There's a nine o'clock feature at The Brattle tomorrow," he says. "I'll watch for you."

"Isn't that risky?"

"If you don't see me it's because I've spotted a cop."

I nod, already looking forward to seeing him, to being able to touch him. "What are you going to do, Cain? Tomorrow, I mean."

"I'm going to see if anyone knows anything about Boo—who might have killed him, who may have had a grudge. There's something that connects all of this...some reason for it all. I just have to find it."

"Is there anything I can bring you tomorrow?"

He looks embarrassed. "I can't use any of my cards with the police watching for—"

I cut him off before he has to ask. "No problem...I have a pile of cash I haven't banked."

He grimaces. "I'm sorry, Freddie."

"Don't be." I smile. "A late-night tryst with a desperate fugitive—what writer worth her salt wouldn't give her eye teeth for that kind of material?"

He laughs. "Your manuscript frightens me a little. How's it shaping up?"

For a few minutes we talk about my work in a way that is surreal for its ordinariness. He says good night quietly, warning me to be careful. And when the screen closes, I sit for a while, feeling wrapped in him, savouring this sensation, the warm intensity of it, despite the circumstances. I'm a little surprised by the totality of my trust in Cain McLeod, my conviction that he is innocent. The writer in me observes my own reactions with a kind of distance. Is this faith based on instinct, a judgement of Cain's character? It makes sense that I would love a man I believe in, surely. But does being in love compromise that judgement? It's a bit of a chicken and egg argument—unanswerable and pointless. The fact is that I believe Cain, and I'm in love with him. There may be a causal link between the two, but that would not make either any less true.

I pull an unused Japanese notebook from the shelf above the writer's desk in the drawing room. The pages of the notebook are made of a single sheet, concertina-folded. I generally use them after the novel is written, to map out the narrative so that I can see the whole story in a glance and make sure that those threads that need tying up are in fact tied up. Now I plot everything I know from before and since the scream, drawing lines of connection between events and people. Lines between Cain and Boo, Cain and Caroline, Cain and Whit, Whit and Caroline, Marigold and Whit. It begins to resemble one of Cain's story webs.

Beside the details of the night Boo attacked Cain, I draw a box, and into it I write in what I can recall of what Boo said. The words which have set seed in my mind. "Does she know what you've done?" He must have been talking about Cain killing his stepfather. I hadn't known then, of course. And there was something else—what was it? He said "I've done it again" or words to that effect. I remember that Cain said once that Boo slept near the Boston Public Library. Could he have killed Caroline?

It's possible, I guess, but while he might have struck out as he did the night he hit Cain with a bottle, I can't see him committing careful murder, one in which he managed to hide the body and himself in a matter of seconds. And how would Boo have known about Whit's mother, or orchestrated the presence of Whit and Cain in the Reading Room?

I find myself pondering Marigold. Is she somehow connected to Cain's past as well, or is she, like me, a random bystander who happened to choose a seat beside impending turmoil? I think about Marigold's determination that the four of us were destined to be friends, her offer to help Cain research Isaac Harmon, and the manner in which she's researched Cain himself. And a little part of me begins to wonder. Could her interest be more than a natural exuberant nosiness? The thought makes me feel disloyal. No. If Marigold, too, is connected to Cain, then she, like the men, was manipulated into being in the Reading Room that day.

I open the notebook I was using back then and glance over my first notes of Handsome Man, Heroic Chin, and Freud Girl. And there it is. A speculation that Heroic Chin was stalking Freud Girl or vice versa. I force myself to relax, deciding to trust that first instinct: Marigold was in the library because she'd followed Whit, taken a seat near him in the hope a conversation, a friendship, perhaps a relationship would begin. It had worked, in part.

It's late. I should go to bed, probably to lie awake and toss and turn and think, but at least in a bed. I notice the folded piece of paper that has been slipped under my front door. It's from Leo, a note that hopes that I'm over the shock of the text messages and that I feel safe, written with his usual charm, his old-world thoughtfulness. He offers a sympathetic ear and red wine, should I need to talk.

Instead, I call my parents. We are no longer the type of family that has long conversations about the meaning of life or the meaning of anything at all. A strange detachment set in after Geraldine died. It's not that we don't love each other—we do—but that our lives don't seem particularly entwined or reliant on one another anymore. We never bother to tell each other about hopes or dreams, nor do we ever touch upon disappointments and fears. Our conversations stay in that safe, removed middle ground, and we talk to each other like someone is listening. They ask about the weather, I tell them about the cold. They mention they've bought a new car, and I enquire about make, model, and colour. There's comfort in the banality of the conversation. Like the ticking of a clock, metered and unchanged by the mayhem into which it sounds.

Dear Hannah,

She's giving him money? To quote my friend Marigold, CHRIST on a bike! With respect to your request, fair enough. I do know what you look like. I have for years because, of course, you're famous! But it is probably time to even the scales. I have attached what is referred to in modern parlance as a selfie, taken in all my masked glory. The baseball cap adds a certain redneck chic and, according to the American film industry, makes the wearer invisible. I like to think of this as my bank-robbing outfit.

Please send the next chapter forthwith!

Yours,
Leo

CHAPTER TWENTY-SIX

I am at Leo's door, though it's not yet eight in the morning.

He answers in his jogging gear. "Freddie! What a pleasant surprise. Come on in."

I step inside and begin as he fetches mugs and pours coffee. "Leo, I need your help."

"Well, of course. What can I do you for?"

"Do you remember when you took me to Magazine Park? There was a journalist there taking photos—"

"Lauren."

"Yes. She works for the *Rag*, doesn't she?"

"Yes, ma'am, she does."

"I was wondering if you could introduce me."

"To Lauren? Why?"

I inhale slightly and begin the story I've prepared. "Caroline Palfrey worked on the *Rag*. I've decided to write a piece on her murder for a paper back home—an 'Australian in America' type piece. I thought someone who worked with her might be able to tell me a little about her."

"Why do you need to know about Caroline for a piece about your experiences in the U.S.?"

"Because being in the library, hearing her scream changed everything about my time here. I want to use her as a symbol of America at its most aspirational cut down by the violence which runs through it." I hold my breath, hoping that it sounds plausible enough.

Leo nods slowly. "Is your novel not going well?"

"It's stalled a bit. I'm hoping writing this article might unblock me a little… And a decent newspaper feature will give me a profile as a writer."

He shrugs. "It's not a dumb idea."

"The only problem is I don't have an *in* of any sort. I want to write Caroline as a real person rather than just a victim—and to do that, I need to know who she really was."

Leo studies me, and I hope the guilt doesn't show. It's not that I think he won't help me if I tell him the truth—I'm reasonably sure he would. And then he, too, would be involved. While I am more than willing to risk my own freedom in helping Cain, it would not be fair to drag Leo into this.

"So I was hoping you might be able to ask Lauren if she'd be willing to talk to me."

"Yes, ma'am, I guess I could. And I reckon she'd talk to you. You might need to talk to her too, though. She'll probably be real interested in what you heard at the library."

"Sure, that seems fair," I reply, confident that I can tell her enough without compromising Cain.

"I'll give her a call."

I smile sheepishly. "I don't suppose you could call her now?"

"What? Right this minute?"

I nod. "The muse," I explain. "I want to begin before she leaves in a huff."

Grinning, he picks up his phone. "Lauren? It's Leo. I'm sorry to call so early… What are you doing this morning?… I have a friend I'd like you to meet. We thought we might take you for breakfast. Sure…you choose the place. The Friendly Toast? Yes, ma'am. Nine o'clock? We'll see you there."

He hangs up with a triumphant flourish.

"Thank you, Leo. I won't forget this."

"It was a phone call, Freddie."

"Still, thank you."

He checks his watch. "Go grab your coat. We'd better head off."

The Friendly Toast is a popular breakfast venue in Back Bay. The decor is modern, the colour scheme primary. Lauren Penfold is already there when we arrive. She is dressed casually, jeans, a fisherman's sweater, and a knit cap over long, dark hair. A khaki down jacket hangs over the back of her chair. She smiles, kisses Leo's cheek, and shakes my hand warmly. Leo introduces me in grand fashion as the embodiment of all Australia's literary hopes and the holder of the Sinclair Fellowship. I tell Lauren to ignore him and call me Freddie. We order French toast on Lauren's urging, and I tell her about my interest in Caroline Palfrey, and its fabricated cause.

"I thought you guys might be able to help each other," Leo says. "Lauren, Freddie met the homeless man who was murdered near the boathouse, and you could tell her about Caroline."

I'm a little startled by this barter on my behalf, but I keep that to myself.

"Sure," Lauren says. "What do you want to know?"

"What kind of stories did Caroline write for the *Rag*?"

Lauren rolls her eyes. "Caroline was a serious feature writer...fancied herself a future contender for a Pulitzer."

"Was she working on anything in particular?"

"Some secret project with Whit Metters...though I'm not sure they were exactly simpatico."

Whit? "What do you mean?"

"She was a lot more serious about it than he was. But then, Whit's not really serious about anything." Lauren's smile broadens unconsciously when she says his name.

"They were an item for a while, weren't they?" I venture tentatively.

"Yes, but I think Caroline was too ambitious for Whit." She lowers her voice. "Whit's a bit of a slut. There were always half a dozen girls calling the *Rag* looking for him. Occasionally, he'd pretend he was with Caroline to get rid of them... Some of them were a bit crazy."

I don't react, and Leo does not give me away, though he knows that Whit is my Heroic Chin, that he is my friend. And for his discretion I'm grateful. "Do you know who these girls were?"

Lauren snorts. "You'll have to ask Whit, though I can't guarantee he'll know their names. He's one of those guys that has groupies. Some kind of animal magnetism, I suppose—the boy that puppies follow home."

"Do you think Caroline might still have had feelings for Whit?"

"I doubt it..." She stops and reconsiders. "Maybe. She was always bailing him out of trouble."

"What kind of trouble?"

"Just stupid things. Whit was always trying some mad scheme or other…
nearly got kicked off the *Rag* I don't know how many times. Caroline would
stick up for him, talk the editor into giving him another chance."

"So they were good friends, at least?" I ask, perplexed that Whit would
keep this from us.

"I guess." Lauren grimaces. "I didn't really hang out with either of them.
Caroline was a bit stuck-up, and Whit was barely around…which is why we
found ourselves taking messages from the poor girls who imagined it was
true love."

"Can you think of anyone who might have wanted to kill Caroline?"
Leo asks. "Would any of these girls have—?"

"Killed Caroline? For Whit?" She raises her brow sceptically. "Who
knows? The heart wants what it wants, I suppose."

I'm jarred by the memory of Marigold using those exact words. But
there is also a growing sense that this means something, that it could lead
somewhere. "Have the police spoken to you about this, Lauren?"

"Not this specifically," she replies, regarding me sharply. "They wanted
to know what Caroline was working on for the *Rag*, whether there was a
story on drug cartels or something that might have got her killed. They
spoke to Whit directly, but I can't imagine he told them he was a player and
Caroline was his front."

Harshly put. "You don't like Whit Metters?"

Lauren shrugs. "I felt a little sorry for some of the girls."

It's my turn to answer questions now. I tell Lauren about Boo, what he
looked like, the way he talked, his volatility, that he slept near the Boston
Public Library, though I wasn't sure exactly where. I leave out mention of
Cain. Again, Leo must realise this, but he doesn't call me on the omission.

Lauren takes notes. She and Leo talk about the boathouse, the details of
the crime scene, which he clearly remembers better than I.

"So what exactly are you writing, Lauren?" Leo asks in the end.

"A cautionary riches-to-rags story," she says. "Shaun Jacobs, more
recently known as Boo, was a doctor—a surgeon—once. He started taking
painkillers, which became a full-blown habit. Lost everything, kicked the
addiction in prison only to return to it and ended up a corpse on the banks
of the Charles."

"Freddie?" Leo is looking at me. "Are you okay? You've just gone white."

"Yes…I'm fine." I scramble for composure. "I think I might have had a few too many coffees today." It's nonsense, of course. I could mainline coffee with no reaction. I smile. "It sounds like a great story, Lauren. It could be a book, really."

She frowns.

"Of course I only write novels," I add hastily, in case she thinks I might steal the idea.

Leo scoffs. "I admit it'll make a great article. A surgeon's fall from grace...but a book? Where's the romance, the sexual tension?"

Lauren laughs, and any territorial awkwardness passes. We finish breakfast, and I try not to be noticeably quiet, though I am preoccupied with what I've learned. I need to be alone to think about it properly, when I can allow what I feel to show without fear of being found out.

It's nearly eleven by the time we return to Carrington Square and another half hour before I can take my leave of Leo without appearing rude or ungrateful.

I bolt the door, let out all the breath in my lungs, and then gasp for air. Shaun Jacobs was a surgeon. Could he have been the surgeon who stabbed Cain? Surely Cain's past could not include two fallen surgeons? Maybe I'm wrong...perhaps surgeons are predisposed to criminality. Maybe it's not unusual to find them in prisons assaulting fellow inmates. But if it was Boo, why did Cain leave that out? Why would he not mention that?

I put on a pot of coffee, more because I need to do something, slow down my thoughts with something ordinary. I find the Japanese notebook in which I tried to plot what was happening earlier, and turn to my notes on the night Cain and I encountered Shaun Jacobs. I close my eyes—it's still vivid in my memory. Cain remained so calm throughout. Surely he wouldn't have been if he knew the man was capable of plunging a knife into his back.

I think about Cain's scar. I can almost feel it under my fingers. Raised, no more than two inches wide, and perfectly straight. A clean wound, precisely placed, and healed without infection. And in the exact place that Whit was stabbed.

I shake my head. Why would Shaun Jacobs stab Whit? I'm overthinking this. It's just a coincidence.

I return to my laptop and spend a couple of hours going over what I've already written, correcting typos, inserting missing words and, of course, commas. It makes me feel like I'm doing something useful without demanding a great deal by way of concentration. It works, in part.

Marigold calls by at about three.

Her face is flushed, her eyes bright and her smile contagious.

"What happened?" I ask, smiling too. "What have you won?"

"Nothing...everything." She grabs my hands and pulls me towards the couch to sit with her.

I laugh, happy for her, though I have no idea why she is so happy. "What's going on, Marigold?"

"You know Whit and I went looking for Cain last night."

"Did you find him?"

"Of course not. We would have called."

"This is a lot of joy for a failed quest."

"Freddie, Whit and I, well we... He came back to my place afterwards."

"Oh."

Suddenly we're teenagers, and Marigold is telling me about a first kiss, the incomparable exhilaration of love returned, and the glory of the often imagined, taking flesh. And she is so, so happy. For a while I'm swept away in the flood of her excitement.

"You and Whit?"

She nods vigorously.

"That's wonderful." In the back of my mind I can hear Lauren Penfold telling me about the girls who would ring for Whit. The broken hearts who called the *Rag*, to be pitied by his colleagues. But who am I to sow doubt into Marigold's happiness?

I listen as she tells me the details of her evening, every loaded glance and utterance that ended with her and Whit in each other's arms. I am drawn in by her guileless elation. Marigold holds nothing back, reserves nothing for caution or dignity. Surely Whit can see this, surely he is a charmed by it as I am. Surely this unmitigated love of hers will not lead to disaster.

"Where is Whit?" I ask when her praise of him finally slows long enough for me to get a word in.

"He went looking for Cain again." She shrugs. "He wanted to go alone. Said I should check on you."

I want to tell Marigold it's okay, that Cain has called me and he's alive, and for the moment safe, but I don't. I'm pretty sure I'm aiding and abetting a fugitive, or at least I will be. There's no need for Marigold and Whit to break the law too—yet, anyway. So I say nothing.

"Has Cain called you?" Marigold asks.

"My phone hasn't rung all day."

"Oh, Freddie, I'm so sorry. Men can be bastards!"

I change the subject. "Marigold, that day at the library, when we all first met…"

"When Caroline was killed?"

"Yes. Why were you there? Honestly?"

"What do you mean?"

"Did you just happen to come to the library that day?"

Marigold blushes. "I suppose it doesn't matter now. I followed Whit." She hugs a cushion in front of her as she confesses. "I was following him…"

"You were stalking him?"

"No…well, maybe… I was trying to run into him." She swallows. "I followed him to the Reading Room and sat down opposite him, hoping that he'd talk to me or that I'd have a reason to talk to him."

"And then Caroline screamed."

"Yes. We might never have spoken to each other if not for that."

"Do you know why Whit was in the Reading Room that day?"

Marigold shakes her head. "I don't know… Maybe he was working on a story for the *Rag*. I've never known him to go to the BPL before. I remember being surprised when he went that way."

I tap my finger on the arm of the couch. Could Whit, too, have been lured to the Reading Room that day? But it was more than that. Whit and Cain were sitting beside each other.

"Marigold, do you remember if Cain was already there when you arrived or if he sat down after the two of you did?"

She frowns and then shakes her head. "I don't remember, Freddie. I know you arrived last and spent a lot of time looking at the ceiling."

I smile, recalling how this all started.

"Why do you ask?"

"I'm trying to work out if it was a coincidence that Whit and Cain ran into each other…or if someone orchestrated it."

"How might they orchestrate it?"

"They could ask both Whit and Cain to meet them there, for example," I reply vaguely.

"But why?"

"I don't really know. But I'm a writer. I mistrust coincidence as an explanation for anything,"

Marigold concedes. "We can ask Whit at dinner tonight."

"Dinner?"

"Yes. Whit says there's an amazing Dominican restaurant in Roxbury, so we thought we'd go tonight. We can check on Cain's apartment again while we're there."

"I can't come," I say firmly.

"Why not?"

"You and Whit."

"What do you mean?"

"You've just discovered each other. I'm not going to be a third wheel."

"But we can't leave you on your own!"

"Marigold, I'm fine. I have work to do, and there's a chance that Cain will come here. I want to be here in case he does."

Marigold's looks at me sympathetically. "Honey, you can't sit here waiting for Cain forever."

I laugh. "It's one night, not forever. Don't get me wrong, Marigold. I'm so happy for you and Whit, but I really don't want to come tonight. You should have some time together."

She studies me intently, and for a moment I think she's going to continue her crusade to have me join them. But she relents. "You'll say if you change your mind?"

"I promise."

"Okay…I have a favour to ask." She looks embarrassed. "Could I borrow a dress? I don't own one, and I thought I should wear a dress tonight…just because…I could buy one but—"

I grab her hand to stop her blithering. "Of course. But Marigold, you don't have to wear a dress. Whit clearly likes the way you look."

"I want him to know that I can look less…out of place," she says earnestly, and I am reminded that she is only twenty-three.

"I'm sure he's beguiled with the fact that you don't look like everybody else, but if it makes you feel any better, my wardrobe is your wardrobe."

Marigold spends the next hour trying on everything I own in various combinations. In the end she chooses my most conservative wool skirt suit. I rarely wear it myself, reserving it for job interviews. Paired with Marigold's close-cropped hair and body piercings, the tattoos visible at her collarbone, it's strikingly incongruent but strangely alluring.

"I can say with absolute certainty that this outfit has never looked so good on me."

"I feel like a princess," Marigold says, swirling.

She actually looks more like an edgy librarian, but if she feels like a princess, fair enough.

"Are you sure you won't come?" she asks at the door.

"Absolutely sure. You two have fun."

———

My dear Hannah,

I'm embarrassed. How could I ever have questioned the moral integrity of your work? I'm very happy for Marigold and a little jealous of Whit. This last chapter was what I call the "yes, of course" moment. Yes, of course Whit is in love with Marigold. How could he not be? It all seems more real now. I should never have doubted you.

With my abject apologies,
Leo

PS—"calls by" is an Australianism. Americans would say "drops in."

PPS—I note you've aged Marigold a bit to account for her being a postgraduate.

CHAPTER TWENTY-SEVEN

It's only after Marigold has gone that I think about the police. Detective Dwyer saw Cain leave my apartment. If they're looking for him, they'll be watching Carrington Square.

I curse. I now want so badly to see Cain. But I know that if I leave at eight thirty for The Brattle, they'll follow me straight to Cain. That can't happen. There's no way I can leave Carrington Square without being seen, but perhaps if I were not here, if I was leaving from somewhere else. I step into the bathroom for a three-minute grooming. Teeth, a hasty check that my hair is not too unruly and a smear of lip gloss. From my bedroom I grab the nearly five hundred dollars in cash stashed in my sock drawer—cash I exchanged before I moved to the U.S. but somehow never used—and slip it into the inside pocket of my navy overcoat. Gloves, scarf, wallet. I glance at the Boston Red Sox cap hanging on the coat rack and think fleetingly of all the recent American films in which a character is rendered invisible by donning a baseball cap. Would that it were true. But I suspect it might be slightly more difficult than that to ensure I'm not followed. I leave my phone behind because I'm not sure if it can be used by the police to track me.

Leo comes out of his door as I'm heading for the stairs. "Freddie, hello. Where are you off to?"

I smile and wait for him to catch up. "I'm going shopping."

"Retail therapy? Excellent. I'll come with you."

"No, you can't!"

Leo pulls back, clearly startled by the force with which I refused his offer.

"I'm shopping for underwear. It's the kind of thing a girl does best alone."

"You're going to spend the entire evening shopping for panties?"

"I'm very particular. And there are also items of corsetry…they need to be fitted. It's not an expedition suited to company."

He holds up his hands in surrender. "Well, then I wish you a successful quest." He pauses. "How's your article coming?"

"Article?"

"On Caroline Palfrey?"

"Oh, yes…okay, I think. I need a break from it…and I need underwear…So two birds."

"Well, let me know if you need a proofreader."

"I will." I feel suddenly guilty about brushing him off. "I need to thank you properly for introducing me to Lauren… Let me take you out for lunch on Saturday."

He smiles. "I'd be delighted to break bread with you anytime, Freddie, but you've already thanked me, and it was no big thing anyway."

"You really are a lovely man, Leo. Let's do Saturday. We'll discuss the progress of our respective romance manuscripts."

He turns to walk back to his door. "Be careful, Freddie. I don't need to tell you there's a murderer on the loose."

I leave Carrington Square aware of the police car parked across the street. I presume there are a couple of officers on foot somewhere too. I have with me a backpack. It contains the change of clothes Cain left in my apartment, which I'd laundered the day before, an extra muffler, a razor, some basic toiletries, and several bars of chocolate.

I try not to be self-conscious and head for the Back Bay subway station on Dartmouth. At this time it's particularly busy with people heading home at the end of the workday or coming downtown for dinner. I spend a few minutes browsing in the small shops outside the front entrance. I purchase a couple of apples from the tiny vegetable market and generally merge into the concentration of people. I stop to give money to one of the street people hanging about the station. He thanks me and I wonder if Cain ever begged here. I feel guilty as I walk on because I'm walking on, because I don't know what else to do.

Slipping back into the crowd past the Amtrak depot, I pick up my pace. My Charlie card is in my hand ready to tap at the ticket gates. I spot my tail. Middle-aged, a little portly, leather jacket. He's about twenty feet behind me and has had to abandon keeping out of sight in order to keep up with me. My heart is pounding. There's something about being followed, even when you know the person in pursuit means you no harm, that makes you want to run. I suppress the instinct because increasing my pace will only draw attention and make me more visible. I step onto the escalators and descend to the Orange Line subway tracks. The platform is packed as I make my way into the middle of the press of people. Still, I catch sight of Portly Leather Jacket pounding down the escalators. I wait until a train pulls into the platform, until his eyes are fixed on those boarding; I take off my coat and run up the stairs and leave the station entirely via the bus depot. From there I make a dash for the Copley subway station. I think I'm clear, but to be on the safe side, I hop onto the next train from the Green Line.

It's difficult to keep the smile off my face. I just shook a police tail! It's absurd, but I feel proud.

I alight at Park Street Station and transfer to the Red Line, getting off again at Harvard Square.

The Brattle is busy. The nine o'clock feature is *An Affair to Remember*. The theatre is full of couples of every age. It feels a little strange to be walking in alone. I take my popcorn, trying hard not to look around for Cain, and find a seat in an unpopular row. I remove my coat and place it onto the seat next to me, hoping nobody will object. Nobody does. I suppose lots of couples meet at the theatre. And I wait. The house lights dim.

"Do you mind if I sit here?"

It's all I can do not to leap out of my seat and throw my arms around Cain. He picks up my coat and sits down. My hand is in his, and his lips are on mine as the opening credits roll. "We'll slip out in about half an hour," he whispers into my ear. I nod, happy to be near him again. My questions will wait. Here in the dark anonymity of the theatre I feel hidden and safe.

About forty minutes into the film, Cain and I make our way out into the dazzling light of The Brattle's foyer. He helps me on with my coat, takes the backpack for me, and we walk up the steps into Brattle Street. The night is cold and damp. Cain still has my hand.

"Come on, I know somewhere we can talk."

Zoe's is on Mass Avenue about half a mile from the Brattle. Large and busy. Rows of booths with red vinyl upholstery, a dozen waiters and wait-resses, extensive menus. We take one of the inside booths, away from the window. Cain orders a burger; I choose a bagel with cream cheese. We're blandly pleasant in our conversation with the waitress, giving her nothing of note to remember. The food arrives almost immediately with bottomless cups of coffee and a jug of water.

Under the bright lights of the diner, Cain looks weary. I reach across the table and lace the fingers of my right hand with those of his left. For a few beats we just look at each other. I start.

"Are you okay? You look exhausted."

He smiles. "I didn't sleep well. But I'm fine."

I resist asking him where he slept. I tell him about Lauren Penfold and Caroline's work on the *Rag*. "She and Whit were working on a joint project, apparently. He seems to have known her better than I thought."

"It might explain why the police interrogated him initially." He frowns. "I wonder if that's why he was stabbed. Could they have been working on something that put them both into danger?"

"The FBI came to see Whit in hospital. Perhaps that's why." I swallow. "Cain, Lauren Penfold also mentioned that Shaun Jacobs had been a surgeon."

He stares at me for moment. "Yes," he says eventually. "She's right. When I was moved to the adult facility, Boo was there. I'm not sure what he'd been doing in North Carolina at all, let alone what he'd done to land him in prison, but he was there. He'd been inside for over a year by then, so he was sober."

"And he stabbed you."

"On direction." Cain's hand tightens around mine. "Boo had aligned himself with a prisoner called Conroy, who basically ran things. Conroy had him take me out. They cornered me. Boo told me if I didn't struggle or move he could stab me in the back and I would survive. It would hurt, but I would be okay. If I fought, there were no guarantees."

"So you let him stab you?"

"No, I fought like crazy. But Boo waited until the others had pinned me properly." He laughs quietly. "He always claimed he'd saved my life."

"But why? Why did this man Conroy want him to stab you?"

"I really honestly don't know, Freddie. I'd offended him somehow…or it may not have been about me."

"What do you mean?"

"When I arrived, Boo tried to look out for me…for Isaac's sake. He recognised me as the kid who had been Isaac's protégé for a couple of weeks. Conroy may have been testing Boo's loyalty to him."

"Oh, God!"

He lifts my hand to his lips. "It was long time ago, Freddie."

"Why didn't you tell me it was Boo?"

"Because I was trying to seduce you." He smiles. "I didn't really want to talk about my prison scars."

I shake my head and pull my hand away.

"Freddie, I'm sorry…Freddie…look at me, please." His eyes are very bright. "Ever since Caroline died, I've felt like my past is trying to suck me back in. I didn't want to lie to you, I didn't think I had…"

"You left a lot out."

"There's a lot I'm trying to leave behind." He reaches for my hand again. "But I am sorry. I never wanted you to feel like you couldn't trust me. You can."

I breathe out slowly. "I do trust you. I just want you to trust me. To tell me the truth, however ugly you may think it is."

He waivers and then he nods. "Okay, what do you want to know?"

I think for a moment. "Can I have some of your chips? I'm still hungry."

A beat and then he sighs. "They're called fries."

I help myself. "So what now? How long are you going to be able to evade the…" I stop, realising that we might be overheard and that the word "police" may by itself attract auditory attention from amongst a background hum of many conversations. "Gladys. How long are you going to be able to avoid Gladys?"

He looks confused for only a second. "I don't know. I want to see what I can find out before I meet up with Gladys."

"I'll speak to Whit—ask him what he and Caroline were working on together." I take another one of his fries. "Do you think it's odd that he didn't mention that he and Caroline were close?"

"They were working together; they might not have been close," Cain replies. "The…Gladys interviewed him…perhaps he was afraid that admitting to a connection would make him a suspect."

"That's absurd. We were all sitting together in the Reading Room when Caroline was...when Caroline left."

"Gladys suspects me of having worked with an accomplice... She might suspect the same thing of him, I guess."

"What accomplice?"

He lowers his voice. "I gather that they believe Boo asked Caroline to leave on my instruction, and then I asked him to leave to make sure he didn't tell anyone, and because I was angry that he'd not managed to get rid of Whit." He finishes, clearly relieved he's managed to maintain the code.

"It's a good theory—"

"What?"

"—except for the fact that Caroline wasn't found for hours." I think about the library, the beautiful stately halls. "Could a man who looked and smelled like Boo really have walked into the BPL, killed Caroline, and hidden her body in less than two minutes without anyone noticing?"

"Whoever killed Caroline also knew exactly where the security cameras were," Cain adds. "They picked up nothing."

"Our locked room in reverse." I gaze at him. "I miss you. Whit and Marigold are terrific, but I miss you."

He leans across the table and kisses me.

And for a time we say nothing. Then I tell him about Whit and Marigold to keep from dissolving into tears. And about Lauren's account of Whit's conquests. He doesn't seem particularly surprised by either revelation.

I confide that I am worried Marigold might end up like those girls who ring the *Rag* in search of him.

"I wouldn't be too worried about that," he says. "Marigold knows where he lives."

I smile, though that worries me even more. I recount Marigold's suspicion that Whit was in the library to meet someone the day Caroline died. "Do you think someone might have orchestrated for you both to be there on that day, at that time?"

His brow furrows as he considers the possibility. "Maybe. But to what purpose?"

"To scare you off maybe?"

"From what? The library?" He shakes his head. "That scream didn't really do anything aside from give us a reason to talk to one another." Cain signals for the check. "We didn't know that anyone had died until later."

I grab the wad of cash from my coat, cover the bill and tip with a couple of twenty-dollar notes, and quietly slip the remainder into the pocket of Cain's jacket. We walk out of the diner in silence and make our way towards the river away from the bustle of people around and about Zoe's. It's still bitterly cold and miserable, but I'm not thinking about that. Cain hands me a cell phone—a model so basic I'm surprised they make it anymore.

"Don't let anyone know you have it," he warns as he places his arm around my shoulders. "It's a prepaid burner. I can call you. The one number programmed into it is this one." He holds up a similar phone. "So you can reach me whenever you need to…or want to."

"Won't the police be able to trace you?"

"Not if they don't know about the phone."

I slip the cell into the inside pocket of my coat. "Thank you."

"It's set on silent so I don't give it away by calling at the wrong time."

I nod. "I'll keep it close." I lean into him as the wind cuts through my coat. "Where are you staying tonight?"

"I don't know, but I'll find somewhere."

"Not on the streets?"

"No—I'll get a hotel room. The police can't be watching them all. I've just got to buy a duffel bag first."

"A duffel bag? Why?"

"Nothing more suspicious than a man checking into a hotel with no luggage." He draws me to him. "I should buy a change of clothes anyway."

"I've got you covered." I tell him what's in the backpack he's been carrying for me.

He laughs. "If I didn't know better, I'd assume you've aided and abetted before."

"Please be careful." I hesitate. "Perhaps you should leave Boston, Cain. Get out of Massachusetts."

"I can't find out who's doing this if I leave," he says gently. "I'll never get my life back if I don't find out."

"Yes, but you'd be less likely to be shot by the police."

He pulls me closer. "I've served my time, Freddie. I made my peace with it, because whatever the reason, I did kill a man. But I don't think I can go to prison for something I didn't do…not without fighting like hell anyway."

I hold on to him, aware I don't want to let go. "Okay, so we fight."

Dear Hannah,

I must admit I'm a little uncomfortable with Freddie lying to Leo. I feel deceived... as though you could be lying to me. It's ludicrous, of course. I must remind myself that Leo is a character and not actually me. That I need to do so is a testament to your talent!

It did just occur to me when I read the end of this chapter. Is Cain Black? Is that why he lives in Roxbury? This whole time I've assumed he's white. If he is Black, the likelihood of being shot by the police is quite high, and this whole fugitive-from-the-law caper is a great deal more dangerous. Now I'm wondering if Freddie is Black. And Marigold. Whit looks like the "hero from an old cartoon," so I know he's white. But I realise now there's nothing in the manuscript which says one way or the other with respect to Freddie, Cain, and Marigold. I just defaulted to white because no one mentioned they were Black. I know you're not white, so maybe your characters aren't either, and it is only my inherent bias that makes me see them as white unless you tell me otherwise.

Wow! My head's spinning.

Yours,
Leo

PS: It is nice to see Leo again even if he's being lied to. Jesus, is he Black, too? You're really upsetting my sense of self. Perhaps he should find the next body.

Dear Hannah,

In answer to your question, yes it does matter what color your characters are. As I've already explained, the police over here are a lot more dangerous if Cain is Black. Even if he walked into a police station with his hands up, they might shoot him. It matters for other things, too, in ways that may affect the story line.

I admire your determination to ignore skin color, but it's a bit like ignoring the virus. It's not realistic. Whether or not a character is Black will affect his story arc...but perhaps that's the point you want to make by ignoring it. Do you want readers to say this couldn't happen to Black people, and then wonder, why not? Is that what you're saying?

Okay, I see your point. But it's risky. You're betting on a level of self-awareness in the reader that might not exist. People who've assumed these people are white may feel betrayed and tricked if they realise that the people they've invested in could be Black. Some folks only want to read about their own kind, and even the idea that a character could possibly be Black means he's not white enough. It's simply the way it is. And, take it from me, you don't want to tick those folks off.

I really wouldn't do this. But it's your book.

Yours,
Leo

Chapter Twenty-Eight

Marigold is waiting in the lobby of Carrington Square when I walk in. Her face is tear-streaked, and she is furious. "Where have you been?" she demands.

Joe looks at me wide-eyed and shrugs. "She's been waiting a couple of hours," he whispers. "She won't go. I was thinking I'd have to call the police."

Marigold removes the suit jacket she's wearing and throws it at me. "I thought I'd better return this to you."

A little alarmed that she might divest the skirt too, I say, "Let's go up. We obviously need to talk."

Her eyes glitter fiercely, but she follows me to the stairs.

Neither of us says anything until I've closed the door of the apartment behind us. And then Marigold explodes. "Where have you been?" She's crying. "You said you were staying home."

"You're upset because I went out? Marigold, what happened?"

I try to put my arms around her, but she pushes me away. "Were you laughing at me? You and Whit?"

"Whit?…Marigold, what are you talking about? Where is Whit?"

"He left!" She shouts. "As soon as he realised you weren't joining us, he made an excuse about something he'd just remembered and left."

"So you put two and two together and got twenty-seven?"

I'm not sure if it's the turn of phrase that confuses her or the fact that I know nothing about why Whit might have run out on her. I hold out my hand. "Come into the kitchen. I'll make hot chocolate and we can figure this out."

She takes my hand like a small child and comes meekly with me. I seat her at the counter and start heating milk and cocoa. "Tell me what happened."

Marigold wipes her eyes with the back of her hand. I place a box of tissues in front of her.

"Whit and I met at the restaurant. When I told him you hadn't wanted to join us, he was upset. He tried to ring you"—her lip trembles again—"to make sure you knew it wasn't a date."

I flinch. I'd left my phone in the apartment to make sure it couldn't be used to track me. I don't know if that's possible—I hadn't wanted to take the risk. If I'd answered, I might have been able to tell Whit to stop acting like a jerk.

"When you didn't pick up, he made an excuse and left. We hadn't even ordered starters." Tears again.

I push a steaming mug of hot chocolate towards her and open a packet of marshmallows.

Marigold looks up at me. "I sat there like an idiot for a while, and then I began to wonder if he'd come here. I came over and your doorman told me you'd gone out. After you said you were staying in. And I thought that you'd gone to meet Whit."

I look at her. "Now that you've said it out loud, I hope you realise how idiotic it sounds, how idiotic it is. I went to a movie, that's all. I forgot my phone. It's on the coffee table in the other room."

"What movie?" Marigold is still a little suspicious.

"*An Affair to Remember*. It was showing at The Brattle at nine."

"Your doorman said you left before eight."

Poor Joe! Marigold had obviously interrogated him. "I did. To be honest, knowing you and Whit were together made me lonely for Cain. I didn't want to sit here feeling miserable, so I went out."

"To look for him?"

"To shop."

"What did you buy?"

"Nothing. Maybe I was looking for him a bit. Either way, I came back empty-handed."

Marigold comes around the counter and hugs me. "I'm sorry. I've just waited so long for Whit...it made me a little crazy."

"I promise you, Marigold, I haven't seen Whit. Even if I was inclined to regard Whit as more than a friend, which I'm not, I wouldn't—"

"I know...I am being hysterical." She returns to her stool and adds a handful of marshmallows to the hot chocolate. "I was so happy yesterday, and then tonight was so strange. I'm afraid I lost my mind for a moment... but it's back." She studies me. "Why are you not more upset?" she asks. "About Cain. I'd be broken."

"I'm older than you."

"And that makes you care less?"

"Not at all. It just makes me more inclined to wait and see." I change the subject. "What are you going to do about Whit?"

"What do you mean?"

"He walked out on you, Marigold." The girls who called the *Rag* linger in my imagination. I don't want Marigold to become one of Whit's discarded conquests. "He should at least tell you why."

Marigold inhales. "You're right. I'll call him now."

The call is short. All Marigold manages to say is "Hello, Whit, it's me. I'm at Freddie's." And then it's finished.

"What happened?" I ask, wondering if there's been a quarrel that Marigold hasn't mentioned.

"He said he was coming over and hung up."

"Oh." It's past midnight. I really want to go to sleep, but it seems I will be required to referee young love.

Whit arrives about twenty minutes later. By then I've made coffee because hot chocolate just doesn't cut it at one in the morning.

Whit hugs me as soon as I open the door. "Freddie, thank Christ!"

I push him away, confused and not a little concerned about how Marigold will take this behaviour. "What the hell is going on, Whit?"

He looks at Marigold and embraces her next. "Hello, Gorgeous. I'm sorry about tonight."

"Right." The hour has made me impatient. "Whit, sit down and explain yourself so you two can make up and I can go to sleep. Actually..." I change my mind. "You don't need to explain yourself to me. I might go to bed now."

Whit shakes his head. "No, Freddie, stay. This concerns you."

I sink into the armchair so they can have the couch. Whit sounds serious, and I notice for the first time that there is no sign of his customary flippancy.

"At about seven this evening," he says, "my mother was attacked. She was working alone in the office—there was no one else about. She seems to have surprised someone trying to break into the files. He left her for dead."

"Jesus on a bike!"

"But she's not dead?" I ask, terrified of the answer.

"No. He just knocked her out. She came to and called the police." He turns to Marigold. "I had just arrived at the restaurant when I got the call. I don't know why I didn't tell you...I was spinning."

Marigold wraps her arms around him. "It's okay." She glances at me sheepishly. "I knew there was a good reason."

"How is your mum—is she okay?" I ask.

"Mom's a tough cookie. And she's on the warpath now." He looks at me. "Freddie, she thinks it was Cain."

I stare at him. "That's impossible."

"Why? Why is it impossible?"

I falter. It was well after nine when Cain joined me at the Brattle. It's not impossible. I can't alibi him. "Because he wouldn't..."

"Where were you tonight, Freddie?"

"I beg your pardon?"

"When Marigold told me you were staying home tonight, I was worried that you were in danger—"

"From Cain? That's absurd."

"Freddie, he attacked my mom!"

"Are you sure...is she sure?"

"She says she is."

"How would he have gotten into a legal office? That doesn't sound possible."

Whit shrugs. He rubs his face. "Mom swears it was him. Freddie, where were you?"

"I went shopping and then to see a film at The Brattle."

"I wonder why the police haven't been here looking for Cain," Marigold says.

"They probably realise Freddie wouldn't risk losing her Fellowship by harbouring a fugitive."

"More likely because they're watching the building." I don't comment on whether or not I'd harbour a fugitive. "They've probably deputised Mrs. Weinbaum and Joe. There's no way Cain could come here without them knowing… And they're following me, so I'm safe," I add by way of alibiing myself.

"They lost you tonight," Whit replies.

"How do you know?"

"You weren't answering your phone, so I came by to check on you. When there was no answer, I called the police. They said they'd lost you in the subway."

"They told you that?"

"My mom's contact in the Boston PD told me."

"If they'd let me know they were tailing me, I would have worn yellow and walked slowly." I am terse now. Angry, though I'm not quite sure with whom.

Marigold leaves Whit to come to me. "I'm so sorry, Freddie. We loved him too."

"He's not dead," I say quietly. I turn to Whit. "I take it you don't believe him anymore?"

"He attacked my mom, Freddie."

A thought occurs. "Was he caught on the security footage?"

Whit frowns. "No. The office archives don't have security cameras… that's where Mom was attacked."

"Cain avoided the cameras in the BPL too," Marigold adds.

I can't halt the resentful flicker of my eyes.

"Freddie, I don't want to believe this of him either, but I don't think we have any other choice."

I nod, tight-lipped. I need to think. Marigold is holding my hand, and Whit is watching me carefully.

"I'm sorry—this has all been a bit of a shock." I swallow and meet Whit's eyes. "I gather you and Caroline were working on something together."

Whit's eyes narrow. "How did you know that?"

"One of the reporters at the *Rag* mentioned it."

"Why were you talking to a reporter from the *Rag*?"

"She's doing a story on Shaun Jacobs…and since I'd met him… Anyway, she said you and Caroline were working on a project."

"Yes, we were," he says carefully.

"You said you barely knew her!" Marigold's accusation has nothing to do with Caroline Palfrey's murder.

Whit sighs. "That was my parents. They told me to downplay my involvement with Caroline."

"Why?"

"Because they know how this sort of thing goes. They didn't want the proud name of Metters dragged into the investigation of the death of a client's daughter. Our project had nothing to do with anything—so I didn't mention it."

"What was it about? The project, I mean?"

"We hadn't decided. Caroline had all sorts of stupid ideas... As I said, it was a very under-baked notion that we'd write a long-form investigative feature together. And, to be honest, I wasn't that keen."

"Why were you in the library that day?" I ask. "Were you there to meet Caroline?"

"Yes, actually," he replies frankly, like he's relieved. "She was supposed to meet me in the Reading Room. I was pretty ticked off she didn't show... And then I met you guys, and I figured it wasn't a wasted afternoon after all." He swallows. "Of course, when I realised what happened to her..." His face crumbles fleetingly.

Marigold returns to him. "It wasn't your fault, Whit. You didn't know where she was. You couldn't have done anything."

"And neither could Cain," I point out. "We were all there when she screamed. He couldn't have killed her."

Whit pauses. "The police now think the scream wasn't Caroline's. They believe it might have been a cleaner or someone who looked under that table and saw the body. That Caroline had been killed sometime before we heard the scream."

"If that's so, why didn't this person who discovered the body tell anyone?"

"The police think that perhaps she was frightened. Or maybe that she realised who the killer was and ran. They're looking into any woman who may have been associated with Cain."

I close my eyes, trying to keep calm, but I'm so tired that it's a struggle to open them again.

"You go to bed, Freddie," Whit says. "I'm going to sleep on your couch tonight, just in case."

"Me too," Marigold adds.

I smile. "Don't be silly, Whit. The police are watching the building. I'm perfectly safe. You take Marigold home and go and be with your mother. You should be with her."

We argue back and forth for a couple of minutes until I announce that I am officially throwing them out. Marigold suggests we meet for lunch, and I agree to get of rid of them. I need to be alone with this mess, to figure out what I'm going to do. Finally, I shut the door on them, relieved and shattered. I turn out all the lights, strip, and climb into bed with the cell phone Cain gave me. And for some reason I can't explain, I pull the covers over my head before I call him. His voice is thick and sleepy when he answers.

"Freddie?"

Dear Hannah,

Wow! Was that just a literary slap? Did you just put my concern over Freddie's flirtation with Whit into Marigold's head? Just to show me how ridiculous I sounded? Well, I deserved that, I suppose.

I see you remain committed to not mentioning the plague. This is a grave mistake, not to mention a missed opportunity. Just think how much easier it would be for Cain to elude the police if he and everyone else were wearing masks. None of us are identifiable. That, combined with the current civil unrest, is a crime writer's dream! This time, this horror, is a gift, Hannah. It would be arrogant and rude to refuse it.

In the hope of showing you what this work could be, I have amended your earlier chapters to set them firmly in the midst of this disease. Please find a new version of your manuscript attached. Give it a chance, read it carefully, close your eyes and see what I see. I know you'll come around.

Writing in an attack on Whit's mother, however, is a brilliant move! It shakes Whit out of his adolescent loyalty to his buddy and makes him finally choose a side. To that end, I wonder if it would work better if Jean Metters was tortured and brutally murdered rather than merely assaulted by Cain. I know you've left her alive so that she can finger Cain, but there may be other ways around that. Killers tend to escalate. It makes sense that Cain's crimes would become more vicious. And I think it might heighten the pace and sense of danger at this stage of the novel.

I've attached a few pictures of a murdered middle-aged woman. As you can see she was clearly tortured before her throat was cut. The injuries to her breasts and pubic region suggest a sexual element to the attack. The mask she's wearing might have made it easier for her killer. I expect that behind it she was no one.

It occurs to me as I'm writing this that Marigold is underused. She's a psych student. If you were to bring her face-to-face with the body of Whit's mother, perhaps she could find a clue in the manner of slaying that identifies Cain as clearly as a victim statement.

Looking forward to seeing what you do with these suggestions. Remember, I'm happy to read rewrites.

Yours,
Leo

CHAPTER TWENTY-NINE

Even alone in my apartment, with all the windows and doors locked and under the bedcovers, I whisper when I speak. And when I cry, I do so silently so he is not aware of the tears which are soaking my pillow under the covers. I ask him where he was before he met me at The Brattle.

"I was trying to find a woman called Mouse. She and Boo were friends of a sort. I was hoping she might be able to tell me if anyone wished him harm."

"Did you find her?"

"No."

"So there's no one who could attest to where you were earlier this evening,"

"No…why?"

I tell him about the attack on Whit's mother, her allegation that it was him.

For a moment he says nothing. Then, "Freddie, I swear I didn't—"

"I know, but she's saying you did, and we have nothing to prove otherwise."

"There'll be no fingerprints or DNA evidence to corroborate her story because I wasn't there, Freddie."

"Why would she say it was you, Cain?"

"I don't know. A mistake? Perhaps she realises who I am and she assumes it was me who attacked her…" He curses. "Who would have thought this could get worse?"

"Cain, you need to make sure you have a lawyer."

"I'll get one before I turn myself in. I promise. But not yet."

I pull myself together and wipe my eyes, hoping Cain can't tell I've been crying. I'm no use to him weeping and falling apart. "I'm going to speak to Jean Metters," I say firmly. "She may be mistaken, as you say, or she may be lying. If it's the latter, we need to find out why."

"Freddie, I'm not sure if you should—"

"Don't worry, Cain, I know what I'm doing."

"Done this before, have you?" I can hear the smile in his voice.

"At least a dozen times."

"Freddie, seriously, you will be careful? Someone has killed two people… Please don't give them reason to even look at you."

"That would be easier if I knew who the hell they were."

"I'm nearby," he says. "Call and I can be there in minutes. I can't let anything happen to you."

I promise him that I will. We wish each other good night and eventually hang up. And I fall asleep wrapped in the idea that he's close.

I don't stir until nine the next morning, and when I rise it is with purpose. Sometime in the night it occurred to me how I was going to speak with Jean Metters, and I wake knowing what to do.

Whit, Marigold, and I have agreed to meet at Marigold's apartment and to go on to lunch from there. I leave Carrington Square at eleven and walk to a nearby florist where I purchase a bouquet of hot-house roses. A moment of wistfulness as I'm reminded that the roses will be coming out at my nana's place. Her garden would look like a box of smarties right now, bright, clashing colour. Nana collected and planted new colours each season, yellow, red, orange, blue, all embedded with no scheme whatsoever.

With the bouquet in hand, I hail a cab and give the driver Whit's parents' address. It's not far, but I'm carrying flowers. The Metterses' home is beautiful—a Back Bay mansion with formally groomed grounds. Whit had moved home to housesit while his parents were abroad some months ago, and had been about to return to his own apartment when he was stabbed. Events and comfort colluded, and somehow he has not yet left.

There are security guards and cameras at the door with its gothic knocker.

I give the security guard my name and tell him I'm a friend of Whit's, with an appointment to meet him for lunch. He regards me in a way that makes me wonder if he thinks I am one of the women who phone the *Rag* for Whit. He makes a phone call and then tells me it's all right to knock.

I'm surprised when Jean Metters answers the door. There's a bruise above her right temple, but she is dressed and made-up for the office, and immaculately so.

"Mrs. Metters." I hand her the flowers. "I'm so glad you weren't seriously injured. Whit told us what happened… It must have been terrifying."

She looks from me to the flowers as if it is some strange custom she doesn't understand.

"Marigold and I arranged with Whit to meet here for lunch," I explain. I glance at my watch. "I hope I'm not embarrassingly early."

"Why don't you come in?" she says, frowning. "Whit's already left—I'll give him a call and find out what's gone wrong."

She places the flowers on a hall table and takes me through the house, into a courtyard with a swimming pool. As we walk, she phones Whit. I hear her say, "Well, clearly there's been some mix-up because she's here. Really, darling, I don't know why you need to go out today of all days… Shall I send her on? Yes, all right. I'm afraid I don't have time to entertain, so just come and get her as soon as possible."

I am starting to regret this plan. It probably wasn't that well thought out.

Jean opens the door to what appears to be a separate guesthouse on the other side of the pool. "It seems there has been some misunderstanding as to where you kids were to meet," she says, offering me a seat in the sitting room. "Whit will be back to collect you in a couple of minutes if you'd care to wait here. Excuse me while I go find a vase for your flowers."

This may be my only chance, so I take it. "Whit said you thought it was our friend Cain McLeod who attacked you. I can't say how shocked and sorry I am to hear that."

"Cain McLeod is a very dangerous young man," she says curtly. "I'm very happy I was able to identify him before he hurt someone else."

I nod. "I've been terrified since I heard. How did he get into your office?"

She looks at me sharply.

"I wonder whether the security in my building is enough, if he managed to get past yours," I add hastily.

"I wouldn't worry too much. McLeod seems to be targeting people, and the families of people, associated with his previous incarceration." She walks towards the door. "But, yes, he does seem adept at evading security and avoiding cameras."

"It's so hard to believe he struck you like that."

"He tried to kill me, Winifred."

"I assure you, we had no idea that Cain was so violent."

"But you knew about his past?" she points out archly.

"Eventually, but the incident he described sounded like self-defence."

Jean rolls her eyes. "Yes, it's always self-defence and a bad childhood." She looks me up and down. "At fifteen Abel Manners was already a hardened thug who responded to his father's attempts at disciplining him by stabbing the poor man in the neck with a knife he'd secreted within reach for the purpose, and then watching him bleed out on the floor. There was no way to defend him. If he hadn't been so young, he would have been facing the death penalty!"

I want to defend Cain, but now is not the time. I say nothing.

"Please, for my son's sake, call the police if you ever see him again."

"For Whit's sake?"

"I'm Whit's mother, Winifred. He's my primary concern, and McLeod has already stabbed him once. Clearly, he feels that I should have got him acquitted, and he is low enough and vicious enough to attack me through my only child as well as directly."

"I'm sorry. I didn't mean—"

"Now if you'll excuse me, I'll say goodbye. The guesthouse has its own entrance, so Whit will be able to collect you without coming through the house. He should be here very shortly—you'll see him pull up through the drawing room window."

I sit primly until she crosses the courtyard again and reenters the main house. The guesthouse seems to be where Whit lives, judging by the masculine, frat-house decor. There's a vague disorder about it, though a marked lack of dust makes it clear that the place is regularly cleaned. It smells faintly of Whit's cologne. There are photographs, both framed and simply pinned to the wall, of Whit playing football, drinking, and draped over smiling women, Harvard memorabilia, and various pieces of technology. I'm impressed by the books on Whit's bookshelf. He is better read than I expected. Literature and the biographies of Pulitzer Prize-winners in the main. A framed article from the *Rag*—his first, I expect—a piece written in investigative style on the use of steroids in college sports. Again I'm surprised. Whit is good writer, and judging by the article, he went undercover for the piece.

The name on the spine of one of the books stacked on the table near the armchair catches my eye.

It's Cain's first novel. I slide it out from the stack.

There's a white barred prison cell depicted on the black jacket. The cell door is open. The book is called *Settling,* and Cain's name appears smaller than the title. I open it to the title pages. A quote from the *New York Times* describes the novel as "primal rage in print"; the *Wall Street Journal* calls it "a visceral tale of incarceration and retribution"; there are starred reviews from the trade journals and terms like "stunning debut" and "tour de force," and a list of awards. The volume is well-thumbed, and a first edition. Whit had read Cain's book before we all met, or perhaps it's a secondhand copy, passed on by someone who'd read it often.

Whit's SUV pulls into the driveway beside the guesthouse. I open the door and step out. He and Marigold are in the front seats. I climb into the back. "I'm so sorry—I thought we were supposed to meet here, Whit. I'm so embarrassed. Your mother must think I'm a total flake."

Whit shrugs. "No big deal. And Mom thinks I'm a total flake, so join the club."

"I'm glad to see she's okay, though."

"Yeah, you'd need some kind of missile to kill Mom. She's part Terminator."

"Well, I'm sorry to have disturbed her."

"She said you took her flowers. That was kind—she probably didn't even say thank you, but it was a nice thought."

I avoid Marigold's gaze. There's suspicion in her eyes. Does she realise what I was doing? "I'm starving. Have you chosen a place for lunch?"

"Whit knows a Mexican place in Cambridge," Marigold says, still watching me carefully. "Unless you have an objection?"

I flash her a smile. "I love Mexican food. Let's go."

Guadalupe's in Cambridge is a high-end Mexican restaurant.

"This is my treat," Whit says as we are seated at a linen-draped table. "To make up for standing you up yesterday."

"You didn't actually stand me up," I point out. "Just Marigold."

Whit ignores my protest. "I'm going to make you both try all my favourites," he says, "so it's only fair I pay for the pleasure of introducing you to the best tacos in Massachusetts." He summons the waiter and orders a jug of strawberry margaritas, and then, without even looking at the menu, a series of dishes. Marigold reminds him that I'm a vegetarian and he adds few more. It seems like an insane amount of food for a Mexican restaurant, but the dishes, when they arrive, do so in small, elegant portions. Even so, the table is laden and we struggle to keep up with Whit's demands that we try this or that. The meal is sensational and the conversation mainly about the food.

It's not until we're attempting to fit in dessert that the focus moves to Cain. "Where do you think he is?" Marigold asks.

"Perhaps he's left Boston," I suggest, mostly because I have to say something.

"No." Whit says firmly. "I think he's still here."

"Why?"

"My mom's okay. So am I. He waited all these years for revenge; I can't see him leaving before the job's done."

"Whatever happened to 'he's served his time'?" I demand, hurt for Cain.

"That pretty much evaporated when he tried to kill my mom." Whit grimaces. "I'm sorry, Freddie. I was on his side, you know that, and if Mom hadn't positively identified him, I would still be giving him the benefit of the doubt...but she's certain."

My nod is designed to pacify, not agree. "Did your mom know who he was before this happened?"

"What do you mean?"

"Had she realised that Cain was Abel Manners who she'd defended as a boy?"

"The police told her a couple of days ago." His eyes narrow. "Why?"

"Because people make mistakes, especially when they're scared or panicked." I explain carefully. "If your mom knew who Cain was, she might have assumed he'd tracked her down and be expecting him to exact some kind of revenge. So when she was attacked, she *saw* him."

Marigold speaks first. "I think you're clutching at straws, Freddie—"

"No, Freddie's got a point," Whit interrupts, "if my mom was an ordinary person. But she's an expert witness...like a cop. She knows what to look for, how to identify someone."

"That doesn't mean she doesn't panic, that she can't make mistakes." I stay calm. "Was there any other evidence to identify Cain as her attacker? Security footage, fingerprints, DNA?"

"He was pulling out my mom's files on his old case, on the trial of Abel Manners," Whit replies.

I falter for only a second. "How did he know where they were? The case was fifteen years ago—any sensible person wouldn't expect your mom to still have a file for a trial conducted in another state fifteen years ago, let alone know where to look. Doesn't that strike you as odd?"

Whit bristles. "What are you saying, Freddie? That my mother's lying?"

"No...I'm saying she might be mistaken. She was hit in the head...she might have been confused."

"Freddie," Marigold intervenes, "we know you want to believe in Cain, but this is absurd. He's dangerous. Isn't it obvious he's the common link in all of this? If you know where he is—"

"I have no idea where he is," I say truthfully.

"Why don't you come stay with me for a while?" Marigold says. "We have an extra bedroom. I worry about you being alone."

I smile. "Well don't. I'm fine. Carrington Square is being watched by the police, and it has security."

"Someone got past all that security to take a picture of your door," Whit reminds me. "Assuming you believe Cain when he says he lost his phone."

I sigh. The conversation is getting more and more tense. I change the subject before it derails completely. "I read your article for the *Rag*—the one that's framed on your wall. It's excellent—I didn't realise you were such a wonderful writer, Whit."

Both Whit and Marigold look surprised; Marigold, a little disgruntled.

"You read that?" Whit asks.

"While I was waiting for you to come back for me. You're a sensational journalist."

"A servant of fake news and the gutter press," Whit says ruefully.

"I take it your mother does not approve of a career in journalism."

"'Not when you could do so much more with your life, Whit. You were born to make the news, not report it.'" Whit imitates his mother bitterly.

"She'll come round after your first Pulitzer," I reply. "Are you going to continue with your project without Caroline?"

"Maybe. It was my idea—I'm not actually sure how Caroline became involved in it. One shouldn't speak ill, but that girl wasn't going to let anyone win a Pulitzer if she could steal it."

"Really?" I try not to sound too interested, because I know they've already decided Cain is responsible for Caroline's death.

"Oh, yeah. Caroline was one those people who was always in the right place at the right time to take the credit, regardless of whose talent or work it really was."

"Gosh—I thought everyone loved Caroline."

"After she was dead—sure. Before that, not so much."

"Oh…anybody in particular?"

He looks at me sharply. He's worked out that I'm interrogating him. "Lauren Penfold."

I try not to react visibly. "Penfold—great name for a writer."

"She thinks so." He's still staring at me. "If Cain wasn't in the picture, I'd suspect Lauren."

———

Dear Hannah,

Are you planning that Lauren Penfold was involved? Working with Cain?

Isn't that breaking at least a couple of Knox's commandments of detective fiction? I don't think Lauren was introduced early enough to allow her involvement to be fair play. Of course, rules exist to be broken!

I see you've decided not to kill Jean Metters. It's a pity, but I suppose it is your book, however involved I may be in its writing. Or perhaps you intend for Cain to try again. Perhaps Whit returns home to find his mother murdered in the way I described earlier. Perhaps part of Cain's torture is to ensure Whit finds her.

As always, I will be checking for your next.

Yours,
Leo

CHAPTER THIRTY

I have Whit drop me at the Barnes & Noble on Boylston Street instead of taking me directly back to Carrington Square.

"I can wait," he offers.

I shake my head. "I want to forget everything and browse the shelves. I could be hours."

"Are you sure?"

"Absolutely. Thank you so much for lunch."

Marigold reaches out and grabs my hand. "If you change your mind about staying at my place, just call. I'll tell Lucas he has to wear clothes while you're around."

I laugh. "I'm not quite sure how to take that, but I'll be fine. You two have fun."

I wave them off and make my way into the bookstore. It is always possible that if I allow myself to start browsing I will in fact spend the rest of the day that way, but I don't have the time. So I ask the bookseller for *Settling* by Cain McLeod. It turns out that he is a fan of the book, and throughout the transaction he regales me with how the story will "blow my mind." The jacket is not the same as that on Whit's first edition. The background is still black, but the graphic is a small, barred window in the upper right of the cover. The words "*New York Times* Bestseller" have been added above the title, and Cain's name is bigger than it was in the first edition.

I purchase the book and return home, pausing to chat briefly with Joe, who beckons me over.

"I found out who's been sending you cupcakes," he says, grinning triumphantly. "It was Mr. Johnson who ordered them."

"Leo."

"Yes, ma'am. You might have yourself a secret admirer…well, not so secret now."

I laugh. Of course. I should have realised. "Leo's just thoughtful."

I stop by Leo's apartment to thank him, but he's not home. I mark the visit for later and return to my own place.

There's a quiet relief to be alone. I slip into my pyjamas, intent on climbing into bed with *Settling*. But first I fish the Japanese notebook out of my satchel and update the timeline I'm building. I write in Lauren Penfold, what she told me about Whit, and what Whit said about her. I go over the meeting with Lauren in my mind, looking for any sign of deception, any indication that what she'd told me might have been self-serving somehow. But to be honest, I can't tell. I also extend the timeline to write in the attack on Jean Metters and her allegation that it was Cain. I wonder what reason she might have to lie, because I do think she is lying. She has to be. But why would she lie? To return Cain to prison? Why would she want that? To prove that she was not negligent in letting him go to prison in the first place, perhaps… That sounds like a stretch. To protect someone? My timeline is becoming crossed with lines pointing to possibilities, but there's no pattern.

I remember suddenly that Caroline Palfrey's parents are clients of Jean Metters'. Could it be their interests that she is trying to protect? I fold the notebook back into its cover. I need to walk away before the puzzle drives me crazy.

I grab Cain's book and climb under the covers.

The cell phone Cain gave me is beneath my pillow—I never let it out of my reach. I think about calling him, but for some irrational reason I feel safer doing so at night.

So, I open *Settling*. There's no author photograph on the back jacket, which is unusual for American hardcovers. I wonder if that was Cain's decision.

I read for the next seven hours, though I'm unaware of the passing of real time. The story is clearly autobiographical in parts—a boy unjustly incarcerated who grows into a man within the prison system. The text is taut with barely repressed rage, which seethes onto the page, exploding occasionally in a scene of particular violence. When released, the protagonist, Caleb St. John, embarks on a quest for vengeance against those he holds responsible for the loss of his freedom. The novel is seeded with a dry black humour. The acts of retribution escalate in violence and yet, despite this, Cain manages to make Caleb sympathetic. The language is raw and authentic, though lyrical in its way, and completely unlike the Cain I know. But he'd warned me as much.

It's half past nine or thereabouts when I finish, exhausted and sobbing. The book is dark but it is a velvety darkness, sumptuous somehow. And it isn't really about revenge but the manner in which judgment can shape both judge and judged. Caleb St. John's anger was honest, his struggle reflective of society's struggle to civilise its own destructive instincts, to disguise vengeance as rehabilitation.

And for seven hours I have thought of nothing else.

But now…now I want to talk to Cain, about his book and Jean Metters, Caroline Palfrey and Whit, and us. I'm intrigued and startled by what was inside him once, and I miss him.

I get up, shower, change into fresh pyjamas, and make the bed for the few minutes that I'll be out of it. Still a bit full from lunch, I fix myself a bowl of cornflakes for dinner…or its American equivalent, which is sweeter straight out of the box. I eat standing up while I flick through my phone for the news. Shaun Jacobs' murder has been superseded by more recent killings. Caroline is still news. There's no coverage of the attack on Jean Metters, but there is mention that novelist Cain McLeod is wanted for questioning in connection with the death of Caroline Palfrey.

A knock on the door startles me. I open it a crack because I'm wearing pyjamas. They're perfectly respectable, and I am not generally so coy, but these days it could be the police.…in which case I'll need to be fully dressed, preferably with a cardigan I can pull over my head.

It's Leo. I open the door properly.

"I saw a light under your door so figured you were still up."

"I am. Would you like a cup of coffee…or a bowl of cereal?"

He peers into the bowl in my hand, which by then contains only a few sodden flakes in leftover milk. "Think I'll pass, unless you have tea."

"I do, as a matter of fact."

Leo sits at the counter as I steep a tea bag.

"I've been wanting to come by and ask how you got on with the police," he says. "You were in a bit of a panic when we came back."

The text message, with the image of my door and Cain's. I'd almost forgotten.

"The police haven't been able to establish anything beyond that it was sent from the phone Cain lost weeks ago."

"By Cain, you mean Handsome Man?"

I laugh. "Yes."

"And he's the guy the police want to question for the Palfrey murder."

"Yes, but as a witness, I expect." I'm lying. Leo probably knows I'm lying.

"Then where is he?"

"I beg your pardon?"

"I read that the police are looking for him…usually means they can't find him."

"I'm not sure where he is…he had some research he needed to do."

"And he's uncontactable?"

"Well, the police took his phone."

"He should turn himself in," Leo says firmly. "For your sake, if not his own."

"I'm not in any danger," I reply lightly.

He meets my eye. "Are you sure?"

I know that he is not talking about that danger emanating from anyone other than Cain. "Yes, I'm sure."

Leo shakes his head. "Freddie, you and I are buddies, right?"

"Yes, of course."

"As your buddy then, I'm a bit worried about you."

"You really don't need to be, Leo."

"But I am. Your good sense is compromised by the fact that you're in love."

"I'm not—"

"You are. Let's not pretend. And being in love is a bit like finding God. You start to act on blind faith. Let me be the voice of reality before you find yourself in Jonestown."

I pull a face. "All right, Voice of Reality, what wisdom do you wish to impart?"

"It seems to me, Freddie, that people have a tendency to mysteriously die when in the vicinity of Handsome Man. So it follows that in his vicinity is not an advisable place to be."

"The people who died mysteriously in his vicinity were also in mine," I point out.

"Well, I suppose you should only worry if you're not a murderer, then. If you aren't, then someone near you is." He finishes his tea. "Face it, Freddie. You believe this guy because you want to, because for some reason beautiful, intelligent women seem drawn to dangerous men—" He stops short as he realises what he's just said. "Not that you're...I mean you're...you know what I mean. Quit laughing!"

But it's too late. The giggles have set in. Who would have thought that in a conversation about whether my lover was a murderer it would take an accidental compliment to make things awkward?

"I'm sorry, Leo," I say, still grinning. "I promise, I'm not about to drink the Kool-Aid. And Cain isn't dangerous."

"No, ma'am, he isn't. As long as you ignore his conviction for murder."

"How did you know about that?" I ask sharply.

"I have a friend who works for the *Globe*, who's working on the story of Caroline Palfrey's murder. I'm afraid the whole world will know very soon. So even if Handsome Man is, as you clearly believe, the victim of a miscarriage of justice, he should turn himself in now."

Damn! I'm aware Leo is watching me. "I really have no idea where Cain is."

He nods slowly. "You know, if you ever feel like you're in over your head, you can turn to me. I know I don't cut the same dashing figure as Handsome Man, but I would do whatever I could to keep you safe, Freddie. Whatever you need, just ask."

Perhaps it's that he's so sincere, or that it's now past midnight, but I feel fraught and emotional. I blink hard and look away to keep the tears from spilling. "Thank you. You really are a mate."

Perhaps he's afraid I'm going to start crying, because Leo stands hastily to say good night. "I shouldn't have called so late—you look exhausted." He pauses at my door and turns back. "Freddie, please be careful. Cain McLeod has proved himself to be a violent man. You may not have seen it yet, but you know he's capable of it. If he tries to contact you, call the police. In America, innocent men get lawyers, they don't go on the run."

I don't argue with him because there's no point. Leo doesn't know Cain. He has nothing to weigh against the allegations, to counter the circumstantial evidence.

I close the door behind Leo. His concern is a little unnerving. I'm tempted to be irritated with him, but I know he's only trying to look out for me. And perhaps on the face of it, my belief in Cain does seem crazy. I realise then that I have completely forgotten to thank Leo for the cupcakes. Perhaps this wasn't the right time. Perhaps I'll bake him some sort of thank you instead. Tomorrow.

I turn out all the lights and climb back into bed, drawing the covers over my head. The phone vibrates uncannily on cue.

"Cain?"

"Hello." He doesn't sound drowsy as he did when I called yesterday. "Is it a bad time? I know it's late."

"No—it's a perfect time. I have things to tell you, and I've just climbed into bed."

"I know."

"How?" I ask, startled.

"I saw your lights go out."

"You can see my lights?"

"Yes…I thought if I waited until they went out, I could be sure you were alone."

I smile. "That's a bit presumptuous." The thought that he's close enough to see the lights in my windows feels strange. Tantalising and frustrating. "Where are you?"

"Nearby."

"The police are watching Carrington Square."

"I know—I can see them."

I'm intrigued and a little alarmed. "Where exactly are you? Actually scratch that. I need to be able to say I don't know where you are. But Cain, isn't it a bit risky to be so close?"

"A calculated risk." There is no background noise. He's somewhere quiet.

I make myself stop trying to guess where he is, in case I do. "I spoke to Jean Metters today."

"How on earth did you manage that?"

I tell him what I did, and about my conversation with Jean Metters. "She's lying, not mistaken, Cain. I'm sure of it."

"Why would she lie? I'm nothing to her…an old case she lost."

"Maybe she thinks you're going to sue or something."

Cain laughs. "She's a lawyer. Half her clients probably want to sue her.

But I doubt that the idea of me doing so is threatening enough to risk her career and possibly jail by fabricating a charge."

"But that's exactly what she did…there has to be a reason."

"Yes, there will be. What else did she say?"

"She wanted me to call the police if I saw you, said that a mother's duty was to protect her son, and that I should turn you in for Whit's sake if not my own."

"A mother's duty," Cain murmurs. "Could she be trying to protect Whit from me?"

"It's possible, I suppose. The police told her who you were. She told me you'd come to Boston to exact some sort of revenge against her through Whit."

"That's a bit Marvel Universe, isn't it?"

"Maybe. Whit was stabbed and Jean Metters does fit the supervillain mould."

"Again, she's a lawyer… But you're right, it's a reason."

I tell Cain about lunch with Whit and Marigold, and Whit's opinion of Lauren Penfold.

"Do you think it's possible?" he asks.

I screw up my nose, though he cannot see it. "If what Whit says is true, she might have had reason to kill Caroline, perhaps even to stab Whit, but why would she kill Boo, or attack Jean Metters?"

"You've decided all four crimes are connected then?"

"They are connected—through you. And since I don't believe you're a murderer, there must be something else at play."

"There must be," he says quietly. He sounds despondent.

I desperately want to put my arms around him, to tell him it will be okay. "I wish I knew if the police were watching all the time" I say, frustrated that he is so close.

"There're a few minutes every now and then when they go for coffee, but it's hard to tell when that'll be. It'd be impossible to get past your door-man, anyway."

"So you could get into the building, just not past Joe?"

"I think so."

"Then I could leave without the police knowing too."

"Your doorman may be under instructions to alert them if you leave."

"I could use the fire escape… You can get out of the building but not into it via the fire door." I sit up, excited now. "I could be ready, you could call me when they next go for coffee, and I could simply walk out."

Silence for a moment. And then, "Okay. When I call, walk out of your building and into the alley one block down. I'll find you there. If I don't show up within a couple of minutes, don't wait. Walk back."

I agree, already scrabbling into clothes by the light of the phone.

"Are you sure you want to do this, Freddie?"

"Absolutely."

"Then dress warmly."

—⁓—

Dear Hannah,

I'm truly touched. You've mirrored our relationship in that between Freddie and my namesake. He is her advisor, honest and true. She can turn to him as you can turn to me. I'm moved to tears to know that this is the way you feel. Corresponding with a celebrated author like yourself is a privilege that I feel keenly. I have learned so much from you; I hope you have learned a little from me. And I have been content to simply be your devoted beta reader. But the idea that we could be more, that we are more, is a dream. Oh, fuck this pandemic. If not for it, you would be here. I would have been your guide; I would have shown you the unimaginable.

Yours always,

Leo

CHAPTER THIRTY-ONE

I stuff a backpack with the travel blanket I bought for the flight to the U.S. It rolls up impossibly small. I throw in a box of crackers, cheese, cookies, and a bag of candy, a small thermos of coffee, the notebook I've been using to plot events, a couple of changes of underwear, and a toothbrush. I realise that I'm not planning on returning for at least a couple of days, though I'm not sure when I decided that. I slip my computer into its sleeve. Perhaps it's absurd to be taking it, but I can't bring myself to leave it behind.

I find the cash I took out that day and slip it into my inside pocket, and I take my passport, just in case.

I'm not sure if what I'm about to do is illegal. It's probably aiding and abetting, but I've been doing that all along. I change the message on my usual phone to say that I'll be incommunicado for a couple of days working on some crucial scenes of my book, so please leave a message. It'll buy me time with family and Marigold, I hope. I leave that phone plugged into the recharger beside my bed, knowing it could be used to locate me.

Breathe, Winifred! I sit down. When I was eight, I packed a bag to run away from home. I never left the backyard, but the excitement of planning the adventure was enough. This is not a child's game. This will have consequences. But still, I am exhilarated by the idea of seeing Cain, of getting out from under the surveillance of the police.

Cain's call comes an hour later. "You have about five minutes."

I slip out into the corridor and make my way to the internal fire stairs. At this time of night the lights in the hallway have been dimmed. The door to the escape is near Leo's, so I am particularly careful to be quiet lest he poke his head out.

I walk down the stairs and out of the building. It's weirdly simple. The street is quiet. The streetlights seem very bright. I don't run or look for Cain but walk evenly down the block. The alley is about twelve feet wide, unlit and silent. It smells rank. Large steel garbage skips sit outside the back entrances to the businesses on either side. And, for the first time, my excitement flags against the reality of what I'm doing. I hear someone and turn hopefully. But it's not Cain. An old man shouts profanities at me as he goes through one of the bins, and I want to run. I stop, not sure what to do now. Terrified to do anything. Where the hell is Cain?

I back deeper into the alley away from the street, away from the man and his bin. I can barely see now. There's a sound at the head of the alley. Footsteps in between the shouting. Thank goodness. I open my mouth to call Cain's name, and a hand a claps over it and pulls me back. I fight, and an arm wraps around me effectively pinning and immobilising me. And my blood chills because though I can't see his face, I know it's Cain.

He drags me down. The old man is shouting again, screaming obscenities. There's someone talking to him.

A whisper in my ear. "Freddie, it's me. I didn't mean to scare you, but that's a cop talking to Zeke."

I stop struggling. In fact, I'm positively limp with relief. "Zeke saw me walk in."

"He won't say anything to the cops. I think the officer is trying to move him on anyway."

A couple of minutes and the policeman runs Zeke out of the alley. We crouch lower as he swings a flashlight in a cursory check before heading back into the street.

I turn finally to face Cain. He kisses me gently. "Hello."

"You scared the wits out of me!"

"I'm sorry. I was afraid he'd see you." He has my hand. "I wouldn't blame you if you want to go back."

I shake my head. "Is this where you've been hiding out?"

His brow rises. "Here? God, no! I wouldn't invite you to come live in an alley."

We leave through the rear of the alley and weave through back streets. Cain knows where he's going; I have no idea. Eventually, I recognise that we have doubled back to the block on the other side of the street from Carrington Square. We cross a small park and climb over a fence, and, suddenly, we're in someone's backyard. Then Cain simply opens a door and we walk into the house. I'm terrified that we are about to be shot by a justifiably angry homeowner for breaking and entering.

Cain bolts the door behind us. My eyes adjust slowly. We seem to have come in through a kitchen.

"The guy who owns this place spends the colder months in the Bahamas. Even in the summer, he's barely here."

"How do you know?"

"He told me. My agent brought me to a party here about three years ago."

"Why do you have a key?"

"There's a statue of Venus in the garden, with a hidden cavity where he keeps his spare key. You have to press Venus's breasts to make it reveal. He was so pleased with it, he showed me. In fact every guy who was at that party knows where the key is." Cain grimaces. "He was a bit of a jerk, to be honest."

"You've been here this whole time?"

"No. I remembered this place and the key last night and tried it on a long shot. As I said, it's been years—he might have sold the house, for all I knew. I come in after dark and leave before dawn, and make sure I don't turn on any lights in the rooms with windows so that no one knows I'm here. When this is all over, I'll tell him and apologise."

"Won't the police think to look here?"

He shakes his head. "He wasn't a friend. This was just one of hundreds of parties I went to on tour. Larry, the owner, is some kind of dot-com tycoon. He seemed to think this place was a bit of a dump... He hasn't bothered to install security. It's a wonder there aren't a bunch of people living here." He grabs my hand. "Come on, I'll show you something." He takes me upstairs and through the house to a bedroom. The curtains are drawn. He directs me to peer through the tiny part in the fabric.

I gasp, surprised, though I knew vaguely where the house was. We're almost directly across the road from Carrington Square. I can see my window. I can also see the police car parked outside, and I realise that Cain must have been here when he called.

He takes me then to an internal room and turns on a lamp. It's a media room with a television screen on one wall and a massive couch against the other. Judging by the blankets folded on the couch, that's where he's been sleeping. Cain's laptop and phone are charging on the floor by an outlet. The room is cold but a respite from the frigid air outside the house.

I smile as I remove my backpack. "I packed for a doorway or park bench. I even brought food."

Cain smiles at me. "Food is good. There's nothing in Larry's cupboards but vodka and truffle oil, and we can't really call out for pizza."

I unpack my supplies. Cain teases me when he sees the thermos but he does not refuse the coffee, and we huddle under blankets on the couch and spread out the folded pages of my notebook. We go over everything together in the hope that our collective memories might shake loose some pattern from the notes I've dutifully made. I remember talking about Marigold and Whit and Jean Metters, the firmness of Cain's chest beneath my cheek and the warmth of him. I'm not sure which of us drifts to sleep first.

I wake because I can feel that Cain has. It's freezing and still dark.

"We'll need to hurry if we want to shower and be out of here before dawn."

"We can shower?"

"Sure. I've been using the en suite in the main bedroom. There's hot water—it might warm you up a little," he adds as I begin to shiver.

"Don't tell me you have towels?" I ask, stretching.

"There are fresh towels in the cupboard in there." He stands up and offers me his hand. "You go first. I'll follow."

The en suite is expansive and luxurious. White tiles and brushed chrome fittings. I grab a couple of towels out of the cupboard and shower quickly. The soap is honey-scented and the shampoo a boutique brand I've never seen. The hot water halts the shivers and blasts away the fuzziness of too little sleep. By the time I emerge, Cain has packed up any signs of us in the media room. I go back to the window while he showers and peer through the part in the curtains again. A police car is still parked on the street within sight, though I cannot say whether it's the same one. I wonder how long it will take them to suspect that I'm not there. I probably have until this evening when I expect they'll wonder why there are no lights on in my apartment... or Marigold calls the police because she can't reach me...which is entirely possible.

My dear Hannah,

How are you? I've been thinking of our novel incessantly for the last few days.

I went for a test yesterday at the pop-up testing station in Copley Plaza. I wasn't sick—just thought I'd try it. I wonder if impaling someone via the nostril would make for an interesting death scene? Perhaps you can't kill someone that way. Maybe lobotomy is the only danger. I'll see if I can find any images of a similar killing. Purely for interest. I suspect you're determined to avoid the subject of the virus. I have given in on that count.

I really liked the last chapter. Finally, momentarily, Freddie wavers in her ridiculous trust of Cain. You could make the scene in the alley even more poignant if Cain was a little rougher with her. Perhaps he punches her or strangles her a little. He might explain it away by saying he thought she was someone else, but for a brief moment we would see his true character.

The more I think about it, the more I am convinced that Cain is Black. You really do need to let people know at the outset. If you don't want to say it outright, perhaps you could have him wear hoodies throughout.

Think about it, Hannie, and think about me.

Ever yours,
Leo

CHAPTER THIRTY-TWO

The sky has not yet begun to lighten when we leave. Cain locks the door and slips the key into his pocket and we leave via the route by which we came.

"Where are we going?" I ask, plunging my hands into the pockets of my hoodie. My knowledge of Boston's layout is shaky at best, and traversing alleys, cutting across and doubling back, I am completely lost.

But Cain seems to know where he's going, where we're going. He grabs my hand. "Breakfast."

"Oh, God…and coffee."

"Sure. Don't say I don't know how to show a girl a good time."

The Old Mate is run by Australians. It serves lattes and cappuccinos, smashed avocado and Vegemite toast. The serving staff all wear brown hoodies which boast an embroidered joey emerging from the pouch, and kangaroo ears. It's a bit cringeworthy, but the place is buzzing with breakfast-goers, many of them Australian.

Cain pulls out a chair for me at a table in the corner. "I thought we could talk here without your accent being noticed particularly."

I might have been impressed if I weren't focussed on real coffee.

Cain signals a waitress who takes our orders. I request a double latte and avocado on Vegemite toast, which, because this is America, comes with fries. Cain orders bacon and eggs, a dish which is apparently made Australian by the addition of a fried banana. I'm vaguely affronted, but I'm hungry and not about to sit on culinary indignation.

After months in the U.S. I find the Australian accents all around us strange and ear-catching, and I realise that my voice would, anyplace else, make Cain and me noticeable. Here we disappear into the buzz.

We talk about Caroline Palfrey's murder first. It seems to be the epi-center of everything that's happened since. I am still reluctant to believe that there is any coincidence to the fact that Cain and Whit met that day.

"Assuming that's true"—Cain pokes the deep-fried banana on his plate like he's checking for signs of life—"the person who brought us all into the library would have known about me, and Whit's and Caroline's familial con-nections to my case."

"Is any of that a secret?"

"Not really, but as you know, it's not something I talk about. You could find it all on record somewhere, but you would have to know to look."

"Jean Metters would not have even needed to look," I point out.

"But why would Jean want to kill Caroline…or to stab her own son? It doesn't make sense."

"Might Whit have been stabbed by someone else in revenge for Caroline? Perhaps this is between the Metters and the Palfreys."

Cain smiles. "This is Boston, not the Ozarks."

I refuse to let him dismiss the theory. "One thing we know for sure is that Jean Metters is lying about you attacking her. Not mistaken, lying. Why would she do that if she wasn't involved?"

Cain frowns. "Unless she's afraid of me."

"I don't follow."

"If she believes I'm a threat to her, or to Whit, she might have decided to *help* the police find evidence against me." He decides to try the banana. "The police told her who I was a couple of days before she was assaulted, so the timing fits."

"Why would you be a threat to either of them?"

"Perhaps she recognizes she did a lousy job defending me and assumes, as she told you, that I'm vengeful." He looks up and meets my eye. "I'm not."

"I know, though I'm not sure why. I would be." I sip my latte and savour the first infusion of caffeine. It's so good it might have been made in Melbourne. "Cain, they're not going to able to convict you, are they? They may suspect you, even arrest you, but they haven't got any actual evidence you killed anybody. Surely it will be thrown out of court?"

"You have a great deal of faith in the American legal system, Freddie."

"But I'm right, aren't I? Everything they have is circumstantial, and they won't find anything more concrete because it wasn't you." I become convinced as I say it. "They haven't got anything."

"I expect they're working on the premise that you don't need evidence if you have a confession."

"But they don't—you didn't—"

"No, of course I didn't. I just mean that's why they may be less concerned about the lack of concrete evidence than you seem to be. They expect that they'll be able to get me to confess."

"We still need to find you a lawyer," I tell him firmly.

He nods. "The moment I retain an attorney, I'll have to turn myself in. I want to make sure that I've found out everything I can before I'm taken off the streets." He puts down his knife and fork. "Boo had come by some money recently. He used it to go on a bender, of course, but apparently he had something on someone."

"He was blackmailing someone?"

"That's what it sounds like."

"Would he have done that?"

"Without a second thought. Boo's moral compass was somewhat pragmatic." Cain frowns. "One of Boo's buddies thinks Boo knew something about Caroline Palfrey's murder."

"Is that likely?"

Cain shrugs. "Maybe. Boo liked the BPL. He might have been there that day."

"So if he did see something, and he was blackmailing the murderer, it follows that the murderer might want to kill him."

"Yes, maybe." He hesitates. "There's a guy called Darryl Leonowski— runs a kind of soup kitchen in East Boston. Apparently Boo was a regular there, played chess with Darryl."

"Have you spoken with him?"

"I was contemplating it."

"But you're afraid he'll call the police."

"There is that chance."

"I could speak with him. The police might not even be looking for me yet."

"Would you? I hate involving you in—"

"I thought we established that I was already involved." I pull a notebook out of my backpack. "What do I need to ask him?"

We discuss questions for a while and then I ask, "Wouldn't he have told the police everything he knows already?"

"Maybe. My experience is that it's hard to run a soup kitchen if the police are hanging about. He may be more willing to take his time with you."

"Should I lose my Aussie accent, you know, to be less identifiable?" I ask the question in my best imitation of Cain's inflection.

He laughs. "No…please don't do that. Ever, if possible."

"How rude! That's exactly what you sound like, you know!"

We pay the cheque and catch a bus across the bridge to East Boston. Cain remains vigilant, constantly scanning for police uniforms, or anyone who might be watching us particularly. I speak as little as possible.

The soup kitchen is in an old church. I leave Cain outside and go in by myself. The church hall is set up with trestle tables and most are filled. Many of the clients are elderly, though some look to me like teenagers. The gathering is quiet. Few people converse as they eat, or if they do, it's in whispers.

I walk up to the counter where hot food is being served. The young man in a sauce-stained hoodie grabs me a plate.

"Thank you, but I'm here to see Darryl," I say. "I'm sorry I don't have a last name. But it's very important that I speak to him. You're not Darryl, by any chance?" I add hopefully.

"No, I'm Jack," he replies, pointing to the large name tag pinned to his chest. I feel stupid for not having noticed it.

Jack looks around. There's nobody waiting in line. "Stay here—I'll get him. If anyone arrives looking for grub, tell 'em I'll be back in a sec."

And so I wait, trying not to let my eyes rest on anybody.

Jack's back pretty quickly. "Darryl's in the storeroom," he says, pointing out the doorway. "Just go through there."

I thank him. The door opens to a long, dark corridor, off of which are several rooms.

A voice from the end. "I'm in here…last door on your left. Watch yourself…the light isn't working."

The hairs of the back of my neck rise, but I tell myself not to be silly. It's an old church.

I find Darryl in the end room. He is man of substantial girth, and indeterminate age. His hair is that pale strawberry blond that speaks of a ginger youth. He wears a black hoodie which declares *Know Christ, Know Life* and is sweating profusely as he opens boxes and stacks cans of foodstuffs on shelves.

I introduce myself.

He shakes my hand. "Pleased to meet you, Winifred. Jack said you want to talk to me."

"I do. I'd like to ask you about Shaun Jacobs."

He looks up sharply. "Shaun? You know he's—"

"Yes, sir, I do. That's the reason I came to see you."

"You knew Shaun?"

"I met him, but I can't say I really knew him. But I believe you did."

He smiles softly and sighs. "Yes. He was something of a curmudgeon and an excellent chess player, even when he wasn't sober." He looks at me. "Why are you interested in Shaun?"

Cain had prepared me for this. "You can't lie to people who work with the homeless. They'll know." And so I tell Darryl the truth.

"The man who the police think murdered Shaun is a friend of mine."

"And you think he's innocent."

"I know he's innocent."

"And how do you know that, Winifred?"

I tell him about the night Cain and I encountered Shaun Jacobs. "If Cain had wanted to kill Boo, he could have done so then, and it would have been self-defence, but he didn't. He wouldn't even call the police or go to a hospital for fear it would mean Shaun would be arrested."

Darryl looks dubious.

"Look, Darryl, in the end I believe Cain. And I know that Shaun had come upon a source of money not long before he died…that he claimed to know something about Caroline Palfrey's murder."

Darryl's eyes narrow. "Caroline Palfrey…the woman in the library?"

I nod. I can see he's realised something.

"Shaun told me a story about a girl who screamed and made everyone think she was dead."

"In the library?"

"He didn't say. I thought at the time it was just another one of his 'women are the root of all evil' stories. I didn't pay a lot of attention."

I try to contain my excitement. This is something. "Is that all he said about the girl who screamed?"

"He said she got hers, and now he was getting his."

"What did he mean by that?"

"I don't know. You gotta understand, Shaun was not always rational or even coherent."

"Do you think he might have killed her…the girl who screamed?"

Darryl thinks and then he shakes his head. "I dunno. Shaun lashes out, but murdering a young woman and hiding the body doesn't seem like him."

I remember Cain saying something similar about Boo lashing out. Could Shaun Jacobs simply be an underestimated murderer? "Did he do or say anything else that you thought was odd?"

"Most things Shaun said and did were odd…but he did bring me a box of donuts. He'd never done that before."

"Donuts?"

"Yes, fancy ones. Flavours devised by someone who was obviously high, but they were good." He smiles sheepishly. "I confess, I've bought the odd box myself since then."

"What was the shop called—where the donuts came from?"

"Around the Hole."

It hits me strangely because I'm not sure what it means, not sure what to think. But suddenly everything from the beginning is uncertain.

I thank Darryl for talking to me. He shrugs.

"No big thing. Shaun wasn't a good man, but he wasn't all bad either. I hope it turns out that you're right about your friend. It's hard to come to terms with being in love with a killer."

And I wonder fleetingly if he's talking about me or himself.

Cain puts his arm around me about two blocks from the church. He was waiting for me outside, but we didn't acknowledge each other in case Darryl or someone else was watching. By the time I can talk to him I am ready to explode with what I have discovered. We walk down to LoPresti Park on the waterfront to talk. There is barely anyone there…a few determined joggers pounding the frozen promenade and the occasional dog walker. It's cold and clear and still, and the view of the Boston skyline is spectacular. We stroll along the pier, Cain shielding me from the wind coming off the water. I begin to tell him what Darryl told me.

"She screamed? But why?"

"I don't know, but it explains why no body was found when they searched. It was Caroline who screamed, but she didn't die then."

Cain nods thoughtfully. "It makes sense, I suppose. But it also means I no longer have an alibi for Caroline's murder."

"But neither does anyone else," I point out. I tell him about the donuts from Around the Hole.

"Marigold's donut shop?"

"Yes." I swallow. "We know she's been in love with Whit since well before we all met. And Lauren Penfold said that sometimes he would pretend to be with Caroline to blow off girls."

"You think she stabbed Whit?"

"What if she felt he betrayed her with Caroline? We know she knew where he lived, and initially, before they got distracted by you, she was the police's prime suspect, if you remember."

Cain exhales. "Okay, I'll concede that's possible, but Boo? She'd never met him."

"Perhaps she had. Perhaps he was blackmailing her because he somehow saw her kill Caroline."

He looks at me. "Does she love Whit that much?"

"I don't know. I love you, but I don't think I'd kill anyone to get your attention—" I stop, mortified by what I've just said. I look at him like a rabbit in headlights.

Cain laughs softly and draws me into his arms. "Me too," he says before kissing me.

We resume walking in silence, letting the moment be untouched for a while.

"We need to talk to Whit," I say finally.

"Why?"

"If Marigold is our killer, he's in danger. She's already stabbed him once, and if he disappoints her…"

"You're right. Call him."

―――

Dear Hannah,

I am a little concerned that you are making Freddie a little too naive. Surely she realises by now that Cain is the murderer—even if she's in love with him. I am also, to be honest, quite appalled by her disloyalty to Marigold. It's understandable that Cain wants to cast suspicion on someone else, but Freddie is supposed to be Marigold's friend, for Chrissake!

Forgive me if my protest is strident, but I abhor disloyalty. It is in my opinion the lowest violation and should be punishable in only the most punitive way. I can only warn you against going down this path, Hannah. You have disregarded many of my previous suggestions, and so I wonder if you might even conceive of making Marigold your ultimate perpetrator.

Perhaps you have become jealous of my fondness for her. But rest assured, she is no threat unless you do this. I cannot tolerate disloyalty.

Yours,
Leo

PS: I didn't fail to notice the proliferation of hoodies in this chapter. I'm hurt by the churlishness of it—I'm only trying to help. You're setting this book in America—you cannot ignore race. It needs to be declared. If a character is not white, you cannot treat him as though he is. It's simply absurd. And if he's white, he cannot live in Roxbury without comment as to why. I note that even after the hours I put into correcting your earlier chapters, rewriting them to include the disease, you have neither acknowledged my efforts nor rectified the omissions in your work. I'm disappointed in the extreme. I wonder if perhaps jealousy is at play here too. Do you fear I can write your story better than you? Needless to say, I suggest you remove all the hoodies and replace them with some fucking masks!

Dear Ms. Tigone,

To confirm our earlier conversation by phone, we have identified the man you know as Leo Johnson. We believe it is possible that he has recently entered Sydney, in spite of restrictions, posing as a returning citizen, medical consultant, or diplomatic official. In the latter case, he might evade mandatory isolation requirements.

We have, of course, mobilized our agents and the Australian authorities to ensure your protection.

Please find attached images of Wil Saunders, aka Leo Johnson. Mr. Saunders has a background in law enforcement which we believe has allowed him to elude the authorities to date. He is a person of interest with respect to several murders in the Boston area. Should you see this man, please do not approach him, or allow him to approach you, and inform our agents immediately.

I assure you this will be over soon.

Sincerely,
Special Agent Michael Smith
Federal Bureau of Investigation

CHAPTER THIRTY-THREE

I find the notebook into which I scribbled Marigold's and Whit's numbers, and I call.

"Freddie! You're speaking to me."

"Why wouldn't I be speaking to you?"

"I thought you might be upset at me over Cain. Honestly, Freddie, if he hadn't attacked Mom, I'd still be giving him the benefit of the doubt. But sometimes you have to cut your losses and give up on people."

"Whit, where are you?"

"At home."

"Are you alone?"

"Yeah. Though Marigold is watching the house."

"What? She's spying on you? Call the police."

He scoffs. "It's just Marigold. It's a little edgy but kind of sexy."

"Whit, it's stalking. You can't—"

"For Marigold it's foreplay. She'll come in once she's worked herself up a bit."

"No. Whit, don't be alone with Marigold!"

"Freddie, I don't know how you do dating in Australia, but being alone is kinda the point..."

"Whit, I think Marigold killed Caroline."

A beat of shock.

"What? Are you out of your mind?"

"Listen to me, Whit. Caroline's scream had nothing to do with when she died…that was afterwards. I think Shaun Jacobs saw something and was blackmailing Marigold… She'd meet him at that donut shop, Around the Hole. It's been Marigold all along."

For a moment nothing. And then, "Freddie, you're clutching at straws. I know you want it not to be Cain, but—"

"Dammit, Whit, don't let her in! Call for help."

"I think you might be the one that needs help, Freddie." His voice is hard, angry. "I know you're upset about Cain, but you can't turn around and accuse your friends." He pauses and when he speaks again, he's less hostile. "Look, just come over. I promise I'll listen to whatever it is you think you've found out. And if you're right, you can protect me from Marigold." I can almost see him rolling his eyes as says the last.

A passing dog barks.

"Is that a dog?" Whit asks. "Where are you?"

I hang up, suddenly panicked.

Cain, who's been standing close enough to have a good idea of the substance of the conversation, gently takes the phone from me. He removes the SIM card and powers off the phone. "Come on," he says. "We can flag a cab on Summer Street."

"Where are we going?" I ask, though I know the answer. What else can we do?

Cain face is grim. "To save Whit," he says.

I hold Cain's hand tightly as we sit in the cab, aware that whatever happens, Cain will probably have to turn himself in as a result. In fact, it's likely that if police are watching the Metters' house, Cain will be arrested the moment we arrive. I suggest that he drop me off and keep going, but he won't countenance the idea.

"Let's make sure Whit's okay, and then we'll tell the police about what Darryl told you," he says quietly. "Maybe there's another explanation."

I concede. Perhaps we owe Marigold a chance to defend herself.

We get out of the cab in front of Whit's house. There is no police presence which, to be honest, surprises me. I would have expected at least a couple of officers to be watching the house, but perhaps it would be stretching the resources of Boston PD too far to have a car stationed with each of us day and night. Even the private security I encountered at the front door when last I was here is absent.

Cain glances at me. Clearly, he too finds the absence of any security odd. Especially since Jean Metters has so recently been assaulted.

"Maybe there's a detail with Whit's mom at her legal offices…or wherever she is," he says, frowning.

I direct Cain to the second driveway, and we walk past the main house and the pool to the guesthouse at the back.

I knock.

There's no answer.

"Whit, it's Freddie." Still nothing.

Cain tries the door—it's open. Now we're both becoming alarmed.

Cain goes in ahead of me.

And then everything happens at once, though the seconds stretch so that each thing is distinct in its horror. The crack. An explosion when the bullet leaves the barrel and the thud when it enters Cain. He twists back and falls before me and my line of sight is cleared for Whit and his gun, and Marigold, ashen and shaking. I drop to my knees beside Cain and someone is screaming. It might be me, I'm not sure. I look for the source of the blood and press my hand over where I think the bullet entered.

And I shout at Whit. "He wasn't going to hurt you, you idiot! We came to help you!"

Marigold goes into another room and returns with towels, then kneels down beside me. "Move your hand, Freddie."

"No."

"A towel will work better than your palm," she says, folding one into a compress.

Slowly, I pull my hand away. She claps down the towel and presses. Cain is conscious, surprisingly calm, though he's clearly in pain.

"Get away from him." Whit has not put down the gun. "He's dangerous…a murderer."

Marigold recoils automatically. I ignore him, replacing the pressure Marigold has released.

"Freddie, get away from him!" Whit screams.

"If I take my hand away he could bleed out."

"He came here to kill us!"

"He came here with me to help you!"

"Freddie!" Cain gets my attention through gritted teeth. "Freddie, Whit sent Marigold to the donut shop...do you remember?" He curses. Probably the pain, possibly the realisation.

And then I remember too. Whit directed Marigold to Around the Hole...it was his haunt before it was hers. I might not have thought anything of it if he hadn't shot Cain. I turn to stare at Whit. "My God, it was you. It was you from the beginning."

"What?" Marigold responds first. "Are you out of your fucking mind?"

But Whit looks almost relieved. He steps across to stand over me and Cain. "You always knew, didn't you, Cain? I could tell you always knew."

Cain clamps his own hand over the towel, rolls onto his side, and drags himself up into a sitting position against the wall. He catches his breath, and then, "I had no idea till just now, you fucking moron. I thought you were too dumb to do anything more complicated than eat donuts!"

"Cain..." I know Whit shot him, but for God's sake, Whit's still holding the gun.

Whit kicks him.

Cain swears, and I try to protect him with my own body.

"Get away from him, Freddie." Whit motions with the gun.

"Why did you kill Caroline, Whit?" I ask, playing for time. Surely a neighbour has heard the gunshot and called the police by now.

"It was just a stupid argument," he says. "I didn't mean to... We were talking and then...then she was dead."

I hear Marigold whimper.

"What were you arguing about?"

"She wanted to pull out. She set it all up, and then she pulled out."

"Set what up?"

"The inside story of Cain McLeod, the bestselling murderer." He shakes his head. "It was her idea...she organized it all. Getting him to the library, giving us a reason to talk..."

"That's why she screamed..."

"She said nothing bonds strangers better than a shared mystery. It was simple, and she was right. Suddenly, we were all pals." He explodes, furious again. "That's what she couldn't stand, that it was me, not her. That I'd be getting the story, the recordings. It would be my observations, my friendship with a murderer. She suddenly decides that it would be better if *she* got close to Cain instead." He shakes his head in disgust. "We met up at the BPL again that night to go over my notes, and she tells me she's changed the plan and I... she...I didn't mean to, but I couldn't let her just step in and take you guys."

Marigold has a phone in her hand. Whit is focussed on Cain and me. I push on. "But Shaun Jacobs somehow saw you kill her...and he blackmailed you."

"Yeah, who knew they let people like him into the library?" Despite his bravado, there are tears in Whit's eyes. "If it hadn't been for Jacobs and his god-awful smell, the security guard might have noticed me...and Caroline. As it was I was able roll her under that table and simply walk away while they were trying to throw him out."

"But then he found out where you lived and he stabbed you?"

"Yeah...he went Batman. Decided he needed to get justice for Caroline. That's when I realized I couldn't simply pay him off."

"So you killed him," Cain snarls.

"Well, considering he had already stabbed me, I'd say it was self-defence." Whit chokes. "He didn't suffer. He didn't even wake up."

"Whit," I say gently. "I get it—Caroline was an accident and Shaun Jacobs was self-defence, or something like it. But what are you doing now? You know Cain wasn't trying to hurt you."

"But he is!" Whit is sobbing now. "You and Cain...even Marigold...digging into things like some kind of idiotic Scooby Gang. You wouldn't leave it alone. You kept talking to people, investigating... It was only a matter of time before you found something. Why couldn't you leave it alone?"

"They want to arrest Cain for what you did!"

"They wouldn't have been able to prove anything—he didn't do it!" Whit is screaming again. A frustrated, thwarted child.

"Whit, we've got to call Cain an ambulance." The towel is now saturated with blood, but the bleeding has not stopped, and I can see Cain fading. "You're not going to be able to hide him under a table and walk away."

"Self-defence," he says desperately. "He's wanted for murder! Who'd blame me?"

"I'd blame you. I'll tell them everything—"

"Freddie, no!" Cain gasps. He pleads with Whit. "She won't say a word. They won't believe her anyway. She's been on the run with me since yesterday. And Marigold's loyal to you. There's no need to worry about them. For God's sake, man, let them go."

Whit hesitates.

Sirens. Cain swears.

"It's too late." Whit is weeping again. "You got hold of my gun and shot the girls before I was able to wrestle the gun back and end it. Jesus!" He aims at my head.

And again the moment seems to stretch. Perhaps last moments do. I look at Cain as I wait for it. He reaches for me. Marigold launches herself at Whit from behind. She is small against his bulk but ferocious. He twists to rid himself of her. I leap up and grab his arm, with no idea what I'm doing but kicking and punching and clawing. I bite his wrist and he loses his grip on the gun, and then Marigold and I become some kind of screaming dervish as we fight to keep him from retrieving it.

I slip on blood and lose my footing.

And so I'm on the ground when the shot is fired, with no idea where it came from. Another shot, and I crawl to Cain. He's barely conscious. I huddle against him and close my eyes, braced for the end.

But there is no third gunshot, only shouting.

When I'm pulled off Cain, I fight, refusing now to die quietly. Someone puts their knee on my back and cuffs my hands behind it, and I realise it's the police. I'm not sure if the Boston PD had ever been thanked by a prisoner before, but I am insane with relief and grateful and terrified. I beg them not to let Cain die. I hear Marigold resisting, cursing, Whit crying like a heartbroken child, and then Jean Metters demanding rights and wanting to know why her son is in restraints.

⁓

Dear Hannah,

I regret that I have been out of touch. The penitentiary rules are somewhat Draconian, and my communication has previously been quite restricted. Still, as Cain once said, prisons have their own societal rules, and I have employed them to enable me to renew our correspondence. I hope you got the basket of cupcakes I sent you. They should have been left on your kitchen counter. I would love to know how your latest book turned out. Did the awesome foursome all survive the finale? How did Freddie come to terms with the fact that her lover was a murderer? I suppose I shall have to request a copy from the prison library when it is released, in order to find out how it ends. For them at least.

I'm afraid I'll be unable to get back to Australia in the immediate future. We had barely laid eyes on each other when I was apprehended. I was wounded that you didn't visit me before I was extradited. I asked for you several times during the two days I was in Australian custody, but you didn't come, and we missed our chance to be with each other while we talked about our work and our lives. No matter. I am a loyal man, and patient. We will encounter each other in the flesh eventually. I look forward to that.

In the meantime, know that I'll be there if you need me.

Your Leo.

CHAPTER THIRTY-FOUR

Justine Dwyer brings me a cup of tea at the station. I ask about Cain for the hundredth time.

"He's in surgery," she says.

"Will he die?"

"I don't know. They're doing everything they can."

She asks if anyone has offered me anything to eat.

"I'm not hungry."

She hands me a bags of crisps. "I grabbed these in case you were. Do you feel up to answering a few questions?"

I tell her everything. It doesn't feel like a police interview. I'm not aware of her asking questions...I just talk. I suppose Cain is not a suspect anymore, and so I'm not a hostile witness or whatever it is you call someone who believes in a suspect's innocence.

She tells me about the plan Whit and Caroline had devised to write an investigative piece for the *Rag*.

"They were aware of Cain McLeod's past through their family connections. Of course, any investigative journalist could have produced a story on McLeod's conviction, and his incarceration. Though it isn't public knowledge, it's not a state secret. Caroline and Whit wanted to go one better. They intended to get close to Cain, and then to put him under pressure...a story on whether a murderer could in fact be reformed."

"How were they going to put him under pressure? Was that why Caroline screamed?"

"No. That was supposed to give Whit a reason to initiate a friendship with Cain. Caroline's idea, apparently. Then they were going to essentially gaslight Cain with similar pranks to—"

"To see if he'd kill someone?" I ask incredulous.

Justine nods. "Something like that."

"But the messages, the images of doors, were sent to me, not to Cain."

"Whit was apparently trying to sow distrust. He's had Cain's phone all along."

"But that means he sent the photograph of his own door the night he was stabbed—"

"Being stabbed wasn't part of the plan. The text was meant to unnerve you, make you wonder if Cain was sending them. My partner has a theory that perhaps Whit intended to attack his mother that night." She shakes her head. "Without Caroline he was making it up as he went…terrified that he would be discovered, unwilling to give up on what he considered his shot. Whit told us he had no idea who attacked him because he was afraid if Jacobs was arrested, he would tell us what he'd seen."

I rub my face. "He told you all this."

"Once his lawyer, who by the way, is also his mother, directed him to say nothing." She shrugs. "Some families."

Marigold and I are released while Cain is still in surgery. The police take us both to the hospital to wait. As first neither of us says anything. Marigold holds my hand in the car.

As we walk up to emergency, she apologises for thinking Cain was a murderer. I apologise for believing that of her. And I tell her I am sorry about Whit.

She laughs through tears. "I fell in love with a murderer."

"That's not the part you fell in love with."

We are escorted through the media pack outside the hospital. The waiting room is crowded. Marigold and I find seats and wait. A surgeon comes down and speaks to an older couple. Perhaps the woman is Cain's mother and the man her partner. I realise that despite the past few days, I have no claim on Cain, no right to know how he came out of surgery, or even if he came out of the surgery.

The woman is crying, the man comforting her. I watch in horror. Has Cain died? Oh, God—is this how it ends?

Marigold swears quietly and stands up. She walks over and talks to the couple. Even as I watch her do so, I'm not really registering any of it. They all turn and look at me and then Marigold beckons me over.

I force my muscles to work, to walk. Perhaps Marigold sees me struggling, because she shouts, "Cain's not dead. He's in post-op!"

A few others turn and look relieved. It seems there are a number of people here for Cain.

I've reached them by now. Marigold isn't finished. "They took out the bullet." She embraces me joyfully. "He'll be okay."

I want to cheer and weep, but I'm not as uninhibited as Marigold, and so I hold myself together, only barely.

The woman grabs my hand. She is, as I imagined, Cain's mother. She thanks me. "The police said that my son might be dead if two young women had not held off his attacker." Her voice is soft.

I tell her that even as he lay bleeding, Cain tried to convince Whit that Marigold and I were not a threat, that he tried to protect us.

Marigold tells her than Cain loves me. Just like that—a five-year-old blurting a secret. "Cain is in love with Freddie, you know."

I stare at Cain's mother, whose name I don't even know, embarrassed.

She is clearly startled by Marigold's declaration, but she recovers admirably. "I gathered there was someone in his life." She still has my hand. "I am Sarah Manners. This is my brother Bill. We're very pleased to meet you."

Bill shakes my hand once his sister releases it. "We're beholden to y'all," he says. "Abel didn't tell us he was in trouble. The first we heard of it was when the police knocked on Sarah's door looking for him."

"I expect he didn't want to worry you," I reply in tentative defence of Cain. "And it all happened so quickly."

"Abel—" Sarah stops, smiles, and begins again. "*Cain* has always tried to solve his own problems."

"Yes, and we all know where that got him," Bill mutters.

"Pay Bill no mind," Sarah tells me. "He loves Cain like he was his own boy."

As Cain will be in post-op for a while, we go to the hospital cafeteria. There, over coffee, Marigold and I tell Cain's mother and uncle what happened. Marigold is frank about her relationship with Whit, declaring it like some kind of confessional penance.

"We all liked Whit," I qualify. "Even Cain. We were all fooled by him."

"He sounds like a troubled boy," Sarah says.

Bill grunts.

Eventually, Cain comes out of the anaesthetic and is transferred to a room and a bed. Sarah and Bill are allowed in to see him.

Marigold and I sit in the waiting room, not sure what to do.

When Sarah and Bill return, she tells us that his doctor has agreed that Marigold and I be allowed to see him too. "He was asking for you," she whispers as I thank her.

Marigold pauses at the door to his room. "I'll give you a couple of minutes alone first," she says, shoving me forward. Subtlety of a brick, that one.

Cain is hooked up to multiple drips and machines. He turns his head towards me and smiles, and I am nearly overwhelmed. "I'm still kinda high." His voice is hoarse. "So don't pay too much attention to anything I say."

"Never did," I reply, taking his hand. There's a cannula in it, so I do so very carefully.

"Mom says we all made it out alive."

"We did."

I feel a faint pressure on my hand. "Good."

Marigold comes in then. "Jesus at the wheel!" she whispers, looking at Cain. She seems suddenly shy.

We talk quietly for a while. I'm not sure we say much. What is there to say? I am aware of feeling deeply happy. Anguished by what's happened, unsure about what's next, but happy. In time a nurse comes in to gently throw Marigold and me out. I kiss Cain and promise we'll be back as I release his hand. It leaves a kind of emptiness against my fingers, and I have to resist the impulse to touch him again.

The nurse buzzes around him, cheerily checking vital signs as we leave.

"God, how are we going to get past the reporters?" Marigold says as we wait for the elevator.

I look down at myself—the blood on my jacket and shirt. Marigold, too, is splattered. There's little chance of slipping past the media throng unnoticed. But right now, I just haven't got the strength to run that gauntlet.

Marigold and I are discussing the logistics of escape when the elevator doors open. And so we don't notice the man in the corner until the doors close again behind us. And then we do.

Leo.

I stare, thrown off balance by the fact that he's here. "What are you—?"

He smiles. "I thought you might need me."

If you've enjoyed *The Woman in the Library*,
you won't want to miss *After She Wrote Him*,
another great stand-alone mystery by Sulari Gentill!

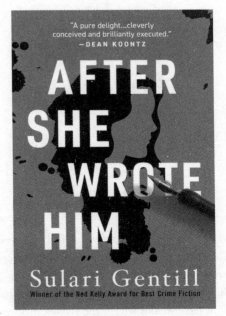

Dean Koontz calls the captivating
psychological thriller a "pure delight, a swift
yet psychologically complex read."

After She Wrote Him is a marvel of metafiction—a wildly inventive twist on the murder
mystery that takes readers on a journey filled
with passion, obsession, and the emptiness left
behind when the real world starts to fall away.

Read the prologue and the first
chapter on the following pages!

PROLOGUE

When the man was murdered, the gallery was full of voyeurs. They'd come to see and be seen, to admire and be admired. In their finery they'd postured and praised the artist, considering each canvas, looking carefully at every mark of the brush, discerning nuance and tone and meaning. They'd eyed each other as rivals in fashion and wit, in the sycophantic ability to recognise artistic genius. The show belonged to art and artists and art lovers. And so no one noticed the writer.

When the body was discovered, there were screams of horror. Some sobbed upon seeing the corpse; others could barely contain their glee. The gallery staff soothed and apologised, management called insurers, the authorities barked orders and asked questions. They listened for guilt, for motive and lies. And no one heard the writer.

When the dead man was identified, many claimed intimacy. Some had worked with him; others had danced in his arms. Several people purported friendship, a few admitted to a mutual loathing. They offered opinions and insights, analyses of character. And yet no one knew the writer.

On Introductions

What if you wrote of someone writing of you? In the end, which of you would be real?

In the beginning she was a thought so unformed that he was aware only of something which once was not.

And there was the idea. The embryonic notions of story. Fragile, swirling mists that struggled to find patterns; sense that was made and unmade and made yet again. In time there were shapes in the clouds and there was her.

They were shy with each other at first. Stiff.

It took the longest time to exchange names. Many were considered and discarded until, finally, one was familiar. One rang true.

She wrote books—quirky, whimsical mysteries with an eye for the absurd. Her pen was light and her voice assured. Even so, she had not been born with the knowledge that she would write, but happened upon storytelling accidentally while seeking some unknown distraction. In writing, she found meaning and purpose and a kind of spiritual joy. And, like many who come late to religion, her devotion to the craft was absolute, her conviction in its power unshakeable.

Yet she hesitated before calling herself a writer lest it seem presumptuous, or affected, or just plain silly. Some small part of her recoiled from claiming her place aloud too absolutely.

Her work had achieved a modicum of success, though she was by no means a household name.

He called her Madeleine d'Leon. Her husband would call her Maddie. She was thirty and—when they first came to know of one another—happy. Madeleine was a lawyer. She'd been a lawyer first. She practised in the corporate sector, but she didn't like to talk of work or even think about work when her time was her own.

"My concern is billable," she'd proclaim when asked about some matter she'd left at the office. "If I'm not being paid, I just don't care."

But she'd married a man who cared all the time. Hugh Lamond was the doctor. Not just a doctor, but *the* doctor. Ashwood was not large enough or gentrified enough to have more than "the doctor" and Hugh Lamond was it. Every man, woman, and child in Ashwood knew who he was and assumed he cared about each small twinge or ache or concern, regardless of whether it was his anniversary or his wife's birthday. They were right.

In the beginning, Madeleine had thought it funny: the god-like status of the country doctor. And Hugh was, after all, charming and committed. If anyone deserved to be a small-town god, it was him. Now, it niggled just a little that she had been lost in his divine glory, a handmaiden to his social deity. But still, she was proud of him.

So Madeleine worked, commuting when she had to and advising from home when she could. During her non-billable hours, she painted and sewed and built a garden that would grow to be worthy of the grand home they would have—whenever they finally got around to renovating.

And then, one day, whilst sitting in a particularly tedious meeting about some technical matter for which a lawyer's presence was merely decorative, Madeleine d'Leon had an idea for a story, and the very first thought of him.

The moment of genesis was strong, a cell of creativity that divided and multiplied until there was life. He had barely any substance at all. Just a space in the narrative for a protagonist of some sort.

She began writing then and there, raising her head occasionally to nod so her colleagues would think she was taking notes about the meeting itself. Every now and then she would arch a brow and shake her head or rub her chin while frowning, or tap the table with her lips pressed tightly together. She called it her boardroom technique: the kind of lawyerly intimations of consideration that made people feel better regardless. It was Madeleine's conviction that her clients demanded the presence of their lawyers at these meetings not because they needed them, or even planned to listen to them, but because the legal profession was a kind of security blanket. She was paid for what she called corporate hand-holding, and the nature of Madeleine was such that she was not too proud to admit it.

In that meeting she discovered just one thing about him, but, oh, what a thing! What a perfect link! He was a writer. It was their connection. He would see the world as she did: in stories, or potential stories, in vignettes and themes. He would judge people as characters, each with their own story. They would look upon his world together.

She called him Edward McGinnity. His friends would call him Ned.

He was twenty-eight when she found him, a young man with the world at his feet and no idea of how he should step into it.

Edward McGinnity had always known he would write. It was as natural to him as breathing, and he suspected the consequences of stopping would be as dire. In his mind there had always been epics, tales that carried on the books he could not bear to end, and new stories with conglomerate characters and modified plots. Eventually he'd picked up a pen.

At first he'd written poetry, as adolescents do. Learned to weave words with angst and defiance and heartbreak. Those old verses embarrassed him now—melodramatic, flowery, pretentious—but every so often there was one line, one phrase that was clear and strong and perfect. As he grew into a man, Edward McGinnity learned to pull back, to leave the louder things unsaid, to call out to the whispers once drowned in waves of passionate literary excess. And he found new stories and a desire to be read.

Maintained by an inheritance, an income born of tragedy, Edward lived well. He did so quietly, aware that the ability to write unencumbered from the first was too enviable to be broadcast, too likely to invite failure as a karmic balancing of luck.

He was sitting on his deck with a notebook and a glass of red when her story first struck him. He knocked over the glass in his haste to grab the pen beside it, allowing the wine to soak and stain the decking timbers as he tried to pin the thought onto his page with ink. In time he stood and paced as he wrote, stopping occasionally to laugh, so giddy was he with the discovery of her. He knew she was a writer before he knew her name.

Madeleine called Hugh that evening, as she did every evening that work took her away. The custom was more utilitarian than romantic—should she pick up milk in Ashwood?—that sort of thing. But this night she was exhilarated, and she loved Hugh Lamond more for the fact that she could share it with him. She knew she was babbling, but the idea was powerful now. It pulled new ideas towards it, building a world of characters and themes and events around itself. Hugh seemed a little bewildered at first, but perhaps whatever it was that possessed Madeleine was infectious, for soon he had suggestions and thoughts. She told him about Edward McGinnity, her well-heeled writer.

"But this is going to be a murder mystery, isn't it?" Hugh asked.

"Yes."

"So he's a crime writer?"

"No. Edward writes literary novels...the kind of worthy, incomprehensible stuff that wins awards." Madeleine paced with the phone, unable to physically contain her excitement. "That's the irony, you see. The hero of my crime fiction wouldn't lower himself to read—let alone write—the stuff himself. He's a serious artist."

"But if he were a crime writer, he'd know what to do to solve the crime."

"That's too predictable, Hugh. The fact that he is so out of place in crime fiction will make it interesting."

"Fair enough. Perhaps his family shouldn't approve of his writing?" Hugh ventured.

Madeleine smiled, touched that he was so interested. "But why wouldn't they approve?"

"They might want him to be a doctor. You know, there aren't enough books about doctors."

Madeleine laughed. "No, I think his family is dead," she said. "An accident of some sort. The story will work better if he's alone in the world."

"Why?"

"I don't know...there's something alluring about the lonely hero."

"He can't be too lonely. He'll need a love interest of some sort."

"Why?"

"Because he's a man. It's what we do."

Madeleine groaned. "If he has a love interest, I'll have to write a sex scene."

"Well, that's to be avoided at all costs," Hugh agreed. "She could be dead too—the love interest, I mean," he said helpfully. "He could be a grieving husband."

"Maybe…" Madeleine considered the idea. The death of Edward McGinnity's family was probably grief enough. She didn't want her hero to be completely withdrawn and bitter. "What if he loves someone who doesn't love him back, but who might one day?" she said. "That way I won't have to write a sex scene because she won't have him. Perhaps Edward is so in love with her that he can't move on."

"Won't that make him look pathetic?"

"It'll make him look deep."

"I don't know, I'm thinking pathetic."

"If I hadn't married you, you would have pined forever."

"Hmmm…yes…forever. Or at least a week. What time will you get home?"

"Should be back before lunch tomorrow."

"Grab some milk on the way in, will you?"

<hr />

Madeleine spent the evening in the familiar, generic solitude of a hotel room. She discarded her board reports onto the small table by the window and heaved her bag onto one of the twin beds. Changing into pyjamas, she ordered room service, settled into the other bed, and opened her laptop.

The novel would begin with him. It had to. That was how crime fiction worked—subplots, clues, red herrings all channelled through a single literary device: the protagonist. The reader would have to know him and trust him for the story to work. So she would open with him and worry about the murder later.

Madeleine closed her eyes. She could see him: sitting on the open deck of his expensive beach house, oblivious to the ocean view as he worked on the great Australian novel. She smiled. Of course he would write longhand, every word chosen after consideration, deliberation, and requisite suffering. The man she saw was handsome. For a moment she wondered when she'd decided that. His hair was dark, blown wild by the salt breeze against which his collar was turned up. The sky and the sea were both grey and turbulent. And yet he continued to write, muttering to himself as he tapped the pen against his chin. It was not until the first fat drops fell that he seemed to notice. Cursing, he closed his notebook against the rain and stepped through the French doors into the house.

The house itself would be tastefully furnished. Modern designer pieces complemented by what might be called sentimental junk. A large basin made of kilned glass was filled with old matchbox cars in anything but collectible condition. An assortment of old cameras—Box Brownies, AGFA Isolettes, leather-cased Kodaks—took up several bookshelves. A professional-quality digital SLR sat on the kitchen bench beside the wine rack.

There was no dust—because, of course, he would have a housekeeper. A quietly spoken, motherly woman called Mrs. Jesmond. Madeleine paused, pleased by the detail. Jill Jesmond had worked with Madeleine at Morrison McArthur. She was anything but quietly spoken, but she'd love being in Edward's story, even as his housekeeper.

There were several picture frames on the sideboard—an eclectic collection of the kind of beautiful frames bought as particular gifts: silver, etched glass, tooled leather. Only one contained a picture, a family photo from the decade before. That must have been his family—parents, brother, little sister—all now gone. Madeleine lingered over that photo, the anguish of losing everybody at once, the loneliness of it. The rest of the frames were empty, blank. He was a man: Perhaps he had just not got around to filling them. Perhaps it was something else.

The rain was heavy now. It curtained off the world around the house with a fall of water, blurring everything without. Edward checked his watch and cursed. It was a gentle, old-fashioned way of cursing that reminded Madeleine of her grandfather. Words not even considered swearing in this age. It was interesting, given the sleek modernity of the décor.

He ran up the iron staircase to the bedrooms on the floor above. Edward McGinnity's bedroom was neat, no random deposits of clothes, the bed made and taut, a dozen or so notebooks of various style and size stacked in an orderly tower on the upended trunk beside his bed. It was a masculine room, functional and unadorned except for one painting: a nude in oil in an Art Deco frame. The composition was simple and the pose direct. The brushwork evoked a certain wistfulness. Somehow Madeleine knew the artist had loved his model: it was perfect.

Edward stripped as he walked into the en suite to shower. The water did little to soothe the tension from his body. Every muscle was tight, wound, ready to begin. He loved this part. Discovery yawned before him, and it was glorious. The sheer possibility, exhilarating beyond measure. How seductive the existential strain between writer and character—almost erotic. Edward was charged with the liminal intimacy of it. Not only would he know her, she would come to know him. And therein would be the danger and the essence of story.

She'd be a crime writer. Edward smiled. He'd always considered authors of detective fiction an interesting breed. They identified with their genre more than other novelists, inhabiting a definite subculture in the literary world. There was a naivety about crime writers that intrigued him, an underlying belief in heroes and justice, despite the darkness of their work. And sometimes, just sometimes, a crime writer would be accepted into the literary elite, lauded for style, despite a dogged commitment to plot and pace. It would allow him to test her sense of literary self, as he intended.

Madeleine d'Leon would begin as a vignette of middle-class success. Professionally and personally contented. A lawyer, with a lawyer's detachment and dedication to reason, she would live in the country in fulfilment of the bourgeoisie yearning for views of trees and cows. But there was an honesty about Madeleine d'Leon, a humour that recognised absurdity. Hers was a mind he wanted to know. Hers was a life suited to prose.

He'd been searching for her all afternoon. In the beginning, she had been elusive, soft, but she was clear now. Small, not conventionally beautiful, but with a smile that made her so. She possessed the kind of face that seemed always to be thinking. She laughed sometimes for no outwardly discernible reason, but because something in the perpetual movement of her mind had amused her.

Edward dressed quickly, knowing he was late. Shirt, cuff links, watch, bow tie, dinner suit. He checked his breast pocket for the invitation, stopping to glance at the naked woman on his wall. He'd purchased her in a small gallery just outside Paris, and she had owned him since then. His muse. Edward thanked her for Madeleine d'Leon.

READING GROUP GUIDE

1. When Freddie, Whit, Cain, and Marigold get coffee together for the first time, Freddie mentions that it was the start of her friendship with a killer. Who did you suspect in that moment?

2. Thanks to the emails, we are regularly reminded that Freddie's story is fiction. Did that change your experience of the mystery at all?

3. Freddie, Whit, Marigold, and Cain become intimate friends very quickly. Have you ever made friends in a similar way? What circumstances (besides manufactured peril) led to these types of sudden, intense friendships?

4. Marigold insists to the others, "A scream is supposed to bring help, and we heard her scream." Do you think of yourself as being responsible for strangers? How effective is bystander intervention?

5. Describe the role of Freddie's neighbor Leo. How does he change Freddie's perspective?

6. Do you think the other characters took Marigold's stalking

behavior seriously? What would you do if your friend was acting like Marigold?

7. Freddie questions herself for trusting Cain several times but never really changes her mind. Where do you think her loyalty comes from?

8. In his emails, Leo insists that Hannah specify the races of her characters, pointing out that it could drastically change their experiences and perspectives in a story set in America. What does a story gain by making race explicit? What are the potential drawbacks?

9. Caroline and Whit planned to test whether they could goad Cain back into a life of crime. If they had executed their plan as they originally intended, what do you think would have happened? What does their experiment reflect about our attitudes toward convicted criminals?

A CONVERSATION WITH THE AUTHOR

The subplot contained in the emails from Leo is chilling, and it adds another layer of fiction to Freddie's story. Why did you decide to use it as a frame?

I was writing another novel, to be honest, when the frame of this one was conceived. That novel, too, was set in the U.S. I live in Australia, and so, to ensure I wrote the details of place correctly, I enlisted the help of a friend of mine—also a novelist and, importantly, an American who was in the U.S. at the time. We'd exchange emails, and he'd do the legwork whenever I needed to research anything to do with location. Now my friend (let's call him Leo) is a very earnest and thorough researcher. He would send me not only information but pictures and maps and footage of things he thought might enhance the sense of place in my story. And so, to this end, he sent me a video file of a crime scene—a murder that had taken place a couple of blocks from where he was staying. The footage was mainly of coroners' vans and police cordons (no bodies), but when I mentioned the video to my husband, his response was "Good grief, I hope Leo's not killing people just so he can send you research." Hmmm. Of course, he wasn't—I promise—but it did strike me as an excellent idea for a novel.

So I guess the decision was made while I was in the middle of writing another book. I put the idea to the back of my mind where it brewed until I finished the novel I was writing. When I was ready to start the manuscript that would become *The Woman in the Library*, I knew it would begin with "Dear Hannah…"

As the emails point out, in the upcoming years, contemporary novelists will have to carefully choose whether to include the coronavirus pandemic or not. How are you thinking about that for your own writing?

In addition to being a disaster on a planetary scale, the coronavirus pandemic presents contemporary novelists with a dilemma. Coronavirus is part of contemporary reality—ignoring it is a little like ignoring cell phones or computers. At best, it dates the novel, and at worst, it makes the story entirely implausible.

Even so, there is a real temptation for writers to, henceforth, set all our novels in 2019. Doing so would avoid the complications and distraction that COVID-19 introduces to a story. It's difficult to confine something like the pandemic, to allow it to play any small part without it taking over the narrative. It's like trying to write a novel set in France in 1917 without it becoming a war story. It can be done, but it is problematic. Moreover, the pandemic is not yet history and may not be for a long time—we are not at this point sure how it will turn all out. It is a changing backdrop to everything, so it's almost impossible to write a contemporary story that will still be contemporary a year from now, and setting a novel in the near future, with the pandemic being over, is a gamble.

That said, just because it's hard, just because it's risky, doesn't mean that one should not try. The challenge is, I suppose, to write about the pandemic in a way that's creative enough that it complements rather than dominates the story you're trying to tell, that is somehow timeless and contemporary, not just now but a year from now and ten years from now. In *The Woman in the Library*, I included the pandemic through this very dilemma. Leo demands its inclusion, Hannah refuses to let it into her story, but through them, I allowed it into mine.

Cain becomes a suspect in Caroline's murder in part because of his first novel. Do you ever worry about something similar happening to you?

Ha! All mystery writers probably have very incriminating google search histories!

Publishing a novel is a scary proposition for so many reasons. A novel isn't just the product of a writer's mind—there's a lot of the writer's heart in it too. Putting that out into the world and hoping that readers will like it is a little like sending your child to school and hoping they'll find friends. It's exciting and kind of wonderful, but also terrifying. You care more than you ever thought you would, and you worry—about bad reviews, slow sales, and most of all, that readers won't like it.

Arrest for murder pales by comparison!

It does also occur to me that if I were a murderer, being a novelist would be a great smokescreen. There'd be so much normally incriminating evidence I could explain as research.

You also write the Rowland Sinclair mystery series. Does it feel significantly different to write a standalone project like this one as opposed to an ongoing series?

In some ways, writing a standalone novel is like writing the first book of a series. Anything could happen because you're not building on a history established in previous books. Every character's past is a mystery to unearth. Each of them has to gain the reader's interest, make the reader care, without the benefit of past adventures together having created a bond. I suppose the big difference is that a standalone novel, as opposed to the first book of a series, requires you to say goodbye. You have to be able to finish with your characters, take them to a place where you are happy to walk away, and leave them to their own devices. For writers, at least, that can be tough. By the time a novel is written, a writer has spent hundreds of hours with the characters of her book... She has been through all manner of peril with them, so it's hard to give them up. I expect there are a few unexpected sequels that exist for no other reason than the writer missed the characters too much to stay away.

ACKNOWLEDGMENTS

This story was sparked by a letter from Boston, written by my dear friend and colleague L. M. Vincent, whose correspondence, guidance, and encouragement I have shamelessly twisted into something sinister. For your generosity and your insight, Larry, thank you.

That glimmer of a story was the recipient of a Create Grant from the Copyright Agency's Cultural Fund, which supported me to write in a year that was, to say the least, difficult. I was honoured to be awarded the grant and remain very grateful for it.

The manuscript was tested for all those things that a story should be by Michael Blenkins, Leith Henry, and Robert Gott in Australia and the wonderful Barbara Peters in the U.S. I can't thank you enough for your time, your support, your advice, and your enthusiasm.

My brilliant, passionate agent, Jill Marr, championed the manuscript and found it the perfect home with Anna Michels and Diane DiBiase at Sourcebooks, who have nurtured it into the best story it can be. Thank you all so much for your belief in my work and your input into this novel. I am truly grateful.

Beth Deveny edited the copy into shape and in doing so ensured readers would have no evidence of my typos. Thank you, Beth.

And then the extraordinary, talented Sourcebooks team turned my story into a book. And here it is. Thank you so much for picking it up.

ABOUT THE AUTHOR

Sulari Gentill is the author of the multi-award-winning Rowland Sinclair WWII Mysteries, a series of historical crime novels set in 1930s Australia about Rowland Sinclair, the wealthy gentleman artist cum amateur detective. The tenth in the series, *Where There's a Will*, was published in the United States by Poisoned Pen Press in January 2022.

Under the name S. D. Gentill, Sulari wrote the acclaimed fantasy adventure series the Hero Trilogy: *Chasing Odysseus*, *Trying War*, and *The Blood of Wolves*.

Her widely praised standalone novel, *After She Wrote Him*, was chosen as a Target Recommends book for 2020 and Apple's Best Book of the Month for April 2020. In Australia, where Sulari lives, it won the Ned Kelly Award for Best Crime Novel and was short-listed for the Davitt Award.

Sulari was part of an Australia Council–sponsored delegation of Australian Mystery Writers who toured the U.S. in 2019 to represent Australian crime fiction to a U.S. readership. Most recently, she was awarded a Copyright Agency Cultural Fund Fellowship.

Sulari lives in a small country town in the Australian Snowy Mountains on a truffle-growing farm, which she shares with her family and several beloved animals. She remains in love with the art of storytelling.